THE RULE OF NINE

ALSO BY STEVE MARTINI

THE
RULE
OF NINE

STEVE MARTINI

**Doubleday Large Print
Home Library Edition**

wm

WILLIAM MORROW
An Imprint of HarperCollins*Publishers*

This Large Print Edition, prepared especially for Doubleday Large Print Home Library, contains the complete, unabridged text of the original Publisher's Edition.

This is a work of fiction. The events described are imaginary, and the characters are fictitious and not intended to represent specific living persons. Even when settings are referred to by their true names, the incidents portrayed as taking place there are entirely fictitious; the reader should not infer that the events set there ever happened.

ISBN 978-1-61664-381-2

**This Large Print Book carries the
Seal of Approval of N.A.V.H.**

I dedicate this book to my loyal assistant, Marianne Dargitz, without whose help my work would not be possible

THE
RULE
OF NINE

ONE

Jimmie Snyder was twenty-three, tall and lanky. He had been in his current job less than two months and he was scared. He knew he had screwed up. He lay awake at nights worrying about it, as if under Chinese water torture, waiting for the next drip to hit him on the forehead. It was all about expectations, mostly his father's.

Snyder's dad was the managing partner in a large law firm in Chicago. Jimmie had graduated pre-law from Stanford a year earlier and his father wanted him to go to law school. But Jimmie wanted to go into film production. His father would have none of it.

As far as the old man was concerned, Jimmie needed credentials to round out his law school application and beef up his less-than-stellar undergraduate grades and middling LSAT score.

Toward that end, his father pulled every string within reach to land the boy a job in Washington. The best he could do on short notice was a temporary position as a part-time guide. The job was a holding pattern until his dad could yank more levers and land something better.

It took him three months and a hefty contribution to a senator in Alabama but he found a spot for Jimmie as a staff gofer with one of the many Senate subcommittees. This particular panel was charged with overseeing sensitive matters of intelligence. As it turned out, the nature of the assignment now made the situation even worse for his son.

It might take a while for the details to trickle back, to filter from one branch to the other, but Jimmie knew he would be called on the carpet sooner or later and asked to explain how he could have done something so stupid. How could he have allowed some middle-aged lawyer from California, wearing a polo shirt and shorts, to talk his way backstage, past all the locked doors and the phalanx of security into the private sanctum off-limits to all but the gods of government? What in an earlier decade might have been a minor transgression, in the age of terror had become grounds for job termination and possible criminal prosecution.

Jimmie had spent a week of sleepless nights trying to conjure up some plausible explanation for why he had done it. Call it bad judgment. Maybe it was because he was angry and bored. He hated the job and the fact that his father had manipulated him into taking it. It was that, but also the fact that the man he met that day was so easy to talk to. Unlike Snyder's father, the guy was affable, approachable, and interested. He listened to everything Jimmie had to say. When Jimmie told him he really didn't want to pursue a career in law, the lawyer, a perfect stranger, gave him absolution. He told Jimmie that the first rule of success in life was to follow your dreams. And then to find out that the guy was a Stanford law alum on vacation, how could Jimmie say no? All the man wanted was to see a few of the rooms off-limits to the public. Jimmie had already finished his tour of duty for the day. What was the harm? It wasn't as if they had done anything wrong. Other than take a few pictures, chat, and look around, you would never have known the man was there. Jimmie still had the guy's business card in his wallet—WARREN HUMPHREYS, ATTORNEY-AT-LAW—with an address in Santa Rosa, California.

Now one of the other Senate staffers told Jimmie that inquiries were being made. Nothing formal as yet, but it was likely to cause waves because the incident could not be contained on the legislative side. Sooner or later Jimmie was likely to be visited by investigators.

Like a bad dream, all the little details tripped through his brain as he walked out the doors of the Hart Senate Office Building. Even now, a few minutes after six, with the sun sailing toward the horizon, the heat of midsummer was oppressive. Most of the members of Congress were gone, back to their districts for the recess, leaving staff to wither in the sultry heat of the national swamp. Beads of sweat ran down the back of his shirt collar as he thought about what could happen. He didn't dare tell his father.

Every little aspect of what had seemed an innocent adventure, a courtesy to a friendly tourist, now appeared much more ominous.

The man's camera was something that hadn't even occurred to Jimmie until later, when he realized he was in trouble. Cameras were prohibited except in the public areas. He wondered how the little point-and-shoot job had gotten through the metal detector without setting off the alarm.

Maybe the man had posted some of his pictures on the Internet. That would explain how they'd found out. He scoured his brain trying to remember whether he might have absently slipped into one or more of the shots. There was no way to be sure, but he didn't think so. All the man wanted was a few snapshots of some of the interiors. He seemed most interested in the walnut-paneled library, which was elegant, and the gymnasium upstairs. The gym was nothing special, just one of those conversational curiosities inside the Beltway.

Jimmie strode onto the sidewalk and headed for the Metro rail and home. It was

a short ride. He lived alone in a small sub-
let apartment in Alexandria. Rent was high
in the area but he was lucky. He had gotten
a deal on the place for the summer. When
the members of Congress returned, so
would the tenant, a lobbyist for the drug
industry, and, Jimmie would have to find
another place to live. If there was a silver
lining to any of this, it was the fact that if
they fired him, he would not have to find
new digs come fall. He would be gone.

A few blocks on, Jimmie ventured onto
the long, steep escalator and down into the
immense cavern of the Metro rail. He
slipped his card into the slot at the turnstile, slid through, and ran for the train. He
caught it just before the doors closed.

The thought of escaping Washington,
even at the cost of failure, left Jimmie to
wonder if it would be enough for his father
to finally give up on him. This and the deep
sense of disappointment he would have to
endure occupied Jimmie as he sat listening to the wheels skim over the steel rails.

Twelve minutes later he emerged from
the King Street station in Alexandria. The
setting sun had finally dipped behind the
buildings by the time he reached the en-

trance to the three-story brick apartment house. There were only fourteen units. They ranged from studios to three-bedrooms, all of them equipped with updated fixtures and hardwood floors. There was no elevator or front desk, and no twenty-four-hour security. The lobbyist who held the lease to Jimmie's unit was looking for a summer tenant to watch the place. As long as Jimmie didn't throw parties and didn't smoke, the single-bedroom apartment was his for two hundred dollars a month until fall. It was a steal.

He climbed the five steps fishing in his pocket for his key to the front entrance. By the time he got there, he realized that the heavy oak door wasn't locked. Something was wrong with the door's overhead closing arm that caused it to stay open just a crack. He had noticed it a couple of days earlier.

He pushed the door and it opened. Once inside he waited for the door to close, then gave it a shove until he heard the lock snap into place. He made a mental note to tell the building manager.

He used his apartment key to check his mail in the locked boxes in the lobby. There was nothing but a few pieces of junk mail and one business envelope from his father's law firm. Probably more suggestions for his law school résumé. He headed for the stairs.

Using his apartment key as a letter opener, he tore a jagged opening in the envelope. He was looking down at the single folded page inside when his peripheral vision caught some dark image in front of him on the stairs. Jimmie glanced up.

There, sprawled across the steps from the banister to the wall, was the hunched-up body of an indigent. Some beggar had wandered into the building. Unshaven, he was wearing a soiled dark trench coat and scuffed-up black shoes with no socks. The guy looked like a dropped sack of potatoes. For a moment Jimmie wondered if he was dead. But as he studied the motionless figure in front of him, he detected the subtle rise of respiration under the wrinkled, dirty coat.

"Excuse me."

The guy didn't move.

"Mister." Jimmie nudged him with his foot.

The body didn't budge.

"If you don't get out of here, I'm going to have to call the cops."

Still there was no movement. A faint odor of alcohol lingered over the slumped form. He had wandered into the building, probably looking for a cool place to sleep, and had passed out on the stairs.

Jimmie nudged him again but the guy still didn't move. He couldn't get around him, so he lifted one long leg, took a giant stride, and tried to navigate three steps while going over the top of the guy. As he straddled the man, suddenly a gloved hand reached out from the trench coat and grabbed Jimmie's ankle.

The kid smiled. "Excuse me!" The man's grip was amazingly powerful for a semi-conscious drunk.

"What are you doing?" Jimmie reached down to grab the hand that was on his ankle. As he did this, he felt a sharp sting on the back of his hand, as if a snake had bitten him.

He tried to jerk his hand back, but just as quickly it was held fast by the gloved hand that had left his ankle.

"What the hell!" A burning sensation spread like fire through the vein on the back of his left hand, between the first two fingers. "What are you doing?"

The ripped envelope fluttered down the stairs like a fallen leaf. It was followed by the jangle of keys onto the stairs. Before the envelope settled at the foot of the steps, Jimmie's vision began to blur. An amazing feeling of euphoria swept through his body, carried by the heat that flushed his veins. He stood there weaving in a broad circle as if floating on a cloud. Sprawl-legged over the man lying on the stairs, a sensation of uncaring bliss flooded his body.

As if in a dream, Jimmie watched as the bum left the syringe still buried deep in Jimmie's left hand. The leather glove reached up and grabbed him by the shoulder. In a rapture, Jimmie settled on the stairs, his delirious gaze focused at the fuzzy edge of the carpeted runner where his cheek landed. His vision clouded. He blinked twice. There was a fleeting sensation of drool as it ran from the corner of his paralyzed mouth, and then nothing as the filament of existence dissolved.

The bum shifted his body and pulled himself out from beneath his fallen victim. He was slight of build, the kind of spindly character who could cross a crowded street and never garner more than a fleeting glance from those who passed him. He had a pockmarked face from an adolescence of acne. But even this did not distinguish him, unless you happened to engage his eyes. If the iris was the window into the soul, Muerte Liquida's glassy stare offered a view of hell. To a growing list of victims it was the last thing they ever saw.

He glanced quickly at the plunger on the syringe to make sure it was all the way in. He didn't remove it but instead grabbed a roll of surgical tape from the pocket of his trench coat. He wrapped three rounds of the tape around the syringe and the dead man's hand to hold the hypodermic in place.

Then, as if in a single motion, he grabbed the keys and slipped down the stairs to retrieve the envelope. Like a jack-in-the-box, he came back up and lifted the body from under the arms and around the chest. For someone so slim he was deceptively strong. Liquida carried the body up the few steps to the second floor. Down the corridor a short distance he found apartment 204.

He leaned the body against the wall and

held it there with his shoulder as he opened the door with the key. Within seconds he and the lifeless body were inside with the door closed. He tossed the keys and the envelope on the chair next to the door.

Now he moved with lightning speed. Liquida lifted the kid in his arms so as not to leave drag marks, and carried him into the bedroom. He laid him on the bed and then removed the dead man's coat, tie, and shoes; opened his shirt collar; and rolled up his sleeves.

Liquida then reached into the oversize pockets inside his trench coat and started pulling out the paraphernalia. This included a short length of elastic surgical tubing; a box of fresh syringes; a tablespoon properly burned and scoured with the residue of heroin; and a small jar with a charred wick, an alcohol burner. To this he added several cotton balls, all of which had been soaked in a solution of heroin and left to dry.

After impressing a thumb and fingerprint from the victim's right hand onto the working end of the spoon and the burner, Liquida lit the burner and allowed some of the residue from the hot spoon to permeate up to the lampshade on the nightstand next to the bed. He put the hot spoon on the wooden surface on the nightstand, where it left a burn mark. He arranged everything on the nightstand next to the bed, except for the tubing. That he stretched out under the kid's left forearm a few inches above the taped syringe that was still embedded in the large vein at the back of the victim's hand. He removed the surgical tape and carefully impressed a single right thumbprint from the victim on the plunger of the hypodermic. Then he ran a few carefully smudged prints with his dead fingers down the barrel of the syringe.

Finally Liquida retrieved six small packets of silvery aluminum foil from the pocket of his trench coat. Four of these contained two small chips, each of black-tar heroin heavily cut and stepped on, any one of which would be unlikely to cause an overdose. The fifth sealed packet contained two deadly doses of pure heroin. He placed these in the top drawer of the nightstand. Then he unfolded the foil on the sixth packet and left it on the nightstand next to the spoon. It contained one small chip of black tar, almost five hundred milligrams of pure heroin. The second chip from the packet Liquida had processed by using the spoon and burner before loading it into the syringe.

When the crime unit processed the scene, they would find an inexperienced recreational user who had gotten a mixed bag of product and overshot his tolerance by not realizing the potency of his purchase.

The job was nearly done. There was only one more item. Liquida grabbed the kid's suit coat from the floor, reached inside, and found Jimmie Snyder's wallet. He opened it and started looking. Sure enough, behind one of the credit cards he found it, just like the man had said. He plucked the business card from the wallet and put it in his pocket.

He was finished, except for one final touch, something special, a personal perk. It was something for himself that the client hadn't asked for but was going to get anyway. It would give Liquida immense pleasure. Time to draw the fly into the web. Fumbling with his gloved fingers he pulled a small plastic bag from his pocket. Inside was a single business card. He lifted the card from the bag.

PAUL MADRIANI
Attorney-at-Law
Madriani and Hinds

He slipped it behind the credit card in the kid's wallet. Then he replaced the wallet in the coat pocket and laid the coat on the foot of the bed, next to the body.

In less than a minute, Liquida was out the door and down the stairs. He stopped only briefly to remove the duct tape he had put on the overhead closing arm at the front door two days earlier to keep it from locking.

Out on the street he mixed in with a few pedestrians. By the time they reached the corner, the disheveled vagrant in the dirty, dark trench coat had disappeared like a lethal wisp of smoke.

TWO

It's tricky to know how good a job the government does at keeping secrets since the only ones we know about are the ones that leak. This morning Zeb Thorpe, assistant director for the FBI's National Security Branch, is trying to wedge all four fingers and his thumb into the cloak-and-dagger dike, which is starting to drip.

Thorpe has us closeted in the federal building out near Miramar for what appears to be a session of truth and consequences.

"Mr. Madriani, Mr. Hinds, Mr. Diggs. I appreciate all of you coming out here this morning."

"I didn't know we had a choice," says Harry.

Harry Hinds is my law partner. He doesn't like cops and had developed a terminal aversion to the FBI when he discovered several months ago that they had wired our office and tapped our phones.

"Nonetheless, we appreciate your cooperation," says Thorpe.

The best he gets from Herman Diggs, our investigator, is a dark-eyed nod. Herman is African American, about six foot four, so Thorpe has to look up at him as he smiles.

"Please come in, take a seat. Can I get you anything—coffee, soda, bottled water?" He directs us toward the long, dark conference table in the center of the room, where a court reporter is already set up behind his stenograph machine. Seated at the table is James Olson, the new United States attorney for the Southern District of California. Seated beside him is a slender, austere man in a naval uniform.

"Just what I wanted for breakfast, coffee and a transcript," says Harry.

"We could have done it surreptitiously, digital tapes and microphones," says Olson.

"That would have felt like home," says Harry. "Just like my office."

Ordinarily Olson would not be doing this himself. He would have assigned it to one of his deputy U.S. attorneys. But given the sensitive nature of the inquisition, I am surprised they haven't dispatched Olson's boss from Washington to conduct it.

"I would apologize for the wiretaps and the surveillance," says Thorpe. He ushers us inside and closes the door, and then motions us toward the three chairs closest to the court reporter. "But we didn't have much choice. You have to understand that at the time, we had no idea who you and Mr. Madriani were working with, where your loyalties lay, or for that matter what you knew. We did what we had to do."

"As I recall, that was the defense at Nuremburg," says Harry.

"And we'd do it again," says Olson.

"You mean the gassing or the wiretapping?" says Harry.

Olson gives him a mean-eyed stare.

"I know you're new to the job and you probably need to practice your law enforcement hard-on for Mr. Thorpe and the court reporter. So feel free to jump right in," says Harry.

The court reporter looks up. "Should I be taking this down?"

"No." Olson fires at him a stony-eyed stare from across the table.

"Gentlemen, please. Let's try to keep this civil and brief." Thorpe tries to moderate. "Mr. Madriani, how about some water for you?"

"I'm fine."

"Mr. Diggs?"

"Depends how long we're gonna be here," says Herman.

"That depends on what you have to say." Olson speaks before Thorpe can open his mouth.

"A bottle of water would be nice," says Herman.

Harry, Herman, and I take our seats and Olson nods toward the court reporter. "Now," he says.

He has each of us identify ourselves for the record and state our home addresses. The stenographer has us spell our names.

"I suspect you gentlemen know what this is about," says Olson. "The events outside the North Island Naval Air Station earlier this year, what the media now refers to as the 'Coronado Assault.'"

For about eight months, Thorpe and his minions have managed to maintain wraps on the central missing detail surrounding the gun battle outside the gates of the North Island Naval Air Station.

"There is no secret to the fact that a group of terrorists were thwarted in their attempt to detonate a bomb-laden vehicle near the naval base at Coronado." Olson looks up to make sure we're all singing from the same page.

"And that in the ensuing gun battle the terrorists, all of them, were killed along with three law enforcement officers. At some point the bomb was defused and the vehicle was removed. Are we in agreement with regard to these basic facts?" asks Olson.

"If you say so," says Harry.

"Do you have some other version of the facts?" Olson looks at him.

"This is your party," says Harry.

"Fine, let's start with you, Mr. Hinds. Have you spoken to anyone in the media, or anyone else for that matter, concerning the events in question?"

"I might have mentioned it to my barber," says Harry. "People want to know. What can I say?"

"But as I understand it, you weren't there that day," says Olson. "You weren't actually near the truck or at the scene, is that right?"

"That's right."

"So where did you get your information?"

Harry glances at me.

"So whatever you think you might know concerning the shootout and the truck, and whatever was on the truck"—Olson puts the emphasis on this last point—"is nothing but hearsay. Is that correct?"

"That's right. So why don't I just go?" Harry starts to get up.

"Sit down," says Olson.

"How about you, Mr. Madriani?" Olson looks at me. "Have you talked to anyone, besides your partner, concerning the events that day and what you think you might have seen?"

"No."

"No one? You haven't mentioned it to other employees in your office?"

"No."

"What about your family? You must have said something to them?" says Olson.

"No. There's just my daughter. And I want to keep her out of it."

"What is her name?" Olson sits poised with his pen over a yellow legal pad.

"Stay away from her," I tell him. "She's not involved."

"Her name?" he says.

"Sarah Madriani."

He writes it down. "Does she have an address?"

"She lives with me. She's just graduated from college."

"Congratulations," he says. "Has anyone from the media tried to contact you concerning the events at Coronado?"

I laugh. "You must be kidding. We've had to change our business phone number four times. For three months we had to move the location of our practice to another office in another city to avoid the horde camped outside our door. That answer your question?"

Olson looks at Thorpe, who nods as if to confirm these details.

"So you're telling us you haven't divulged any information concerning the details of what happened that day?"

"By details, do you mean the fact that

the device on board the truck was nuclear?" I say.

"You don't know that," says Thorpe.

"So what do you think it was?" says Harry.

"According to the information I have, it was an IED, an improvised explosive device," says Thorpe.

This is the official line, and technically correct. After all, it was a forty-year-old nuclear bomb originally designed for the belly of an obsolete Russian cruise missile and modified sufficiently to be loaded into the bed of a rental truck. The government has offered no other details and has blunted further inquiries on the grounds of security and because the device is the subject of an ongoing investigation. No doubt the investigation will be ongoing in perpetuity. Nobody wants to explain how close we came to a moon-size crater at the north end of Coronado or the annihilation of most of the inhabitants of the city.

"The fact of the matter is," says Thorpe, "none of you has anything but suspicions."

"Then why are we here?" I ask.

"To make sure you haven't spread those suspicions to the media or to anyone else," says Olson.

Somewhere, someplace, someone has talked. They're trying to find out who and stanch the flow before the tidal wave overwhelms them.

"If you recall, at the time of our initial interrogation we were instructed by you, by the FBI, that under no circumstances were we to reveal any information concerning the nature or details of the device," I tell him.

"That's correct," says Thorpe.

"The question is have you revealed such information?" says Olson. "I put the question to you, Mr. Madriani."

"No."

"Mr. Hinds?"

"What would I know?"

Olson looks at him.

"No," says Harry.

"And you, Mr. Diggs. Have you said anything to anyone concerning the device?"

"Nobody ever talks to me," says Herman.

"Does that mean no?" says Olson.

"That's what it means."

"I remind you all that this is part of the ongoing criminal investigation. That you are talking to law enforcement officers in these regards. So any deception or mis-

information could have criminal consequences. Do you understand that?"

Each of us replies in the affirmative and
the court reporter takes it down.

"That's all I have," says Olson. "They're
all yours. We're off the record."

The stenographer starts to pack up his
machine.

"You mean we're not finished?" I say.

"Not quite," says Thorpe.

THREE

It takes several minutes for the stenographer and Olson to gather their belongings and clear the room. The entire time Thorpe is seated in his chair in total silence, shooting furtive glances at us, so by the time the door closes the atmosphere over the table seems charged.

"Is this when we're supposed to believe that we're not being taped?" says Harry.

"You're not," says Thorpe. "I'm not asking for information. I'm imparting it. What I'm about to tell you is for your own safety." He reaches down into a briefcase at the side of his chair and pulls out a large manila envelope. He lifts the flap and slides out several glossy photographs, eight-by-tens.

He assembles these into packets of three, one for each of us, and then slides them down the table toward us.

The top photograph appears to be something from a crime scene, a young man, a head-and-shoulder shot. You might think he was sleeping unless you looked closely and noticed the slight blue cast of his face, cyanosis.

"Do any of you recognize the man in the first photograph?"

I take another look, and then shake my head as I glance toward Harry.

"No," he says.

"Never saw him before," says Herman.

"He was found dead, an apparent drug overdose in an apartment in D.C. a few days ago. In his wallet was your business card, Mr. Madriani."

When I look up at Thorpe, he is staring straight at me. "Do you have any idea how it got there?"

I shake my head. "No," and then look at the photograph again. "Do you have a name to go with the picture?"

"James Snyder," says Thorpe.

"Doesn't ring any bells," I tell him. "I can check our files, see if his name pops up in the computer, but I have no recollection of him at all."

"I don't think you'll find anything in your firm's records," says Thorpe.

"Why do you say that?" I ask.

"Because we lifted a latent thumbprint from the back of your business card, the one that was found in his wallet. Ordinarily you wouldn't expect to find much, especially if the card's been slipped in and out of a wallet several times. You might get a smudged print. But this one was pretty clear. What's more, the print didn't belong to the victim. And it wasn't yours. We checked. When we ran it through our computer, the thumbprint on your card matched an unidentified print we lifted from another crime scene. Next picture," says Thorpe.

We flip to the next eight-by-ten glossy.

At first it is difficult to determine what the image is until I realize it's a human body. It is charred, burned so thoroughly that the gases, body fat, and oils have erupted from the abdomen, leaving a darkened cave of encrusted and exposed ribs. Both legs end

in sharpened stubs somewhere below
the knee. The head looks like a burned
volleyball, all the facial features gone.

"Okay, if you're trying to scare me, you've
succeeded," says Harry.

"I wouldn't expect you to recognize him,
Mr. Hinds. I don't think you ever saw him,"
says Thorpe. "But both of you, Mr. Diggs
and Mr. Madriani, did see this man, possibly
more than once. He was at the scene that
day near the gate to the naval base. He was
one of the terrorists. In fact, we believe he
was the leader. His name was Alim Afundi.
We know that from the DNA we were able
to extract from the body. He had been in
federal custody at one point. I'm not at liberty to tell you where he was confined, but a
DNA sample was taken at that time. He apparently escaped. Suffice it to say, we did
not take him into custody at the scene in
Coronado."

"So contrary to Mr. Olson's statement,
the terrorists were not all killed at the
scene?" says Harry.

"No," says Thorpe. "We found his
charred remains two days after the shootout in Coronado at a location near National City, a few miles north of the Mexican

border, which is where we lifted the unidentified print matching the one found on
your business card," says Thorpe.

"But you don't know who the print belongs to?" I ask.

"No. But we do have rumors as to who
killed Afundi. There's some sketchy information from sources across the border that
the person who killed him is a Mexican hit
man. According to the information, he's a
professional assassin known only by reputation, mostly among aspiring young guns
trying to claw their way to the top of the professional pyramid. To them, none of whom
claims to have actually seen the man, he is
known variously as the Mexicutioner, sometimes Muerta Liquida. It means liquid
death," says Thorpe. "Others just call him
Liquida."

"Charming," says Harry.

"From what we're told by the Mexican authorities, he's connected to the Tijuana drug
cartel. But he also freelances. We think he
may have been working with the people
who transported the device to Coronado."

"You mean the IED," says Harry.

"Any of you ever heard the name Liquida?" Thorpe ignores Harry. "Perhaps during your sojourn down south?"

"You mean the trip to Costa Rica?" says Herman.

"That's what I mean."

Herman and I had gone south to find a witness and gather evidence in a criminal case. It was how we got caught up in the events surrounding the attack in Coronado.

"Do you have any description of this man Liquida?" I ask.

"Nothing," says Thorpe.

I remember the pockmarked cheek and the evil eyes stalking me from a moving car that night as I hid in the shadows under a parked vehicle in San Jose. All I got was a fleeting glance as fear forced my face into the gravel, not enough to provide a reliable description. Still, I may have a name to go with the evil eyes.

"If Liquida was working with them, why would he kill this guy Afundi?" says Herman. "If Afundi was the boss, I mean."

"Maybe to silence him," says Thorpe. "We don't know. As you can see, the body was badly burned. But the medical examiner did find what appeared to be some indications of torture before he died. It's possible the two of them, Liquida and Afundi, got sideways, and Afundi came out second best in a grudge match."

"Yeah, I'd say whoever did this has a problem with anger management," says Harry. He is looking at the photograph of the charred body.

"The question is, assuming the information from Mexico is accurate, how did Liquida's thumbprint, if it is his, end up on your business card in the wallet of a drug overdose in D.C.?" says Thorpe.

I look at him with a blank stare. "So what is it exactly that you're telling us?"

"It's possible that you show up on this guy's radar screen," says Thorpe, "and that's not a place you want to be. Just a heads-up. If I were you, and this goes for each of you, until we know more, I'd be careful going out anywhere alone, especially after dark. And if you have any security devices at home, you might want to make sure they're turned on."

FOUR

Josh Root was a man who could always make time for an old friend. He and Nicholas Merle had come of age together in the counterculture trenches of the sixties. So when Root called him on his cell phone and asked to meet for a drink, Nick didn't think anything of it.

"The usual place?" said Nick.

"Why not?"

"Give me twenty minutes."

Neither man felt comfortable venturing into the other's office. It was one of those unwritten rules of government etiquette.

The "usual place" was a quiet upscale

restaurant in Columbia Heights, not far from the Capitol and the court building. The restaurant possessed a lounge dripping with old-world charm, dark wood, and equally dim lights.

Root arrived first, dropped off by his driver, who parked in a garage across the street and waited. He ordered a drink and took a seat at the booth in the back corner.

When it came to their meetings, Nick was usually late, mumbling something about circumspection and Caesar's wife. It was part of Nick's cautious routine. He always had to be certain that no one had picked up on their private meetings, especially the ever curious rumormongers from the press corps. Josh always gave him a hard time about it. If they ran into each other at a cocktail party or an embassy fling, it was fine. But a one-on-one meeting in a bar would cause tongues to wag, not that anybody could do anything about it. Still, why end up in the gossip sheets?

A few minutes later Nick came through the door. He smiled the moment he saw Root. In many ways they were like night and day. Nick was as organized as Josh was

THE RULE OF NINE

chaotic. Nick was tall and slender, had a kind of stately appearance, and was reserved in his manner, whereas Josh was in your face. Josh's suits, no matter how well tailored or expensive, never seemed to fit his paunchy body. If Nick was the smile of life, Josh was the scowl. Yet with all their differences the two men remained fast friends.

Nick had been losing weight for the past several months. He didn't look good, at least not to Josh, whose mind was increasingly focused on thoughts of mortality. Nick was working too hard.

He ordered soda water, no twist, just ice. Nick never allowed alcohol to pass his lips during business hours. He took the glass from the bartender, headed for the booth, and took a seat on the other side of the table. "I thought you were out of town, back in Oregon."

"I was until yesterday," said Root. "I came back to take care of some business."

"I should be out of here myself, but I'm interviewing some new clerks for the fall," said Nick. "What a pain. Kids. Still, a couple of them are pretty bright."

"Remember when we were that age?" said Root.

"I don't think I can remember that far back."

"Sure you can. Berkeley, sixty-eight," said Josh.

"Jesus, don't remind me. Seems like another age," said Nick.

"It was."

The two men had known each other for almost half a century. Their paths had crossed and careers intertwined so many times that Root could not begin to count them. He often wondered how it happened that two people following such different courses could end up on the same trajectory, as if they were touched by some stellar fate.

Nick had graduated from Berkeley. Josh was a senior at San Francisco State. They met at an antiwar demonstration during Vietnam, and in the months that followed sucked down enough tear gas and tossed enough bricks to form a kind of bond that usually coalesces only in the heat of battle.

After that Nick went on to law school at Yale. Josh graduated and then seemed to drop out of life. He disappeared for more than three years. It was what Josh came to remember as "his dark time." He talked to no one about it, not even his friends. That he was able to pull himself out of it, resume a normal life, and come so far in the decades that followed was an absolute wonder. It seemed that he had gone off the track and somehow, as if by magic, had wandered back. Still, he often saw himself as a failure. The demons of his youth continued to haunt him. Only now they appeared distorted by the contradictions in his life and the looming horizon of death.

"Do you ever wish we could go back to the time?" said Josh. "You know, the smell of tear gas in the morning."

"Are you kidding?" said Nick. He laughed.

"You don't miss the sense of commitment—the crusade?"

Nick thought about it for a second. "It had its place, but the moment has passed."

"You're wrong. That moment never passes. The world is what we make of it. And we never lose our ability to change it for the better until we lose our grip on life."

"You were always more ambitious," said

Nick. "I gave up trying to warp the world a long time ago."

"I know," said Josh. It was a major disappointment. Nick believed that radical thought was something you outgrew, like toys in an abandoned sandbox. To Josh it was a core element of his being, as essential as breathing.

"We've both been pretty damn lucky," said Josh. "What is it they say? 'It's better to be lucky than good.'"

"We've had this conversation before. Don't sell yourself short," said Nick. "You are where you are because of talent. Otherwise you wouldn't have survived as long as you have."

"I know. Luck is only as good as what you do with it," said Root. Still, there was no way to get around the fact that his career rested on the pillar of an accident.

In the years after pulling himself together, Josh got a job teaching at a small college near Portland, Oregon. The problem was he was bored. He hated it. He talked endlessly about changing the political system. He often went on a rant at faculty meetings. He had failed to change the system from the outside and now all he did, it seemed, was complain. When one of the other faculty members laughed at him and told him he should run for office, Root filed papers in a bid for a seat in Congress. For months it was the standing joke on campus.

Josh found himself up against a seven-term incumbent from a solid Democratic district in the party primary. His opponent was so invincible that the Republicans didn't even bother to field a candidate in the general election. As far as they were concerned, the man was anointed.

Then two weeks before the primary, political fortune ran its errant fingers through the golden locks of Joshua Root. The incumbent did a face plant into his chicken Kiev at a fund-raiser in Portland. The man died of his heart attack before the peas had run off his plate.

As the only surviving candidate on the primary ballot, and with no opposition in the general election, Josh found himself with a ticket to Washington and a seat in Congress.

It was where he and Nick crossed paths once more. By then Nick had graduated from law school. After spending a year

clerking for a judge on the federal circuit
court in D.C., he was working in the office
of the solicitor general. The two men re-
newed their friendship.

Cynical though he might be, Josh was
learning how to survive in office. If the only
way to effect political change was to turn
to the dark side, Root was prepared to do
it. He mastered the finer arts of duplicity.
He seemed to thrive in the shadowed crevices that form the boundary between perjury and politics. He won two more terms
in the House before a vacancy in the Senate yawned open before him. He ran and
won.

It was there that the light of good fortune finally spread to encompass Nick.
Four months after Josh arrived in the
Senate, a vacancy developed on the Supreme Court. The president filled it with a
nomination, but his candidate soon found
himself in trouble. The nominee had a history of recreational drug use in his youth,
something he had not disclosed to the
White House.

As it turned out, the high court candidate was a native of Oregon. He sat on
the Ninth Circuit Court of Appeals. As a

matter of courtesy, the White House con-
sulted the senior senator from the state.
This was not Root; still, he was sufficiently inside the loop to have influence and
to know how to use it. The question was
whether the senior senator from Oregon
would continue to back the man from his
home state.

Root discovered that on the short list of
other candidates for the appointment was
the name Nicholas Merle. Nick was still
working in the solicitor general's office. He
was a dark horse for the high court, but he
had a subtle advantage, and Josh saw it
immediately.

Though Nick had argued cases before
the Supreme Court, he had never handed
down a decision or an opinion because he
had never been on the bench. Conse-
quently he was a clean slate with no controversial baggage that might erupt in a
battle during Senate confirmation. Caught
in the crosshairs of a drug scandal, the
White House was already gun shy, Root
realized. Josh convinced his senior cohort
in the Senate that they could no longer afford to support the current candidate. It was
the political kiss of death. The nominee

withdrew his name from consideration the next day.

That was more than fifteen years ago.

As Root sat there sipping his Amaretto in the dimly lit lounge, it seemed almost surreal. His friend who had sucked tear gas with him and thrown bricks at police on the barricades had now spent the past decade and a half on the United States Supreme Court while he himself served as chairman of the Senate Select Committee on Intelligence. Surely the gods must be laughing.

"I wanted to talk to you about something," said Root.

"Shoot," said Nick.

"Have you ever thought about retiring?"

"What?" Nick looked up at him.

"Fifteen years on the bench is a long time. You're not getting any younger. And now might be a good time to think about stepping down."

"Josh, I know you had your own set of health issues. We all start to feel our own mortality at some point in life, but I'm not quite there yet."

Most of Washington was aware that Senator Josh Root had serious health concerns even though his staff tried to keep a lid on the details. He had been in and out of Bethesda Naval Hospital as well as several other treatment facilities for the past two years. What troubled Root most was his increasing loss of short-term memory. Whether it had to do with the new medications or other factors Root couldn't be sure, but there were periods of time for which he could not account. He collected his thoughts for another pitch to his old friend.

"The president would be able to fill the vacancy with someone younger who would have a much longer tenure on the court," said Root. "And he would have no problem with confirmation since we control the Senate. If you wait until after the midterm elections, that may not be the case."

Merle looked at him. "Has someone sent you here to ask me this?"

"No, of course not. I'm speaking as your friend. Look at yourself. Every time I see you, you've lost another ten pounds. You're working yourself toward an early grave. If you stay on the court until the current administration leaves office, and there is no assurance of a second term, you may find yourself in a partisan vice, unable to get off without changing the balance of the court. Think about it."

"Go on," said Nick, "I'm listening."

"If you end up with a Republican in the White House, and if he gets two terms, you'll be well into your eighties before he leaves office, if you can live that long. Nick, I'm telling you as a friend, now is the time to think about getting off."

"The administration has two more years on its current term," said Nick. "That's if they don't get a second term."

"Yes, but the confirmation process takes time. If you wait until the election is on top of us, there's no way to be sure that the president will be able to make the nomination, and that it won't get blocked in the Senate. Now is the time."

It was a problem. Everybody knew how the game was played. It was why the balance on the court never changed, at least not in recent decades. There was a time when presidents made mistakes and unwittingly appointed moles from the other side of the philosophic divide. Now that was nearly impossible given the mind meld of interrogation to which candidates were subjected. So unless there was a sudden death on the court, which was rare, the balance was static.

Root realized, as did most observers, that the court was the only real agent for permanent and lasting change in the system. Its members were immune from the whimsy of voters and the restraints of the ballot box. Once confirmed by the Senate, they were there for life. They could pick and choose the cases they heard and in this way dictate the policy agenda for the country. If the voters rebelled and elected a hostile Congress and president, the court could strike down any new laws that were enacted. A long-term change in the political balance of the court was tantamount to a revolution. It was why Roosevelt tried to pack the court with additional new seats that he could appoint during the Depression. Sooner or later the balance on the court would change. The only question was which direction the revolution would take.

FIVE

Life has turned upside down in the eight months since the shootout in front of the naval base. I have trouble sleeping at night. Like a turtle shrinking into its shell, sudden noise has me compressing my neck until my head is between my shoulder blades. The doctor tells me that this will pass in time.

Who could have ever guessed that a chance meeting with a young woman, Katia Solaz, in a grocery store would have led her to become a client in a murder case, or that the quest for evidence in that case, and the search for a witness in Latin America, would have ensnared us in an attempted nuclear assault on an American military base. It is like an ongoing nightmare.

In the hours after the shootout, before the smoke had even settled, federal, state, and local police held a chaotic news conference not far from the scene. My name, along with Herman's, got mentioned as "persons of interest" already in custody. It didn't matter that the cops told the press we were not necessarily suspects.

In less time than it takes to boil an egg, the names Paul Madriani and Herman Diggs ricocheted from one cable news network to another. It was a story with global reach. Within an hour, people in Hong Kong supping on Chinese glass noodles with chopsticks were seeing file photos of Herman and me on television. Bad news travels fast. News of a terror attack travels at the speed of light.

It began as a routine homicide case, the murder of Emerson Pike, a somewhat secretive old man who dealt in rare coins and whose past seemed shrouded. To the police the motive was obvious, theft. And when Katia was arrested with coins belonging to the victim in her possession, her guilt was self-evident. But then no one knew of Pike's background, except the federal government, and they weren't talking. In the end it was history that ensnared us, Pike's past, and that of Katia's grandfather, the old Russian, and the specter of the Cuban missile crisis.

When it was all over, the feds held us for five days. They picked up Harry and planted the three of us, Herman, Harry, and me, in separate cells at the federal lockup in San Diego so that we couldn't talk and compare notes. Then they interrogated us around the clock.

When I asked them if they were going to read me my Miranda rights and allow me to have legal counsel, I was told I was not a suspect, at least not yet. When I demanded that they either arrest me or let me go, they ignored me. After conferring with his lawyers, Thorpe then told me I was a material witness. He intended to hold me as long as necessary, for my own safety.

Because of the circumstances, they couldn't be sure whether they had all the perpetrators. If some of them were still at large, they might try to silence me. At least that was the story.

What they wanted was information. Short of violating attorney-client confidences, I told them everything I knew. At one point they brought in experts. Whether they were military or CIA wasn't clear. There were no introductions. The questioning went on until I lost track of time. Inside, with no windows, I couldn't tell whether it was night or day, or how long I had been there. I wondered about Harry and Herman and assumed that they were getting the same treatment.

Once they were certain they had squeezed us for everything they were going to get, they brought Harry, Herman, and me together in a room. There Thorpe, flanked by a lawyer from the Justice Department in Washington, warned us in the strongest possible terms to say nothing to anyone about the events leading up to the assault on the naval base. In particular, they told us not to mention the explosive device. They told us that we could be charged criminally if any of the information we had given them turned out to be knowingly false.

Given the stress we were under, the multitude of details, and the fact that none of us could be sure whether our stories conformed entirely, truth was largely in the eye of the beholder. It was the sword Thorpe held over our heads to assure our silence.

Before they let us go, Thorpe warned us that the press was waiting outside. He offered to take us out through the basement and give us a ride. At first, I turned him down, but then he showed us the photograph.

It was a picture taken that afternoon of the area outside our law office. A sea of cameras and lights blocked the entire sidewalk in front of the Brigantine restaurant, near the arched entrance to Miguel's Concina where our office was located. There were satellite trucks double-parked on the street out front from one edge of the photograph to the other.

He explained that they were also camped out on the front lawn at my house, and that the media trolls had found Harry's apartment and Herman's place as well.

I asked about my daughter.

The FBI had taken Sarah out of the house that afternoon. She was fine. They were providing protection. They had a place for us, a kind of "safe house" near Balboa Park, until they could figure out some way to get the media heat off us. We didn't have to accept his offer. It was up to us. We could go to a hotel, but there was no assurance that the press wouldn't find us. It was clear Thorpe didn't want us in front of the cameras. There was no telling what we might say.

All I wanted was to see Sarah, hold her in my arms, and bury her head in my shoulder. We took him up on his offer. If we had to, we could make other arrangements later.

* * *

It was the beginning of a long nightmare. Harry, Herman, and I spent weeks hiding out in an office tower in San Diego. We shared two condos near Balboa Park, Sarah and I in one, Harry and Herman in the other. When the FBI tried to gather some clothes and personal belongings for us from home, stories on the cable channels with film footage showed authorities presumably removing evidence from the residence. There was nothing Thorpe could do to set them straight without revealing that he knew where we were, and that there was a reason for hiding us.

Work files from the office were shuttled by secretaries, driven by the FBI to the office across the bay. Local police ran cover in squad cars if the media tried to follow them.

Sarah was unable to tell her friends where she was living. She couldn't go anywhere without an FBI chauffeur.

It became impossible for me to show my face in court without being questioned by print reporters on the courthouse beat. The two times I appeared in the courthouse, a near press riot erupted when word got out that I was there. The FBI decided it was not a good idea. I was forced to step away from a case that was scheduled for trial. When the judge threw a fit, the U.S. attorney's office quietly went behind closed doors and got a continuance along with a substitution of counsel. The bottom line was I could no longer practice.

Over time the details of the shootout unfolded, a little more each day. Other names surfaced, most of them foreign sounding, all perpetrators who were dead.

Slowly, like leaves from a tree in autumn, the satellite trucks in front of our office began to thin out.

The authorities made it clear that the investigation now centered on those who had planned the attack. To their knowledge there were no other active perpetrators. The shooters and those carrying out the plot had all been accounted for.

In time the myth of the IED was unveiled. A news blackout was thrown over the contents of the truck, all part of the continuing investigation.

Thorpe was worried that if he simply went to the press and told them right up front that Herman and I were not involved, it might look suspicious. A sharp reporter would wonder what we knew that might cause the FBI to carry water for us. So instead, Thorpe posed one of his undercover agents as a journalist during a news conference. After all the hot questions were asked and answered, the agent, with his notebook out, his pencil at the ready, prefaced his question by saying, "This is sort of ancient stuff, but as I recall, just after the scene was secured outside the base, didn't you arrest a local lawyer and a private investigator? Can you tell us, were they involved in any way?"

Thorpe mustered up his best toothy grin and said, "No. They were taken into custody and questioned, but they were cleared. They weren't involved in any way. As I recall, they just happened to be in the wrong place at the wrong time." Then he pretended that he couldn't remember our names, until one of his minions behind him whispered in his ear.

"That's right. As I recall, Mr. Madriani was the lawyer and I think Mr. Diggs was his investigator. They . . . no, as I remember, I think they just happened to be in the area talking to a witness who lived in the neighborhood regarding a totally unrelated matter. And they got pulled up in the net. It's regrettable, but it happens. No, they were cleared long ago," he told them.

Thorpe watched as some of the reporters in the room jotted down notes. "Next question."

It took a full day for the gardener to clean up the mess in my front yard after the media horde pulled out. Crushed paper cups, cigarette butts, and discarded sandwich wrappers covered the lawn. Part of the top rail on the low fence separating the garden from the sidewalk was gone. The flower bed behind it was flattened and the shrubs around it trampled where the fourth estate had decided to blaze a new trail to the house.

The office fared a little better, but only because the owners of the building hired security to keep the cameras and equipment out on the sidewalk. Miguel's Cocina sold enough coffee and chips with guacamole that Harry was afraid they might frame us on other charges just to get the customers back.

We've been back in the office now since early May, a couple of months. The first few days we noticed a black town car parked across the street in the same spot each day. The shadowed silhouette of two men could be seen in the front seat. Thorpe was probably trying to make sure that we weren't inviting any journalists in for coffee. No doubt they were tailing us but it was hard to tell. After a while we noticed that the car was gone. Apparently the FBI was satisfied that Harry and I had developed a terminal aversion to publicity.

We brought in a professional security service to check the office for electronic bugs, wires, and taps on our phones. Everything tested clean.

The print press, always the first to find a story and the last to give it up, made a few calls to the office, mostly voice-mail messages that we never returned. One enterprising reporter tried to inspire a new angle with the rumor that we were preparing to sue the government for defamation and invasion of privacy. He wanted to know if it was true. Before Harry could warm to the idea, I shot a one-line e-mail back to the guy telling him, "No truth to the rumor and no further comment." A lawyer unwilling to file a lawsuit; this seemed to kill the last vestige of the beast. Life had finally returned to normal.

SIX

Bart Snyder sat staring at the half-packed cardboard transfer box resting in the middle of his desk. One of his fleet of meaningless mementos was sticking out of the top like the prow of a sinking ship. The wall of respect behind his executive leather chair now stood stripped nude except for the patchwork quilt of nail holes and little brass hooks.

It seemed that this was all Snyder had to show for forty years of labor in the trenches of the law. He had resigned his position as managing partner with Todd, Foster, and Williams, a firm with more than three hundred partners and associates and with offices in five cities. Snyder was waiting for the man who might be able to give him at least some clue as to why the stars, moon, and sun had caved in on him. Certainly the Washington Metropolitan Police were no help. They would call if they had any further information. That was three weeks ago, and Snyder hadn't heard a word. Bart Snyder wanted to know who had killed his son, Jimmie, and why. And he wasn't taking no for an answer.

The phone rang on Snyder's desk. He punched the com line on the speaker. "Yes."

"Your two o'clock is here," said the receptionist.

"Show him in."

A few seconds later the door to his office opened and a tall young man with dark, closely cropped hair wearing a blue serge suit with broad shoulders entered his office. He was carrying a light leather briefcase and all of the expression was in his eyes; he had a serious face that looked a lot like the actor Russell Crowe's.

"Mr. Snyder, I'm Special Agent Joseph Wallace."

Snyder got up from his chair. "Yes, of

course, please come in. Can we offer you anything—coffee?"

"No, thanks. Your secretary already offered."

"Please have a seat."

The agent took one of the client chairs on the other side of the desk and Snyder picked the half-packed box up and put it on the credenza behind him. "You have to excuse me. I'm in the process of moving to another office down the hall. I'm going to be taking some time off for a while."

"I understand," said the agent. "First let me express my condolences and those of the entire bureau for the loss of your son. I know it's difficult, and I'm sorry for the intrusion at a time like this. But it's necessary that we gather as much information as quickly as we can."

Snyder settled into his chair. "I understand. And I want to help in any way I can."

"Good," said Wallace. He reached down and pulled a notepad out of his briefcase, then drew a pen from the inside coat pocket of his suit with the dexterity he probably used to draw a gun.

Snyder couldn't help but notice that the agent was probably no more than a few years older than Jimmie, but in terms of force of character and focus there was a galaxy of time between the two. It was a painful thing for Snyder to accept.

"First let me say that some of my questions may be difficult for you, and I apologize for any pain they might cause, but they are necessary."

"Please, ask away."

"To your knowledge did your son ever use narcotics or any other form of illicit or illegal drugs?"

"No!" Snyder said it emphatically, then leaned forward and planted both hands flat out on the desk as if to punctuate the point. "Jimmie never used drugs. I know that to be a fact."

"No pot, no pills?"

"Nothing," said Snyder.

This was the conclusion the FBI was leaning toward as well, as the result of a thorough postmortem and interviews with most of James Snyder's friends. The victim possessed no apparent history of drug use. For his first experiment in the recreational world of narcotics to be a full-blown hit of heroin was unlikely.

The agent then covered the usual questions, whether Snyder knew anyone who might want to harm his son, and whether Jimmie had been depressed or may have wanted to hurt himself.

"No. Jimmie was a good boy. He was never in any trouble, even when he was young. He was an easy child to raise," said Snyder. "Sometimes a little too easy, if you know what I mean."

"No, why don't you tell me?"

"Well, there were times when I wished that he might have been a little more headstrong. You could say he was easygoing, but Jimmie never seemed to argue with anyone, over anything. He seemed to have very few personal boundaries that others couldn't invade. You didn't have to push him. All you had to do was touch him and he'd move in any direction you wanted. I'm not saying he was weak," said Snyder. "Please understand. I know he had a solid sense of values, and I'm sure there were limits beyond which he would not go. But I have to say, I couldn't tell you what they were."

"Except for the use of drugs?" said the agent.

"Well, there you go. You're right," said

62   STEVE MARTINI

Snyder. "There's one right there. The things a father never sees."

"Did you know that your son was in some difficulty at work?"

Snyder looked up at him. "No. What kind of trouble?"

The agent told him about the breach of security, the fact that authorities were looking into it, and the discovery that James Snyder had been informed of this by a coworker, something the FBI turned up in their preliminary interviews.

"Was it serious? I mean, was he going to lose his job?"

"I don't know," said the agent. "But it's one of the threads we're checking out."

"Did it have anything to do with Jimmie's death?" said Snyder.

"We don't know. As I said, we're still investigating. There are a couple of other items," said the agent. He reached into his briefcase and pulled out three glossy color photos, five-by-sevens. "I'd like you to take a look at these pictures and tell me if you recognize the other man walking next to your son."

The photos were freeze-frames from the surveillance video in the building the day James Snyder had violated security with an unidentified man.

Bart Snyder looked at them closely. Two of the pictures showed his son in various strides walking with another man down a stark white hallway. There was nothing on the walls except a single sign over Jimmie's shoulder in the distance in one of the shots. The other man looked as if he was late middle age, overweight, heavy jowled, and, from what Snyder could see, he possessed a fair-size gut hanging over his belt. He was perhaps an inch shorter than Jimmie and was wearing a baseball cap, so it was difficult to make out the features of his face in two of the pictures. The third shot looked like an enlargement taken earlier in the sequence, because the sign on the wall was larger and he could actually make out some of the lettering. When he read the few words that were visible, Snyder knew instantly where the pictures had been taken. He had often heard about it, but he'd never seen it. It was off-limits, like the holy of holies, one of those insider places in D.C. that the active set among the power elite talked about, like playing the back nine at Spyglass in Carmel. It had been in the news recently because the president wanted to use it. He didn't have one like it. The picture showed only the head and shoulders of the man in the baseball cap. Here his face was a little clearer, but the angle of the shot was still bad, so the bill of the cap continued to obstruct a clear view of one eye and put a shadow across his face.

"Have you ever seen that man before?" said the agent.

Snyder started to shake his head.

"Perhaps a friend of the family or a relative, someone your son might have known?"

"He's no relation. I know that." Snyder studied the photographs a few seconds longer, then shook his head again. "I've never seen him before."

"You're sure?" said the agent.

"Yes." He handed the pictures back to the agent.

"Just one more thing," said Wallace. "Do you know whether your son might have taken a trip recently to the area around San Diego in California?"

Snyder thought about it, and then shook his head. "Not that I know of."

"Do you know whether he recently conferred with a lawyer regarding any legal
matters?"

"If he needed a lawyer, I assume he
would have called me."

"I see. But you say he didn't tell you
about the problem at work, the security
breach."

"No. Was it that serious?"

"We don't know. Did he ever mention a
name to you, a lawyer named Paul Madriani?" asked Wallace.

"How is that spelled?" said Snyder.

The agent spelled the last name for him
as Snyder wrote it down on a pad on his
desk and looked at it. "It sounds a little
familiar, but not off the top of my head. Do
you know where he practices?"

"The area around San Diego," said the
agent.

"I see. Do you know what field of law?"

"Did your son ever mention that name,
Mr. Snyder, or could you have referred him
to someone by that name?"

"No," said Snyder. "And I can't recall my
son ever mentioning him. What makes you
think my son talked with this lawyer?"

"I'm sorry, but I can't discuss that."

Thorpe and the FBI were reasonably certain that Madriani's business card had been planted on James Snyder's body by whoever killed him. Still, they were crossing all the *t*'s and dotting all the *i*'s. There was always the long shot that Madriani wasn't telling them everything he knew. He could be involved with whoever killed Snyder. Then again he could be hiding something that wasn't necessarily criminal but which fell into the dark hole of lawyer/client confidence. It anyone knew, it was likely to be Snyder's father, who as next of kin now stood in his son's legal shoes. It looked like a dead end.

"I think that's everything, Mr. Snyder. I want to thank you." The agent picked up the photographs and started to put them back in his briefcase.

"I wonder if I could look at those one more time," said Snyder.

"Sure."

Wallace handed them to him and Snyder looked at the pictures one at a time, very closely, for almost a minute.

"Jimmie had a lot of friends, people I didn't know. It's possible this man is somebody that Jimmie knew from right here in Chicago. If I could have a copy of these I could show them to some of his friends and see if anybody recognizes him. Would that be possible?"

"It's possible," said the agent. "At least for the time being. We've got copies. You can keep those, for now. You will call us if you get any information?"

"Of course."

The agent gave Snyder a card with his name and phone number on it, thanked him for his time, and left.

Snyder immediately turned to his computer and hit one of the icons on the desktop. The page popped up on the screen. Martindale-Hubbell is a directory of lawyers with detailed profiles by name, location, fields of practice, education, and experience, whatever you want to know. Snyder typed in the name Madriani and the location, San Diego, California. A few seconds later the computer coughed up a note indicating no hits. Snyder tried again, this time with only the name. This time he hit pay dirt. Paul Madriani's office was located in Coronado, not San Diego, and his field of practice was criminal law.

SEVEN

He had used so many names over the years that it was hard to remember some of them. Whether he called himself Dean Belden, Harold McAvoy, James Regal, or cloaked himself in the persona of Warren Humphreys, the amiable lawyer from Santa Rosa, the people who hired him knew him by only one name, Thorn. There was no first name. Most of his clients couldn't be sure if it was a surname or a code name. Thorn liked it that way. The less they knew the better.

This morning he sat hunched over one of the hotel's computers in an office just off the lobby of the Hostal Conde de Villanueva, a nineteenth-century mansion turned boutique hotel in Old Havana. Thorn had slipped the staff a few American dollars to use the computer for a few minutes. There was no Internet connection in his room and no Internet cafés that he knew of. He was busy scanning the online edition of the *Washington Times* for a news article someone told him was there. It was the perfect location, close to the States but beyond their governmental grasp. He could relax, send out e-mails, do some recruiting, and refine the plan with the confidence that no one was looking over his shoulder, at least not anyone who would care. Thorn had flown to Cuba from Mexico on a Canadian passport two days earlier.

There was a time years ago when he favored travel documents from South Africa. They were easy to get because of connections he had with apartheid security forces in the country. But those days were gone.

Ten years ago if he needed an article in a foreign newspaper he would have called their morgue or a clipping service and had it copied and mailed or faxed. True, it was slow. The Internet was faster and more convenient, but it came at a cost. Technology was closing in, laying nets and throwing bands around the chaotic, free-wheeling world in which Thorn had once thrived. They were closing the frontier, reining it all in so that it could be digitized, watched, and regulated.

The use of embedded holograms and the encryption of personal data in bar codes on passports made it increasingly difficult to find anyone who could make a credible forgery any longer. If your life depended on it, as Thorn's did, a good one could cost you almost seven thousand euros, ten grand in the United States.

He now had more than forty thousand dollars tied up in false passports that had a limited shelf life and could probably be used only once. After that the instinct for survival kicked in and sound judgment told you to toss it.

Once they started implanting biometric chips into the passport covers, passport fraud would be a thing of the past. It would no longer be possible. Thorn estimated that for most of the countries where he did business this might be no more than three to five years away. As the new high-tech passports came on-line and the old ones expired, so would Thorn's career.

If he couldn't alter his identity to some disposable facade and slip into a country with ease, he couldn't work. The notion of trying to cross a border with a herd of ille-gals didn't appeal to him, especially if, when the job was done, he couldn't get out quickly.

As far as Thorn was concerned, change sucked, and passport security wasn't the only thing that was changing. For years he had used numbered accounts in bank-ing havens around the world to salt away cash. In Thorn's line of work, you didn't take checks. Money was wired into num-bered accounts in Swiss banks, or on the Isle of Man, sometimes in the Caymans or Belize. These were places where you paid the bank to hold your money and where the marketing brochures read like Mafia primers on secrecy.

Thorn had used a small Swiss bank in Lucerne for years. Now Uncle Sam was knocking on the door trying to bring down the curtain on private banking all over

Europe. They needed more money to feed the swirling black hole the politicians had punched in the American budget. So now they were turning the screws on other countries, looking for taxes in numbered accounts.

Maybe it was just that he was getting older. But the world was changing, and the shadows he used to hide in were fast disappearing. For Thorn the writing was on the wall. It was well past time to retire. If it hadn't been for the meddling woman from Washington State and her dead friend from Holland, he would have been out of the business long ago. Instead Thorn had been forced to hide out in Mexico and go on the lam along the horn of Africa, living in Somalia and other hellholes for almost four years while the CIA and the U.S. military tried to hunt him down. When the twin towers went down, their focus changed to Bin Laden. It was the only thing that had saved him. It allowed him to go back to work, but with a much lower profile, and for a fraction of what he had once been paid. After 9/11 it was a whole new world, with much tougher rules.

It was the reason he took the contract.

Ten years ago he would never have even looked at it. If anyone had approached him with such a wild idea, he would have run screaming.

He felt safe in taking the job because it was brought to him by someone he knew and trusted, another soldier of fortune who at one time had been with Delta Force, the American special ops unit that, according to the U.S. government, didn't exist.

From this contact Thorn was handed a sealed envelope with a single folded page inside. It spelled out the details of the job, the target, the time frame, and the terms of payment. Thorn was to be paid in two installments, half up front for planning, acquisition of materials, equipment, and training. The other half was to be wired into his account twenty-four hours before the operation was launched. If Thorn didn't receive confirmation from his bank in Lucerne that the final payment was there, it was understood that the mission would be scrubbed.

After opening the sealed document and reading it, Thorn was instructed by the former Delta contact to burn it there and then, which he did. The contact then told Thorn that he didn't want to know what the document said, only whether Thorn was willing to take the job on the terms stated. He told Thorn that those making the offer were well funded and possessed first-rate intel to provide him with vital information.

Thorn agreed to do the job. But he wondered whether his old friend from Delta might have been commissioned to kill him if he had said no. If the people behind it were as serious as the man said, it would be absolutely essential to keep the contents of the then-destroyed document secret until they had a chance to find another operator to carry it out.

Thorn was then given a second sealed envelope. This one contained a long list of telephone numbers with area codes from all over the country. Each one had a separate date next to it. In order to communicate with his employers and to receive instructions or critical intelligence, he was to call each of the numbers listed on the dates printed next to them. From the time he'd started, about five weeks ago, there were a total of forty-five numbers, one for every other day, for a period of ninety days. By then the job was to be completed.

When Thorn called the first number, he found himself listening to instructions from a digitized voice synthesizer. He was told to repeat several lines of the verse "Mary had a little lamb . . ." and so on. Finally the instructions on the machine told him that in the future it would not be necessary to identify himself by name or in any other way, but that he should call one of the listed numbers every two days for further updates and information.

Thorn guessed that they were using voice-recognition software to identify him, a digitized voiceprint that could not be replicated by anyone else. Any other person calling in and the machine would shut down. The phone numbers on the list were no doubt patched through to wherever the voice-mail and message machine was located. The equipment could be sitting in the middle of an empty room anywhere in the world. If they cleared all messages and instructions each day, anyone seizing the box would get almost nothing by way of information. And they couldn't tap the phone line because it changed every other day. Because of the voice synthesizer, there was no way for Thorn or anyone else to pick up on an accent.

It was a onetime venture. Whoever did it would never work again. The risks were enormous, but so were the rewards. The initial offer was two and a half million dollars. That was his fee, but with the proviso that money was no object. The success of the mission was everything. Who else but the Middle Eastern merchants of terror would have that kind of money?

They agreed to cover the cost of the ordnance, all the transportation, and the crew. And Thorn was not above padding these to increase his take-home pay. He was already thinking along these lines when his eyes caught the headline near the left side of the screen. A single column about two inches long:

"Senate Staffer Found Dead"

Dateline: Alexandria, VA.

"Police are still investigating the death of a staff member for the Senate Select Committee on Intelligence who was found dead in his Alexandria apartment last month. The victim, James Snyder, 23, was found dead following an apparent drug overdose. Police are looking for anyone with information regarding the victim or his whereabouts on the evening of August 2. They are asking anyone with information to call the Alexandria Police Department, Investigation Bureau." The phone number followed.

Thorn had been following the little bits and pieces of news ever since the kid's murder. From the news stories it didn't sound as if the cops had any particular suspicions. It was standard procedure to look for witnesses who might have seen the person in the hours before he died, if for no other reason than to narrow down the time of death.

To the extent that Thorn was capable of such feelings, he had a fleeting pang of regret. It lasted a couple of seconds. He had nothing against the kid. It was the luck of the draw. Thorn picked him as the pigeon to gain access because he stood out.

Thorn had observed three young guides from a distance for more than an hour before settling on Snyder. The kid seemed lonely, as if he was desperate for a friend, but never seemed to mix or chat with the other two. He was the odd man out. The only person he talked to was the clerk behind the counter in the gift shop downstairs. That's how Thorn had found out Snyder went to Stanford and was trying to get into law school, by listening from behind a pillar as Jimmie chatted with the clerk during his break.

From that sparse information Thorn tailored the friendly lawyer Warren Humphreys. The rest was easy. The kid was so anxious to find a friend that Thorn didn't even have to ask him for a private tour. Snyder offered, and in less than forty minutes Thorn had everything he needed.

Thorn found out that his unofficial tour of the building had been discovered and that Jimmie Snyder was about to be questioned. He was tipped off by his employer. Whoever they were, they had boots on the ground, and big ears.

The kid could no doubt identify Thorn even without the heavy makeup and the rubber gut glued to his stomach to create a paunch under his polo shirt. Thorn had used padding in his cheeks for jowls and wore a broad-billed baseball cap that he kept pulled low over his eyes. All of these were intended to mask Thorn's appearance from the security cameras in the building. What was more threatening, however, was that Snyder could tell authorities exactly what it was that Thorn did as they went through the building, the fact that he had this rather strange-looking camera and that he kept using it to snap pictures from odd angles inside some of the rooms. Jimmie had even commented on it, wondering out loud how the camera had gotten through the metal detector without setting off the alarm. The reason was that the device contained no metal. Thorn had had it fabricated from plastic and carbon fiber using off-the-shelf hardware and parts.

Considering what the kid had seen and what he knew, Thorn had no choice. He hired the Mexican he had used several times before, and silenced Jimmie Snyder forever.

Thorn scrolled back to the first page and glanced at a few of the other headlines on the screen. He read the banner at the top: "Deficit Grows to Six Trillion."

He scanned enough of the story to conclude, at least in his own mind, that the old superpower up north was going down fast, in one final orgy of spending. To Thorn the whole thing seemed comical. For a century and a half, it had sucked taxpayers dry, forcing them all to pay for Social Security and Medicare several times over while Congress refused to lock up the money and pissed it all away on other things, including the Congressional gold-plated pension plan. Now they wanted to give everybody health care so they could play the same tune over again, only louder this time.

Einstein was right; only two things are infinite, the universe and human stupidity.

Two thousand years since the Romans disappeared, government was still dealing in bread and circuses. Perks to the people in return for their votes, all of it to be paid for by the rich, if you believed the people pulling the levers. And all they wanted was merely to serve, to maintain their death grip in the wheelhouse even as the ship went under.

Thorn would have to move fast if he was going to catch it before it sank; it would be like shooting fireworks off the deck of the *Titanic*. He would give them a light show they would never forget, just as the country slipped beneath a financial tsunami.

EIGHT

The United States Senate was without question the most exclusive club in the world. But tonight Joshua Root was wishing he had joined the Rotary Club instead. He was sitting alone in the darkened living room of his home in Chevy Chase holding a single sheet of paper, a printout of a personal e-mail from his computer upstairs. It was the second message in less than a month from an old acquaintance, someone he hadn't seen or heard from in years, a former friend from the dark days of his youth. Root had promptly responded to the earlier e-mail and thought it was over. But apparently it wasn't.

He had survived in the snake pit of Washington politics for three decades. Now in his senior years, he thought about the fact that at the peak of his power, his past was finally catching up with him. It seemed that everything around him was suddenly collapsing. He seemed to be suffering from increasing bouts of anxiety and confusion. Whether it was age or his worsening physical condition he couldn't be sure. But lately it seemed that he was constantly perspiring.

The mess in Washington, the disarray within his own party, was rapidly transforming the achievements of the previous year into a nightmare. They had come to power on the shoulders of voters with a promise of fresh politics and openness in government. Now, little more than a year later, they were left to founder on an agenda of costly social reforms that few on either side of the aisle embraced. In the end they had to be negotiated in the middle of the night behind locked doors, and purchased with billions of dollars in pork.

Root had been through tough times before, but never anything like this. With high unemployment and an ever present recession, voters across the country were growing restive. Their mood was increasingly ugly. An invitation to a tea party could mean anything from tar and feathers to a lynching.

The powers in Washington had lost control. In their place was a mob of itinerant Internet bloggers, constantly picking through political trash looking for dirt. The minute they found it, the story would play in a continuous loop over the national bullhorn, the round-the-clock cable news networks looking for ratings.

To Root, the delusional mood among leaders in Washington resembled the sense of serenity at Versailles the night before the French Revolution. Of course, his sense of dread was heightened by the knowledge he possessed.

The most odious scandal in American political history was bubbling like a hot yellow cauldron just beneath the surface of the nation's capital. And with millions pounding the streets looking for work, the timing couldn't have been worse.

For as far back as Josh could remember,

senior members of Congress had been
raking in large sums of money from interested parties on legislation. The casual ob-
server might ask, "What else is new?" But
this money was not in the form of campaign
contributions, and the sums being transferred would have dwarfed the national
treasuries of a few small countries. It had
been going on for years, long before Root
arrived in Washington, and was without
question the best-kept secret in town. Over
the decades sizable personal fortunes had
been transferred from multinational corporations, and in some cases foreign governments, into secret numbered bank accounts
owned and controlled by powerful key
members of Congress.

It was never discussed. No one ever
talked about it. It was considered the poor-
est of form ever to put anything in writing.
Votes were peddled with a wink and a
nod, and the money wired in from overseas accounts where U.S. authorities had
limited reach. The practice was of long
standing, and was clearly understood by
all the players, almost as if it were written
in invisible ink and included in the Senate
rules.

Virtually all of the numbered accounts were in Europe, in countries where the sanctity of bank-secrecy laws was not only time honored, but a principal pillar of the national economy. For a considerable fee these banks would quietly roost on your growing bag of gold with never a name attached to it, just a number, along with written instructions for periodic disbursements.

Senior members of Congress, including Root, were now sitting on stacks of money that would have shamed the Rothschilds. This while they beat their gums and railed over bonuses paid to corporate executives, people who were forced to genuflect because they flew into town on private jets.

For Root, his lifetime under-the-table earnings now amounted to more than a billion dollars, all of it illegal and on which he paid no U.S. tax. After all, the 1040 IRS form didn't include a line for "income derived from bribery." It must have been an oversight.

Then it happened. Forty years of corruption and incompetence and the national economy suddenly tanked. Who could have guessed? They found themselves busy holding hearings and pointing fingers, mostly at everyone else, when some do-gooder at Treasury lit a fuse that legislative leaders on the hill were still trying to stamp out.

The government was strapped for cash, so it was natural that the Treasury Department would be looking for a new group of taxpayers to shear. It didn't take long to find a pigeon. Who more deserving than American citizens hiding large amounts of income in banks offshore? Somebody slipped an amendment into a bill allowing Treasury to turn the diplomatic and economic screws on foreign banks holding deposits belonging to U.S. citizens. What they wanted were the names of Americans holding secret numbered accounts so they could impose taxes and penalties on undeclared income. And it would be an added bonus if they threw a few of the tax dodgers in prison as a warning to the rest.

Before Root and his friends could move to kill the bill, a number of foreign governments similarly strapped for cash jumped on the idea. What had been a private food fight in Washington suddenly turned into an international free-for-all and was threatening to get out of control.

Neglecting to report a modest amount of income on foreign rental properties was one thing. Explaining away vast fortunes in numbered accounts in what was clearly an institutionalized system of public corruption dating back decades was another.

Root and his friends began scrambling for some way out. They couldn't transfer the funds without creating a paper trail and shooting off international warning flares for money laundering.

Quietly they appealed to the manhood of their Swiss bankers, questioning whether any sovereign nation should cede such intimate powers as bank secrecy to a bullying superpower. If the bankers would only push back, members of Congress would quietly knee the Treasury Department in the groin from behind.

It took nearly two years of testy negotiations with the State Department and Treasury before Josh and his friends could get the genie back in the bottle and hammer the cork into place once more.

Under the plan only a limited number of

American account holders would be identified. These were to be selected at random. At least that was the theory. Since no one could be sure whether they would be in the group to be outed or not, the theory was that the random disclosures would force a large number of U.S. citizens to come clean. It was a good argument, except for one thing. The names of current and former members of Congress suddenly went off the banks' official books. They would never be dropped in the hat, and therefore would never be disclosed. Business would go on as usual. At least that was the dream before Josh received the first e-mail.

Root couldn't be sure, but he had a good idea of who the man was. In the two e-mails received so far, he'd signed off using the name "the Old Weatherman."

The Weathermen were a loosely knit organization of student radicals dating back to the late 1960s. They were a splinter group of the Students for a Democratic Society. Their goal was the violent overthrow of the United States government. Eventually the organization died like everything else, of old age.

Root knew all about them because he

had once been a member. It was during
the early seventies. Using a different name
and a false ID, Josh had participated in a
number of acts, including the bombing
of two federal buildings and a Bank of
America in Southern California. The bank
bombing, which had taken place in the
middle of the night, resulted in the unintended death of a guard no one knew was
present. It was this that brought Root to
his senses. He quietly dropped out of the
organization a few weeks later and cy-
cled back into the real world.

But the Old Weatherman, now sending
missives to him, knew about it. Not only
did he know about Root's past, but he had
details and evidence that could tie Josh to
the bank bombing.

Root looked down at the single sheet of
paper in his quivering hand. He'd known
when he made the first payment that there
would be no end to it. Now he wanted another half million. This to keep quiet. Or
else he would send the information to the
police. The Weatherman had already collected two and a half million, wired from
Root's Swiss bank account to another
numbered account in Lucerne. The Old

Weatherman was forcing Root to take dangerous chances wiring large sums of money around in the open. It was almost as if he was enjoying it. No doubt a true believer who never gave up the cause and was angry with Root, who had sold out and was now part of the power structure.

It was as if he knew that Josh had a bottomless pit filled with cash. But how could he know? He crumpled up the e-mail in his hands, balled it into a tight wad, started to throw it at the wall, then saw himself in the mirror and stopped. Sooner or later he would have to deal with the man, one on one. Root couldn't chance going to anyone else. "Better the devil you know than the one you don't."

NINE

My daily calendar sheet says her name is Joselyn Cole. She is from the state bar association. According to our reception-ist, she called late yesterday afternoon, demanded a meeting, and mentioned something about irregularities in our client trust account. Given the recent chaos it's probably a minor bookkeeping mistake, but it's not something I can ignore. I've had to shoehorn her into my calendar this morning.

As I cross the threshold into my office she is already seated in one of the client chairs in front of my desk, attractive, sleek, and from appearances all business. She is wearing a dark blue suit and packing a briefcase, black leather, that is slung from her shoulder on a strap like that of an assault rifle.

I close the door behind me and step around the desk and into my chair on the other side.

I introduce myself. "Ms. Cole, is it?"

"That's right."

"What is this about, our client trust account?"

She looks at me a little sheepishly and smiles. "I suppose I should apologize for that. I have to confess I'm sailing under false colors. It's true my name is Joselyn Cole. But I'm not with the bar. So you can relax. As far as I know there is nothing wrong with your client trust account."

As soon as she says it, I'm like Bambi in the headlights.

"Who are you? What do you want?"

"I'm sorry for the deception but it was absolutely essential that I talk to you."

She looks to be in her early forties, with blue eyes and shoulder-length sandy hair. There are just a few specks of gray, enough to let you know she is more interested in what she's about than how she looks.

"I am with a group known as Gideon Quest. We're a nongovernmental organization, an NGO." She slips me a business card from across the desk.

"I don't make contributions or respond to solicitations in the office." I talk as I examine her card.

"I'm not here looking for money, Mr. Madriani. Our organization is involved in the international effort to stem weapons proliferation, both weapons of mass destruction as well as certain classes of conventional weapons. So I suspect you probably know why I'm here," she says.

An electric chill runs down my spine, the kind of feeling you got as a kid when the nun called you to the front of the class with a ruler in her hand.

"No. I'm sorry, I don't. And I have a very busy day, so I think we're going to have to cut this short."

"Part of my job involves incident inquiries, events that may represent a threat to public safety, and that may go undetected and unreported for any number of reasons."

She ignores me. "Events don't always get covered in the general press."

"It's all very interesting, but as I said, I'm busy."

"We're one of a number of organizations that report on a regular basis to the International Atomic Energy Agency, the IAEA. I assume you've heard of it."

I'm still looking at her card, trying to collect my thoughts to figure out whether to toss her out now or let her go on to find out what she knows, if anything.

"I've got some questions I'd like to ask you," she says.

That cuts it. "I'm sorry, but I don't have time for this."

"It's very important," she says. "It's not often that we see an incident like this. The fact is I've seen it only once before. And a friend was killed. They covered it up then too. I tried to warn people back then but no one would listen. The government made it sound as if I was crazy. So I did the only other thing I could do—I found others who shared the same concern and we founded Gideon Quest. Yes, accidents happen, but an attempted intentional detonation in a population center is a seminal event. You really have a moral obligation to talk about this."

"Excuse me. You come here under false pretenses, scare the hell out of me with some story about problems in our client trust account. Then you tell me you're with an organization I've never heard of . . ."

"I told you I was sorry, but it was the best I could do on short notice," she says.

"No, you could have told the truth," I tell her. I'm trying to shift from angst to indignation, so I can gain the moral high ground to get her back on her heels and out of here.

"If I'd told you the truth, you would have refused to see me." The facts being what they are, she is dead on. So I try again. This time I get up out of my chair as if emphasizing my moral outrage.

"You come here misrepresenting who you are and what you want. Flying, as you say, under false colors, and you expect me to take time out of a busy day . . . Get out." The words come out as if I'm trying to shoo some cat out the door. "Get out of my office. Now! Please."

There is a moment of silence as she looks at me with a kind of quizzical expression, as if she has gas. It starts with a

modest grin, then the laugh lines around
her eyes begin to flex. A second later any
attempt at composure evaporates in a
wave of laughter. It seems my attempt at
fury has waddled across the desk, rolled
over in front of her, and died.

"What's so funny?"

"You," she says. There's a tear running
out the corner of one eye. "You should
never try to do pompous, angry bastard.
You're terrible at it."

"Is that so?"

"You lack the paunch and jowls." She's
still laughing, wiping the tears from her
eyes. "If you want to do anger, you should
do silent and steely eyed. You know, quiet
rage and maybe avoid getting out of the
chair. I'm sorry, but the words just don't
comport with the picture. Pompous, angry
bastard belongs to fat men. You just don't
make it. Besides, your eyes are all over
the place. You're looking at everything in
the room except the object of your
fury—me. You were avoiding eye contact.
You know what that says to me?"

"No, but I'm sure you'll tell me."

"Man with a secret, trying to hide it under a bushel of feigned fury. And your body language . . ."

"What's wrong with my body language?"

"It's dead," she said. "You're supposed to be angry. You should be pointing at the door when you tell me to go, and you never, never, never end by saying please. It sounds like you're asking permission to go to the bathroom. Trust me. I've been thrown out of better offices than this. I have a lot of experience. I know what I'm talking about."

"Thanks for the dramatic critique," I tell her. "Now you can go."

"That's better," she says. "I mean I'm still not convinced that you're about to turn the desk over on top of me. But at least you didn't say please. It's a step," she says.

I stand there looking at her. I'm not sure whether to laugh or cry.

"Now I've hurt your feelings," she says. "I'm sorry. I didn't mean to. Listen, it was cute. Really. And I'm flattered that you would do it for me. To take the risk, I mean, to put yourself out there like that. That takes a lot of courage. Let me guess. I'm going to bet that you don't have a lot of authority with little children or dogs. Am I right?"

"Now I'm starting to get angry," I tell her.

"Good," she says. "It has to be real. It has to come from the gut or no one's gonna believe it."

"I want you to go." I point toward the door.

"Yes, but how badly do you want it? I don't see any real passion."

I try to hold a stern expression but I can't. I start to laugh.

"There you go," she says. "Back to my question now about children and dogs."

I'm shaking my head as I laugh. She's destroyed me.

"I thought so. They have a sixth sense for false anger. They can read it in a heartbeat."

"Is that so?" I slump back into my chair.

"Children just laugh, but dogs will try to take advantage of you. They'll turn you into a littermate." The laugh lines come to life deep within her tawny complexion as she smiles at me.

"I'm not your enemy. Believe me. You can call the police and have me thrown out, or have me arrested if it makes you

feel better, but do me the courtesy of answering at least one question."

I would ask her what, but sound judgment tells me not to.

"I want to know why you haven't told
the press or the public what you know
about the events in Coronado. Why you
haven't made any public statement about
what was on that truck. You see, we already know the device was nuclear. What
we don't understand is why you haven't
said anything. People need to know how
close they came. The next time they may
not be as lucky."

"I don't know what you're talking about."

"Acting talent and confidence skills come
from the same area of the brain," she says.
"Your gifts must be elsewhere because you
don't lie very well either."

"Now that's something you would know
about," I tell her.

"They put pressure on you, didn't they?
The FBI, NSA, the Justice Department?
They've threatened you, to keep you quiet.
What did they say?"

"I'm practicing being silent and steely
eyed," I tell her.

"You can trust me," she says.

"Of course I can. You come with such sterling credentials." For all I know she could be working undercover with Thorpe, sent here to test me, to see if I'll talk. The way she's holding her briefcase under her arm, pointed at me, it could easily be concealing a digital minicam and a mic. My face might be playing on a television at this moment in the back of a government van parked out in front.

She notices me looking and glances down at her bag. "Ah. I see. You don't trust me. You're a careful man," she says. "That's good. Here." She opens the briefcase, pulls out a file, two pens, a yellow notepad, and a small case for eyeglasses. When she opens the case, a pair of glasses fall out and clatter onto the top of the desk. She drops the strap from her shoulder and turns the briefcase upside down, shaking it to show me that it's empty. Then she slides it across the desk toward me. "Go ahead, check it yourself. I want you to be comfortable. And I'm not wearing any electronics if that's what you think. You can pat me down. I'll even take my clothes off if you like."

"What then? Scream rape? No thanks.

Don't get me wrong. It's not that I don't trust you. I'm a criminal lawyer after all. I'm used to being lied to. People lie to me all the time. Some of my best clients lie to me. But then, that's all part of the lawyer-client thing. You expect a client to lie, at least from time to time. It's like the husband-wife thing, when one of them tells the other they're not having an affair. But we're not married and you're not a client, so we don't have a thing. We're strangers, so it's much trickier trying to figure out when I'm being lied to and why. Do you understand? I know it's confusing, but trust me on this."

"You haven't answered my question," she says.

"You noticed. I'm sorry to tell you this, but if you keep asking I'm afraid you're gonna have to get used to it. I am better at asking questions."

"Go ahead. What do you want to know?" she says.

"Who sent you here?"

"No one."

"What makes you think I know anything?" I ask.

"Now who's lying?" she says. "Okay, I'll tell you. We don't think. We know," she says. "Your name, along with all the details, was given to me."

"By whom?"

"That I can't tell you. But I can guarantee you that the information I have is solid—direct from God's lips to my ear," she says. "You wouldn't be revealing any secrets to me if that's what you're afraid of. In fact, I suspect we know things you don't. We know that you were on the truck, along with Mr. Diggs and a woman from Costa Rica whose name we have. We know that the device was of Russian design, gun type, using highly enriched uranium, and that it dated to the Cuban missile crisis, 1962 to be exact. At some point it became a loose nuke in the hands of Middle Eastern terrorists. We know that a defector from the Russian military with technical skills armed the device either when, or before, it was delivered to Coronado and that this man was shot and killed on the street outside the naval base. We know that you were there when he was shot and that you witnessed it. How am I doing so far?"

"If you know so much, why don't you go to the press?" I ask her.

"Because we can't. It would jeopardize our source of information. This is a valuable and continuing asset that we cannot afford to lose. The source is irreplaceable, not just with regard to weapons of mass destruction, but other weapons systems as well. Precision-targeted high-tech stuff that we believe presents unacceptable risks to civilized societies in the future. If we said anything, they would know where the information came from. And even if they didn't, the source would never talk to us again. But you have independent knowledge. You were there. That's why we need you and Mr. Diggs to come forward."

"It's an interesting story," I tell her. "But I can't help you."

"My god, what did they do to you?" She reaches for her briefcase and pulls it back across the desk. "I mean, to put the fear of federal wrath into you so deeply that you're willing to cooperate in covering up a major nuclear incident? They must have done something horrible. You poor man," she says. She starts to load her stuff back into the briefcase.

"Appealing to my sense of manhood will get you nowhere."

"Obviously," she says. "Contrary to popular belief, they don't kill all the lawyers, they just neuter them. That's funny, they must have missed me," she says.

"You're a lawyer?"

"I don't practice any longer."

"That's good, because going around passing yourself off as an investigator with the state bar could probably get your ticket punched."

"I'm licensed in another state," she says.

"For your sake I hope it's the state of grace, because there's a good chance you're gonna find yourself up to your high heels in some serious doo-doo if you continue pursuing this line of inquiry."

"You won't say anything," she says. "Not about what I told you. Not about our source."

"Why not? If I've been as emasculated as you suspect, maybe there's something I want that they can give me in return."

"Like what? Courage?" She's up out of her chair. "You're no lion and this ain't no yellow brick road. Just the same, you won't tell them."

"How can you be so sure?"

"Because refusing to help me is not the

same as helping them. And you know as well as I do that they can't be trusted."

"And I thought I was a skeptic."

"Every government in the world thinks it owns the cartel on virtue," she says. "Of course, none of them would use the bomb. Those that have it would love to get rid of it, but they can't. They need it to keep other less noble and more warlike pricks from using it on them. And the angels who don't have it would never pursue it, unless of course they have an excess of spent fuel rods that need to be put to some useful purpose, wasted resources being a terrible sin. In the meantime, bombs like the one on your truck have become war surplus, like old canteens and frayed fatigue jackets. I used to ask how long before some nutcase on a crusade got his hands on one. Now I guess I'm gonna have to come up with a new question, because we both know the answer to that one, don't we?"

I don't answer.

"Have it your way." She slings the briefcase over her shoulder, stands up, and heads for the door. As she gets there, hand on the knob, she stops to look at me one more time. "You're a hard sell," she says. "You're sure there's no way I can persuade you? Make no mistake. It's a watershed event. News of this would flash around the world before you could blink. It would force people to wake up. It would produce a back- lash that those in power would not be able to ignore. Right now they're asleep. What is it going to take to get their attention? Do you have any idea how many people would have died if that device had detonated? This office probably wouldn't be here," she says. "And we must be at least two miles away."

"You know a lot. It was nice meeting you. And thanks for the stage direction. I'll try to keep the dogs from humping my leg."

She smiles. "You do that."

"One piece of advice. I'd stay away from Mr. Diggs. He's not as understanding as I am."

"Is that right?"

"Yes. If you try to lie your way into his of- fice, he won't have any difficulty at all gin- ning up anger. And as for his body language, you may find yourself suspended by your panty hose from the flagpole in front of his office."

"Really?"

"Really."

"I'll be sure to wear pants," she says. "I'm pretty good at it."

I make a mental note to call Herman and warn him.

TEN

Dad, what is your problem? I'm just going out with a friend for the evening. I'm not running away. Though the thought has occurred to me." Sarah stands near the foot of the stairs in the entryway, her arms folded as she taps her toe nervously on the hardwood floor. She looks at me with a twinkle in her eye and a maternal smile on her face, like flashing neon that says, "Poor Dad's slipping around the bend."

"I know, but it seems like I never get a chance to see you anymore." I'm just getting in from the office and Sarah's getting ready to go out.

"You mean, besides the three months camped out together in the condo?"

"I know. That couldn't have been fun . . ."

"How can you say that? Do you know any other girl who gets to pick up her dates with an armed agent riding shotgun in the front seat? 'Hello, Bill. This is Special Agent Smith. He'll be frisking you before we leave.'"

"It couldn't have been that bad," I tell her.

"Yeah. You weren't there. Most of my dates were more interested in the driver than in me. One of them wanted to see his gun. Then he wanted to know how he could apply."

"I wouldn't go out with that guy if I were you." I drop my briefcase on the floor and pry my dress oxfords off my feet without untying them.

"Not to worry, Dad. I'm sure he won't call again. That is, of course, unless he's filled out his application and wants to file it."

It is a sore point with my daughter. And it's not the first time that cameras and paparazzi have stalked us in our own house. It has happened before during trials.

At this moment she looks so much like

her mother, Nikki, she could pass for her sister, auburn hair pulled back in a pony-tail and the same dappled freckles across the nose.

"But you could stay home tonight," I tell her.

"Dad, I'm twenty-two. I've been away at college for four years, on my own. Nobody was there to take care of me and I made it just fine. You have to learn to let go," she says.

"I know. You're right. I just need a little more time to get used to the idea. You have to remember, you're all I have left."

She glances at me. The sarcasm melts from her face as she drops the defensive posture and the folded arms. "Oh, Dad!"

In two strides she closes the distance between us, throws her arms around me, and we hug in the hallway, right next to the old register clock hanging on the wall. "I'm not going anywhere," she says. "I'll always be around. You're not going to lose me."

My wife, Nikki, Sarah's mother, died more than fifteen years ago, leaving the two of us to fend for ourselves. As I hold Sarah the clock ticks in my ear and floods my mind with memories of a million happy mornings; of hastily cooked breakfasts, tuna sandwiches in waxed paper, fruit and cookies tossed into brown paper bags. And always capped by the hectic morning road race to school. I still drive the old yellow Nissan, the one I used ten years ago to ferry Sarah back and forth. A hundred and fifty thousand miles and I cannot bear to part with it. I am afraid that when it dies, so will I. It is my time machine, filled with remembrances of better days, echoes of laughter, and a few tears. I love the grown woman who returned from college, but I miss the little girl who once sat next to me in that big yellow car.

While she still has her arms around me, I start in again. "I just thought that maybe you could stay home tonight and we could enjoy an evening together."

"I know, but I already made plans to go out with Jenny." She gives me a final squeeze, slides her arms from around my shoulders, and looks at her watch. "She should be here any minute. You've never met Jenny."

"No."

"She's really nice. You'll like her."

"I'm sure I will. Listen, I've got an idea. I could order out, get a movie, whatever you girls want to watch. If there's someone else you want to invite, call 'em up. Now that you're back in town, I'd like to meet all your friends. And you know me, by ten o'clock I'll hit the sack and you guys can have the run of the house."

"Gee, we could put on our pajamas and have a sleepover." She rolls her big brown eyes toward the ceiling and laughs. "Dad, please . . ."

She turns and glances through the double-glazed window in the front door, then checks her watch again. "Late as usual. Jenny's a lot of fun, but she needs a clock."

"You can do whatever you want. Have a party. Drink. Bring in guys. I don't care. But why not do it here?" I tell her.

Sarah turns back and looks at me. "What is this? What's going on?"

"What do you mean?" I give her a look of innocence.

"Is there something you're not telling me?" she says.

"No. Why?"

"Dad! I mean it." She folds her arms again

and looks at me straight on—the brown-eyed truth machine.

"I swear. There's nothing." My voice rises half an octave in denial.

"Are you sure?" She puts the same female glare on me that Joselyn Cole used to unravel me in the office. Where they learn this I don't know. You could bottle it and dispense with trials by jury. "I don't believe you." She comes to the same conclusion Cole did. The woman was right. Children and dogs, they'll get you every time.

I shrug my shoulders and shake my head. "There's nothing," I tell her. I raise my right hand, three fingers held tightly together.

"What's that?"

"Boy Scout sign," I tell her.

"When were you in the Scouts?"

"You don't have to belong to know the sign."

"Exactly, and stop trying to change the subject." Sarah studies me for a couple of seconds. "Dad, I'm worried about you."

"Why?"

"Because you're a basket case. I know we've both been through a lot. The last several months haven't been easy for either of us. But it's over. Look out there." She points toward the front window in the living room. "The cameras are gone. Those people are off our front lawn. And unless we've moved to hell, they won't be coming back. You don't have to worry anymore."

"I know."

She glances down toward the floor for a moment and collects her thoughts. "You know, Dad, I've been thinking. It might be good if you got some help," she says.

"Excuse me?"

"I'm talking about professional help," she says. "Since what happened at North Island you're not the same person anymore. You're never happy. You're always worried. It seems like you're constantly looking over your shoulder, as if something bad is about to happen. Is there some reason for this?"

"No . . . I guess I'm just . . . well, you know . . ."

"No, I don't!"

"A little jumpy!" I snap at her.

"That's what I mean. You need help," she says. "I know you don't want to talk to me about what happened that day. And if it makes you uncomfortable, I understand. But you need to talk to somebody."

She stands there looking at me.

At first I don't say anything. When the words finally come out, it's as if they are emitted from some feeble golem-like ghost buried in the depths of my soul—"I'm all right."

"I don't know everything that happened that day, only what I read in the papers. But I know it must have been awful. It had to be—the noise, the violence, people being shot and killed like that. I am guessing that you saw a lot of it."

"You know what they say: 'As long as the right people get shot.'" I try to make light of it.

"Don't even joke," she says. "It doesn't matter whether they were good or bad or what they were doing. They still died and you had to watch it. There's no shame in seeing a therapist," says Sarah. "There is such a thing as post-traumatic stress." She pauses for a moment and looks away. "I didn't want to say anything, but I found the pistol in your nightstand."

Whoops!

"When did that start?" she asks. "We've never had a gun in the house before. Not that I know of."

"No. You're right." A set of headlights flash as a car turns into the driveway out in front.

"I should have told you. Thorpe, you remember, the man from the FBI. He told Harry and me and Herman that there's probably nothing to worry about, but until they tie up all the loose ends, it wouldn't be a bad idea to keep some form of self-protection in the house."

"What kind of loose ends?" says Sarah.

"Nothing you need to worry about. Go ahead and have a good time with your friend. Do you have your cell phone?"

She nods.

"Do you mind telling me where you're going tonight? You don't have to if you don't want to."

She shakes her head. "No, no, it's all right," she says. "I think we're doing Café Coyote for dinner. It's a Mexican place in Old Town."

"I know it," I tell her.

"And then I think we're going to a club somewhere in the Gaslamp area. I don't

know the name. Jenny's been there before."

"That's okay."

"If you want me to stay home, I will," she
says.

"No. That's all right. You go and have
fun. And don't worry about anything. It's
fine."

The doorbell rings. Sarah grabs her
coat and opens the door.

"How are you?"

"Sorry I'm late." There is a lot of chatter
and giggling at the door.

"Come in. I want you to meet my dad."

A second later a tall, blond young
woman, nicely dressed, long legged and
a little ungainly, steps through the door
and under the lights in the entry hall. She
looks well scrubbed, blue eyes and rosy
cheeks, wearing a nervous smile and high
heels that make me think of a newborn
fawn trying to find its footing. She is gripping a tiny sequined bag to her stomach
with both hands so tightly that the little
glass beads are about to pop off.

"Jenny, I'd like you to meet my dad. Dad,
this is Jen."

"Is it Jen or Jenny?"

"Either one," she says.

"Well, it's good to finally meet. Sarah's told me so much about you I feel I already know you." I reach out. She releases the death grip on her purse and gives me a fleeting fingertip shake.

"Same here." She nods and smiles and does a little nervous genuflection on the tall stiletto heels.

Take off the makeup, put her in tennis shoes, jeans, and a T-shirt, shrink her down ten years, and Jenny could pass for any in the battalion of Sarah's "little friends." This was the legion of noise, the siege of laughter and yelling that rampaged through the neighborhood with light sabers and squirt guns a decade ago. Even now sometimes when I see one of them, grown and tall, and I have to look at them to say hello, if someone asks me who they are, I will slip and refer to them as "one of Sarah's little friends." My daughter gets angry. She tells me not to say it, especially in front of them; her dad, the loose cannon. Of course I would not. But if I live to be a hundred and see them with grandchildren, in the crevices of whatever is left of memory, to me they will always be part of that lost and noisy brigade—"Sarah's little friends."

"So you guys are doing Mexican tonight, is that it?" I ask.

Jenny glances at Sarah and smiles. "And then I thought we'd go to a place downtown."

"A club?" I ask.

"Yeah. Place called Ivy. They have good music."

"Listen, you guys have a good time," I tell them. We all head toward the door.

"I'll be home by two." Sarah kisses me on the cheek. "Don't wait up."

"You have your key?" I ask.

"Got it, Dad. And don't worry. We'll talk more tomorrow," she says as they head to the car.

"Good night. Have fun." I stand outside under the porch light watching as Jen's Camry slides down the driveway and backs into the street. A few seconds later the taillights fade into the distance and disappear down the block.

* * *

He sat in a rickety ladder-back chair that wobbled and teetered just a little each time he leaned forward to type.

The room was small and dark. It resembled a closet more than an office. A single naked lightbulb hung from a wire dangling from the ceiling, just above his wispy strands of unkempt gray hair. The shiny crown at the back of his balding head gleamed with illumination, revealing only a subtle hint of the energy and purpose that blazed within.

The Old Weatherman could almost feel the political ground shifting beneath his feet as he pounded the letters on the computer's keyboard. Outside, turbulent public attitudes turned like a weathervane in a cyclone. It was a sign of the times, a measure of people's fears and their uncertainty about what lay ahead.

The window of opportunity was already beginning to close. He had only months for the entire train of events to play out. The doctors had told him that he would be dead by then. The cancer was already in his lungs and brain. No matter. He had time. He would set in motion the change that would take America into the future, a transformation of the system that no politician or political party could ever bring about; he would "breach the monastery."

Back in the late sixties and early seventies, when they were young and stupid, they set off isolated bombs in federal buildings and courthouses around the country. Such a waste. None of it had any effect except to give Nixon the excuse to crack down on all forms of dissent. Other than to cause some localized terror and largely regional headlines, their actions failed entirely to bring about their ultimate goal, a permanent change to the system. One that would take the country in an entirely new direction, away from the corporations and the capitalist underpinnings that had taken America down the wrong path since its inception.

Then, in 2001, foreign terrorists struck the World Trade Center. Flying commercial jets loaded with fuel and passengers into the twin towers, they killed more than three thousand people. They also hit the Pentagon, causing hundreds more to die. And what was the effect? Did they bring down the country? No. Did they destroy the U.S. economy? No, at least not immediately.

Economic markets recovered in less than a year and came raging back to hit peaks never before seen. The damage to the Pentagon was repaired in a few months and the U.S. military set about to crush two of the regimes thought to be most antagonistic to American interests.

As he clicked on the keys, the Old Weatherman thought about his old comrade, Senator Joshua Root. He had voted for the war along with the rest of them. Back in his day, when he was young, Root used a different name. He didn't call himself Josh to pander to voters. No, back then he was spouting a different rhetoric, the words of revolution—power to the people, throwing rocks and Molotov cocktails. That was before he saw the error of his ways and sold out.

The Old Weatherman wondered if Root had ever seen him coming, or if the good senator had been completely blindsided by the first e-mail message. Of course, like himself, Root had a number of private e-mail accounts where he hid out in dark corners, places where government censors, auditors, and investigators could not see his personal musings and sins. The Old Weatherman had found them all. Even if Root closed one, the Old Weatherman could go to another. It was because the Old

Weatherman had an inside connection, someone Root could never get rid of.

People like Root never expected to be held accountable for anything. Their sense of privilege and entitlement blinded them. And, of course, Root couldn't go to the police and tell them that he was being blackmailed. The truth would destroy him.

The Old Weatherman stopped the pounding of the keys for a moment and thought about it. It had to be the work of the gods, all of it. It was too perfect.

The attack on the World Trade Center accomplished something that no one realized at the time. What became a series of protracted and unpopular wars distracted many in Washington, particularly in the White House, from the real danger. A rapidly expanding bubble of false fortunes and speculation in the nation's housing market was threatening to take the country where it hadn't been in more than seventy years, into the grip of another Great Depression.

When the bubble burst on the eve of the national election, it came with such swiftness and public shock that the country

was left reeling. Overnight the reactionary
forces in the White House and Congress
were swept from power in a way that hadn't
been seen almost since the Civil War. It
was something that no one could have pre-
dicted even a month before.

When all the dust had settled, the Old
Weatherman sat back and pondered the
stunning political landscape that lay before him. For the first time in modern American history, all of the stars were aligned,
the set pieces in place. He couldn't believe
his eyes. A young, liberal president, some
called him radical, was installed in the White
House. His party controlled both houses of
Congress with majorities that could not be
overridden or stalled.

For at least the next two years, until the
midterm elections, they had a free hand.
It was the perfect storm and the Old
Weatherman was about to add the coup
de grâce. While Congress and the White
House argued over health care and taxes,
unemployment and trade, a new subterranean agenda of change would be moving
on a parallel course, one that the powers
in Washington could never anticipate.

The system was now vulnerable to true

endemic change on an order that had not been seen since the founding of the country, change that, if successful, and if done soon, would alter the direction of America for the next hundred years.

ELEVEN

The house had a dangling For Sale sign planted in the dead grass of the front lawn. A large old elm tree near the sidewalk provided shade, so he pulled up to the curb and parked. Even the words "For Sale" hung vertically from a partially broken chain. It appeared that the place was deserted, nobody there who might get nosy and come out and see what Liquida was doing.

He knew it could take hours. For Liquida it was an act of amusement on its way to becoming a labor of love.

For the man they called "the Mexicutioner," pursuing a vendetta was a high art form. It was not something to be hurried or rushed.

He knew there was a limit to the level of physical pain a human body could endure. Liquida had often tested this boundary, looking for new horizons. But at some point the brain's natural defenses always seemed to kick in and the object of his attentions would lose consciousness. He was able to revive the barbecued Arab three times while probing all of his nerve endings with an arc welder and tongs before the guy finally latched on to the only sedative that Liquida had never been able to reverse— death.

This might be okay for some of his guests, but not for the lawyer. For him there was no amount of physical pain sufficient to quench Liquida's thirst for revenge.

In a single stroke Madriani had transformed Liquida's plans for his own future into cinders.

Among his various paid chores several months earlier, the Mexican had used a chef's knife from a Del Mar coin dealer's kitchen to turn him into sliced sushi. As the soon-to-be cadaver lay shivering on the floor, Liquida couldn't help but notice the glitter of heavy metal all around him, coins everywhere.

While he knew he'd been a good boy, the thought that Santa might come flopping down his chimney with a load of gold anytime soon didn't seem likely. So Liquida decided to help himself. He hauled off enough precious metal to set up his own gold reserve and form a country, and then played the wizard doing alchemy as he transformed the rare coins into gold ingots that couldn't be traced.

Until he could wrap it and put on a bow, Liquida stashed his early Christmas present in a safe-deposit box at a bank in San Diego under the name John Waters. With visions of sugarplums, warm sandy beaches, and bikini-clad courtesans dancing in his head, Liquida started browsing pictures of villas in exotic locations in the *Wall Street Journal* and on the Internet. It was about then that everything came crashing down.

Liquida was starting to get nervous. He hadn't checked on the gold in a while. Something told him it was time to move it, and it would take a few trips. They had to roll it in and out of the vault on a heavy steel cart because of the weight. Liquida didn't want to spend time hanging out at the bank while some clerk fished for signature cards and he did an eye tango with the security guard or anybody else who happened by. So he called the bank to tell them he was in a hurry and to ask them if they might have a signature card ready when he arrived. When he gave them the name John Waters and the box number, the clerk did a quick check and told him that, under a court order, the box was sealed.

Liquida wanted to crawl over the phone line to get at her. He asked why, and all they would give him was the lawyer's name— Paul Madriani. If he wanted to get at the box, John Waters would have to file an objection and go to court. And Madriani knew that whoever owned the box couldn't do that. If they showed up in court, they'd be met by a firing squad.

Some way, he didn't know how, Madriani must have traced the name John Waters. Liquida couldn't figure out how else it could have happened. He had picked the name himself from out of the blue. It was a play on words. "Liquida" meant water in Spanish, but he couldn't

understand how the lawyer would have either name. So how did he find the box? It
would probably be the first question he
asked when he got Madriani on the working end of a blowtorch.

The next thing he knew, the cops were
at the bank with a drill for the lock and
Liquida's dreams of an indolent life on the
beach went up in smoke.

The timing couldn't have been worse.
With the economy tanked, now every teen-
ager in Tijuana with a rusty razor was
undercutting his prices. You could hire a
quick death for the cost of a Big Mac. Throw
in fries and they'd make it look like an accident.

Each day he watched as the spot price
for gold soared like a rocket while his venom
toward the lawyer turned more toxic.

Liquida steered away from the drug cartel at the border and instead began nosing
around the fringes of the international terror trade. He had heard enough frantic bar-
gaining from the fevered mind of the Arab
before he died to know that there was
money there. The only things deeper than
the primeval grievances that fueled their
hatred were the pockets that paid for the

revenge. Even at current prices, there was always more oil money.

Liquida ended up taking a job from an Australian who thought he was fooling the stupid Mexican with his lousy American accent. The word was that the man was wired into a major contract being paid for in euros, most likely money from the Middle East.

He took the job, but he figured there was no harm in stirring a little enjoyment in with his business. Liquida knew he'd left at least three fingerprints on the Dumpster where he'd dropped the burned body. As soon as they figured out who Liquida's grilled guest was, they would connect the roasted remains to the fireworks in Coronado. The FBI would land on the Dumpster as if it were a national treasure. It would take them a while to sort out all the prints, the guys who drove the hoist trucks and the ones who unloaded them, Dumpster divers who fished through the trash for goodies, and drifters who saw the container as a five-star condo and tried to move in. In the end they would come away with a few prints they couldn't identify and could not clear. These would end up in the

FBI's big mainframe, a computer somewhere in West Virginia.

Liquida then filched one of Madriani's
business cards from the reception counter
in his office. He did this during the chaos
of the Paparazzi Putsch when he realized
that the two lawyers were nowhere to be
found. He superimposed a single patent
thumbprint on the back of the business
card, using a little graphite so they couldn't
miss it. Then he waited for the right opportunity. It came when Liquida killed the young
tour guide in Washington. He had no idea
why the Aussie wanted the kid dead. What's
more, he didn't care. He knew the card with
his print would set off all the bells and whis-
tles in the FBI database, roping in the lawyer and leaving the feds to wonder what
the connection was between the two cases,
and whether Madriani had told them everything he knew.

*   *   *

It was just a little after seven when the
flash of headlights roused Liquida from
behind the wheel. He saw the car pull into
the driveway. He lifted a pair of field
glasses and peered toward the front of the
house half a block away, on the other side

of the street. He watched as a tall, skinny blonde got out of the car and climbed the steps to the front door.

A few seconds later someone opened the door. In the light he could see another woman just inside, talking to the blonde, who was still standing on the porch. They were laughing. A few seconds later they both went inside and the door closed.

As he waited he wrote down the license-plate number from the blonde's sedan, parked in the driveway.

Several minutes went by. Liquida was looking at his watch as the door to the house opened once more. This time both women came out, the blonde followed by a shorter woman with brown hair who was carrying a light jacket. She was smiling as the two of them came down the steps and headed for the car.

From the corner of his eye, Liquida caught movement up on the porch. He shifted the binoculars, refocused them a little, and there he was. Standing in the doorway waving toward the car in the driveway was the lawyer Madriani.

Liquida had seen his picture splashed all over television enough times that he now had visions of him in his sleep. As he glanced back and forth between the lawyer and the two women, he realized that the brown-haired girl belonged to Madriani, probably his daughter.

Liquida watched as the car with the two girls backed out of the driveway onto the street. Its headlights shone down on him as the car approached. Liquida leaned over on the front seat until they passed, then looked up just in time to see the front door at the house close behind Madriani.

There were many forms of pain; physical was only one of them, and perhaps not the best. Liquida started the car, and pulled away from the curb in a slow U-turn. He focused his gaze on the taillights of the Camry, already a block away as they turned left and headed off toward the bridge.

* * *

I grab the wireless house phone from the cradle in the kitchen and punch in the number. It rings three times before he answers.

"Hello!"

"Herman, Paul here."

"Whassup?"

"I need some help. I'm sorry to call this late, but Sarah's out on the town."

"Why didn't you stop her?" he says.

"I tried. She wouldn't listen. There's probably no reason to worry. But I'd feel much better if somebody was close at hand."

"Understood," says Herman.

"There's no need to race down there, but you're closer than I am. She's out with a girlfriend, a tall blonde named Jenny. They're going to have dinner at a restaurant in Old Town, Café Coyote."

"I know the place."

"They just left, so it'll take 'em a while to get there. No need to bust your hump. After that they're headed to a club in the Gaslamp Quarter, but I'll take care of that."

"You sure?" says Herman.

"Yeah, I got it. If you can cover the dinner, just stay with them until they're in the car. Then you can go home and get some sleep."

"Okay," he says. "Call me if you need some help."

"And, Herman, if you can, try not to crowd them."

"I never do," he says.

"If Sarah finds out, she'll be on the warpath for a month."

"Gotcha," he says, and hangs up.

Sarah doesn't know it but Herman has been her guardian angel on and off for the past five weeks, ever since the FBI pulled out and we came home. He follows her to and from work and keeps an eye on her from a distance whenever she has something going on outside work. Tonight she caught me by surprise. I had no idea she was going out.

I head upstairs, grabbing my briefcase and oxfords as I go. Moving at a quick clip I drop everything on the bed in my room and start to change. In less than a minute my suit jacket, pants, shirt, and tie have joined my oxfords in a heap up near the pillows. I throw on some jeans and a thin navy blue sweatshirt with a hood in case I need it to mask myself from my daughter. I slip on a pair of running shoes, check my watch, and walk to the nightstand.

Inside the top drawer is a two-tone stainless and blued .45 automatic. It's a Springfield Arms ultracompact, with a three-and-a-half-inch barrel. And contrary to what Sarah might think, it's not new.

Though she's never seen it before now, I've had it for years, ever since she was a little girl. And on one or two occasions I've felt the need to keep it close, but always in the office.

Herman is an investigator. He's had a license to carry for years, though he doesn't often use it. Harry and I are new to this. Though I've done my share of target shooting over the years and at one time did some loading with a friend who had the equipment, I've never had a desire for a permit to carry a concealed weapon. Now, in light of what's happened, and the warning from Thorpe, the county sheriff has issued permits to both of us.

In the last two years, three lawyers in this county have been shot. So far the scorecard is one wounded and two dead. Deterrence is a problem since the sentencing guidelines for shooting a lawyer in this state call for ten minutes of probation to reload while they frame the certificate of merit to be awarded to the shooter by the local prosecutor.

I don't do divorces, the most dangerous area of law, because I don't like surprises. Why should I allow some angry husband to pop into my office without warning or even the courtesy of an appointment, and shoot me while I'm behind my desk? If the maggot wants to defend his honor, then give me a pistol and tell him to turn and take five steps so I can shoot the crazed bastard before he gets there.

In criminal law you usually know what you're dealing with. It's normally your own client who will jump you, and he's often confined, for good reason. If he's not, you probably want to keep your eye on him. You have to figure he wasn't arrested for good housekeeping.

Of course, you can always draw the odd client, the mental three-headed hydra who opens as Mr. Rogers and shows up a week later playing Darth Vader without the mask, and his friends who insist on testifying the minute Satan releases them from the ninth circle of hell and they can get to your office to prepare their perjury. It happens.

So it's easy to see how a spirited disagreement can quickly escalate beyond the normal civility of single-fingered hand gestures and four-letter name-calling. The one time I had to pull the gun, I was happy to have it. When somebody leans across my desk with a needle-sharp shank angry over the result in his case and questions the need for my continued existence, it's comforting to be able to mediate by citing the case of Mr. Springfield pointed at his groin from the kneehole of my desk.

I punch the button on the side of the pistol and check the clip—seven rounds, eight if I want to load a live one in the chamber. The .45 ACP jacketed hollow point is a short, stubby little bullet with enough wallop to make an elephant's eyes water. It's designed to spread on impact. So if you have to shoot, you want to hit your target in the mass of the upper body where all the energy will be absorbed. You never want to shoot an idiot in the head where the bullet will pass through the vacuum and kill somebody behind him.

I slam the clip home, pull the slide back, and let it go, chambering the first round, then lower the hammer with my thumb and click on the safety. The pistol fits into a leather fanny pack with Velcroed webbing that I snap around the weapon to hold it in place. Then I zip up the pack and strap the belt around my waist.

Anyone itching for a permit to pack might want to carry a four-pound diving weight in their back pocket for a few days. It's a good prescription for a cure. The dead weight of the pistol and three loaded clips makes my behind feel as if it's lost the battle with gravity. No wonder cops all seem to be shrinking. With the load of gizmos on their belts, it's a wonder they can stand up.

I head toward the stairs and down to my car in the garage.

TWELVE

It was nine o'clock. Thorn was packing his bags, getting ready to pull out of Havana the following morning, headed for his next port of call, when the phone next to the bed rang. Unless it was the front desk, it was trouble. Only two people on his crew knew where he was, and both of them had been told not to call unless it was an emergency.

He dropped the folded shirt into the bag and grabbed the phone. "Hello."

"Cheeef, is Victor here. We got problem."

Thorn immediately recognized the voice. Victor Soyev was his procurement man.

The Russian was a former army ordnance sergeant who'd found himself without a chair when the music stopped in the Soviet Union. Like many other Russians with an instinct for business, Soyev quickly learned that change can be good. His talent lay in the murky world of international arms trade and its shipping sideline, what Soyev called "special handling" but most normal nations viewed as smuggling.

"Victor, we may be on an open line here." At times Soyev could be an idiot. It provoked Thorn, but then it probably didn't matter. The two men had never met, only voices on the phone. Soyev knew Thorn only as Mr. Bell, one of his many aliases, and neither man particularly trusted the other. It was a symbiotic relationship only because it produced money for both.

"Understood. It's an open line," said the Russian. "But it was necessary I talk to you." Thorn was telling him to keep it cryptic in case the Cubans or anybody else was listening in. "Our shipment got diverted."

"When?"

"Last night. I just found out. Apparently some engine problem. They had to put down in the land of smiles."

Soyev was telling him that the giant IL-76, a massive four-engine cargo plane carrying one of the critical items, had apparently been forced down in Thailand.

"Did they fix the problem?" said Thorn.

"No. Seems they got more serious problem now. Open cargo door," said Soyev. "I am told that it cannot be fixed. I'm sure you see something about it in tomorrow's paper."

Open cargo door could mean only one thing. Thai customs had discovered what was on the plane. They had seized the entire load. The wire services and the press were already on it.

Thorn looked out the window and thought for a moment. "Which, ah . . ." He collected his thoughts. "Which of the passengers was onboard?" he said.

Soyev didn't know what to say. He understood the question, but he was afraid to use the code words over an open line. He might as well telegraph Washington. Thorn thought it was cute. It was his plan, and he was in charge, so there was nothing Soyev could do to stop him from using the terms. But what the hell was the use of code names if you couldn't use them? He also talked about "breaching the monastery," though Soyev had no idea what it meant.

"Tell me," said Thorn. "Which of them had the boarding pass, the big guy or the little kid?"

"Big guy," said Soyev. Thorn had solved the problem for him.

"I see," said Thorn. If it had to be, this was better than the alternative.

"The kid will take a later flight," said Soyev.

"Make sure he goes first class," said Thorn.

"You bet. I will take him by the hand and make sure he gets a good seat. By the way, I'm still here," he said.

Oh shit, thought Thorn. Soyev was calling from North Korea. Might as well just hang a neon sign in the sky.

"I'm gonna have to go," said Thorn. "Can't talk any longer."

"The man has a brother." Soyev spoke before Thorn could hang up.

"Really?" The North Koreans had made not one, but two of the devices.

"Yes."

"Do you know if the brother might like to visit?" Thorn was asking if it was for sale.

"I think so."

"Then we would love to have him," said Thorn. "I think we can make the same accommodations." Thorn was going to need more money. They had already paid for the device. Now they would have to pay again. He would have to get on the phone, to the link with its elaborate voice synthesizer, and leave a message. No problem. They would call the oil sheiks and dial up a few more million. After all, what's money when you have all that oil?

"Good," said Soyev. "I let you know tomorrow if he can come."

"Good. You have my schedule?"

"Yes."

"Call me," said Thorn.

"You bet." Soyev hung up.

If the Russian had his schedule, then he knew where to call him tomorrow, either on his stateside cell or at the hotel in downtown Manhattan.

* * *

Liquida moved quickly across the grass in the backyard until he stood beneath the window where he had seen the light go out a few minutes earlier. She was the last to turn her light out after arriving home. The room upstairs had to be her bedroom. And now the house was dark. He crept along the side past a coiled-up hose and a small bench. He kept his feet on the brick pavers.

Halfway to the front Liquida found what he was looking for, a partially open window, a slider someone had left ajar just a crack, probably for fresh air. Through the dark glass, he could see the glow of green light from the digital clock over the stove—3:18 A.M. The window looked out on the side yard from a small dining nook just off the kitchen.

With the window open Liquida knew it was unlikely that there would be any electronic contacts to trigger an alarm. Nonetheless, he scanned with his eyes along the inside frame behind the glass. He could see no metal contacts and no security catch that might prevent the window from opening all the way.

Using the needle-sharp point of his knife, Liquida gently punched a hole in the screen. Then he maneuvered the long stiletto until it released the metal clip inside. With gloved hands he removed the screen and set it on the ground, propping it against the side of the house. He used two fingers to gently slide the window open, and then with the feline agility of a cat, Liquida slipped inside.

He reached out and grabbed the window screen and gently dragged the bottom of the aluminum frame through the sandy, dry loam of the planter bed outside. This would prevent anyone from gaining an impression of the soles of his shoes.

Inside, the house was still and entirely dark except for the glow from the kitchen clock and a narrow shaft of light streaming in from down the hall. By now they were both asleep, in separate bedrooms upstairs.

Liquida moved swiftly and without a sound through the kitchen and down the hall until he came to the front entryway. The light was streaming in through the living room window from a streetlamp out in front. Quickly he stepped through the shaft of light, turned, and climbed the stairs two at a time.

When he reached the top, Liquida saw a closed door immediately to his left, just a few feet down the hall. To the right were an open door and another door farther down that was closed. The open door in the middle had to be a bathroom between the two bedrooms. He crept slowly toward the open door until he saw the porcelain pedestal of the sink, then slipped past the opening to the closed door at the end of the hall. This was her room, where Liquida had watched the light go out from the yard down below.

He quickly glanced over his shoulder toward the other bedroom down the hall. Satisfied that no one stirred, he transferred the knife and carefully gripped the doorknob with his gloved right hand. With the care one might use to unthread the fuse from a bomb, Liquida turned the knob until he felt the gentle click of the lock as it slipped from the brass striker in the door frame. He held his breath and gently eased the door open just enough to quickly slither inside.

Holding the door behind him, his gaze fixed to the front, Liquida scanned the darkness like a bat searching for its quarry. He held the inside knob turned tight so that the bolt was retracted all the way into the door. Then with his hip he silently pressed it closed.

In the dim light of the room he began to make out the soft muslin landscape of the thick comforter. He couldn't see her, but she was in there somewhere. He hoped that the padded hills and valleys would somehow define her body so he could find the right spot.

Slowly he rotated the wrist of his right hand behind him until he was certain that the door was latched closed once more.

Then Liquida turned his full attention to the front. He glanced quickly around the room, sizing up the terrain around the bed to make sure there was nothing in the way, shoes to be kicked or clothes he might trip over. Once he was certain he had a clear path, Liquida took the knife in his right hand and moved slowly around the foot of the bed.

His eyes were fixed on the girl's subterranean form, buried somewhere under the rolling hillocks of the covers. He could see the steady rise and fall of her breath as he approached from the right side. Her head was partially buried under the pillow, shutting out whatever light and noise might interrupt her deep sleep.

Liquida assessed the situation. It wasn't as easy as it looked. If he tried to pull the bedcovers off her to get a clear strike, she might scream before he could silence her. He gauged the thickness of the bedspread against the length of the blade in his hand, and wondered if the comforter was filled with goose down or something harder. Hopefully it wasn't Kevlar.

He crept forward, searching with his eyes for the area just above the small of her back. As he drew closer he could make out the definition more clearly.

Liquida was two feet from the edge of the bed. His foot found a weak spot and the floor squeaked as he lifted off it. A second later the body on the bed began to move. He froze in place and stared at the moving mound. He was prepared to pounce if he had to, but he knew if he did they wouldn't be alone in the room for long. He watched as she shifted under the covers and prayed that she would not roll over and open her eyes. Instead she stretched out, took a deep breath, and settled back in. Liquida was thankful, because in the process she flattened enough of the hills to show him his target. If only she would stay still.

He looked at the floor and quietly took two more steps. It put him at the edge of the bed. He looked down. He couldn't see her head. But he knew where it was, under the pillow.

He leaned over the bed, held his breath, and in a single fluid motion Liquida grabbed the pillow with his left hand and forced it down against the side of her face as he plunged the needle-sharp point of the knife through the covers and into her back. A few flakes of down floated like snow around his gloved hand as he pressed the knife home.

Liquida was lucky and he knew it. The blade slid cleanly between her ribs. Her body jolted with the shock. She tried to scream, but her face was buried deep in the mattress and sealed by the pillow. Liquida pressed down hard, with all of his weight. He had the knife in her but it was like riding a tiger. She was stronger than she looked. Before he realized it, she was struggling into position to do a push-up. If she got her face out of the mattress and let out a scream, they would hear it a block away.

Coming up onto the bed, Liquida forced his knee into her lower back and collapsed her arms. She struggled to escape the searing pain as he moved the blade around in the wound. Her legs thrashed at the covers and her fingers clawed the sheets, but Liquida wouldn't let up. He searched for the sweet spot before she could throw him off. He angled the knife handle down and jammed the blade upward under the ribs as hard as he could. Jenny arched her back in a rigid bow. He felt the penetration as the tip of the blade sliced through the sac and pierced her heart.

Liquida sat on her like a jockey, his knee still planted in her back. He could feel the life force beneath him dissolve as her body settled back into the mattress.

He took a second to catch his breath, and then he lifted the pillow from her face. Her left eye was wide open, but it was too dark to see if the pupil was dilated. He swept the long blond hair away from the side of her neck and felt for the jugular. There was no pulse. Leaving the knife where it was, Liquida hoisted himself off her and back onto his feet, at the side of the bed. Then he reached over and pulled the knife out as a crimson stain seeped slowly, in a broadening circle, through the thick white muslin.

Liquida had followed the two women all night, but from a safe distance. He parked up on a hill near a hotel and watched them through his field glasses down below as they had dinner in the restaurant's outdoor plaza. He also saw Madriani's detective. How could he miss him? The biggest thing moving in Old Town that night. Liquida had seen him before, months earlier, in Costa Rica. He wasn't someone you were likely to forget. A man the size of a mountain, with a shiny, bald black head that looked as if he spit-shined it at night. He stood there on the wooden boardwalk in front of the shops, smoking his cigar as he watched the two girls from a block away.

The moment he saw the investigator, Liquida knew he had the lawyer's attention. So he followed the two women, but kept his distance. When the blonde dropped Madriani's daughter off at home, he followed the blonde. If he killed the daughter, the FBI would throw another blanket over the lawyer and Liquida might not be able to find him again. They had done it once before. But kill her friend and there was no way to prove that Liquida was involved. After all, she was a perfect stranger. And there would be no fingerprint left behind this time. The police would start looking for jilted boyfriends or anyone who might have been stalking the blonde. But Madriani would be left to wonder. The minute his daughter told him that her friend was dead it would begin to gnaw at him.

It is true. There are things worse than physical pain and death: the certain knowledge that these are coming, not only for you, but for those you love.

THIRTEEN

It's not quite noon. I'm in a booth at the Brigantine waiting for Harry to join me for lunch and I am about to be ambushed.

Joselyn Cole sits at one of the bar stools across the room, one shapely leg crossed over the other as we pretend not to notice each other in the largely empty restaurant.

Yesterday she went to see Herman and he slammed the door on her as I'd warned her he would. So unless Coronado is suddenly on the way back to her office in D.C., I'm assuming she's back for one more shot at me.

The cocktail waitress cruises by to take my order.

"Gin and tonic, hold the lime," I tell her.

Cole glances at me in the mirror over the bar, and as the waitress leaves, Joselyn swivels on her stool and steps down. This morning she looks very different. A white sweaterdress of thin-ribbed wool clings to her body like water on its way down to midthigh over skintight black leggings. She dangles a small purse from her arm as she nurses her drink with both hands and moves toward me with a kind of arousing feline elegance. New day—new tack.

"I thought it was you when I heard the voice," she says.

"You come here often, do you?" I give her a big grin.

"Your secretary told me you were having lunch here," she says. "You don't mind?"

"I'm going to have to talk with my secretary."

"Oh, I hope I'm not getting her in trouble," she says. "I told her we were meeting for lunch and I forgot the location. So it really wasn't her fault."

"There you go, you did it again," I say. "Did you tell her who you were this time?"

"I told her who I was the last time. It was only the stuff about the bar that I lied about. And yes, I did tell her who I was."

"And she believed you about lunch?"

"I'm here, aren't I? If you have a problem with me, you need to tell your secretary. After all, the woman doesn't have a crystal ball. For all she knows we could be having a tryst."

"I'll make a note," I tell her.

"I don't like lying, really," she says. "But you make it very difficult to tell the truth."

"You're talking about your attempt to ambush Herman?" I say.

"The least you could have done was give me an open field shot at the man."

"If I'd known you could dress up and look like this, I would have gone over personally and nailed his door shut," I tell her.

"Well, thank you, I think." She smiles, standing there all hippy and slinky in high heels, curves in all the right places. "Besides, I can tell, you're not really angry."

I shoot her a glance.

"At your secretary, I mean."

"We're back to clairvoyance, are we?"

"Care if I sit?"

"Would it make a difference?" I ask.

She sets her drink down and slides into the booth across from me. "Tell me, is the food good here?"

"Would you like a menu?"

"No. I'll just have what you're having," she says. "Do you usually eat here alone, or is someone else joining us?"

"My partner," I tell her.

"That would be Mr. Hinds."

"I take it you've met Harry?"

"Not yet, but his name is next to yours on the sign by your office door. Perhaps you could introduce me." The way she says it, I can tell Harry is on her hit list to be questioned. If she looks like this when she does it, she can mount Harry's head on the wall next to the sign on her way out. Harry will spill everything he knows, and guess at the rest.

She smiles at me over the tumbler as she nibbles playfully on a chip of ice, pursed glossy lips and white teeth. "You're making this much more difficult than it has to be," she says. "All I'm asking for is a little co-operation."

"What the spider said to the fly," I tell her.

The waitress brings my drink, then looks at Joselyn and asks if she'd like another.

"I don't know, should I?" Cole looks to me for the answer.

"Depends on how long you're going to be here," I tell her.

She looks at the waitress and smiles. "I'm afraid he's a hard case. Better bring one more for each of us, and keep his tab open. We may both need more medicine before the day's done."

The waitress laughs and looks to me. I nod.

"Thanks," says Joselyn. "And I thought I was going to wait and get drunk on the plane tonight. You're a bad influence."

"You're going somewhere?"

"Home." The sliver of ice slips through her lips as she says it. She reaches up to trap it with rose-painted nails on long delicate fingers. "Excuse me." She giggles as she presses the melting sliver back between her lips. "And don't look so satisfied. I won't be gone long, and I will be back."

"Not on my account I hope."

"You don't really think I was going to let you say no and slip away just like that, do you?"

"What time's your flight?"

"Not to worry. We have plenty of time. Six o'clock shuttle to LAX, and then the red-eye to Washington. So we can drink all afternoon."

"Must you leave so soon?"

"I have a hearing tomorrow. Testimony before a Senate committee." Then a twinkle in her eye as she looks at me. "Of course, you could always join me. With what you could tell them we could turn it into an extravaganza. Cuba in the age of Camelot, Excalibur gone nuclear. Of course, they already know it, but they've pulled the national security curtain down so nobody else does. We could do a press conference on the steps of the Capitol that would set the place on fire . . ."

"No thanks."

"Then I'm afraid you're condemning them to some terribly boring stuff at tomorrow's hearing."

"Go as you are, and I'm sure they'll be all ears, and eyes," I tell her.

"Yes, but the topic," she says. "The future threat of aging precision weapons. It sounds like the surgeon general's warning on the side of a box of Viagra."

"It does, doesn't it?"

"Put another way," she says, "does the lack of collateral damage really matter when a hellfire missile takes out the Oval Office?"

"Well, that should get the attention of the Secret Service," I tell her.

"The last time I looked, they didn't have a seat either in the House or the Senate," she says. "Did you ever wonder if the man who invented the stick thought for a moment what would happen when somebody else got his hands on the fabulous new weapon and beat him with it?"

"You mean Igor-the-red-ass?"

She laughs and toasts me with her glass. "To Igor, whose descendants now sit in Congress," says Joselyn.

"Do you testify often?"

"Only when I have to. Just enough to keep my hand in, and let them know we're still around. We don't have money to throw into the campaign flames, so unless we're carried along on a tidal wave like 9/11 no one pays much attention. Since the war in Iraq, the press has turned WMD into a four-letter word. The topic is no longer politically chic. So until somebody ignites one over the Capitol Building nobody wants to pay attention. A dozen rogue regimes around the world are now making nuclear bombs and what's the attitude of the West? 'If you have to do it, fine, just shut up and do it quietly.'"

I steal a glance at my watch.

"Your partner's running late. Is he in court?" she says.

"No. He's in the office. Maybe I should run over and get him."

"Oh, why do that?" She blocks me with her high-heeled foot from across the table. "We can just sit here and talk. I'm in no hurry. Have another drink," she tells me.

"Plying me with liquor will do you no good."

"And why is that?"

"I'm a cheap drunk. I'll just pass out all over you."

"Yes, but do you talk in your sleep?" she says.

I laugh. "I don't know."

"And how can that be?"

"Do you hear yourself when you talk in your sleep?"

"That lonely, is it?" she says.

"As much as I hate to admit it, it's been

a while since I've had any witnesses in a position to tell me."

"I see." She stares at me from piercing blue eyes, her parted, glossed lips now finished with the ice. "Is that an invitation? Or do you just want me to drive you to a sleep clinic?" There is a kind of sensual ozone in the air. I feel as if my hair is being lifted by a static charge waiting for the bolt of lightning to strike me somewhere farther down.

I take a sip of gin to cool off before I stammer around a little the way men often do when they are frontally accosted by a beautiful woman. I don't deny the urge. Instead I say: "What difference does it make? You have a flight. And I draw the line at sleep experiments in the backseat of my car."

"There's always another airplane," she says. "And I noticed a beautiful hotel just across the street."

"What about your testimony tomorrow?"

"I suppose we could talk about precision weapons if you like. But I was thinking we could do some other things."

I give her a smirk.

"There are more important things than Congressional hearings."

"Yes, but my ego isn't sufficiently inflated to think that I'm one of them."

"Don't sell yourself short," she says. "You have to remember that there is always the quality of your pillow talk."

"Ah, there you go spoiling the moment. And I thought you wanted me for my body."

"How could I possibly know when I haven't seen it yet?" She ups the ante just as Harry comes breezing through the door.

"Sorry I'm late."

"Go away," I tell him.

He looks at me and then turns behind him to see Joselyn seated in the booth. "Am I interrupting something?"

"Nothing important," she tells him. "Your partner was just having a dream. Nothing a towel can't fix. We haven't met." She reaches out and takes Harry's hand, brushing her fingernails along the inside of his palm. "I'm Joselyn Cole. You must be Mr. Hinds."

Harry looks at her over the top of his reading glasses for a better appraisal before he grabs the spectacles from his face and pockets them.

"Nice to meet you." Harry looks like he's been hit by a dumdum round. Still holding her hand, he gives her the big, broad grin as she slides to the back of the curved booth to let him in.

"Joining us for lunch, that's wonderful," says Harry.

"Leave him alone. He's an old man," I tell her.

"I never discriminate on the basis of age," says Joselyn. "In fact, older is better."

"He doesn't know anything," I tell her. "Harry has only hearsay."

"So he knows what you told him," she says.

I give her a face of concession.

"That's fine, we can start with that," she says. "Besides, press conferences don't have rules of evidence."

"What's this about?" Harry slides into the booth.

"You don't want to know," I tell him.

"Let me be the judge of that." Harry is smiling at Joselyn. "Where did you two meet?"

"How about a drink?" I raise my hand and call the waitress over.

"I work undercover for the state bar. I'm a female decoy for illicit relations with clients," she tells him. "I'm wearing a wire and very little else. And you want to know how your partner and I met?"

"Sounds like entrapment to me," says Harry. "I'm game. Besides, you're not my client, and if you nailed him, I own the firm. So I'm not only old, I'm rich."

"She's pulling your leg."

"I have two of them," says Harry. "So anytime you want, just yank away." He smiles at her. Harry can be a charmer when he wants to be. Suddenly he turns a stern expression on me. "You and I have to talk. Janice told me to tell you some guy is waiting for you back at the office."

Janice is my secretary. Somebody waiting in the office catches my attention since I don't have any appointments on my calendar for this afternoon.

"Who is he?"

"I don't know who he is," says Harry, "but he's insistent. When Janice told him you might not be back for the rest of the day, he apparently planted himself in one of the chairs in the outer office and told her he'd wait."

Ever since the events in Coronado and the warning from Thorpe, I get edgy when visitors show up at the office unannounced. "What did he look like, did you see him?"

"Tall, lanky, sunny side of fifty maybe, well dressed, suit and tie, dark . . ." Harry's gaze rises as he talks to me. "Speak of the devil."

Before I can turn, a shadow settles across my shoulder and onto the table in front of me.

"Are you Paul Madriani?"

I look up and he is silhouetted against the bright daylight from the window behind me. The stupid things that race through your mind at a moment like this. His face has the shadowed clarity of the dark side of the moon. I find myself looking down toward his hands to see if they're packing anything.

"Who's asking?"

"My name is Bart Snyder. I think you may have known my son, James."

FOURTEEN

Zeb Thorpe stormed into the small conference room at FBI headquarters like a man running on afterburners. "Gentlemen. Sorry to be so late." He had been racing all day through a series of meetings. This one had been dropped on his calendar at the last minute in a telephone call from his assistant, Ray Zink, with no time to talk—only a message that it was urgent.

"I take it everybody's here?" Besides Zink there were only two others present, an air force officer sporting brass birds on the epaulets of his dress jacket, and another man, a civilian Thorpe didn't recognize.

He moved at speed toward the head of the table, took his seat, and opened the file in front of him. Thorpe started to scan the file as he talked.

"Hope this won't take too long. I've got a dinner meeting with the director in a little over an hour. And somehow between here and there I have to struggle into a tux that's down in my car." He looked at a photograph in the file, a large military transport plane parked on a tarmac, its cargo ramp down and the rear bay open. "You want to do introductions or should we just get started?"

"Greg Sanchez, National Security Agency." This from the man in the suit at the other end of the table. He looked to be in his early thirties, with short dark hair and intense eyes.

NSA operated out of a set of glass towers at Fort Meade, in Maryland.

"I don't think we've met before. What division at NSA?"

"Infosec, international relations."

"That covers a lot of sins," said Thorpe. "How long you been out of the navy?"

"Is it that obvious?" said Sanchez.

"Lucky guess," said Thorpe.

"Two years."

"When you see George Simmels, tell him Jughead says hello." Simmels was Sanchez's boss. He was an old salt who never hired anybody who hadn't first paid his dues bounding on the main. He and Thorpe, a former marine, went back almost twenty years.

Thorpe also knew that Simmels was soon for retirement, whether he wanted it or not. For decades the navy held a firm edge in the field of encryption, code making and breaking. Throughout the Cold War this was the NSA's fundamental mission. But no longer. That had all changed with the attack on 9/11. Now the NSA's job was to read everybody's e-mail and listen to their telephone communications, or at least as many of them as could be sucked out of the ether by the supercomputers at Fort Meade. The job was to scan it all, searching for the code words of terrorism. On that score the air force held the whip hand. They controlled most of the critical communications satellites.

"Sir, I'm Colonel Nelson Winget." The man in the uniform slid a business card down the table toward Thorpe.

"You can call me Thorpe, Zeb, anything

but sir," said Thorpe. "That one's reserved for my five-year-old grandson and only when he knows he's been really bad." He looked at the business card: ASSISTANT COMMANDER, AIR FORCE SYSTEMS COMMAND, WRIGHT-PATTERSON AIR FORCE BASE. "Who wants to start?"

Zink jumped into the void. "The plane in the file photo is Russian made, an IL-76, registered in the Georgian Republic. As to who owns it, it's anybody's guess. Title seems to be a bit cloudy. The aircrew is a mixed bag, three of them out of Belarus, and one Chechen. They were flying out of North Korea. The plane was forced down by mechanical problems and landed at Don Muang airport in Bangkok two days ago. Thai authorities found thirty-five tons of arms and munitions on board, all of it in violation of the UN Security Council ban on exports from North Korea."

"And who says serendipity never works for our side?" said Thorpe.

"We did tip off Thai customs as to what we thought was on board," said Sanchez.

"You don't have to explain to me," said Thorpe. "As long as they land outside the country and it doesn't start a war, you got my vote. So far it sounds like an issue for the State Department or Defense, not us." He started to close the cover on the file in front of him.

"We don't know the intended final destination," said Zink. "You can probably draw a big circle around the Middle East and throw darts at it."

"But there appears to be a problem," said Sanchez, "and if we're right, it's gonna likely fall in your court sooner or later."

"Go on," said Thorpe.

"Yesterday we intercepted telephonic communications between an individual in Pyongyang, North Korea, and someone in the area of the northern Caribbean," said Sanchez. "They were using a satellite link we don't control, part of the old Soviet system. And the receiving end in the Caribbean wasn't using a cell phone. It was an old analog landline."

"Cuba," said Thorpe.

Sanchez nodded. "It gave us some problems with transcription since our computers and our software are weighted toward digital signals. So we didn't get the entire conversation."

"Was it encrypted?" said Thorpe.

"No. It was clear and in English," said Sanchez. This meant it probably wasn't the North Korean military or its government talking to their counterparts in Cuba.

"It appears to have been a private-party conversation. The transcript is in your file, the parts that we were able to pick up."

Thorpe had the file open again and was turning pages until he found the transcript and started to read.

"The scanning software at one of our stations picked up the phone call because of the location from which the call originated, in North Korea. It became a full intercept when key words were recognized," said Sanchez. "You'll see those words highlighted in the transcript."

"The man calling in from Pyongyang was reporting to his friend in Cuba that a certain cargo plane was forced down in the 'land of smiles.'"

"Thailand," said Thorpe.

"It was clear there was something on board they were interested in. The man at the Cuban end of the conversation seemed to be in charge. He was worried that the communication might be intercepted. They beat around the bush for a while and finally

out came the words 'big guy' and 'little kid,'"
said Sanchez.

"And that's when all the lights and buzz-
ers on your computer went off." Thorpe had
already keyed on the highlighted words in
the transcript.

"It's not just words or phrases, but us-
age," said Sanchez. "The way these words
are employed in a conversation that trig-
gers the computer to recognize them. They
were among a number of similar words or
phrases designed to capture a particular
reference."

"Fat Man and Little Boy," said Thorpe.

"Yes," said Sanchez. These were the
two atomic bombs dropped on Japan to
end World War II.

"We lost bits and pieces of the conversation. But it appears that the subject in
the Caribbean asked the man in Pyongyang
which of the two was on board the plane.
And the man in North Korea said 'the big
guy.'"

"I see it." Thorpe sits up straight in his
chair. "Do we know what was on that
plane?" He looks at Zink.

"We sent two agents over from the embassy in Bangkok late yesterday, before

we knew about the telephone intercepts," said Zink. "But Thai customs wasn't sure how much they could cooperate until they had approval from a higher authority."

"So we still don't know what's on that plane?" said Thorpe.

"We do now," said Sanchez. "When the phone intercept came in, we alerted the military. The navy dispatched one of their nuclear weapons officers from Subic, in the Philippines. When the Thai military saw the guy in a Hazmat suit with a yellow Geiger counter the size of your mama's kitchen stove, they stepped aside and set a world speed record for deplaning."

"And?" said Thorpe.

"Good news and bad news," said Sanchez. "Good news is, there was nothing nuclear on board."

Thorpe issued a deep sigh of relief and settled back into his chair.

"The plane contained a bandit's bazaar, everything the well-armed terrorist wants for Christmas," said Zink. "RPGs, rocket launchers, missile tubes and the missiles to go with them, shoulder-fired surface-to-air stuff, enough Kalashnikovs to restart the Russian Revolution. All of it crated up in wood and labeled as tools. Thai customs is still doing an inventory.

"Don't get too comfortable," said Zink, "'cause we're not off the hook yet. There was one big surprise, a wooden crate about half the size of a small house, marked 'oil drilling equipment.' It took us a while, but we finally convinced the Thais to let us take a peek. At first nobody knew what it was. It looked like a very large, oversize hot water heater."

"Go on," said Thorpe.

"They tested it for radiation but it wasn't hot. Well, maybe I shouldn't say that yet."

"Why not?"

The air force colonel leaned forward at the table. "Because according to our ordnance people, it's thermobaric, and it's the biggest damn thing they've ever seen," said Winget.

"You mean like McVeigh's truck bomb in Oklahoma City?" said Thorpe.

"Similar principle," said Winget, "but on a much higher order of technology, and far more destructive. It is a fuel-air device and considerably larger than anything we have in our own arsenal. We don't know the exact magnitude. So far our experts have only seen pictures of it. We have two of them on a plane now, on their way to Thailand to examine it. But based on the photos they've seen, they're telling us it looks like a Russian design."

"Why would the Russians—"

"We don't think the Russians built it. It probably has 'Made in North Korea' stamped on the bottom of it, part of the technology transfer from back in the eighties. The Russians got a big jump start on us in the field of thermobaric weapons before the Soviet empire went down. We had to play catch-up when we first went to war in Afghanistan. You remember the mountain caves at Tora Bora?"

Thorpe nodded. "I remember seeing pictures."

"We used B-52s and bunker-busting thermobaric bombs in an effort to penetrate the caves and incinerate whoever was inside. We believed it was Bin Laden. If it was, he slipped away.

"Based on the size of the device in the photographs, if its power is true to scale and if you could set it off in the right spot under the right conditions, you could boil a fair amount of the water in the Chesapeake."

"You're kidding," said Thorpe.

"I wish I was," said Winget. "It's only half a step to a step down from a nuclear device. There's no fallout from radiation and the blast effect is more confined. That's the good news. The bad news is that once you master the technology and perfect the design, which isn't that difficult, the weapon is easily replicated, and the technical know-how is readily transferable to others. We know that terrorist groups have been experimenting with fuel-air designs for some time. The bombing in Bali a few years ago showed signs of fuel-air design."

"It stands to reason that this is the cargo the man in Cuba was talking about with his friend in Pyongyang," said Sanchez. "The big kid."

"What you're saying is that somewhere there's a smaller one still floating around," said Thorpe.

"Worse than that," said Winget. "Look at the rest of the telephone transcript."

Thorpe turned back to the file and read to the end of the transcript. "The North Koreans have a replacement for the one on the plane."

"It looks like it," said Winget. "We're talking a very serious problem here. Ground-ing that plane may have slowed them down but it didn't stop them."

"It appears the North Koreans are sell-ing this stuff to private contractors," said Sanchez. "There's a lesson to be learned here, if you ever get a chance to testify and they ask your opinion."

Thorpe looked at him.

"Before the embargo the North Koreans were shipping their military wares mostly to other friendly regimes in return for hard currency," said Sanchez. "As we push the UN to tighten the screws on the embargo, all indications are that more of this stuff is going underground. Major weapons sys-tems finding their way onto the black mar-ket and into the hands of people who don't own territory or possess national flags. You want my opinion, embargos are not only weak because they're hard to enforce. When you do enforce them, the result can turn out to be even more dangerous."

"Unfortunately, we can't resolve that one here," said Thorpe. "It's above our pay grade. For the moment let's stick to the problem at hand. What are we dealing with? The device itself. How does it work? And what type of targets are most vulnerable? Let's start with how it works." He looked at Winget.

"In a nutshell?" said the officer.

Thorpe nodded.

"They use liquid high explosives in a vaporized form, mixed with delayed accelerants, in most cases aluminum powder or other flammable metal dust, magnesium, titanium, any of these will do. The bomb doesn't kill or destroy in the conventional manner of most high-explosive ordnance, through fragmentation or shrapnel. It uses intense heat and massive concussion. It's a two-stage process. On ignition the device will deploy a large volume of powdered flammable metal dust into the air. This is followed by the detonation of a superheated high explosive that creates the first of two pressure waves, in this case an out blast. A fraction of a second later, the powdered metal in the air will ignite, setting off the second and much larger pressure wave, this one called a back blast. It's not unlike an implosion. This will collapse all but the most hardened structures and rupture the internal organs of anyone inside.

"Walls, even if they're concrete, don't provide much protection. The powdered metal, once it starts to burn, creates a superheated slurry that forms a molten plasma. This will find its way into even the smallest crevice in a wall and cook everything on the other side. If the target structure by some miracle stays intact and remains sealed, say an underground bunker or a hardened cave, the heat will suck the oxygen from it. So if the heat doesn't kill and the initial blast doesn't burst the lungs, the vacuum that follows will collapse them. If you're in the target structure, it's almost impossible to survive," said Winget. "It's a thorough and relentless killing machine."

"What kind of delivery system would be required, say, for the item crated up in Thailand to reach and destroy its target?" asked Thorpe. "And please tell me it's a heavy-lift airplane, something we can track on radar and shoot down before it reaches its target."

"Aerial delivery might be optimal but not necessarily the only method," said Winget. "In the proper setting a truck will do just as well. Unlike nuclear, you're not looking for an air burst to obtain maximum effect. We used B-52s at Tora Bora with earth-penetrating ordnance because it was the safest and most efficient way to reach the target. You can use fuel-air bombs on the open battlefield, but that's not the most optimum deployment. Maximum destruction and lethality would be obtained in a large enclosed structure. Thermobaric devices are perfect for underground bunkers, caves, tunnels, and they can be used to flatten large buildings. It's most effective to get them inside the structure before detonation. Then again, McVeigh didn't drive the truck into the federal building in Oklahoma City. He parked it at the curb in front. And we all remember the level of damage and loss of life there. So there are no hard-and-fast rules."

"Let's go back to the two men on the phone," said Thorpe. "Any idea where that plane was going to deliver this thing, if it hadn't gotten waylaid in Thailand?"

"Best bet's Cuba," said Sanchez. "They have airfields capable of landing and could provide cover for the device."

"You think the Cuban government would allow an air attack on the U.S. from the island?" said Winget. "I don't think so."

"I didn't say that," said Sanchez. "But

once it's on the ground these guys could always transport the device by ship, move it from one vessel to another, and sooner or later it arrives in a U.S. port boxed as industrial tools and they could haul it by truck. You said so yourself."

"Possibly," said Winget.

"In other words, we don't have a clue," said Thorpe. "Mr. Sanchez, when your agency alerted the Thai government that there were arms on board that plane, I take it NSA had no idea that this device was there?"

"Correct," said Sanchez.

"How did you know about the small arms?" said Thorpe.

"Communications intercepts and, from what I understand, some satellite surveillance."

"What other agencies are already in the loop?" asked Thorpe.

"CIA and military intelligence branches have already been informed," said Sanchez.

"What about Homeland Security?" asked Thorpe.

"I don't know," said Sanchez.

"We notify Homeland Security, the White House, U.S. Customs, especially at the ports. Tell them what to look for. Send them photographs if you can."

Zink was taking notes. "We'll need to tell the State Department."

"Why?" said Thorpe.

"Just in case we're not the target. Somebody's gonna have to decide whether to inform foreign governments, and if so, which ones. What if the target's in Europe, or the UK?"

"It's not likely," said Thorpe. "But okay, alert them, but ask them to keep it low-key and on a need-to-know basis only. I don't want to be seeing it on CNN in the morning."

"Homeland Security is going to want to know what the threat assessment should be. What do I tell them?" said Zink.

"Tell them what we know, the telephone intercepts and the nature of the device in Thailand. They'll have to make a judgment call," said Thorpe. He turned back to Sanchez. "If NSA can give us even a hint as to the identity of the two men on the phone, we need it yesterday."

"Understood," said Sanchez. "We did get voiceprints. We've got the computers checking for matches on overseas and domestic calls. If we get a match, we'll try to nail down a location and turn it over to your people or the CIA to run it down, depending on where it is. Preliminary voice analysis indicates that the voice in Pyongyang displayed indications of a Slavic accent, possibly Russian. It was impossible to be certain since the entire conversation was in English. The other man appeared to be a native English speaker, possibly from Australia or New Zealand. He was very cagey. He kept trying to slip into a South African English Boer accent, but our analyst didn't buy it."

"Stay on it," said Thorpe. He turned to Winget. "We will need all the satellite surveillance we can get over North Korea until this thing's over."

"We're on it already," said Winget.

"Any hint of these devices being moved or transported we need to know about it immediately," said Thorpe.

"Chances are any shipment will already be crated before it comes out into the sunlight," said the air force officer.

"Then get the dimensions on the box from Thailand, and anything that matches it we want tracked," said Thorpe.

"Will do." Winget made a note.

"We'll end up chasing a lot of false leads, but right now we don't have a choice. I'll have to tell the director over dinner," said Thorpe. "See if I can get him off alone for a minute and unload on him. We meet tomorrow. What's my calendar look like?"

"You've got an opening at four o'clock," said Zink.

"Afternoon or early morning?" said Thorpe.

Zink, who was still taking notes, held up his left hand, rubbing his thumb and forefinger together, as if to play the smallest violin in the world.

"Yeah, well, if I can't get any respect, I certainly want a little pity. Four o'clock it is. Can you make it?"

Sanchez nodded. "I'll be here," said Winget.

"Bring any and all information you can find. Anybody who can help, drag them along. We'll meet daily until we get some kind of a handle on this thing."

FIFTEEN

Snyder . . . ?"

The name doesn't click in my brain until he says: "My son was murdered in Washington a few weeks ago."

"Ah . . ."

"I'm afraid I followed your partner over here. I'd like to talk to you," he says.

"Sure, drag up a chair."

"It might be best if we could talk where we have a little more privacy," he says.

"Listen, I can go," says Joselyn. She's trapped in the curved booth between Harry and me.

I put my hand on her arm as she starts

to slide toward me to get out. "We haven't had lunch yet," I tell her. "Have you had lunch, Mr. Snyder?"

"No."

"Then please pull up a chair and join us. You already know my partner. I keep no secrets from him. And this is Joselyn Cole, our resident mystic psychic for whom my head is a glass display case. She knows all my most intimate thoughts."

He gives Joselyn a cautious once-over. "How do you do?"

"He's joking," she says and gives him a simpering smile.

"You want to talk here, it's fine with me," says Snyder. He drops a leather portfolio on the corner of the table next to Harry and grabs a chair. He slides it over and finishes up the foursome, sitting at the outside edge of the booth.

I flash the waiter to bring us menus. We take a couple of minutes and we order lunch. As soon as the waitress leaves, I turn and look at Snyder. "So what can I do for you?"

"I may as well cut to the chase. Why waste time?" he says. "I am told that my son discussed certain legal matters with you prior to his death. I want to know what these matters regarded, what the two of you talked about."

"Who told you this?"

"Does it matter?"

"Yes, because the information you've been given isn't accurate. The fact is, I never met your son, never talked to him, never communicated with him in any way."

"Listen, if you're worried about violating privileged communications we can go to your office and talk. It won't take five minutes. Besides, any privilege died with my son. I too am a lawyer," he says. "And even if the privilege didn't die, I'm the executor of my son's estate. I stand in his shoes. So what you could say to him you can now say to me."

"It's nothing to do with lawyer-client privilege. There's nothing to talk about because I never had any dealings with your son."

Snyder looks perplexed, casing me with his eyes. "Then why would they give me your name?"

"Who?"

"I'd rather not say."

"Then there's nothing more I can tell you." It's going to be a long, silent lunch. He thinks about it for a few seconds. "All right. I was interviewed a week ago by the FBI. They asked me if I knew whether my son had recently hired a lawyer. They mentioned you by name," he says. "So if you never met Jimmie, why would they give me your name?"

"What exactly did they tell you?" I ask.

"Just what I said."

"They gave you my name. They didn't say anything more? No other details?"

Snyder shakes his head. "No."

"What they didn't tell you is that at the scene the police found my business card in your son's wallet. That's how the FBI had my name."

"But you say you never met Jimmie?"

"That's right."

"Then how did my son get your card?"

"I don't know. The FBI asked me the same question and I told them the same thing. I didn't have a clue."

Snyder thinks about this for a moment. "It doesn't make a lot of sense. I mean, it's possible somebody else gave Jimmie your card, one of his friends, on a referral. Maybe he was going to call you and never got around to it. You do criminal work?"

"Right."

"Do you ever handle drug cases?"

"No."

"That's what I thought. I knew Jimmie never did drugs." He seems at least relieved by this thought. "Still, he was in Washington. You're in California. Regardless of what the problem is, I'd get somebody local. Wouldn't you?"

I nod. What can I say without telling him everything?

Harry has a pained expression. We could just sit here and allow Snyder to wander down this posy path, coming to all the wrong conclusions, wondering if his kid was a closet addict and maybe got a flawed legal referral from some drugged-out junkie.

"The cops are horsing you around," says Harry. "Sending you here to talk to Paul with only a fraction of the facts."

"The FBI didn't send me," says Snyder.

"Oh, yes, they did." Harry's looking at me from under arched eyebrows, shirtsleeves rolled up, his forearms sprawled on the table. "And I think you deserve all the answers." Harry says it to Snyder, but he's still looking at me.

"Okay, so you think we should tell him?"

"Hell, yes. If it was anybody else, I'd say no," says Harry. "But given the circumstances . . ."

"Tell me what?" says Snyder.

"There's a tad more to the story," says Harry.

"Do we have your word that you'll keep what we're about to tell you in confidence?" I ask Snyder.

"Sure." Or at least until he can get outside, whip out his cell phone, and call the FBI to kick the crap out of them, demanding whatever they have on the man Thorpe called the Mexicutioner.

"When the police found my business card in your son's wallet they also found some other forensic evidence. Based on that, there's reason to believe that your son may not have been the one who put my business card in his wallet."

"Explain," says Snyder.

Plates arrive juggled up the waitress's arm. Over lunch I tell Snyder about the thumbprint that the cops found on the back of my business card, the fact that the print was somewhat obvious. I tell him that, according to the police, this unidentified print matched a second unidentified print found at the scene of another murder in Southern California committed several months before his son was killed. I'm careful not to give him Afundi's name or any of the details in the other murder. With Joselyn tuned in, it would probably take her a nanosecond to connect this earlier murder to the shoot-out in Coronado. This would only ignite her candle all over again.

Snyder asks whether any arrests were made in the earlier case or whether the police have any suspects.

"Arrests, no. Not that I know of. But they may have a lead. Call it a rumor."

I tell him about the tidbit from Thorpe, that the Southern California murder may have been the work of someone called the Mexicutioner, aka Liquida.

"According to the FBI, the narco buzz out of Mexico is that this man is connected to the Tijuana drug cartel."

With the mention of drugs, Snyder lifts his eyes from his plate, snaps a quick look at me, and grabs a notepad from the leather portfolio at his elbow.

"What did you say his name was? Liquida? How do you spell that?"

I give him my best guess.

"He deals in drugs?" says Snyder.

"I don't know. It's only a name," I tell him. "I know nothing about him other than what the authorities told me, which was very little. It's possible I may have seen him one time, just a fleeting glimpse, but I can't even be sure of that."

"When was this?" says Snyder.

"About a year ago, down in Costa Rica. We were working a case. It was late at night, dark, and as I say it was just a quick glimpse. This guy had a swarthy, pock-marked face, looked like acne, and a set of evil eyes you could never forget. Of course that's assuming it was even him."

"Why didn't the FBI tell me about Liquida?" says Snyder.

"I don't know. Probably for the same reason they didn't tell you about my business card. It's part of their continuing investigation."

"So why did they tell you?" he says.

"I don't know."

Harry looks at me. I cut him off with a glance. I don't want to tell Snyder about the warning from Thorpe and the fear that Liquida may be playing out a vendetta against

Harry, Herman, and me. If I go there, Snyder will want to know the rest, like pulling a thread on a sweater. How was it that we ended up on the death list of a man we don't even know? Pretty soon we'll be sitting here naked in front of Joselyn and her friends in the media trying to explain Liquida's part in the events leading up to the attack at the naval base, the details of which I don't fully understand myself.

"Go on," says Snyder.

"There's not much more to say. The FBI was unable to match the two thumbprints, the one on my card or the one at the earlier crime scene, to any known person in their database."

"But," says Joselyn, "if the information out of Mexico is accurate, that this man Liquida is responsible for the murder in Southern California, the FBI must be operating on the assumption that it must be his print that they found at that scene. Correct?"

"I assume so."

"Hmm . . ." She goes back to nibbling at her salad.

"Let me get this straight," says Snyder. "They don't have any background on this guy Liquida?"

"If they do, they didn't share it with me," I tell him.

"Who was the victim in the Southern California case?" says Snyder. "And what city was it? I'd like to look at some of the press reports, and maybe talk to the local police."

"I'm sorry, I don't have that information." I wink at Harry, but he's looking down, taking a bite out of his sandwich when I do it.

He wipes his mouth with a napkin. "Yes, we do . . ."

"No, Harry. That information was wrong. I checked with Thorpe. They had the wrong name. It was a different victim. When he found the right information, he refused to give me the name."

"Are you sure?"

"Trust me, I checked."

Joselyn is listening to the words, smiling as she looks at me, deciphering the facial language of lies.

"You say so." Harry shakes his head and goes back to his sandwich.

I don't want Harry dropping Afundi's name in front of her. I can't be sure how much she knows from her own sources regarding the attack at Coronado. She may already be aware of Afundi's name.

"Lemme get this straight." Snyder's looking down at the pad in front of him, scrawled notes. "If the fingerprint found at the scene here in Southern California belongs to this guy Liquida, then he also owns the print on the back of your card in Jimmie's wallet. If so, that means he did both murders."

I shrug my shoulders. "I assume that's what the cops are operating on. But your guess is as good as mine. Now you know everything I know."

"Not quite," says Joselyn. "What's your connection to this man?"

"Who?" I look at her like a spotted owl caught in the headlights of a lumber truck.

"This Liquida. What's your connection to him?"

"None. What makes you think there's a connection?"

"Well, he didn't take my card and put it in Jimmie's wallet," she says. "Why would he pick you?"

"Who knows?" Any second she's going to lean over and sniff the sweat on my forehead, analyze the acid content in her gas chromatograph, and her buzzer will go off.

"It's possible he could be an unhappy former client," she says. "Didn't like the result, got out of prison, and used your card as a kind of consumer complaint." Joselyn looks at Snyder. "Sorry. I don't mean to make light of your son's death."

"No. I wanna hear." Snyder is all eyes at me.

"No. I don't think he's a former client," I say.

"Why not?" she says.

"Yeah," says Snyder, both of them waiting for an answer.

Harry looks at me as he fills his face with another bite of sandwich. I know what he's thinking: "You got yourself into this with one lie; you're going to have to get yourself out of it with another."

"The thought crossed my mind. We checked our records. But there's no one we can think of." Then the afterthought, like a stroke of genius. "Besides, if it was a disgruntled client, someone unhappy with my services, they would have been booked and fingerprinted at the time of arrest. Their prints would be on record with the FBI." Take that!

Harry gives me a wink, good job.

"Right. Of course. How stupid of me," she says.

"All I have is a name—Liquida. No physical description. So that's it. That's everything. That's all I know." I'm still smiling when she says it.

"That's too bad."

"Why?"

"Because it must be hard on you."

"What do you mean?" It's one question too many. What they teach you in law school is to stop when you're ahead.

"Because that thumbprint on your card is no accident," says Joselyn. "It may be your business card, but it's his calling card on the back of it. You did say the print was on the back of the card?"

"It's what the FBI told me," I say.

"You must have done something to really piss this guy off," she says.

I refuse to ask why. I don't want to play in her sandbox anymore.

"Do you have one of your business cards on you?" Joselyn looks at me.

"Yes." I'm gritting my teeth as I say it.

"Can I see it?"

"Sure." What else can I say?

I reach into my pocket and pluck a business card from the small cardholder I carry. I reach over to hand it to her.

"You just proved my point." Joselyn doesn't look up from her salad or take the card from my hand. Instead she leaves me there, my arm extended, holding the card, as she sweeps a small piece of lettuce into her mouth from her fork. "Do you see . . ." She wipes her mouth with her napkin.

"You see how you're holding the card, thumb on one side, first finger on the other? I never practiced much criminal law, but anyone handling a business card, unless they held it by the edges, in which case they won't leave any prints, would hold it like you are, front and back, thumb on one side, finger on the other. Even if they were smudged, you would still find two smudged prints, one on each side of the card, not one clear thumbprint. To get that you would probably put the card on a table or a hard surface and press down with your thumb. Besides, isn't it normal for a professional to wear gloves at a crime scene? Wouldn't that be part of the uniform of the day? And yet he left thumbprints at both scenes. It's a conscious act." She punctuates this statement of fact with a sip of wine she had ordered in a stemmed glass and then places it back on the table next to her unfinished drink in the tumbler. "I wouldn't want to worry you unnecessarily, but it seems to me he's sending you a message."

"Is that why he killed my son?" says Snyder.

"I don't know. But then it wasn't my card that he used." Joselyn looks at me with a Cheshire-like grin. "Do you have any ideas?"

"No." I slip the business card back into my pocket.

"What could you have done to make him that angry?" says Snyder. "I wanna know how you know this guy. What's the connection between you and him?"

"I told you. I don't know him. I don't have a clue. I wish I did."

"That doesn't tell me why my son was killed," says Snyder. "He wasn't involved in drugs. That I know. So how would he come in contact with someone like this—this Liquida?"

"Maybe he didn't," says Harry. "Maybe this man Liquida came looking for your son.

It's how he earns his money. He's hired to kill."

"No. Why would he be hired to kill Jimmie? My boy wasn't involved in anything that would put him in that kind of danger."

"Obviously he was," says Harry, "or else he'd be alive."

"What do you mean by that?" Snyder starts to get out of his chair.

"Relax." I put a hand on his arm. People at the other tables are starting to look at us. "Harry didn't mean anything."

"I'm sorry if I offended you," says Harry. "If what you say is true, then Jimmie was probably in the wrong place at the wrong time. For all we know he could have been killed by mistake. The information we have on Liquida is sketchy at best, only that he works for the cartels and hires out. The people employing him would have the moral judgment of a cancer cell. If they thought the rain was a threat, they'd shoot the weatherman. So it might not have taken much for your son to get killed. If he saw something, heard something, and he may not even have realized it."

"They would kill him for that?" At this

moment Snyder has the look of a clerk who has rung up a sale and is calculating the change.

"What?" I say.

"Nothing," says Snyder. "Only . . ."

"Only what?" I ask.

"It was just a minor problem, trouble he had at work. It's why I thought he might have come to see you."

"What was it?" says Harry.

"Jimmie violated some security protocols in the building where he worked. At least that's what I'm told. He took someone into a secure area without authority, and apparently he got caught."

"Your son told you this?" says Harry.

"No, the FBI, when they interviewed me. They showed me some pictures, Jimmie and another man. They didn't tell me that this was the actual event, but I have to assume . . ."

Snyder reaches into the leather portfolio next to his elbow and pulls out what appear to be three glossy prints. He hands them to me. I look at them. I recognize Jimmie Snyder from the death scene photos shown to us by Thorpe that day at the FBI office. The other man is pudgy looking, a little shorter than Snyder's son, wearing a baseball cap, Bermuda shorts, and a polo shirt.

I hand the photos to Harry. "Did they say anything else?"

"No. They showed me the photos in hopes I might recognize the man. They let me have them so I could run them by Jimmie's friends to see if anyone knew who the man was. I thought that if Jimmie talked with you about the problem at work, he might have told you who he was."

I shake my head.

"Hard to tell what he looks like from the pictures. The hat's down over his eyes in two of them." Harry zeros in on the other photo, the enlarged close-up. Over the shoulder is just a piece of a sign, the words "basketball and weight lifting" and a line below it that was out of focus. Harry studies it for a moment, then lays it on top of the other two and pushes them off to the side.

"When were these taken?"

Snyder looks up at Joselyn. "I don't know. Why?"

"Do you mind?"

"Go ahead."

She picks them up.

"I'm pretty sure they are stills from a security video camera," says Snyder.

"That's exactly what they are," says Harry. "Where were the photographs taken? What building, I mean?"

"Oh, God." Joselyn is leaning over the enlargement, peering down at it on the table. She's white as a sheet, and slack jawed.

"What is it?" I say.

"It's like a bad dream," she says. "I thought he was dead. They told me he was dead."

"Who?"

"National Security Agency." She coughs, covers her mouth. "Gimme—can I have some water," she says.

Harry motions for the waitress, but she doesn't see him.

"There's a pitcher and glasses on the side table near the bar." I point.

Harry starts to get up, but Snyder's closer. He makes a beeline for it just as Joselyn topples sideways onto the booth seat.

I grab her before she can fall. Snyder scurries back with the water. He's got it in a glass, but Joselyn's not going to be drinking. She's out cold. I dip my linen napkin into the glass and wipe her forehead. The shock of the ice water on her skin causes her eyelids to flutter. A second later she opens them.

By now the waitress is over. "Is she all right? You want us to call 911?"

"No!" says Joselyn. "I'm okay. Really, it's nothing." She struggles to right herself on the booth seat.

Her skin is clammy, with cold sweat on her arm. "Sip a little water," I tell her.

She gives a feeble shake of the head. "No, my stomach right now . . ." I steady her so if she goes down again she doesn't bang her head on the edge of the table. "Yeah, you're just fine," I tell her.

"I think she'll be all right." Harry looks up at the waitress. "We'll get her back to the office. We've got a couch in the conference room. She can lie down. If she needs help we'll call from there. Can you bring the check?"

"We'll deliver it to the office. Go," she says. "Take her on over. We'll catch up."

SIXTEEN

He's older, and he looks heavier in the photograph, but it's him," she says. Joselyn is flat on her back on the couch.

"Keep your head down, don't try to lift it. Keep your eyes closed." One of the girls from the outer office is holding a cold compress across Joselyn's forehead and eyes.

"Do you have a name for this guy?" Snyder is holding the single enlarged photo in his hand, his notebook open on the conference table in our office.

"When I knew him he was calling himself Dean Belden."

Snyder writes it down.

"But that was what? Nine years ago now. I was told later that he had a number of other names he used, but according to the people I talked to he usually worked under the name Thorn."

"How did you meet him?" I ask.

"He came to my office. I was still practicing law back then. Up in Washington State, near Seattle. He said he . . ." Joselyn lifts the wet compress from her eyes and shifts her body on the sofa to get her head up onto the armrest.

"Don't try to sit up," I tell her.

Harry hands her a pillow and helps her to slide it under her head.

"Thanks. I'm feeling a little better. Besides, I have to get my feet under me. I have a flight to catch tonight, remember?"

"As you said, there are more important things than Congressional hearings," I remind her.

"You were telling us how you met him," said Snyder.

"It's been so long. He was calling himself Dean Belden. He showed up at my office one day and said he was a businessman. Said he had some corporate legal work for me or something. No. No, I remember now."

She lowers her feet onto the floor and sits up. She holds her head for a moment with both hands as if it's ringing like a bell.

"Are you all right?" I ask.

"Yeah. Gimme a second." She takes a moment to compose herself. "The offer of corporate work came later. The first thing he told me was that he had been subpoenaed. That was it. He was under subpoena to appear before a federal grand jury in Seattle. He told me that as far as he knew, it had nothing to do with him. He was not the target of the investigation. It was somebody else, another man he just happened to do business with. He claimed he didn't even know why they wanted to talk to him. He offered a large retainer and told me that if I did a good job on the grand jury thing, especially if I could get it quashed, there might be some corporate work for me later. I was starving at the time, in a solo practice, ready to take anything that came through the door, and like a fool I said yes. That's when the world caved in on me."

"How do you mean?" says Snyder.

"All of it was a lie—his name, his business, the reason he was being called before the grand jury. He knew I couldn't get the sub-

poena quashed. The government was closing in on him and what he needed was a
witness, so he could disappear."

"Go on," says Sydner.

"His business, which was nothing but a
front, was located in the San Juan Islands,
in Puget Sound. He invited me out, supposedly to prep for his appearance before
the grand jury. He had a pilot's license
and a small floatplane. The day he was
supposed to appear before the grand jury
he decided we'd fly.

"I was impressed. I was young and stupid. He set the plane down on Lake Union
in Seattle and we took a cab to the federal
courthouse. He was cool as a cucumber.
We got inside and while I was engaged in
small talk with one of the marshals, Belden
took a powder. It was a few minutes before I realized that he was gone. But there
I was, standing all alone holding the bag. I
assumed that Belden had a case of last-
minute nerves, simply got scared and ran.
It's what he wanted me to think. I grabbed
a cab and headed back to Lake Union
hoping I could catch him before he got into
the air. I thought I could talk him into coming back to the courthouse.

"As it turned out, I didn't quite make it. I got there just in time to watch him push off from the dock, climb up into the plane, and lift off. I heard the engine sputter and watched as the plane cartwheeled into the lake. To this day at least that's what I think I saw. He was very good. It was all meticulously choreographed. Of course, the divers didn't find his body in the wreckage, but then they didn't have to. The police had me as a witness. But the feds didn't buy it."

"So they already knew about him," says Snyder.

"Oh, yes. He wasn't just the target of their probe, he was the bull's-eye. They told me that he worked under the name Thorn and that he was a hired mercenary. That his specialty was the transport of dangerous cargos."

"What kind of dangerous cargos?" says Snyder.

"Nuclear, biological, chemical, that kind," says Joselyn.

"A terrorist," says Snyder.

"That was a word that had not quite come into its own back then."

The puzzlement on Snyder's face as he

tries to snap all of these amorphous pieces into the puzzle of his son's murder might be funny if it wasn't so sad.

"I know how you feel." She looks at him. "While Thorn didn't pull the trigger, I know he is responsible for the death of a dear friend, a man named Gideon van Rye."

"Ah."

Joselyn looks at me. She nods. "He died trying to stop something that Thorn had set in motion. It's a long story."

The story of how Gideon Quest came to be.

"Do you know where he might be now, this man Thorn or Belden or whatever he's calling himself these days?" says Snyder.

"No. For a short time, maybe a year or so after the plane went into Lake Union, he was up near the top of the FBI's most wanted list. Not only did they not buy his drama of accidental death, they didn't even treat him as missing, except for the fact that he was a fugitive. I heard they had him cornered somewhere in Africa and supposedly it was only a question of time. Then the World Trade Center went down, 9/11, and all the priorities changed. Have you seen the FBI's most wanted list lately?" She looks at me.

I shake my head.

"If you don't wear traditional Arab head-gear, you don't get on it."

"Can I see the photographs?" I ask Snyder.

He hands them to me. In one of the photographs, Jimmie and the man Joselyn calls Thorn are laughing.

"Any idea how this man might have gotten on your son's blind side?" I ask Snyder.

He shakes his head. "Jimmie was much too trusting. I tried to warn him. Some people would take advantage if he wasn't careful. But you know how kids are."

"I'm learning," I tell him.

"You have a son?"

"A daughter."

"How old?"

"Twenty-two."

"Almost the same age as Jimmie. You think this man, this Thorn, may have killed my boy?" Snyder directs the question to Joselyn.

"I have no idea. He's not Mexican, I know

that. But from what I saw, what I know, he was certainly capable of it."

"If he was on their wanted list, the FBI must have some kind of file on him," says Harry. "Give them the names, Thorn and Belden. They should be able to connect the dots."

"You better tell them that the photos you've got there aren't going to look the same as the ones in their old files," says Joselyn.

"Do you think it's his print on your business card?" Harry directs this to me.

"I don't know how far back the FBI fingerprint database goes," I tell him, "but if that print belongs to him, it should have spit out a name, Thorn or . . ."

Behind me the door to the conference room suddenly opens. "Paul!"

I turn, and it's my secretary, Janice. By the look on her face I can tell that something is wrong. "Phone call for you. It's urgent. Your daughter."

"What is it?"

"You want to come right now, and take it in your office," she says.

SEVENTEEN

Josh Root sat at the committee rostrum, gavel at hand, completely oblivious to the noise and commotion going on around him. This afternoon his mind was on other things. The Old Weatherman had struck again. This morning Root had gotten up and found it on his personal computer at home, another e-mail in the middle of the night, like a bomb blast.

But this time the fear that had been so palpable in Root following the first two communications was replaced by anger. The Old Weatherman was demanding an additional two million dollars, and he was giving Root only two days to come up with it.

The prick must have thought he was made of money. The thought of it produced bile in his throat. He coughed a few times and covered his mouth with the back of his hand. He took out a handkerchief and wiped a bit of phlegm from his lip.

"Are you all right, Senator?" One of his aides was hovering over his shoulder.

Root took a sip of water from the glass in front of him. He cleared his throat. "I'm fine. We'll get started in a minute."

"Sure. Can I get you anything?"

"Nothing."

The kid sat down again.

Root was beginning to suspect that someone at the Swiss bank had talked. How else could anyone know that he had that kind of ready cash on hand? Two million dollars. People with that kind of money usually had it tied up in investments. It could take anywhere from a few days to a week to sell stocks and reduce them to cash. But the Old Weatherman seemed to know that it was just sitting there, waiting to be wired from one Swiss bank to another. For the moment, how he knew wasn't the problem.

Getting rid of him was. And by now it was clear that buying him off wasn't an option. Knowing the man as he did, Root knew that this would only serve as an invitation for him to come back for more.

The trick was to find him. The key was the Old Weatherman's e-mail account. Somewhere there had to be a record with an address, some point of physical contact. Ordinarily Root would turn this over to one of his staff members and within a short period they would have an answer for him. But this time Root couldn't do that. He would have to do it himself, in the same way that he would have to deal with the Old Weatherman.

He looked up at the clock on the wall at the far end of the room, picked up the gavel, and slapped it hard, twice. "The committee will come to order." He cleared his throat again, took another quick drink of water, and slapped the gavel once more. "The committee will come to order."

The voices in the room began to quiet. "We're going to pick up where we left off this morning." Root looked down at his schedule of witnesses. "Next witness is Joselyn Cole. Is Ms. Cole here?"

A man was sitting at the witness table. "Are you here on behalf of Ms. Cole?"

"No, sir."

The next thing Root knew there was a hand on his shoulder from behind and lips in his ear. "Senator, I think you're looking at the wrong schedule." One of his staffers was pushing a piece of paper in front of him. "You're looking at Tuesday's schedule."

"Ah, sorry," said Root. "My mistake. Seems I'm getting ahead of myself." He laughed. A few in the audience laughed with him. But to Root his was a nervous laugh, a small measure of the forces now coming to bear on him. The Old Weatherman's e-mailed threats, Root's diminishing physical and mental condition, and all the other pressures and demands were now descending on him.

* * *

Ever since the destruction of the World Trade Center, the authorities had tried to erect a series of impermeable security barriers around the entire southern tip of Manhattan. Probably nowhere on earth was there a piece of hallowed ground more protected than this. Thorn was certain that if the local police and the federal authorities could shrink-wrap the whole area in Kevlar, they would.

This evening he stood on the pedestrian overpass and surveyed the work spread out below through a small rip in the blue plastic tarp. The overhead pedestrian walkway was bounded on both sides by chain-link fencing, which in turn was wrapped in plastic tarp material to keep prying eyes from seeing what was happening down below.

Where the twin towers once stood there now existed only a cavernous concrete hole three or four stories deep, housing communications equipment, generators, and the other machinery necessary to run the subway sixty feet down, below the streets. For nearly a decade arguments raged over whether the twin towers should be rebuilt in some manner, or if the site should be transformed into a park or a memorial for those who died on 9/11. In the vacuum of leadership that marked the new century, the concrete cavern remained as a symbol of American indecision.

It was nearing five in the evening, and the stream of human traffic scurrying across the overpass was beginning to resemble some of the rapids on the Colorado, people running to catch the subway down below or one of the buses on Broadway.

Thorn waded into the stream and through the escalating rush-hour crush of people to the other side. At one point he had to grab the chain link to keep from being washed along with the masses. He found a short section of the fence where the walkway widened for just a few feet. He settled in and staked out this little nook as if he owned it.

The plastic tarp blocking his view cracked in the stiff breeze off the Hudson. He looked around to make sure there were no cops on the walkway. Then, using two fingers, he reached up and ripped the tattered tarp just a few inches so that he could claim a clear view out.

He wasn't interested in the site of the World Trade Center. Instead his attention was drawn to an area a few blocks to the south and east of where he was now standing. It was the intersection of Fulton and Broadway, almost dead center in the middle of the Financial District. Wall Street was only a stone's throw away.

The Cold War may have been over, but the Russians and Americans were still locked in a death spiral of ever more lethal weapons. When the United States introduced its largest thermobaric device on record, the Massive Ordnance Air Blast (MOAB), and nicknamed it "the Mother of All Bombs," the Russians responded with the largest vacuum bomb ever constructed. Dubbing it "the Father of All Bombs," it was used to level an entire block of multistory steel-reinforced concrete buildings. In testing it, they set off the largest man-made nonnuclear blast in history.

Now that the Russian cargo plane had been forced down in Thailand, Thorn had to assume that the American government was well aware of the type and size of the device on board. While he hadn't planned it, the downing of the Russian plane played right into his hands. Like a big, flashing neon sign.

The feds would be racking their brains looking for high-risk targets. Thorn was already well ahead of them. The solid fuel-air device was much more effective in an oxygen-controlled environment. If you could introduce the device inside, solid

concrete walls would serve only to mag-
nify and focus the blast. The stronger the
walls, the higher the pressure wave, the
farther it would travel. Of course, American military ordnance experts would know
all of this. They would be advising the FBI
and other law enforcement agencies ac-
cordingly.

Identifying prime targets wouldn't be too
difficult. The problem was there were too
many of them. The authorities couldn't
possibly cover them all. Adding to their
problems, Thorn was already engaged in
devilish games of misdirection, forcing
them to look in one place while he was in
another.

He wondered if anyone had ever considered what the blast from a large thermobaric weapon might do to the hardened
concrete structure surrounding the reactor
of a nuclear power plant. Particularly if the
device were delivered from the air in the
form of a bunker-busting bomb.

That reminded Thorn. He was going to
have to make a call for more cash. His es-
timates of the cost to buy the airplane were
too low. You would think that with the dis-
mal state of the airline industry and the

number of commercial jets now littering boneyards all over the desert, there would be a fire sale. But it wasn't the case. He had gone online and checked prices.

The banks that held the mortgages on these planes were now sitting on piles of taxpayer cash. Having been bailed out, they were demanding top dollar for their securitized loan assets, in this case airplanes for which they had vastly overpaid during the boom-boom times before the crash. The politicians and the central banks had stepped in it big time, up to their hips. And why not? They knew that if the banks went under, there wasn't enough money in the Federal Deposit Insurance Corporation to cover even a small fraction of the claims filed by depositors. So they ran the presses, printed more cash, and deferred the inevitable to a future date when some other new regime could be left holding the bag. To Thorn it was a rat's nest of political and financial corruption, with a new generation of liars at every turn. At least for the moment, acquiring more money didn't seem to be a problem for his employers. What the devil could do if he had cash.

Even if the feds were able to track each

of his moves, as long as he could stay ahead of them, Thorn knew they would have their hands full trying to guess what was coming next.

He trained his eye through the hole in the tarp toward the Fulton Street project. He could see the boom of a high-rise crane moving slowly, like the neck of some gentle giraffe, over the site. It was the answer to Thorn's dreams, nearly half a billion dollars in federal stimulus money for a single piece of construction. It was the once abandoned Fulton Street Transit Center. Total cost, 1.4 billion dollars for a transportation palace, complete with a crystal dome that would have shamed the Wizard of Oz.

Scheduled completion was four years off, but Thorn didn't care. All that mattered was that they had broken ground. The giant excavators had already ripped a two-hundred-foot wound in the earth directly above one of the busiest subway hubs in New York. According to the project schedule, the hole would be open for at least four months while they worked on foundations. This gave Thorn plenty of time. With the city providing the open aperture above the subway, the method of delivery became simple—gravity. The only question was how? And Thorn already knew the answer to that one.

EIGHTEEN

It's like a nightmare. I want to wake up, but I can't. I keep thinking she's going to call me any minute and tell me she's okay, but she doesn't. Dad, she can't, because she's dead." She starts to cry all over again.

Standing in the living room, I hug her in my arms and pat her on one shoulder as she sobs.

"Who would do this? Jenny never hurt anybody. Why, Dad? Tell me. Why?" She looks up at me, searching for an answer I don't have. Her eyes are as red as road flares. She has been crying on and off for more than an hour, ever since hearing the news that her friend Jenny Beckfeld was found dead in her house early this afternoon.

"When she didn't show up for work, I figured she was sick. I tried to call her but she didn't answer."

"What did the police tell her parents? Do you know?" I ask.

She eases out of my embrace and reaches for the Kleenex box I had tossed on the coffee table. Tears run down one cheek. My daughter does not cry easily. In fact, I can recall seeing her like this only once before. Sarah was seven when her mother died.

"They've told them nothing!" Sarah gives me a merciless look. She turns her back to wipe her eyes, and begins to pace across the front room once more. Her shoulders are hunched up tight, one hand at her side holding a wad of Kleenex.

"Why don't you sit down and relax?"

"I don't want to sit. I want to know what happened," she says.

"Herman went over to Jenny's to see what he could find out," I tell her. "I called him from my cell on the way home and asked him to go by and get whatever information he could."

She turns to face me and sniffles into the Kleenex. "And what exactly are they going to tell Herman if they won't even talk to Jenny's family?"

"Herman has his ways," I tell her. "Relax. We'll find out when he gets here."

According to Sarah, Jenny's older brother, a CPA with one of the big firms downtown, went to her house and they wouldn't let him in. They held him on the front lawn and refused to answer any of his questions. When he got angry, they threatened to arrest him unless he calmed down.

"So much for your police," she says. The gulf between sorrow and anger in Sarah at this moment is narrow, and increasingly tapered toward fury. She wants answers, and if I know my daughter, at this moment she wants revenge.

"All they would tell him is that Jenny was dead and they were treating it as a homicide. Nothing more." She turns to face me again. "So somebody killed her, right? It couldn't be suicide, right? What am I saying?" She throws her hands up and tosses the Kleenex in the air. "Jenny would never kill herself."

"If it's homicide, it's death at the hands of another," I tell her.

"I can't believe it. Damn it!" She stamps one foot on the carpeted floor hard enough that it rattles the glassware on the shelf behind me. "It makes me so mad. They wouldn't even tell her brother or her mom and dad how she died."

"They're just doing their job," I tell her. "Is anyone with her parents? Do they have family in the area?"

She nods. "And a minister from their church."

"That's good."

Sarah starts to tear up once more.

I walk over to her and try to comfort her.

"No." This time she feebly pushes me away and steps back. "You know what I've been thinking? Why would someone want to kill Jenny?" She looks directly at me.

"I don't know," I tell her.

"I think maybe you have an idea." She looks at me with bloodshot eyes. "Tell me what's going on."

"What do you mean?"

"When Jenny and I went out, you didn't want me to go. Why?"

"It had nothing to do with Jenny," I tell her.

"Maybe yes, maybe no," she says. "But you didn't want me to go out and it wasn't because you wanted me to stay home and visit. I want the truth."

I turn my palms up and begin to launch an expression of denial. "What—"

"Don't you dare treat me like a child. I want to know what's going on and I want to know now."

"It had nothing to do with Jenny."

"What had nothing to do with Jenny?" She reads me like a book, and snaps it closed before I can turn the page. "So there is something?"

The same question has been plaguing me ever since Sarah's phone call to the office telling me that Jenny was dead. My own private nightmare, the thought that Herman and I may have screwed up and missed something when we followed them. It's a selfish notion, one I can't help but harbor. If it must be that Jenny is gone, I hope and pray that the cops have a clear suspect or at least an evident motive for why she was killed, something unrelated to me or my daughter. Call it guilt.

"What is it that you're not telling me?" says Sarah. "I want to know."

"It's nothing."

"If you don't tell me, I'll get it out of Uncle Harry. You know I will. Harry can't keep a secret. Not from me."

"I was just worried because of everything that's happened. That's it. That's all."

She looks at me askance. "Then you won't mind if I go out this weekend," she says. "On a date."

I hesitate for only a second as I think about this. "Sure. No problem." I call her bluff.

"Sure, because you know I won't. Like I'm going to go out dancing on Jenny's grave. I want you to tell me what's going on. Tell me or you won't be able to leave this house."

"What are you going to do, ground me?" I laugh.

"No. But if you leave, I won't be here when you get back," she says.

I take a long, hard look at her. Sarah has me in a box and she knows it. "I was just worried that, well . . . that what happened

out at the base might not have been entirely over."

"What do you mean?"

I'm saved by the front doorbell, followed
by a sharp rap on the door.

"That'll be Herman." I can see him
through the glass sidelight in the entryway. I head toward the door.

"Don't think for a moment that you're off
the hook," she says.

I open the door and Herman steps inside, all six foot six of him. He's wearing a
nervous smile and whispers, "You guys all
right?"

"Why wouldn't we be?"

When he hears her voice, Herman looks
toward the front room and sees Sarah
standing there.

"Hello, Herman."

"There's my girl. How you doin'?" One
look at her and he knows the answer.
"Stupid question," he says. "Sorry to hear
about your friend."

He turns back to me. "I stopped by out
there like you said, and made a couple of
phone calls." He glances toward Sarah.
"Maybe you and I should talk privately."

"You can talk right here," she says. "Dad was just about to tell me what's going on when you rang the bell."

Herman gives me one of those uncomfortable looks reserved for an untimely entry into a family feud.

"What did you find out?" I ask.

"The house is cordoned off. Cops all over the place. Homicide dicks, one of 'em I recognized."

"Was he helpful?" I ask.

Herman shakes his head. "Not that friendly. Brant Detrick."

Herman and I went toe-to-toe with Detrick on a case two years ago. He is not likely to help us out. If Herman started posing questions, Detrick would assume that we already had a principal suspect lined up as a client.

"Told you he wouldn't get anything," says Sarah.

"Had to go a different way," says Herman.

"How's that?"

"Paramedics," he says.

"I would have thought they'd be long gone," I tell him.

"They woulda been, except two of 'em were held over to do shoe impressions for forensics," says Herman.

I raise an eyebrow. "Was she alive when they got there?"

"Nuh-uh. They got a call, so they had to respond. Tramped through the crime scene before they realized she was dead."

"You think the cops have a shoe impression from the perpetrator?" I ask.

"I don't know."

"Go on."

"So I talked to the paramedics," says Herman. "Both pretty friendly. According to them, the landlord found the body. He was called by somebody who didn't identify himself. This unidentified voice told the landlord the victim didn't show up for work and they were worried about her. So the landlord called the vic's cell phone. When he got no answer, he figured he'd check the house with a passkey."

"So the door was locked," I say.

"Uh-huh. If whoever did it came in that way, they either had a key or picked the lock," says Herman.

"Or maybe she let him in?" I say.

Herman shakes his head. "Not according to the paramedics. It looked like she was in bed alone. Whoever got in caught her lying there facedown. Whether the perp made noise and she woke up they couldn't say. But the way the blankets were laid out covering the body, and the blood pattern, they were guessing she was surprised."

"How was she killed?" I ask.

"Stabbed. Of course, they couldn't verify that as the cause of death. But according to them it looked like she bled out."

"Sarah, you really don't need to be listening to this," I tell her.

"I want to know."

"Fine. Then please tell me you didn't have a key to Jenny's house."

"No. Why?"

"I'm just checking." Unless the police already have a primed and warmed-up suspect, they are likely to throw a wide net. They will want to talk to everybody who knew Jenny. And unless they identify another point of entry, they'll be asking about keys and who had them. "The police are probably going to want to talk to you at some point."

"Why would they want to talk to me?"

"You were probably one of the last people to see Jenny alive."

"But I can't tell them anything, that is unless you tell me what's going on," she says.

"In a minute," I tell her. "Did Jenny have a boyfriend?"

"No," says Sarah.

"Nobody she broke up with recently?"

Sarah shakes her head. "Nuh-uh."

"Did she have any male admirers who weren't welcome?"

"Not that I know of. She never said anything to me."

"Go on. Anything else?" I look back at Herman.

"Yeah," he says. "The landlord panicked when he saw the blood, called 911, and asked for an ambulance. He didn't wanna go inside, and he couldn't tell if she was dead. According to the paramedics, it's not a pretty scene. Reason for the shoe impressions, there was a lotta blood. They stepped in it. Whether anybody else did or not they didn't seem to know, or if they did they weren't saying."

"When you say a lot of blood, did it sound like a rage killing?"

"No," says Herman. "That's the problem.

It's more like whoever did it knew what they were doing. They couldn't be absolutely certain, but according to the paramedics it looked like there were only two stab wounds." Herman stops and looks at Sarah. "You really don't want to be listening to this stuff," he tells her.

"She was my friend. I want to hear it all. Every bit of it. I want to know who did it and why."

Herman looks to me for a reprieve.

I shrug my shoulders. "She's an adult, as she keeps reminding me."

"You're the one's gotta stay up with her when she gets nightmares. Both wounds were well placed. Seems they caught all the vital organ systems. To get that much blood it's either that or a main artery. They didn't get a real good look at the two wounds. They weren't doin' a postmortem," he says. "As soon as they confirmed she was dead, they backed out of the room and tried not to disturb anything any more than they had to. But one of 'em said the wounds looked small and narrow. It was not a wide-bladed weapon, but deep, like maybe whoever did it might have used a long-bladed shiv or a stiletto."

Herman can tell this has my attention.

"Anything else?" I ask.

"Like what?"

"Like maybe fingerprints?"

"You mean . . ."

"Yeah." My darkest dream, the one I will curl up with tonight, is that forensics will find an itinerant thumbprint at the scene, one they cannot exclude or identify.

"It's too early." Herman turns his nose up. "They wouldn't have had time to pull all the latents yet and check 'em against the victim and anybody else who had regular access to the house."

"So there's no way to know," I say.

Herman shakes his head. "We'll have to wait and see," he says.

"Wait for what?" says Sarah.

"To see if they can identify a perpetrator from the fingerprints," I tell her.

"I see."

Herman looks at me, round eyed, as if perhaps I should tell her.

"Oh, I am," I whisper to him. "Got no choice now."

"You gonna tell her all of it?" he whispers back.

"All of it, including what you and I did," I tell him.

"What are you two talking about?" says Sarah.

"I was asking Herman if he wanted to join us for a cup of coffee in the kitchen."

"I'd like to, but I gotta go," he says.

"Nonsense." I have one hand on his shoulder, steering him toward the kitchen. "Come on, Sarah, there are some things we need to talk about."

NINETEEN

Snyder slept fitfully on the red-eye flight from L.A. back to Chicago. By the time he arrived at O'Hare, it was five in the morning and he was exhausted. He couldn't remember the last time he'd had a full night's sleep. It was before his son was murdered, of that he was sure. Even with all the medications given to him by his doctor, a cornucopia of antidepressants and antianxiety drugs, Snyder was unable to dodge the pain.

He looked down at the notepad lying on his lap—"aka Dean Belden." The man's photograph walking next to Jimmie was now branded on Snyder's fevered brain. He hoped that Cole was right. If so, it was something he could feed to the FBI and perhaps harvest some information in return.

One thing bothered him. Snyder was convinced there was something Madriani wasn't telling him. Whether it had to do with Jimmie's murder he couldn't be sure. The tip-off was in the needling current of inquiry directed by Cole at Madriani during lunch, her observations about the business card in Jimmie's wallet and the thumbprint, her uptake on Liquida and the danger this posed to Madriani, and the obvious fact that the lawyer was already well aware of this but wasn't saying anything. What else did he know that he wasn't telling them?

It provoked questions regarding some of the background research Snyder had done on Madriani. The night before he left for San Diego he ran a couple of online news site searches and Googled Madriani's name. Most of what came back was the usual stuff you might expect concerning a criminal defense lawyer, news on cases Madriani had tried.

But there was one item, more recent, that caught his attention. Madriani's name popped up in connection with the attack on the Coronado naval base. This was one of those seminal events that the entire world knew about because of the blanket coverage on the cable news networks. It never rang any bells with the name Madriani until Snyder read the news articles online. At first he figured Madriani must have defended someone in connection with the case until he realized that the lawyer had been taken into custody in the shootout. When he saw this, and knowing that Madriani's business card was found in his son's wallet, the adrenaline began to spike in Snyder's body. He was sure he had something. He wasted two hours reading news articles until in the end it all turned out to be smoke. Or was it? According to the FBI, Madriani and one of his employees happened to be in the wrong place at the wrong time and were caught up in the law enforcement net after the shootout.

The second he got home, Snyder dropped his luggage inside the front door and headed for the study. The large, stately home in the North Shore area of Chicago was dark and empty. Snyder had lived alone ever since the divorce from his wife five years earlier.

He turned on the floor lamp, plopped himself down in front of his desktop, and hit the browser button.

Snyder had already hired a private investigator. Now he would feed him all of the information he had gathered on his trip to San Diego. He fired off an e-mail to the investigator, giving him the name Liquida and the term "the Mexicutioner" along with the rumor that he worked for the Mexican drug cartel in Tijuana. He laid it all out, including the thumbprint on the business card, and then typed in the name Thorn and his alias, Dean Belden. He told the investigator to gather any information he could find under the name Belden regarding a federal grand jury investigation and a floatplane crash on Lake Union in Seattle and gave him the approximate time frame for the events. Snyder told the investigator that he needed whatever information he could find, and that he needed it immediately. He told him he was willing to pay a premium by way of fees for thorough and prompt service and that he would be waiting for a reply ASAP. He hit the Send button.

Then Snyder pulled out his wallet and located Joselyn Cole's business card. The meeting in San Diego had come to an abrupt end when Madriani had to leave his office, something about a family emergency. Cole and Snyder exchanged business cards and agreed to keep in touch. Snyder told her he would lay heavy hands on the FBI turning over the information on Thorn, and promised to keep her informed as to what he learned.

He entered her name and all of the contact information from her business card into the contact list on his computer. Then he synchronized it to his BlackBerry so that he could call her or shoot e-mails to her from the road.

He navigated to one of his tailored news sites on the Web and hit the button for advanced searches. He went to the line that read "Find results with the exact phrase" and typed in the name Joselyn Cole in the box next to it. Snyder scanned down the page to make sure he would capture everything back for a period of one year. Then he hit the Search button. He knew he wouldn't find anything on Thorn or Belden or the grand jury stuff in Seattle. Those events went back too far, beyond the time of Internet news sites. And not many newspapers made their news morgues available online, even for a fee.

The search under Cole's name produced a few news articles, one reporting on a press conference held by Cole's organization, Gideon Quest, dealing with the issue of land mines in Africa and Asia. Cole and her organization seemed to have a particular brief for arms merchants and the manufacturers who produced their wares.

One of the stories caught his eye. It involved testimony before a Senate committee dealing with nuclear weapons and their proliferation in Third World countries. Toward the bottom of the article Snyder saw the name Gideon van Rye, for whom the organization Gideon Quest had been named. He remembered Cole mentioning the name over lunch in San Diego.

According to the article, van Rye was a Dutch physicist who died of radiation poisoning following an accident at Lawrence Livermore National Laboratory in California. The article described the accident as somewhat mysterious and never fully explained. Mysterious was right. It didn't make sense, not to Snyder, not if Cole was telling the truth. According to her, Thorn, alias Dean Belden, was responsible for van Rye's death. If so, how could it be an accident?

He printed out the story and then turned his attention to the Web. He Googled Cole's name and found several more news articles, all of them dealing with various weapons systems, testimony before Congress on Defense Department appropriations, research, and development. Joselyn Cole seemed dedicated to her work. She couldn't be making much money doing what she did. She was a woman with a cause. This struck Snyder as positive, someone he could probably trust if he needed information, or if he had to share some. If he had to pick a face to bond with around the table in San Diego, he felt safest with Cole.

He ran a search for the names Thorn and Belden just to be safe, and as expected came up with nothing useful. He searched using the name Liquida as well as the Mex-

icutioner. "Liquida" was the Spanish word
for water. He found sites where the word
was used in connection with products, but
nothing else. Without a first name it was
impossible. For "the Mexicutioner" Snyder
found multiple pages with links to a Mexican prizefighter. That was it.

By now the sun was up and streaming
through the window in Snyder's study. He
checked his watch. Seven minutes after
eight, 9:07 in Washington. He pulled out
his cell phone, entered the name Joseph
Wallace, and pressed the little roller ball.
His contact list offered him two options: the
FBI agent's office phone or the cell number
that Wallace had penned on the back of
his card. Snyder opted for the cell line.

It rang twice before he answered. "Agent
Wallace here."

"Mr. Wallace, this is Bart Snyder, Jimmie Snyder's father."

There was dead air at the other end for
a second as Wallace tried to place the
name.

"Killed in his apartment, drug overdose,"
said Snyder. Jimmie's murder was already
slipping through the cracks.

"Oh, yeah, yeah. Yeah, I remember."

"You left those photographs with me, do you recall?"

"Sure."

"I think I may have something for you." Snyder could hear a lot of noise in the background, sounds of traffic. He had obviously caught him at a bad time. "Are you on your way to your office?"

"No," said Wallace. "Another case."

"I see. Do you have a pen and paper?"

"Gimme a second."

Snyder could hear the rustle of the phone as the agent juggled the cell while looking for something to write on and a pen to do it with.

"Okay. What have you got?"

"A name for the man in the photographs. Last name Thorn." Snyder spelled it for him so there would be no mistake.

"Any first name?"

"No, but there's an alias, Dean Belden." He spelled it again.

"Any address?"

"No. But you should have something on him," said Snyder.

"How's that?"

Snyder told him about the grand jury

proceedings in Seattle and the crash of the floatplane, the fact that Belden or Thorn or whatever his real name was had appeared on the FBI's most-wanted list ten years ago and that they should have photographs of him, and possibly fingerprints. "Check your files," said Snyder.

"Where did you get this?" asked Wallace.

"I'm not at liberty to tell you that right now," said Snyder.

"Was it one of your son's friends?"

"Can't tell you. Not right now. But I'll tell you what. You tell me what you find and I'll tell you more," said Snyder.

"Wait a second," said Wallace. "If you're withholding information, I can have you arrested."

"Do you think I care? My son's been murdered. I want to know who did it."

"We're working the case, Mr. Snyder. Your cooperation would be appreciated."

"That's what I'm doing, cooperating," said Snyder.

"We need to follow up on the information," said Wallace. "We have to know if your source is reliable."

"She's reliable." Snyder shook his head.

He realized he'd given away her gender. He knew he shouldn't be doing this when he was so tired.

"Then I assume this woman you talked to must have met or had some involvement with the man in the photographs?" Wallace was fishing for more.

"Let's just say they met some years ago," said Snyder. "That reminds me, she told me to tell you that the photographs you gave me may not bear a striking resemblance to the old file photos that you have of Mr. Thorn. You may have to look closely. But she was absolutely certain it was him."

"She must have known him well," said Wallace. "Listen, I'm pretty busy right now. Can I call you back?"

"When you have some information," said Snyder. "I want to know what you have on this man. You tell me what you know and I'll tell you what I know."

"Are you trying to bargain with me?"

"In a word, yes," said Snyder.

"You have to understand, I cannot open our files to you. If that's what you're thinking, you're wrong," said Wallace. "Confidential law enforcement information in our files is strictly controlled. I can't reveal it to anyone."

"I'm not just anyone, I'm the father of the victim."

"Even so," said Wallace. "There's a limit to what we can tell you. You need to tell me what you know and let us handle it. And be patient. It may take a while."

"What do you mean?" said Snyder.

"I mean we have other cases. And we're stretched thin right now."

"You said you were working on my son's case."

"We are. Along with a few dozen other open files. Listen, I can't talk right now," said Wallace. "Can I call you back? May not be till later in the week. Can I reach you at this number?"

Snyder knew when he was getting the runaround. "Call me after you've looked at your files on this man Thorn."

"Call you back," said Wallace, and the line went dead.

He had a sinking feeling. Snyder now knew he was on his own. The police and the FBI might continue to pursue the case, but not with the urgency that it required.

To them it was just one more open file. He could sit on his hands and do what others did and "leave it to the authorities"—one more cold case, or worse, they would close it with the finding that Jimmie had died of an accidental drug overdose. Snyder wasn't going to let that happen.

TWENTY

I have been chasing Zeb Thorpe at FBI headquarters in Washington by phone all morning. Three separate phone calls so far. The number he gave me for emergencies several months ago rings through to a secretary near his office. I get the sense when I talk to her that I am now old news.

"What was your name again?"

"Paul Madriani. He gave me this number in case there was a problem."

"I know. I think I told you before, Mr. Thorpe is in a meeting. I believe he already received your earlier message."

"But he didn't call."

"No, he's busy. I'm sure he'll call you back as soon as he can."

I have already left the information about Jenny's murder, and the fear that it may have been Liquida sending me another message and that he may be targeting my daughter. Herman and I are unable to get any further information, as the police have dropped a curtain around everything at Jenny's house. What news there is, and there are local reports every few minutes on cable, is offering less than we already know.

"I'll get the message to him that you called again, just as soon as he gets out."

"Listen, it may be a matter of personal safety, we just don't know," I tell her.

"If there's an emergency, you should call the local police," she tells me.

"I don't know if there's an emergency. We don't have enough information to know. If I have to, I will. But I don't think Mr. Thorpe would want me to call the local authorities."

"Why not?"

"If I call them, I'm going to have to tell them why. If I have to tell them the details, your boss is going to be very upset."

"What is this regarding?" she says.

"The attack on the Coronado naval base."

"Oh!" she says. "Just a moment." She puts me on hold.

I wait. Herman is grousing around out in the living room, where he slept last night. I see him scratching his chest through his tank-top undershirt, yawning as he ambles barefoot for the bathroom at this end of the hall.

"Who you callin'?"

"Thorpe."

"He didn't call you back?"

"Not yet."

He steps into the bathroom and closes the door. Herman spent the night with a pistol stashed under the cushion of the couch where his head rested. While upstairs I kept watch with my unzipped fanny pack and the loaded .45 next to my pillow.

Every few minutes I would look in on Sarah. She didn't sleep much. Each time I opened the door to her room, she was lying there wide awake. The information I gave her about Liquida, the FBI's warning, has shaken her. She understands now why it was necessary to stay away from home for so long. Worse, she is now beginning to labor under the burden of guilt for her dead friend. She told me yesterday that if she had known about the threat from Liquida, she would never have allowed Jenny to come anywhere near our house.

I told her that for all we knew, Jenny's death may have nothing to do with Liquida. But to Sarah it didn't matter. The thought that she may have been putting others at risk was enough. In other words, I should have told her. I will have to live with it.

"Hello." She's back on the line. "Mr. Thorpe will take your call in his office. It'll be just a moment."

I wait on the line. I've begun to sense how a mobster must feel when he's being squeezed by prosecutors with the less than subtle hint that his life is in danger. It's the reason I have been scrupulous in keeping quiet about the nuke at Coronado. It has less to do with the threat of criminal prosecution, the fear that the government might drop the hammer on me if I talked, and more to do with the knowledge that Liquida is out there. I can't afford to alienate Thorpe. Regarding Liquida, he is my only source of information, and if push comes to shove, to protect Sarah there is nowhere else I can go.

A second later Thorpe comes on the line. "Mr. Madriani."

"Yes. I'm here."

"I'm sorry to keep you waiting," he says. "We've got a major crisis going on. I couldn't get away. It's terrible news about your daughter's friend. I'm sorry to hear it. I take it your daughter was not a witness to any of this?"

"No. But they were out together that night. My investigator and I tried to provide some cover. We tried to follow them from a discreet distance. Apparently we didn't do a very good job."

"You shouldn't blame yourself. First of all, you're making a lot of assumptions. I take it you didn't tell your daughter about Liquida," he says.

"I have now. I know you didn't want me to."

"Only because it would raise questions about what happened at Coronado. Did she ask you about that?"

"No. Right now she's too upset to think about anything."

"I understand," he says. "You did what

you thought was best. You said you followed the two girls that night?"

"We did."

"Did you see anything? Anyone who
looked suspicious? Might have been following them?"

"No. Nothing. Not that I noticed. Of
course, I'm no pro. My investigator has a
better eye for this stuff than I do and he
didn't see anything either. And we were a
fair distance away. We didn't want the girls
to know."

"I understand."

"They went to a restaurant and a club;
both places were crowded. It's possible he
could have been close and we just couldn't
see him."

"Do you have the names of these places?"

"I do."

I give them to him over the phone. Thorpe
tells me he'll have some of his agents from
the San Diego field office check it out to
see if anyone who works there might have
seen or heard something.

"Assuming it was him, do you think he
could have made you?" says Thorpe.

"What do you mean?"

"If it was Liquida, do you think he might

have seen you or your investigator and kept his distance until later?" asks Thorpe.

"The thought never entered my mind. You seemed to think it wasn't him."

"Have you told the police any of this?" he says.

"What's to tell? We didn't see anything."

"Of course." There's a long pause at the other end. "I don't know what to tell you. As soon as I got your first message, I had one of our agents contact San Diego homicide. He didn't find out much."

"Then am I safe to assume that the killer didn't leave a calling card this time?"

"Not that they found. At least not yet. We checked. We told them to pay particular attention to prints. Of course, they'd already dusted the place. They'll go back and take a second look. We told them anything they couldn't identify to run it through our computers. We'll authorize it to be expedited. We told them so."

"Did they ask you what your interest was?" I say.

"They did. We told them we couldn't discuss it unless there was evidence linking it to a couple of cases we have open. For the time being, unless they find something else, I'm afraid that's all I can do. Unless we can make some connection, we'd be hard pressed to say it's him."

"What about the MO, the knife and the wounds?"

"How did you know about that?" he asks.

"Local sources," I tell him.

"I see." Thorpe is wondering if I've talked to the cops and if so whether I've lied to him. "There's nothing there to connect it either to Afundi or to the kid in the apartment in D.C.," he says. "Liquida, if he exists at all, may use a knife, but we have no record of it."

Now, suddenly, it seems Liquida doesn't exist at all, but is a figment of my imagination.

"I didn't dream this guy up," I tell him. "You're the one who warned us about him. Remember?"

"Well, but we just don't know," said Thorpe.

"You have two matching thumbprints at two separate crime scenes, one of them on the back of one of my business cards. What is it exactly that you don't know?"

"Who those prints belong to for starters," says Thorpe.

"You can be sure of one thing. It's not a coincidence," I tell him.

"Of course not," he says.

"And according to my investigator—he talked to the paramedics—Jenny's death looked like a professional hit. This wasn't a girl who ran with drug dealers or gangbangers any more than Jimmie Snyder did," I tell him. "You can trust me on that one."

"I don't doubt you," says Thorpe. "But without more we can't connect your daughter's friend to the other two cases or to the prints."

"Do you know if the local police have any other suspects? Anybody of interest?" I ask him.

"According to our agent, at this time the answer's no. The detective in charge told him it was too early to know."

"So what do I do?" I ask.

I can hear him take a deep breath on the other end. "I really don't know what to tell you," he says.

TWENTY-ONE

The old tarmac seemed to have more cracks than solid surface. With weeds sprouting up through the fissures, it looked like the prairie. Some of the taller grass came up to his hips. From a distance, as he drove in off the highway, Thorn could swear that he was looking at a farmer's fallow field instead of what it was: one of a score of abandoned army airfields left over from World War II. These dotted the island of Puerto Rico like the measles, as they were used to guard the entrance to the Panama Canal. Anyone with a map who wanted to take the time could find them.

Thorn spent the better part of two days surveying four of the old airfields. Two of them had landing strips that looked good on paper but were too short for the plane and its final cargo when he measured them. Some farmer had cut a trench across one of them before he realized that the old oil-soaked tar macadam and the three-foot gravel bed underneath it weren't exactly the best soil for growing crops.

The third field was long enough, with a good surface. It was well maintained. But there were too many prying eyes. The airstrip was a hangout for the local general aviation crowd. There was a small fleet, maybe a dozen single and twin-engine props. If he landed the big bird there, the amateur pilots would be crawling over it in minutes, asking him what he was doing and if they could watch.

This one, the prairie field, seemed to have everything Thorn needed. The oil surface looked as if it hadn't been sealed since the fifties. But the runway was long enough, and it would only have to take the heavy load twice, once coming in and once going out.

Thorn paced it off, taking nearly two

hours to make sure there were no surprises. There were no buildings, just some
footings and a large concrete slab, probably what was left of an old hangar. After a
thorough inspection, Thorn decided that,
all in all, it was in good shape.

Best of all was the location. It was isolated. The runway lay in a narrow valley between low-lying hills along a rugged stretch
of coast about a mile in from the ocean.

If there was a place on the island where
a large plane on a single approach might
not attract much attention, this was it.

Thorn turned and looked out toward the
sea. He planned it all out in his mind. If he
dropped down, say, a hundred miles out,
and skimmed the waves coming in, he could
slip in under the radar from the airport in
Mercedita ten miles to the south. The airport presented problems, but it also gave
him cover. Anyone seeing the plane come
in over the water would assume that he
was either on an approach to the airport or
was circling around for another shot.

His biggest concern was the AWAC
flights manned by the U.S. military. These
were large four-engine jets or prop jobs
with radar domes on top. They flew regular

missions over the Caribbean, mostly for drug interdiction. They were a problem for Thorn because he couldn't get under their radar. If they picked him up coming in, they would notify drug enforcement. Within minutes Thorn could expect a flyover from an unmanned drone or a helicopter doing followup surveillance. An hour later he'd be up to his hips in DEA agents with their dogs sniffing his crotch.

He turned and looked back at the runway. Somebody would have to knock down the weeds. Otherwise the friction from the wheels or the blast from the engines would start a fire. A man with a harvester could do it in a day, crop it all down close enough that it wouldn't matter. Thorn could rent a small combine harvester on the island, and one of his men could operate it.

He surveyed the trees at the far end of the field, mostly scrub brush with a small grove of tall palms casting long shadows in the late-afternoon sun. Some steel cable, a couple of come-alongs, and enough camouflage netting and they could fashion their own hangar. Taxi the plane under the trees, drop the netting, and no one would see it.

With the right equipment, supplies, and a little labor, they could kick the plane into shape in two weeks. Thorn would do a title search, find out who owned the land, and lease it from them for six months.

He made a mental list of what they would need. At the top of the list was a wheeled electric starter motor for the engines, unless he could find his dream plane, an airliner that didn't require one. Most large commercial jets, once the engines were shut down, could not be restarted again without an external power source.

A good-size front-end loader rigged with a tow bar could push the plane around to maneuver it, that is, if they lined it up empty on the runway for takeoff before they fueled it. Some paint, welding equipment, and a load of Jet A fuel, and they were in business. Oh, yes. And one big mother of a bomb.

With the calculator running in his brain like the tape from an adding machine, Thorn already knew that the costs were going to climb faster and higher than the plane could fly. It was little wonder that no one had ever tried this before. Thorn hoped his employer's pockets were deep enough, because the good old days of hijacking somebody else's plane and flying it into a building were over.

Thorn headed for his car knowing that he'd done a good day's work. Halfway there, the new BlackBerry on his belt began to vibrate. The new phone was becoming a pain in the ass. He had purchased it along with a data service plan under a two-year contract using a phony name, a bad billing address, and a stolen credit card. All he wanted to do was see how the thing worked.

It vibrated again. He knew it wasn't a phone call. Those rang. It was either an e-mail or something from the World Wide Web. Probably another ad from the phone company. It was reaching the point that Thorn wasn't sure if he would even wait until the end of the thirty-day billing cycle to drop the thing in a Dumpster. He couldn't sleep at night because it kept vibrating all over the nightstand next to him. And if he turned off the vibrator, it would beep instead. How to turn that off, he wasn't sure. The phone required an advanced degree in computer engineering before you could operate it. It was no joke that they'd offered him a two-day course over a weekend, and Thorn had just laughed. That was before he started losing sleep.

It vibrated again. He ripped the thing from the holster and tried to work the tiny roller ball with his big thumb. Thorn was spitting four-letter expletives, looking at the screen as he tried not to trip over the weeds.

It was an e-mail from Soyev. He was on his way back from North Korea, holding over in Hong Kong: "Big brother in the bag." What it meant was that the Russian had closed the deal on a replacement for the mammoth blockbuster they'd lost in Thailand. This one would ship by sea and not from North Korea, where the Americans would be watching. Other arrangements were being made.

There was a postscript: "You will be interested in the attached."

He almost put the phone away, figuring he would read it later. Then curiosity got the better of him. He stopped in the field for a moment and worked the trackball to call up the attachment.

It was a news article, something from the *Washington Post.* The moment he saw her name, he knew it was trouble. Thorn had been watching Joselyn Cole from the sidelines for years, ever since he'd tangled with her in Seattle.

She had very nearly run him into a hole in East Africa, exhorting the feds to hunt him down. Not that they needed much encouragement. Now she was causing problems again. Cole was a busybody. She was testifying before a Senate committee. But it was her words quoted in the story that sent a chill up Thorn's spine, the reason the Russian had sent it to him.

> The hellfire missile you use today to kill a carload of accused terrorists on a dusty road in Afghanistan may, in time, find its way into the hands of their children. What do we do then when this same relentless, unerring weapon is aimed at the West Wing or Ten Downing Street?

She was talking about precision-guided weapons. It made the hair on the back of Thorn's neck stand up.

> These systems, originally designed and sold on the notion of avoiding collateral damage, have now become the weapon

of choice for acts of very precise mass assassination. Think about that. We reap what we sow. A laser-guided missile can kill with more lethality and certainty than a bullet fired by a sniper. Why? Because it can reach its target in an enclosed vehicle or a building where the victim suffers from the illusion of security.

He should have killed her in Seattle, thought Thorn.

Make no mistake about it. Soon there will be no place left for leaders of any stripe to hide.

It was intended to get their attention, and it did. Standing in the empty field, rolling the little trackball, Thorn devoured the rest of the story. She took a few shots from the right, members who asked if she was equating Al Qaeda to leaders of recognized political states.

She told them they were missing the point.

For the most part the committee got the message. They wanted to know what they could do to ensure that this wouldn't happen, that someone wouldn't get their hands on these weapons and target their sorry asses.

Without even realizing it, Cole was directing the spotlight just where Thorn didn't need it, and at the worst possible time.

Of course, the bitch had a long list of recommendations, all of them designed to tighten the screws on the tools of Thorn's trade. To make it more difficult to get the weapons he needed. Not that she would ever be able to shut down the market. But she could surely make it expensive.

If she continued to whip this horse, he would have to find a way to shut her up. It would be just Thorn's luck if she stumbled into his party and somehow unraveled it all before he could move.

TWENTY-TWO

So then I take it we're all agreed?" The four of us are seated around the kitchen table at our house in Coronado.

"I don't see that we have any other choice," says Harry.

Herman nods. "I agree." Three days since they found Jenny's body and we're all running on empty from lack of sleep.

"Well, I don't," says Sarah. "I don't like it. Besides, you're only doing this because of me. Why should we let him chase us out of our home?"

"We don't move, we're just playin' into

his hand," says Herman. "He killed your friend to send us a message—that he can reach any one of us anytime he wants. If we move and do it the right way, we take that away from him."

"How do we know it's even him? How do we know he killed Jenny?"

"We know. Trust us on this," I tell her.

"Why can't we go to the police? Aren't they supposed to provide protection?" says Sarah.

"They gotta have evidence," says Herman. "So far they got nothing linking Liquida to Jenny's murder."

"At least not yet," I tell her. "We gave them his name and some other information. They're going to investigate—"

"You mean they can't provide protection?" says Sarah.

"They might send a patrol car by the house every few hours to keep an eye on us," I tell her. "But that's all."

"And that ain't gonna cut it," says Herman. "Not with this guy. His game is to play with our minds. Man's evil, but he's got patience. He knows that sooner or later we're gonna get tired, give it up, and go back to livin' a normal life. That's when he'll hit. He's toyin' with us like a cat that has one of his claws in a mouse."

"I should have taken Sarah and run," I tell them. "The minute Thorpe told us about Liquida. Jenny would still be alive."

"Maybe. But one of us'd be dead in her place," says Herman.

"What do you mean?" I ask.

"Harry or me," he says. "You gotta understand what you're dealin' with. Liquida's a mental case. One sick son of a bitch. Excuse my language." Herman glances toward Sarah, then looks at me. "If you run, it's the way he'd bring you back, reach out and kill somebody close. It's why I had you shut down the office."

"You closed the law office?" says Sarah.

"Had to," says Herman. "He killed Jenny, so what's to think he won't go after one of the secretaries? Can't take the chance."

Herman has managed to stay half a jump ahead of Liquida for the past few days. Otherwise, by now one of us would probably be dead. He is beginning to get a sense for the twisted mind that is shadowing us. Herman's take is that Liquida probably hasn't taken the time to tail any of our staff to their homes yet, because he thinks he has the four of us under glass, where we can't move.

"So we sent everybody from the office home," Herman explains to Sarah. "Told them to stay away from the office till they hear from us, and to take all the home addresses and other identifying informa-tion out of the office so Liquida can't find any of it. You did do that?" He looks at Harry.

"Took care of it this afternoon," says Harry. "The staff is on paid leave for as long as we can manage it. Told them to take all their personal stuff home and told them the reason. I had the IT people put everything behind passwords in the com-puters and cleaned out all the personnel files. I can't guarantee we got everything, but he'd have to hunt like hell to find it. Take him days. I had the phones rolled over to the answering service, locked all the windows and doors, and turned on the full security system—doors, windows, mo-tion sensors, the whole nine yards."

"So now it's down to us," says Herman. He looks at Sarah.

"If we do this. Assuming I go along. How

long do we have to stay away?" Sarah looks me dead in the eye.

"Until the police and the FBI can nail him," I tell her.

"Oh, yeah, that's great! How do we know they're even looking for him? Besides, what good is the FBI? Harry tells me that when you call them, they put you on hold," she says. "We lived with them for three months, now they forget our names?"

I shoot Harry a look and he winces. "Sorry."

"Sarah, I know it's short notice, but it's the best we can do. If you have a better idea, let's hear it."

"Let me have a gun. Teach me how to shoot and I'll take care of myself," she says.

"What, and go off on your own?" I say.

"Why not? I'll stay away. Get another job. If he can't find your staff, he won't be able to find me."

I roll my eyes, shake my head, and glance at Harry. "You talk to her."

"Not that I want to discourage you from exercising your god-given right of self-defense," says Harry, "but I don't think this is a good idea."

"You don't think I can do it?" she says.

"Oh, I don't doubt it," says Harry. "Nobody in their right mind would come after you if they knew you were armed. But if Herman's right, Liquida's a mental case. So he's not likely to be dissuaded by the fact that you're packing a gun. Even if he knows it's there."

"Good. Then I'll kill him," she says.

"Just like that," says Harry.

"You bet. Give me a gun and show me how to use it," she says.

"Not me. I haven't figured out how to get the pistol out of the fanny pack yet," says Harry.

"Where is it?" I ask.

"Not to worry. It's in my car. Locked in the trunk. Right next to the shotgun," he says.

"What shotgun?" I ask.

"One I bought yesterday. Biggest twelve-gauge pump I could find, a barrel longer than my uncle Willie's dick. If I'm gonna have to pack a gun, I want him to see it. That way, even if Liquida's crazy, maybe he'll be less likely to come visiting."

"Your uncle Willie's dick?" says Sarah.

"A manner of speaking," says Harry.

"Well, there you go," says Sarah. "So now we have an extra gun."

"It's not a matter of guns," I tell her.

"Why not?"

"Your dad's right," says Herman. "It's a question of sleep."

"What do you mean?"

"Look around the table and tell me what you see. Four tired people," says Herman, "all of us on edge. And it's only been three nights since they found Jenny. A couple more nights and some of us are gonna get the jitters. At that point I'm gonna be collecting all the guns. Otherwise we'll be shooting each other in the dark. We won't have to worry about Liquida. Besides, you go off on your own and he comes after you, he'll come when you least expect it. Gun or no gun. He'll wait until you get too tired, or till you think it's safe. He'll come when you're asleep, like he did with your friend Jenny. Or when you're walkin' to your car after work. You'll have to grow eyes in the back of your head, and stay awake around the clock. You think you can do that?"

"I don't know, but I can try," she says.

"And do you really think your dad's gonna let you do it alone?" He smiles at her because they both know the answer to this.

"Give it up 'cause it ain't gonna work. We gotta find somewhere safe, simple as that, and there's no way around it," he says.

"And what about all of you?" she says. "Where are you going to hide?"

"Harry's going with you, at least for the time being," I tell her.

"So you've worked this all out?" she says.

"We have," says Harry. "You can ride shotgun during the drive."

"May I ask where I'm going?"

"Not right now. But shortly after you leave, Herman and I will disappear," I tell her. "We've got some work to do."

"And if I don't go?" she says.

"Then you're putting all of us in jeopardy," I say. "Because we can't get out of here unless you do."

"So that's it," she says.

"I'm afraid so," I tell her.

"I still don't like it," she says.

"None of us do," says Herman. "Had my way, I'd kill the bastard now and get a good night's sleep. Problem is I don't know where he's at."

"If we knew where he was, we could call the police," says Sarah.

"Why waste a dime?" says Herman. "Besides, cops and courts are like fishermen—catch and release. Far as I'm concerned, a man threatens my life, it's open season." He stands up and almost hits his head on the light fixture high over the table.

"You mean you'd just shoot him?" she says.

"Not necessarily," says Herman. "I might not want to make that much noise." Herman gives Sarah one of his big smiles.

"Is he kidding?" She looks at me.

"I wouldn't bet on it."

"Good. Then I'll go along with the program on two conditions," says Sarah. "You keep me posted on everything that's happening. No more secrets."

"Agreed. And what's the second condition?"

"I want Mr. Diggs to teach me how to shoot when he has some time."

"You got it," says Herman.

"Make the call," I tell him.

Herman takes the cell phone from his belt and starts pushing buttons as he strolls toward the living room.

I spend the next hour helping Sarah

pack. About forty-five minutes in, I hear a vehicle pull into the driveway out in front. I step into my bedroom and look through the front window. It's a large white van, two guys getting out. They're wearing white overalls and baseball caps. One of them is pushing a small laundry hamper filled with coiled sections of large, ribbed gray rubber hose.

"It's my people," Herman whispers up from downstairs. "Don't worry, you got plenty of time. Paul, can you come down? One thing we need to take care of."

"Be right there," I tell him. "Can you finish up?" I ask Sarah.

"Yes." She's on her computer taking care of some last-minute business.

"Be right back." I hear the men coming through the front door with their equipment. I head for the stairs.

"What do I do with my mail?" says Sarah. "Can I have it forwarded?"

"I don't know. Let me think about it. Why don't you wait? We can talk about it when you get back there."

"I don't want to wait."

"Gimme a second," I tell her.

"Besides, I've got a paycheck coming. Everything's gonna pile up in the mailbox. Did you think about that?"

"No, it won't." I hold up on the stairs so she can hear me without my yelling. "I had my mail and the household stuff sent to the business PO box. The secretaries will take care of it there and pay the bills. I set it up so they can write checks."

"Oh, right," says Sarah. "Took care of your stuff. Sounds like you've been thinking about this for a while. Nice of you to let me in on it."

"Give me a minute," I tell her.

Herman introduces me to his crew and we talk about how it should go down, the number of bags to be loaded, and I make sure they have the right address for the next stop.

The two men spend the next twenty minutes connecting the sections of hose, hooking up one end to the motor in the back of the van while they haul in carpet-cleaning equipment for the other end. They turn on the motor in the back of the van, loud enough that half the neighborhood can now hear it. For the next forty minutes, one of them puts his hand over

THE RULE OF NINE

the open suction hose every so often to drown the motor down while the other one starts a routine rolling the laundry hamper back and forth. The first load contains Sarah's two rolling luggage bags laid in the bottom of the hamper under several large white towels. On the second run I shake Harry's hand.

"Not to worry. I'll take care of her," he says.

"I know you will. Let her share the driving. It's a long trip. It'll help keep her mind off things. What do you figure, how many days?" I ask him.

"Four, maybe five. Depends on the weather and traffic."

"Drive carefully."

"Will do." Harry sits down in the hamper. They cover him with the towels and he goes for the ride. It takes both of the guys to lift the heavy hamper inside the van, out of sight. A minute or so later they come back out with the empty hamper.

I hug Sarah, hold her as tight as I can, and give her a kiss on the cheek and the forehead. "I love you. I'll call you tonight. Keep your cell phone charged. And don't send anything with your address on it, no e-mails, no letters, don't tell any of your friends."

"Got it, Dad."

"We'll get past this. I promise. I know it's hard."

"Don't worry about me. Love you." She is starting to tear up. "Please be careful," she says.

"Not to worry," I tell her. "Herman is with me, remember?"

"I know," she says. "Still . . ."

"I'll be careful."

A few seconds later, she's in the hamper, covered with towels and being rolled out the door.

"I'm gonna keep watch," says Herman. "When they pull out, I'll wait a few seconds and follow 'em to the bridge. If anybody looks like they're tailing the van, I'll know it."

"Do it," I tell him.

TWENTY-THREE

Carrying the heavy pistol strapped to the hip pouch on my side, I load Herman's luggage and mine into the trunk of my car. It's parked in the garage behind the house. Then I head back inside through the door to the kitchen. I go upstairs and check all the windows to make sure they're closed and locked. Downstairs I do the same.

Herman has been gone about ten minutes. I'm beginning to wonder what's keeping him.

The van carrying Harry and Sarah will take them only a few miles, across the Coronado Bridge to a private parking structure in San Diego used by repo agents to store recovered vehicles.

This morning before dawn a driver in a carrier tow truck hauled Harry's car from the parking lot behind his apartment to this same repo facility. Harry's luggage, along with the two firearms, a .45 auto and the shotgun he purchased, are in the trunk of his car.

I look at my watch. In less than an hour, if all goes well, Harry and Sarah will be on the road, headed east, across the country to my deceased wife's sister. Sarah's aunt Susan lives on a small farm with her husband outside Groveport, Ohio, not far from Columbus. They are retired. When I told them what was happening, they insisted that I send Sarah out of harm's way immediately. It's a good fit. Fred, Susan's husband, is a retired highway patrol officer. In his spare time he breeds and raises Dobermans for guard duty, and he is armed to the teeth. He knows every law enforcement type in the county. Sending her to the farm is like boarding her at a fortress.

It was the best place I could think of. And for the moment, it's certainly safer than my own house in Coronado. By now Liquida has marked every aspect of that like a dog peeing on a bush. I have wondered more than once whether he's been inside casing the place when we were gone, and if so, how many times. Even with the sophisticated alarm, I don't trust it.

Sarah was right about one thing. There is no assurance that the FBI or anyone else is breaking their hump to find Liquida. In the meantime, we know that he is stalking us. This is no longer surmise. We can't move on with our lives unless we can put an end to it. And for the moment we have only one lead. It's where Herman and I are headed, to meet with Joselyn Cole.

The key is the man she identified as Thorn. If Joselyn is correct, and I don't think she is one to make mistakes, Jimmie Snyder is linked to Thorn by the photographs that Snyder's father had. From all accounts, according to the FBI, and assuming the thumbprint on my business card means anything, Liquida killed Jimmie. Why, we don't know. But based on the information Joselyn gave us as to Thorn's background, it's not a far reach to assume that Thorn and Liquida know each other, and that

Jimmie's murder may have been contracted by Thorn for a reason.

Liquida is a shadow, a wisp of smoke. But Thorn has a face, and according to Joselyn, some record of information, whether a rap sheet or an investigative file with the FBI. If so, it's possible that our only way to Liquida is through Thorn.

A second later I hear a rap on the front door. I walk lightly down the hall until I see Herman's large hand near the glass on the sidelight. I check to make sure he's alone, then I open the door.

"I followed the van to the bridge." Herman is a bit breathless as he comes in and I close the door behind him. "From what I could see, they were in the clear."

I check my watch. "I'll give them twenty minutes and then I'm gonna call Harry or Sarah, and make sure they got there okay. What I'm afraid of is if he knows they're on the run he may try to make his move now."

"I don't think so," says Herman. "My two guys in the van are armed and they know what they're doing. Once he and Sarah get on the road, Harry's got the shotgun. If you want, I can have one of my guys go with them, just for the first night or so."

"No. I'm just worried that maybe we missed something," I tell him.

"No. I think we got it covered," says Herman.

"The luggage is in the car."

"Good," he says. "Then we better make tracks." He starts to head down the hall.

"Did you see anybody watching the house?" I ask.

"No. And I went around the block on my way back. A few cars parked at the side of the road, but I slowed way down and didn't see anybody inside any of 'em."

He stops just inside the kitchen door, turns, and looks at me. "You sure you got everything you need?" he says. "'Cause once we leave we don't want to have to come back."

"I think so. I got the laptop for communications, cell phone, cords and wires for everything, credit cards and cash. I took nine thousand out of the bank. You think that's enough?"

"I'm hoping we don't have to go out of the country. Can't take more than ten thousand if we do," he says.

"That's what I thought."

"What about your passport?" he says.

"Damn it. Knew I forgot something. It's up in the safe."

"What about Sarah's? Did she take it?" I'm already headed down the hall toward the stairs.

"No, it's there too. I'm sure," I tell him.

"Get 'em both. That way we can send it to her if she needs it."

I'm wondering what else I may have forgotten.

Five minutes later we're in the car backing down the driveway. The house is locked and the alarm is set. I punch the button and the garage door starts to slide down.

"I packed a box of extra ammo if we need it," I tell him.

"Coulda saved the weight. We blow through more than half a clip, we'll know we're in real trouble," he says. "Where are you supposed to meet her?"

"L.A. A hotel out near the airport. Joselyn's flying in tomorrow afternoon."

"Joselyn, is it?" Herman looks over at me and smiles. "I assume she has other business out here?"

"Not that I know of."

"You must have made an impression," he says.

"Business," I tell him. "She has information I want. I have information she wants. Nothing more."

"You don't have to convince me." Herman is still smiling. "I met the lady, remember? You had me lock her out of my office. Nice looking as I recall."

I ignore him.

"I hope this meeting isn't too close to the airport." He fills the void as I shift into drive and head down the street.

"What's wrong with the airport?"

"We'll have to shed the firearms the minute we get near a plane. And while I'm not personally too fussy, the permits to carry are only good in California."

"So that means we use the car as long as we can," I say.

"That's good, 'cause any big hops, and we're gonna be traveling naked," he says.

* * *

Liquida smiled to himself as he watched the car cruise by the house, the lawyer at the wheel. He was standing in the empty living room looking through the blinds with binoculars in his hand. It was the same house, the one that was for sale when he'd scoped out the two girls a few days earlier.

He was flattered by all of the sleight of hand, the trouble Madriani and his friends had gone to. He wondered if the guys from the van actually cleaned any of the carpets.

They could have saved themselves the trouble. Liquida knew they were on the move the minute he got out of bed that morning and checked his computer. The only reason he came by today was because he was curious.

Did they really think he had nothing better to do than sit there and watch them twenty-four/seven? Liquida was a busy man. There was always somebody new to be killed. He had to work for a living, unlike some people who could stay home and hide in their houses.

Killing the blonde had put a bolt of lightning up their collective asses. They'd turned the lawyer's house into a bunker. And now they were all packing guns. This was like trying to run with a load of lead in their pockets. They couldn't fly, not commercial, not with all the metal. The guns would tend to keep them grounded and offered little protection as far as Liquida was concerned. He liked to work in close with something sharp.

Liquida knew something was up the minute the other lawyer's car moved in the middle of the night—3:42 in the morning to be precise. It went from the parking lot behind the lawyer's apartment to a location in downtown San Diego.

This was strange because for two days running, the car's owner had been shacked up in Madriani's house, barricaded with the rest of them.

Since Madriani and the investigator were in the car that just went by, Liquida figured that the girl and the other partner must have been in the van. He knew the house was empty. He'd watched Madriani going to all of the windows, locking everything up. It didn't take a law degree to figure out where the van was headed. Liquida could take care of business, watching his computer, until the other lawyer's car, the one in San Diego, started to move again. There was nowhere they could hide that he couldn't find them. If they crawled under a rock, Liquida and his stiletto would be there waiting for them.

TWENTY-FOUR

The phone rang in his study and Bart Snyder picked it up. "Hello."

"Mr. Snyder?"

"Speaking."

"Volney Dimmick here. Got your message. Sorry I couldn't get back to you sooner. I've been meaning to dictate a report and get it off to you, but I've been so damn busy . . ."

"Don't worry about the report. Tell me what you found out." Snyder was no rube. The fact that Joe Wallace, the young FBI agent, had refused to share information wasn't going to slow him down.

Dimmick was a private investigator in a Washington, D.C., agency known as the Brownstone Group. Brownstone had a reputation for cherry-picking many of their employees from key government agencies, including the FBI, CIA, and Defense Department. They were well connected. Besides investigations they did consulting and had a number of high-profile clients, including some major corporations. Snyder knew that if you couldn't get information one way, you could always get it another.

"We're still working on it but we have some information," said Dimmick. "First off, the police are now operating on the theory of foul play, that your son's death was not an accidental overdose."

"I knew it," said Snyder. "What did they find?"

"This is confidential," said Dimmick.

"I understand."

"If word leaks, the police will know where it came from and it's going to be very difficult to get further details."

"Yeah, I know. What did they find out?"

"The point of injection was on the back of the hand," said Dimmick, "which is very unusual, especially for somebody who is inexperienced in shooting up. The veins can be harder to find. So you have to ask yourself why he would pick that location instead of the inside of the forearm."

"That's it?" said Snyder.

"No," said Dimmick. "It was the fact that the injection was in the back of the left hand that caught their attention."

"Jimmie was left-handed," said Snyder.

"Correct," said Dimmick. "He'd need his left hand to operate the syringe. If he was going to shoot up, he'd do it in the back of the right hand."

"That's why the police asked me whether Jimmie was right- or left-handed," said Snyder.

"Evidently. And there's more. Forensics found loose hair and fibers on the body. The fibers didn't match anything your son was wearing that day, and the way they laid on the surface of his clothing indicated that they were transferred after he was on the bed. Long and short of it is somebody else was in the room when your son died, and no doubt was handling the syringe."

"Good work," said Snyder. "Did you get any information on the Mexican?"

"Nothing solid. No mug shots, no rap sheet, but according to our sources at DEA, drug enforcement, he does exist. Up until about a year ago he was one of the Tijuana cartels' major badass soldiers. Word is he would kill anybody for a fee and was highly efficient at what he did. Of course, if he was involved in your son's murder, he stepped in it."

"How could he know Jimmie was left-handed?" said Snyder.

"Good point."

"You said up until a year ago he worked for the cartel. Who's he working for now?"

"According to the information he's always been freelance, but the cartel was his principal client. According to DEA he's branched out. He was involved last year, you probably read about it, in that attack outside the North Island Naval Air Station near San Diego."

"I'll be damned," said Snyder.

"What is it?"

"Never mind." Suddenly the pieces started to snap together, the Internet research he'd done on Madriani. His name had popped up in connection with the same event. And according to Madriani,

Liquida was after him. "Go on," said Snyder.

"It's not exactly clear what Liquida's involvement was in the San Diego thing, but word is he's now hiring out to multinational terror groups. I don't know if you remember, back in the seventies, Carlos the Jackal. It's like that except without the ideology. Apparently, according to our sources, the only thing Liquida believes in is money."

"Do they have any idea where he is?"

"No. A man like that doesn't leave forwarding addresses. I may be stepping out of line," said Dimmick, "but I'm not sure exactly why you're doing a parallel investigation with the police. Although I understand that families sometimes just want to stay on top of things. You're paying us, so it's none of my business. But if you want some advice . . ."

"What's that?"

"If this guy is involved, this Liquida, you do not, repeat, do not want to be looking for him yourself. Leave it to the police."

"Do you know if they're looking for him in connection with Jimmie's death?" said Snyder.

"We ran the name by them, but our sources didn't know," said Dimmick.

"There you go," said Snyder. "What about the other name, Thorn?"

"You were right about that one. The FBI does have an open file on him. We should be able to get some photos, wanted posters, in a day or so. We went to the Internet, but the online Justice Department photos don't go back that far. I have to say the FBI was not terribly helpful," said Dimmick. "But we did find information elsewhere. One of the intelligence agencies has a good-size file on this guy Thorn. And the fact that it's open would indicate to us that they still see him as active."

"Can we get a copy of the file?"

"No chance," said Dimmick. "They won't even let us look at it. But they did give us a few tidbits. They confirmed everything you told me. In fact, they wanted to know where I got the information."

"Did you tell them?"

"Of course not. Thorn, under the name Dean Belden, was subpoenaed to appear before a federal grand jury in Seattle about ten years ago. But he never showed. He was reported killed in a plane accident shortly afterward, but the accident, according to the authorities, was staged. Thorn was apparently involved in a terrorist plot in D.C., though the details were sketchy and the agency we talked to would not provide clarification. A few months later, U.S. authorities tracked Thorn to Africa, Somalia, where he was in hiding. After that, nothing."

"Any associates, contacts, people he knew?" said Snyder.

"No."

"So all they would tell us was what we already knew," said Snyder.

"A few other items," said Dimmick. "Thorn, aka Belden and a score of other aliases, is believed to be Australian. He specializes in weapons technology and transport, mostly aviation. He's done a lot of business with the boneyards over the years."

"What's that?" said Snyder.

"Places out in the desert," said Dimmick. "It's where old planes, commercial jets, go to die. According to the intelligence file, Thorn would buy one under a fresh alias each time. Then he and the plane would disappear overseas somewhere. Scary thing is nobody knows what he did with them, whether he sold them, and if so, to whom."

"After 9/11 you would think somebody would be watching this," said Snyder.

"You would think," said Dimmick. "Still, what do you do if there's a buyer, a company with cash, and a seller who has a used plane sitting on the ground? Sooner or later he has two choices, sell it or scrap it. From what I understand, the boneyards are overflowing with grounded planes right now, airline travel being in the pits. According to the information in the intelligence reports, Thorn was partial to four of the boneyards, three of them considered major aviation parking lots and one other smaller one. They think he may have done repeat business at these over the years. One of them is in California, at Victorville; two others are in Arizona, near Tucson; and the fourth is in New Mexico."

Dimmick gave Snyder the details regarding names and specific addresses for these facilities and Snyder took notes.

"Apart from that, intelligence says he's former military, but they wouldn't tell us

which country. First hired out as a mercenary to small Third World countries about
twenty years ago. Somewhere along the
way he turned to the dark side and started
taking pay from subnational terror groups."

"It sounds as if he and Liquida are on
the same career arc," said Snyder.

"Kinda does, doesn't it? You want me to
write it up, put it in a report?" asked Dimmick.

"No, it's not necessary. But I would like
you to do one other thing. Is there any way
we can find out whether Thorn might have
shown up out at any of the boneyards recently, say within the last year or so?" It
was a long shot, but the fact that Thorn
was bumping around in Washington and
showed up in pictures with Jimmie meant
that he was back in the world and up to
something. There was a chance that somebody at one of the boneyards might recognize him, and if so, it could provide a lead
as to what he was up to, or better yet, where
he was.

"It will take shoe leather and money,"
said Dimmick. "It could get expensive. We'd
have to take the photographs you gave us
and the pictures from the FBI's wanted

posters, when we get them, and send somebody to each of these places to ask questions. See if anyone recognizes him."

"Don't worry about the expense," said Snyder. "Do it."

"You got it," said Dimmick.

"Thanks. Call me when you have more," said Snyder. Then he hung up.

Snyder swiveled around in his chair to face the computer. He opened his e-mail, hit Compose, and started to type in the name Joselyn Cole. Before he got to the *l* in her first name, the computer produced her e-mail address. He typed "Liquida and Thorn" in the subject box, and began to unload all the information the investigator had just given him. He laid heavy emphasis on Thorn and his presumed activities at the boneyards, underlining the name of each place and their locations.

Snyder left out the fact that he had hired an investigator and told her instead that the information had been obtained from undisclosed but highly reliable sources. This made it sound more important, the inference being that he had more than one. He told her that these sources had credible information that Liquida was involved in the attack on the naval base near San Diego a year earlier. Then Snyder mentioned that he had seen Internet news items in which Madriani's name appeared in connection with this same event, and asked whether she knew anything about this. He wondered if this would surprise her, or if she already knew. Snyder wanted to believe that he could trust her. He desperately needed an ally, and Cole had history on Thorn.

She was also a mover and shaker with friends in high places and access to the press. For the last several days file footage of Cole coming down the steps of the Capitol and reports of her testimony before Congress had been on the airwaves. She had ignited a firestorm of debate. Snyder was impressed. He studied how she'd done it.

Joselyn had emphasized the danger of precision weapons by telling the panel that these were the dream weapons of future assassins. As far as the cold logic of the weapon was concerned, the only difference between a carload of terrorists and a room filled with elected officials was the finger on the trigger and the selection of targets. The suggestion that in time this might change was all it took. Cole pushed their button and suddenly the weapon was a threat to them.

It was an obvious point, but it wasn't lost on Snyder. All politics is local, and nothing is more local to most politicians than saving their own asses. If Cole could do it in the halls of Congress, why couldn't he do the same thing outside, on the streets of Washington? Hold a news conference and go public.

He had already sent letters to the Metropolitan Police in Washington about Liquida and Thorn. He'd received nothing in reply. Follow-up phone calls netted the usual response. They couldn't discuss the investigation, talk about persons of interest, or identify suspects.

The fact that Dimmick, with his inside sources of information, was unable to confirm whether the police were actively looking for Thorn or Liquida convinced Snyder that he was getting nowhere.

Dimmick had given him plenty of information, especially on Thorn. Snyder had the photographs from the FBI showing Thorn with his son. He could blow them up into posters. That would play well on television. The fact that he could now identify Thorn by name and provide details about his background, the fact that he was a merchant of death, that he bought airplanes and was linked to terrorists and wanted by the FBI. Snyder started to smile at the thought. It could be a hot story if it was handled the right way, the way Joselyn Cole had done it in front of the committee.

He could toss out Liquida's name, the fact that he was a former hit man for the drug cartel and was now believed to be associated with terrorists, and that his fingerprint was found at the scene of Jimmie's murder. He wondered about Madriani and what he might say. It was Madriani who'd told him about Liquida and his thumbprint on Madriani's business card. Snyder could skate around it at the press conference. Just tell them there was a fingerprint. No need to tell them where it was found. Let the police deal with it.

His son was murdered because, as Madriani or his partner had said, Jimmie was in the wrong place at the wrong time. He was a victim. Now, from what Snyder could see, the police were looking for his

killer in all the wrong places. Either that or
they weren't looking at all. Crime was like
everything else. Cases went cold because
cops got lazy. He wasn't going to allow
that to happen to Jimmie's case. To Snyder, the investigation of his son's murder
was like a living, breathing soul. It was all
he had left. It galled him that there was no
death penalty in the District of Columbia, a
place where violent crime was the local
sport. If the killer was arrested before Snyder could get his hands on him, Snyder
would move on to the trial and live for that.
And if the killer was convicted, he would
live for the trial's penalty phase. And if you
cornered him and asked him what he would
do once the killer was marched off to prison
and locked away, Bart Snyder couldn't tell
you, because he didn't know. To him the
concept of closure was a lie.

But for now he would be satisfied to
have the media asking questions, demanding to know why the cops weren't develop-
ing the information he had given them on
Thorn and Liquida. He would blow the lid
off the investigation, smoke out the people
in charge, and force them to answer his
questions. He was tired of standing on the

outside looking in, calling and getting no answers. It was his son who was dead. He had a right to know what was happening. And he wasn't going to sit around and wait to find out.

TWENTY-FIVE

I'm getting a little hungry. Would you mind if we stop?" Harry looked over to discover that Sarah had dozed off in the passenger seat next to him.

"What? What did you say?" She blinked, rubbed her eyes, and stretched her arms. "You want to stop?" She yawned. "Sure. Where are we, do you know?"

"Somewhere west of Gallup. I'm not sure how many miles. We crossed the Arizona–New Mexico line a ways back," said Harry. "Just passed a sign. There's a restaurant and truck stop just up ahead."

"How far to the next town?" she asked.

"What, you don't like truck stops?"

"If you want to stop, it's fine with me," said Sarah.

"We're going to need gas anyway. How are you doing?" Harry looked over at her and smiled.

"I'm fine. Rather be home."

"Wouldn't we all," said Harry.

"After we gas up and eat, I'll drive if you want. You can rest up."

"Sounds good."

"You must be tired," she said.

"Actually, I am a little." Harry had been up half the night, keeping one eye out the window of the motel room toward the car. He had parked it almost a block away, under a streetlight in front of another motel across the road. He had told Sarah it was too dark in front of the motel where they were staying and they had a lot of stuff in the car.

She called him Uncle Harry, told him he was weird, and asked him if anybody had ever told him that before.

"No. Just you. Oh, and maybe a half dozen judges in town."

Harry had known Sarah since she was three. Until she was six, Sarah thought he was her uncle. When she was finally told they were not related, it was like finding out that the tooth fairy was a fraud. Harry hung around the house more than most of her relatives. He was often there for dinner. And when her mom, Nikki, died, it was Harry who sat with Sarah for long hours and played games with her, cards and anything that came in a box out of her closet. While Paul arranged the funeral, Harry tried to keep Sarah's mind from grasping the permanence of death.

The images of him in that effort were forever engraved on her memory. She could still see his hulking form scrunched up sitting on a ridiculous little chair at her play table, looking like the giant who'd lost his beanstalk. He would move the Parcheesi pieces around the board with his thick fingers and he would cheat just to keep her mind on the game whenever she asked an uncomfortable question, like what they were doing to her mom at that place where they'd taken her, or where Dad was going with one of Mom's pretty dresses on a hanger.

There were times when Sarah still called him Uncle Harry, but usually now it was only to get his goat, to remind him of how old he was getting. But Harry didn't care. Harry was timeless, like a comfortable old pair of jeans. The fraying and the holes only added character. He would be there forever, at least in her memory.

"Explain something to me," she said.

"If I can."

"How did we get in this mess?"

"You mean Liquida?"

"No, I mean the stuff with terrorism. The attack on the base in Coronado, 9/11 and the World Trade Center. All the hostility from the Islamic world. How did it happen?"

"Why don't you just cut to the chase and ask me what happened before the big bang?" said Harry.

"No, really," she said. "I was just a little kid when most of it happened. Now we're caught up in it. Dad, you, me, Herman. I'd like to have a better understanding."

"Fair enough. Where should I start?"

"The Middle East. I didn't take any world history," said Sarah.

"Oil and money, what can I tell you? From the history I've read, it began before the First World War with the Western powers when their warships went from coal to oil. When the war ended, the winners carved up the Middle East and installed friendly leaders to get oil. The national boundaries didn't make much sense. They didn't take into account many of the ethnic groups, clans that had been warring with each other for centuries. Some of the poorer countries got none of the oil but had most of the population. Add to that the creation of Israel in the late forties, the loss of Palestinian lands, and you get a region that's a boiling cauldron. We shared in the division of spoils from the oil. Saudi Arabia and the shah of Iran fell into our sphere."

"Iran?" said Sarah.

"Yeah. Strange as it seems now, we were thick as thieves with the shah before he fell. It started in the fifties when a CIA-inspired coup brought him to power, but got real ugly in the late seventies. Yeah, I'd say that's when the real trouble started. The origins of jihad and the terrorist movement.

"Then once in a while you get a leader who decides to do what he thinks is right, by that I mean morally correct. Jimmy Carter was one such soul. He had his share of failings, but most agree that his heart was in the right place. Unfortunately, in the twisted world of foreign affairs that's probably a disability. Carter's big thing was human rights.

"But you see, it's not that easy. After a couple of thousand years using avarice, malice, greed, and tyranny as the steady diet of the body politic, a sudden dose of human rights can make the patient upchuck. The shah had all the jails in Iran bulging, some of them with political prisoners who wanted to replace him. Every once in a while he'd stick 'em with cattle prods and do other nasty stuff. Needless to say, this didn't go over big with Carter.

"He turned his back on the shah. The message to the world was that unless the shah cleaned up his act, we wouldn't support him. It was a new day. Human rights were suddenly in vogue. But the regime was already sitting on a powder keg.

"The shah saw the fuse being lit and left town. The army threw down its guns, students overran the palace and the American embassy, and suddenly the Islamic revolution was in full swing.

"You would think the students in the

streets would be grateful to Carter for his stand on human rights. But they weren't. Everyone in the U.S. embassy became a hostage. Carter became a victim of the law of unintended consequences.

"After that it was like a house of cards. It led to the Iran-Iraq War. We backed our good pal Saddam Hussein, the tyrant in charge of Iraq. A few million people got killed. Saddam lost a lot of face when we got tired and the war ended up in a draw. In Middle Eastern politics, loss of face is a terminal condition. Generals seeing their dictator walking around with half a face figure they could do a better job and they start measuring the other half to see where a bullet might look good.

"A few years after this, Al Qaeda declared war on us, but given everything that was going on, we didn't notice. They set off a bomb in the World Trade Center. We treated it as a criminal matter, made a few arrests, and shook it off. A few years later they blew up two U.S. embassies in East Africa. We lobbed a few missiles at Al Qaeda training bases and then went about our business. They attacked a U.S. warship in port in the Middle East, killed a bunch of sailors, and we started another round of investigations. Then came 9/11.

"We went after Al Qaeda in Afghanistan, ousted their allies, the Taliban, only to have them come back later.

"Which leaves us with Iran, their quest for nukes, and their continuing threats to use them on Israel the moment they get them. And of course Al Qaeda, who would like to borrow a couple of these for use in gift baskets to New York and Washington."

"So what are we doing to stop them from getting the bomb?"

"Oh, the State Department's on top of it. They're talking to the Iranians through third parties. Trying to convince the international pariah that they wouldn't want to be viewed as an international pariah. Threatening to isolate them with economic sanctions. And trying to make sure that if Israel incinerates them, they do it on a day when the rest of the world is upwind."

"You are a cynic." Sarah laughed.

"I know. What can I say? I founded the party and our numbers just keep growing. We have our government to thank for this."

"Whatever happened to Jimmy Carter?"

"He lost to Ronald Reagan in the next election. Reagan wrinkled his brow, took one look at Iran on his way to take the oath of office, and the Iranians released all the hostages that day."

"Reagan was that strong?"

"He had a big advantage. He was standing tall, on top of the heap of mistakes made by Carter. It's always easier when someone else has cleared the way through the minefield. Carter tried to negotiate the release of the hostages. The Iranians used the negotiations to humiliate him. It failed. He tried a rescue mission. A U.S. plane and a helicopter collided in the dark in the desert, and that failed. The Iranians knew that the American public had reached the end of its tether. Americans weren't just angry, they were mad as hell. It was the reason they elected Reagan. He had a mandate to kick the crap out of Iran, and the Iranians knew it. And he wasn't coming into office on a platform of human rights singing 'Kumbayah.' It's a noble concept, but worn on a presidential sleeve and advertised to the world as the guiding principle, it tells the devil more than you want him to know. The Iranians figured they'd milked the hostage crisis for all they could get. So why put Reagan to all the trouble of fueling up the B-52s?"

Harry could see the sign and the off-ramp coming at them fast, up ahead. He eased to the right and took the ramp up the incline. At the top he hung a right, went a little ways, and pulled into the truck stop. There were fuel pumps off to the left under a large corrugated metal roof. To the right was a hexagonal building with signs out in front, what looked like a shop and a restaurant.

"Tell you what, that looks like the restaurant, and maybe a small shop next to it," said Harry. "I'm gonna drop you off right in front and go get gas so that we're ready to go when we're done. I'll be over at the pumps. Why don't you check out the menu, and here, get me a bottle of water." Harry reached into his pocket for some cash.

"Don't be silly. I've got money. You're the one who's hungry. Why don't I get the gas, and you can go in and check the menu and get some water?"

"No," said Harry. "Listen. I want you to go in and look at the menu. See what the place looks like. If you don't see anything you like, we'll go on to the next town."

"Whatever."

He drove over in front of the building. Sarah grabbed her purse and got out. She closed the door and Harry drove away slowly, heading in the direction of the fuel pumps about a hundred yards away.

Harry watched Sarah in the rearview mirror as she went inside the restaurant and closed the door. He wasn't comfortable leaving her alone, even for a minute. But he had no choice. He glanced down at the car's fuel gauge. He still had a quarter of a tank, plenty of gas to get to the next town.

Harry had been nervous as a cat since the previous evening when he'd failed to find a good truck stop to take care of business. It was why he'd parked the car so far from the motel the night before. If Sarah had known, she would have been in his face. It violated her rule of no more secrets.

Harry counted seven large trucks, sixteen-wheelers, parked in the back along a gravel strip just beyond the pumps. Off to the right there were four more big rigs.

These were over behind the back of the restaurant.

Harry took one look and turned right. He figured there was a better chance that the drivers of these four trucks would be down out of their cabs, probably inside the restaurant having lunch. The last thing he needed was an ugly confrontation with an angry truck driver.

Three of the trucks were long-haul jobs with sleepers behind the cabs. One of them was hauling an empty flat-bed trailer. He didn't like the rigs with the sleepers. Harry couldn't be sure that somebody wasn't up inside taking a nap. Instead he picked the red Peterbilt. The load on the back was covered by a tarp. It was perfect, and unless the driver was stretched out low across the seat, sleeping, the truck's cab was empty.

Harry drove all the way around the back of the semitrailer, pulled up behind it, and turned off his engine. He stepped out of the car and stood behind the open door for a second, then looked around to make sure nobody was watching. He reached down into the wheel well of the car and pulled the lever. He heard the latch pop.

Harry quickly closed the driver's-side door, went to the front of the car, and lifted the hood. He didn't have to waste much time looking. Herman had done a good job. For Harry, driving with it for two days, knowing it was there, was like driving with a bomb under the hood.

Herman had located the GPS tracking devices a week earlier, about the time Jenny was murdered. He'd discovered them while doing an electronic sweep of the office and Paul's house. The sweeps had become routine after they'd discovered a year earlier that the law office had been bugged during the period just before the attack at Coronado. Herman found nothing in the office or the house. But he got a weak signal from the front of Paul's car, in the driveway, where he found the GPS device affixed to a magnet under the front bumper.

At that point he checked all the cars. He found similar tracking devices on Sarah's VW bug, his own car, and Harry's. The vehicles belonging to the rest of the office staff were clean. It was the reason they were confident that if they got the staff out of the office now, they would be in the clear. Liquida hadn't targeted any of them because he figured there was no need. He could easily keep tabs on the two lawyers, Sarah, and Herman.

The tracker was smaller than the palm of Harry's hand. It had a tiny antenna about the size of a toothpick and was shaped like a twig that swiveled out to pick up the satellite signal. For long-term power it was connected to the car's battery by a wire from underneath up into the engine compartment.

The day before they left, Herman purchased two small batteries and went to work on Harry's and Paul's cars, the two they were going to use.

If he pulled the trackers and tossed them, Liquida would know it. So he disconnected the wire from the car batteries and reattached it to the new ones. The small battery would provide power for about five days. In Harry's car the extra battery was held in place by bailing wire in an open area along the side of the engine compartment.

Harry used his fingers to unwind the wire. In a few seconds the battery came loose. He reached underneath and pulled the tracker off the bumper, and then fished it up from the inside using the power wire connected to the battery.

The normal GPS most people use plots the position of a vehicle on a map and shows it to the driver on a software-provided map displayed on a small screen located in the receiver. You key in your destination and the GPS either talks to you and tells you when to turn or shows you waypoints on the map.

But not the little tracker Harry had in his hand. It gathered positioning data and sent it to a remote receiver where it could be plotted in any number of different forms, including map references. You could purchase this service from several different vendors. It was used by employers to make sure drivers weren't off on some private frolic when using a company vehicle. It could locate a stolen car or track a load of freight across the country, making it easier to project delivery schedules. In Harry's case it would allow Liquida to track them right to the farm in Ohio, where he could stalk them at his leisure.

Harry glanced around to make sure nobody was watching. He walked over to the back of the semitrailer, lifted the tarp, and slid the battery underneath. Quickly he ran a loop with the bailing wire around the battery connecting it to the load under the tarp so the battery wouldn't slide around. Then he dropped the tiny tracker into one of the steel postholes along the rear of the truck bed. He heard the metallic click as the magnet attached. Harry used his fingers to push the thin power wire from the battery into the crack between two of the scarred wooden boards on the bed of the truck. Then he checked the antenna. Unless the driver was neurotic, there was now a tiny twig that no one should notice just sticking up out of the posthole.

Less than two minutes later, Harry was in the restaurant. Sarah was waiting for him, seated at a booth. He walked over. "Did you already order?"

"No. Thought I'd wait for you. Did you get the gas?"

"No. They want an arm and a leg," said Harry. "Listen, why don't we go on to the next town? We can fill up there and get something to eat. The gas will probably be less."

"What, you think you're going to save

three cents a gallon? Besides, the waitress already brought me water," said Sarah.

"Good." Harry picked up the glass and downed the whole thing in a single gulp, then wiped his mouth with the back of his sleeve. "Now I don't need to buy any. Let's go."

"God, Uncle Harry, gimme a minute. Let me get my purse."

Harry was guiding her by the arm.

"Anybody ever tell you you're a penny pincher?" she said.

"Yeah, matter of fact, most of the women I've dated. Probably why I never got married."

"I can understand that," said Sarah.

For the moment all Harry wanted to do was put distance between themselves and the tarp-covered trailer in the parking lot behind the restaurant. If they were lucky, the driver was headed to Mexico. Then Liquida could follow it home.

TWENTY-SIX

I'm sorry to hear about your daughter's friend. I don't think I have to tell you that. I think you already know. You're in a great deal of trouble with this Liquida." Joselyn looks at me over the rim of her wineglass as she sips a little Chardonnay. "What exactly did you do to make him so angry?"

"I don't know."

"Oh, come on. You can tell me," she says. "It's just the three of us sitting here and I'm willing to bet that Mr. Diggs already knows."

"If I knew I would tell you. But I don't."

"Why don't you tell me the truth?" she says. "Or else . . ."

"Or else what? You're going to get your crystal ball out, smack me in the head with it, and do another mind meld?" I say.

"If you like. We can do that."

The three of us, Joselyn, Herman, and I, are seated in a dark corner of the lounge at the Brasserie in the Crowne Plaza Hotel on Century Boulevard, a stone's throw from LAX.

"Have you given any more thought to what we talked about the last time we met?" she says.

"You mean before you turned white and slid under the table?" I ask.

"Yes, before that."

"As I recall, you wanted to know whether I talked in my sleep?" I say.

"And you said you didn't know. As I recall, because there were no witnesses."

"Actually, it all depends."

"On what?" she says.

"On the other thing we talked about."

"Which was?"

"You may be clairvoyant but you have a bad memory," I say. "The question was whether you wanted me for my mind or my body."

Herman is fondling the beer bottle in front of him nervously, as if he's wandered into the middle of a conversation on birth control.

"I've had some time to think about this," I tell her.

"Have you?" She looks at me over the glass, feline oval eyes and a sultry grin. "And what did you conclude?"

"That if you wanted me for my mind, I'd probably put us both to sleep. But if it was my body you were after, I doubt if I'd talk."

"And why is that?"

"I don't think I'd get much sleep."

"Yes, but you might talk," she says. "It would depend on how I tied you to the bed."

"Interesting hypothesis."

"Perhaps we need to conduct an experiment," she says.

"I take it you have a lab upstairs," I say.

"I do."

Herman clears his throat. "You guys wanna get a room, don't let me get in the way," he says. "I'll just go out front, stand in the fountain for a while. Maybe light up a cigar so's I can ask you how it was for both of you when the experiment's over."

"Perhaps you should join us," she says.

"No, thanks," says Herman. "I draw the line at that."

"You could take notes," I tell him.

She laughs. "I think we've embarrassed him," she says. "We were joking."

"We were?" I give her a crestfallen look.

"Of course. I think so. Anyway, we have business to discuss," she says.

"You mean that wasn't it? Glad to hear it." Herman, for all of his earthiness, is a prude.

"I'm sorry about getting sick the last time," she says. "You can imagine my shock when I saw Thorn's face in that photograph."

"Now we're down to talking points," I tell her. "What else do you know about Thorn?"

"What do you mean?"

"Can you tell us anything more about him? Did he ever say anything that might have given away where he was from? Any associates of his you might have met?"

"You want information?" she says.

"If you can help us, yes," I tell her.

"And do you mind if I ask, what are you offering in return?" she says.

"My body," I tell her.

"We're back to that. No. I mean of value," she says. "Do you have anything of value to offer in return?"

"That's pretty mercenary," I tell her. "Besides, you probably don't have much on Thorn. Not that's current anyway. It's been what, ten years since you saw the man. Still, you might have something, some small item that might help us run him down."

"And why would you want to find Thorn?" she says.

"He's the key to Liquida," says Herman.

"I see. Thorn is in the picture with Jimmie Snyder. Jimmie is killed by Liquida. And you know that because his fingerprint is found on your card in Jimmie's wallet. Is that right?"

"Thumbprint," I tell her.

"Excuse me. His thumbprint. And of course the authorities know this because they have one of Liquida's matching prints from an earlier crime scene in Southern California. What was the name of that case again?" She looks at me. "You remember?

Your partner was just about to say the name when you stopped him."

"Tell you what," I say. "You tell me everything you know about Thorn. And I'll tell you what I know about Liquida and the earlier case. How's that?"

"You know what I want?" Joselyn gives me an exasperated look. "I want your testimony concerning what happened at Coronado," she says. "Both of you. All the information you have about the nuclear device and the Russian who was killed outside the base. Agree to go public with that and I will help you in any way I can with Thorn and Liquida. That's the price. Don't forget, I have some very good sources of information."

"Can't do it," I tell her.

"Why not?"

"I just can't."

"Why, because you think the FBI, your friend Zeb Thorpe, might keep Liquida off your back?"

"What do you know about Thorpe?" I say.

"I know he headed up the investigation following the attack at Coronado. That he provided protection for you, your daughter, your partner, and Mr. Diggs here for the better part of three months. But it didn't have anything to do with Liquida. All he wanted was to keep you quiet. To keep you away from the press."

Joselyn knows more than I thought.

"Then what makes you think that Thorpe's involved in any way with Liquida?"

"Give me a break," she says. "Liquida killed Afundi. That's your earlier case. The one with Liquida's matching thumbprint."

"Whoops," says Herman.

"She's right," I tell him. "She does have good sources."

"So stop lying to me," says Joselyn. "I know everything already. It's just that I'm not a percipient witness. Everything I have is secondhand, from reports and documents, and other sources," she says. "I don't have copies, but I've been allowed to look at them. Problem is it's all hearsay. But you, you both saw it, the bomb and everything that happened. More than that, you can corroborate each other."

"We saw a device," I tell her. "Neither of us is an expert. We can't verify that it was nuclear."

"What, does it have to go off before we know this? You talked to the Russian."

"He didn't speak English," I tell her.

"But his daughter did. And she told you it was nuclear. She knew it was. Her father was the guardian of that device. We know that. I've even heard him referred to as the 'Guardian of Lies.' He was the expert, right from the horse's mouth."

"Sounds like she knows everything already," says Herman. "So the only question is whether we'll talk."

I look at him. "What do you think?"

"Feds aren't giving us anything anyway," he says. "Of course, they might try and throw us in the slammer."

"Not after you go public," says Joselyn. "They wouldn't dare. It would look like the biggest cover-up in history, which is exactly what it is."

"Okay, but it depends on what you can give us in return. If the information you provide leads us to Thorn and Liquida, I'll talk. Otherwise no." I look at Herman.

"That's good by me," he says. "Let's hope your sources are better than Thorpe's. They don't seem to have squat on Liquida." He looks at Joselyn. "Of course, if what you got is ten years old and cold as a witch's tit it probably ain't gonna help us much anyway."

"Then we have an agreement?" she says.

"Agreed. But the information has to net Liquida," I tell her. "If we bag Thorn in the process, great. But Liquida's the key. If the information we develop results in his arrest and conviction . . ."

"Or his death," says Herman.

"Or his death, then we'll go public, in any forum, any way you want to do it."

"Agreed. One other thing," she says. "Some of my sources are confidential. Not all, just some. And on those I can't disclose their identity. Is that understood? I can assure you the information is golden."

I look at Herman. He nods. "Agreed," I tell her.

"Good. Then I have some information for you," says Joselyn.

"Already?" I say. "Just like that. Damn it." I look at Herman. "She probably would have given it to us anyway. Wouldn't you?" I put it to Joselyn.

"I don't know. You weren't looking terribly pathetic today. I'm not sure. But based on what I know, Thorn is very big on planes. Which I already knew. Apparently he's qualified to fly commercial aircraft, large jets. That I didn't know. According to my information, over the years he's purchased more than one plane from places called commercial boneyards. Out in the desert, here in California, Arizona, and New Mexico. I have a list of names and addresses for these."

"I assume this is from one of your confidential sources?" I ask.

"No, as a matter of fact it came from Bart Snyder. I got an e-mail from him a few days ago."

"Where did he get it?" I ask.

"I don't know. He just said he got it from unidentified sources."

"And this is your golden information?" I look at her.

"I don't know. I guess we'll have to find out."

"Maybe you could call him and find out who his sources are and whether they're reliable before we chase all over the Southwest?" I say.

"If you want, I can do that," she says.

"Why didn't he copy us on this e-mail?" I ask.

"I don't know. You want me to ask him?"

"No."

"Perhaps it's your demeanor," she says.

"What's wrong with my demeanor?"

"You tend to put people on the defensive. Like right now, you're angry because you think you might have gotten this tidbit for nothing. You need to drain some of the lawyer juices."

"Snyder is a lawyer. So are you," I tell her.

"Yes, but I've had time to develop a soft side and shed the bristles."

"That's true. You slid under the table like a slinky, in that clingy, soft sweaterdress. Certainly nobody could call that abrasive. That must be why he communicated with you. What else did he say? In the e-mail, I mean."

"Now you sound jealous," she says.

"Why would I be jealous?"

"I don't know," she says. "Did you like the dress?"

"Very nice."

"It's up in my luggage. I packed it in case I needed it again."

"You wear it like a weapon, do you?"

"Only if I need to." She's already search-ing the Web on her phone. "One of the boneyards is in Victorville, north of here. We could cover that one by car, and then book flights to Arizona and New Mexico if necessary. I have copies of the pictures of Thorn, the ones Snyder showed us. He scanned them into his computer and sent them attached to his e-mail. I printed them out."

"I've got copies in my briefcase too. I got them when he was at the office," I tell her.

"See, he didn't withhold everything from you," says Joselyn.

"We could split up, but I don't think we ought to fly," says Herman. "It'd be a long drive to Arizona and New Mexico, but we'll have to use the car." He winks at me. We have already ditched the tracking device from my car, and Herman took care of the other two, the one from his Chevy and the one from Sarah's VW. By now they are crisscrossing the country on the back of sixteen-wheelers, so Liquida must be get-ting dizzy.

"If you and I split up, we don't save that

much time. If the place in Victorville turns out to be a dead end, whoever is headed to Arizona wouldn't be that far ahead," I tell him.

"I could fly to Arizona," says Joselyn. "Besides, why would we want to drive? It could take a week or ten days to cover all that ground."

"And what if you do get lucky and run into Thorn by yourself at one of these places?" I ask.

From the look on her face, she hadn't thought about that.

Herman opens the flap of his jacket and shows her the butt of his pistol. "Bertha gets airsick," he says. "And I'd rather not leave her behind."

"I understand," she says.

TWENTY-SEVEN

Nine o'clock at night and Liquida was angry. He had a naturally short fuse, and Madriani and his buddies had taken nail clippers to it by sabotaging his eyes in the sky.

Liquida knew something was wrong when all four of the devices started moving at once. He was pretty sure the girl's Volkswagen bug was still in the garage at the house.

Then he received word from the satellite-monitoring company that clinched it. They told him that one of his GPS tracking devices was found on the trailer of a big rig

when the driver went to deliver his load in
Phoenix. The trucking company wanted to
know who had put it there and why. Liquida typed an e-mail back, telling them he
didn't know, that someone must have stolen it and was using it to play games. He
knew that if Madriani found one of them,
the others would be turning up soon.

Faster than snot on a kid with a cold,
Liquida headed for Madriani's law office.
He found the place dark and buttoned up
tight, with a sign inside the glass on the
front door saying CLOSED UNTIL FURTHER NO-
TICE.

Obviously the lawyer, or somebody helping him, had thought this thing through.
Liquida began to wonder if the FBI was
involved. Maybe killing the blonde was a
mistake. He should have killed the daughter and taken his chances on Madriani going to ground. The lawyer would have had
to hang around at least long enough to go
to his daughter's funeral. Otherwise people
would talk. Liquida could have popped
an IED in the open grave. Some Simex
and a detonator wired to a cell phone,
one-button quick dial and they could have
shoveled them all into the same hole as

soon as they picked all the pieces out of the trees.

Liquida was furious. The two lawyers, the daughter, and the investigator were gone, and now he couldn't find anybody in the office to kill.

He checked the windows and the doors; the office was wired, and probably monitored by a security service from a central location. Through one of the windows he could see motion detectors, at least two of them on the ceiling in the reception area. He could toss a potted plant through the window. Security would call the police and then whatever number they were given for the client. If it was Madriani or his partner, they would tell security to have the window boarded up and to reset the alarm. They might even hire security to be posted inside. If security called one of the employees, it wasn't likely that they would show up at the office, not if Madriani had sent them home and told them why. Even if Liquida could get into the office, he weighed the prospects of finding anything useful there and decided it would be better to case Madriani's house before trying the office. What he wanted was some clue as to where they were hiding. There had to be something.

Liquida suspected that the two lawyers didn't get rid of the tracking devices immediately. The online data from the satellite company showed continuous travel of the two cars from the point of departure at the house for Madriani and the location in San Diego for the partner. He couldn't be certain regarding the partner's vehicle, but Liquida had seen Madriani and the investigator drive away from the house. The tracking data showed him going north on I-5. The first time the vehicle stopped was a few miles south of Santa Ana. According to the tracking data, the vehicle was still traveling north on I-5, but was now somewhere near Medford, in Oregon. It was probably on the back of a truck. Liquida was guessing that they dumped the tracker at their first stop. And they could have been going north, just to throw him off. But there was a chance that if Madriani was going north, his destination was in that direction.

The other tracker was more problematic. Assuming it was still on the partner's vehicle when it left San Diego, the partner and Madriani's daughter were headed east.

They took I-8 and didn't make any stops for more than a hundred miles, until they reached El Centro. That would be a long way to go just to throw somebody off your track.

By the time Liquida reached Madriani's house, it was almost ten o'clock. He parked his car down the block in front of the same old For Sale sign. The place was beginning to feel like home. He grabbed a small black day pack from the backseat, stepped out, and closed the car door. He didn't lock it in case he had to beat a hasty retreat. Then he casually strolled across the street and down the sidewalk. The neighborhood was dark except for interior house lights and the blue haze from a couple of television sets. Liquida reached into the bag and pulled out a black ski hood and a pair of gloves. By the time he arrived in front of the house, a half block down, he had the gloves on his hands and the hood rolled up on top of his head like a hat. He looked for security cameras, the big ones that cities sometimes mount on lampposts. He didn't see any. He walked slowly up the driveway toward the backyard, no furtive moves, very calm and deliberate, as if he owned the place. At the same time he rolled the hood down over his face and head. He checked the neighbor's windows to make sure nobody was looking out, and then stopped for a moment to glance toward the front porch. He was looking for any small security cameras that might be tucked up under the porch roof, not that he could see them even if they were there. Some of the new cameras were not much bigger than an eraser on the end of a pencil. He wanted to flash his little pen-size Maglite up under the eaves for a better look, but the bright beam might draw attention.

He headed toward the back of the house and, like a cat, settled on the top step at the back door. Four days earlier Liquida had seen Madriani and the man called Diggs, the big, bald, black investigator, go out this way. The bald head and the man's mountainous size were engraved on Liquida's memory from their first encounter down in Costa Rica almost a year ago. They had never come face-to-face, but Liquida had gotten a good look at him from inside as Diggs tried to pick the lock on the front door. As far as Liquida was concerned, that was close enough. If and when he had to deal with the man, he would want to make sure that he had a considerable edge, preferably long and sharp, and a good deal of surprise.

Liquida had a set of lock picks in his bag. The problem was, if he opened the door, it would trip the alarm. He could see the small control panel on the wall in the kitchen with its flashing red light. The alarm was set. Cutting power to the house wouldn't disable it, at least not immediately. Most of the systems had battery backups and would shoot off a signal over a dedicated phone line the second he opened the door.

He didn't see any infrared motion sensors. These were usually housed in tiny plastic units up near the ceiling and sometimes showed a small flashing red light when they were on. This was good. It meant that if he could somehow get inside the house without triggering the alarm, he would be able to move around freely and presumably leave the same way he'd gotten in. Liquida decided to scope out the rest of the house.

It was bungalow style, probably built

before the war and remodeled several times since. Older bungalows, especially those in Southern California, often had a soft spot in terms of entry. Unlike the newer ranch homes that were built on concrete slabs, the old bungalows sat on cement piers with short posts holding up the floor joists. There was a dirt crawl space under the house. And because the bungalows were small, with limited storage, in many of the originals, not having a garage, contractors would often excavate a small eight-by-ten-foot hole under the house somewhere, line it with concrete walls, and advertise the house as having a cellar. You couldn't always tell because many of these small concrete cellars had no exterior exit or entrance. The only way in or out was a trapdoor, usually in a closet floor with a built-in wooden ladder going down to the cellar.

Liquida poked around the outside of the house for several minutes before he found what he was looking for. It was a small lattice panel, two and a half by three feet wide, held in place by two hook-and-eye hasps, the kind you might use to latch a gate. He popped the hooks out of the eyes and lifted the lattice panel away from the siding, then reached into his bag and found the Maglite. He flashed it into the crawl space under the house; peers and posts, and twenty feet away a rough edge of concrete. Shazam! Liquida could see a set of wooden steps disappearing below the top of the concrete wall, spanning the gap between the crawl space and the floor above.

He didn't have any coveralls. Liquida would have to crawl through the dirt under the house in his street clothes. He shimmied through the opening, crossed the span of dirt on his belly like a snake, and lowered himself over the wall and into the cellar. Holding the Maglite in his teeth, he dusted his clothes off with both hands, then quickly climbed the ladder.

He pushed on the overhead trapdoor. It rattled along the right side but wouldn't budge on the left. Liquida realized it was hinged on the left and locked on the right. He focused the Maglite into the slender crack along the right edge and saw the reflection of a yellow glint. Liquida smiled. Ten thousand dollars in home security equipment, and a two-dollar sliding brass latch.

Liquida reached into his bag and found the cordless quarter-inch minidrill and fitted

it with a long metal cutting bit. He checked
with the Maglite to line it up so that the tip of
the drill bit was centered in the crack directly under the sliding latch on the lock.
Holding the light in his teeth, he pulled the
trigger on the drill and pushed the bit through
the wood and into the soft brass of the lock.
He reversed the drill, pulled the bit out, re-
positioned it, and drilled again. On the third
attempt he severed the slide on the lock,
dropped the drill in his bag, and pushed up
on the trapdoor. It lifted.

Liquida climbed up and found himself in
a closet off the downstairs hallway. He
stepped out and moved cautiously from
one end of the hall to the other, checking
the ceiling in each room for motion sensors. There were none. There was a small
windowless study off the kitchen, a desk
with a computer and a monitor against one
wall, a file cabinet, and some shelves. He
could ransack the file cabinet, but it wasn't
likely Madriani would have left a trail there.
Instead he fished through the wastebas-
ket near the desk looking for any last-
minute handwritten notes or printouts that
might provide a clue. He found nothing.
He turned on the computer and checked

the browser history to see if the last few searches the lawyer or his daughter had done might reveal travel plans, hotels, or flight arrangements. There was nothing. He tried to get into the e-mail and data files and found they were locked behind a password.

Liquida turned his attention to the trash can in the kitchen under the sink. It was empty. They must have dumped it before they left. He could see the large rolling trash container outside in the yard, against the garage. He would have to check it on his way out.

He headed down the hall toward the stairs at the front of the house. Just as he got to the foot of the steps he saw several pages of newsprint scattered on the floor of the entry, what looked like pages from a throwaway advertiser. It had been pushed through the mail slot in the door and missed the box underneath. Staying away from the windows, Liquida made his way to the front door and looked in the box. There were three envelopes. He plucked them out, pieces of junk mail, one from a furniture company, another from a financial consultant looking for business, and a business

reply envelope from the postal service.
The last envelope had a cutout for the re-
cipient's name and address. It was sent to
"Sarah Madriani." Liquida recognized the
envelope format immediately. He ripped it
open. Sure enough, it was a form letter,
what the postal service calls a "Move Vali-
dation Letter." The post office was confirming that Sarah Madriani had used the
postal online services to forward her mail
to a new address. The purpose of the form
was to make sure that someone hadn't
done this without her knowledge. It was
one of the tactics used to steal mail as well
as identities. The letter didn't reveal the
daughter's new address. The postal service had learned not to do this for reasons
of privacy and security. For one thing, it
wasn't terribly healthy for abused women
on the run.

But Liquida didn't care. He no longer
needed to scrounge around upstairs. The
postal form told him everything he needed
to know. Sarah Madriani had forwarded
her mail, and Liquida could pick up right
where he'd left off.

TWENTY-EIGHT

Mid-September, the clock was running, and for once everything seemed to be coming together nicely.

Thorn had struck a deal with the property owner in Puerto Rico, slipped the man ten grand in cash and taken a six-month lease on a hundred and fifty acres of worthless scrubland including the old airfield. Happy to have the cash for the worthless ground, the man didn't ask any questions.

Thorn brought in his crew and readied the airfield. They knocked down the grass with a harvester and put up the camo netting.

While the crew was finishing up in Puerto Rico, Thorn had gone to work lining up the plane and all the equipment at the bone-yard. He found the old 727-100C online, and gathered all the documentation, including maintenance records, long distance, hav-ing the paperwork sent to a commercial mailbox in Tampa. Thorn didn't want to spend any more time than necessary deal-ing face-to-face.

The plane's airframe was old, dating to the early seventies, but the engines showed less than a thousand hours since the last overhaul. He checked the records and found that none of the engine work had been outsourced to any of the overseas re-pair stations where skill levels were some-times questionable and parts could be unreliable. The avionics were dated, but for the single flight he had in mind it didn't matter. There were no passenger seats to remove since the plane had last been used for hauling freight.

The seller was a regional bank in Texas. Thorn could tell by the tone of the e-mails coming back from the boneyard that the bank was wetting its pants trying to unload the plane and get it off their books. Passenger volume had imploded along with the economy. Airline leasing companies were holding fire sales on new planes that made the old 727 look like something out of the Wright brothers' bicycle shop. It was probably no more than a few months from being parted out and cut up for scrap.

Thorn made them squirm while he negotiated long distance on the extra equipment he needed. This included a good-size generator and a new mode C transponder unit. The boneyard agreed to throw in the transponder for free if the deal on the plane went through.

Thorn knocked the price down to rock bottom in a series of e-mails and made the final purchase subject to approval by the buyer's representative, one Jorge Michelli of Bogotá, Colombia.

When Thorn arrived at the boneyard as Jorge "George" Michelli, an expat commercial pilot out of California, the pump was already primed and ready to go. He kicked the wheels and checked the critical onboard components. He had them start up the engines and reverse the thrust for braking to make sure it would work when he got to the airfield. Then they checked the hydraulics and looked for leaks. The two items he checked carefully were the landing lights and the altimeter. He had one of the service attendants at the yard make sure the altimeter was perfectly calibrated and then checked the external pitot tubes to make certain they weren't plugged with debris. Except for two breaker switches that needed replacing, the plane was in good shape for its age.

Thorn had the title put in the name of a Colombian corporation, Gallo Air, SA, and paid for everything, the equipment, the plane, and a full load of fuel, with a certified check. He told the boneyard that the plane was destined for overseas service, a small regional freight carrier in Latin America. Nobody seemed to notice that the word "gallo" in Spanish meant rooster, and that roosters don't fly.

The yard crew loaded the extra equipment on board and in less than two hours Thorn was taxiing down the runway headed for Puerto Rico.

The flight was uneventful, but for Thorn the approach for the landing was white-knuckle time. Flying in at wave-top altitude in the dark, in the middle of the night, re-

quired either a kind of sixth sense or a
twisted death wish. He slipped in under the
radar, over the line of white water splashing
on the beach ten miles south of Ponce and
the airport at Mercedita. Thorn's crew had
put out the portable beacons so that the
perimeter of the field was outlined, at least
enough for Thorn to see it. Depth percep-
tion was tricky, as Thorn waited until almost
the very last second to turn on his landing
lights. The wheels smoked as they hit the
grass stubble over the crumbling macadam
and Thorn threw the engines into reverse.
In less than three minutes he taxied to the
end of the runway and with the help of his
crew salted the plane away under the camouflage netting. They buttoned it, and all of
them disappeared into the darkness.

Thorn watched the airfield and the plane
for four hours from a distance with field
glasses to make sure no one came by to
investigate. When they didn't, he knew he
was home free. The plane wouldn't have to
move again until the day of the operation.

The ducks were aligned. He now had
both of the fuel-air devices, Fat Man and
Little Boy, in hand. One of them had arrived
by sea in the port at San Juan two days

earlier. It was in a box labeled INDUSTRIAL TOOLS. U.S. Customs opened and inspected it only to find exactly what the label said, a large industrial compressor with an air tank almost nine feet long. Customs had one of the dogs sniff around it for drugs, then nailed the crate closed and tagged it as inspected. The crate was loaded onto a rental truck driven by one of Thorn's crew members.

Little Boy now rested quietly, still in its wooden crate under the camo netting, no more than thirty feet from the plane.

With all of the ordnance now in his possession, Thorn started thinking about cutting his overhead. He no longer needed Victor Soyev.

The Russian arms merchant had screwed up and nearly cost him the job when the plane carrying Fat Man was forced down in Thailand. Thorn wondered if Soyev might not have planned it that way so he could hold him up and make Thorn pay twice. He wouldn't put it past the Russian to cut a side deal for a kickback with his North Korean hosts. As far as Thorn was concerned, they all played in the same sandbox, where the name of the game was "screw over the buyer."

The Russian had served his purpose. Now it was time for him to serve another. Besides, there was the cost factor to consider. Thorn had paid Soyev half up front for the two devices, with the balance due on delivery. If Soyev wasn't around to collect, Thorn could put the second half of the payment in his own pocket and Thorn's client would never be the wiser.

Three days later and seventeen hundred miles to the north, Thorn was now busy in upstate New York. He was scrambling to finish work on the delivery vehicle for Fat Man.

The place where they were working was a large commercial garage rented from a boarded-up GM truck dealership just outside Albany. As far as Thorn was concerned, it was great having the U.S. economy in the dumps. Not only were commercial airliners cheap as dirt, it seemed whatever he needed was readily available, and at cut-rate prices. Now if he could only figure out some way to pad his bills and make sure the country didn't blow away and disappear before he could destroy it, everything would be just peachy.

There were only three of them, a welder from Thorn's crew, a Muslim taxi driver from Manhattan who'd quit his job two days earlier to join them, and Thorn. For muscle they were using a three-ton electrical chain hoist on rollers suspended from an overhead I beam. The welder had been working for nearly a week on a giant steel barrel that now encased Fat Man.

The barrel was slung under the chain hoist using heavy nylon tow straps and rolled along the overhead beam until it was centered over the open frame of the truck. Carefully they lowered it into place.

"Once I do this it ain't gonna turn anymore. You sure you want me to do it? You want I could make it so it could turn? Might take two, maybe three extra days," said the welder.

"Don't worry about it," said Thorn. "Time's running out. Get it done."

"Your call." The welder had already made a small fortune. The job had taken the better part of a week. Five days earlier he had removed the large metal paddles from the inside of the barrel. Using a torch the welder then cut the huge steel barrel in half.

Working alone with nothing but the hoist, the welder had lifted the rear half of the barrel away with the chain hoist and spent three hours of backbreaking labor maneuvering the bomb into the remaining front half of the barrel. Another two days was spent cutting angle iron and welding the bomb in place. He kept reminding himself to keep the hot end of the arc welder away from the area that housed Fat Man's initiating charge. Otherwise the authorities would be searching for his identity from the spray of DNA taken from air samples in the stratosphere.

Now that the two halves of the barrel were back together, Thorn wanted it welded to the frame of the truck where it wouldn't move, giving the bomb a stable platform. As the welder worked, throwing sparks of hot metal around the truck, Thorn spent his time assembling the parts for the detonator.

This was the one item he hadn't purchased. It was supplied and delivered by his employer, a last-minute change in their agreement. As Thorn examined it closely, he realized why. It was clear that they didn't want any mistakes on this.

The truck's driver, the Muslim taxi man, was handpicked by Thorn based on references from some very nasty associates he'd met while hiding out in Somalia. Whether they were pirates or jihadists, Thorn trusted the Somalis because he knew they would go to their deaths either for their wants or for their beliefs.

The driver was to be well armed, both a handgun and two fully automatic AKs with half a dozen spare clips. He was to reach his target at all costs, driving through barricades and shooting his way in if he had to. It was without question a trip to paradise. Whether there would be virgins waiting at the other end, Thorn would leave to the driver. But he began to reassess his earlier assumptions as to the national origins of the people who had hired him. It wasn't oil money that was fueling the venture. He was now certain of that. They were not part of the jihad. The detonator had been made in Germany by a well-known industrial electronics manufacturer. It had come to Thorn by way of a circuitous route that took it through a buyer, an unnecessary middleman in Yemen. The detonator carried with it, like a neon sign, a paper trail of invoices and shipping labels. At first Thorn thought this was a bold and naked claim of accountability, until he looked more closely at the detonator itself. Thorn didn't ask any questions. It was what the client wanted, and he was paying the freight.

Time was now getting tight. By morning Thorn had to be headed back south and he couldn't wait to be gone. He had a mountain of work ahead of him in Puerto Rico.

He carefully soldered the two lead wires from the mercury trembler switch to the terminals on the electronic detonator. Then he climbed the metal ladder and crawled into the opening up high on the rear of the barrel. Once inside, Thorn wired the detonator to the initiating charge on Fat Man. Then he taped the detonator to a piece of metal angle iron using three rounds of electrical tape and another round of duct tape to make sure that the detonator wouldn't be torn from the bomb by the impact of the fall, that is, if the driver reached his final target.

Thorn had to crawl on his back and

squeeze his gut under the massive bomb in order to rig the final set of wires. These were about thirty feet in length. They had to be fed through a small hole drilled in the front end of the barrel and from there through a hole in the back of the truck's cab.

Inside the cab was a small metal box, and inside the box was a toggle switch. This was a manual trigger designed to detonate the bomb if all else failed.

It took him several minutes and a lot of sweat to drag his body under the bomb once more and climb out of the slippery steel barrel. By the time Thorn had his feet on the ground again, he was huffing and puffing. He was getting too old for this.

Time for a break. He grabbed a cold beer from an ice chest in the corner and sat down for a minute to check his e-mail. He used a small Netbook with a 3G connection.

Two minutes to boot it and Thorn opened his messages. There was one from Soyev asking why his money on delivery hadn't been wired to his overseas account, a couple pieces of junk mail from the 3G provider, and a news story from Thorn's customized Google news site.

The last item caught his attention. Thorn had set it up to provide regular searches for news items that turned up any of a number of names, the recent aliases he had used as well as the name Thorn itself. If the authorities were looking for him, it was one way to stay alert. He could discontinue the use of an alias the second he had any warning.

He opened the e-mail and started reading: "Chicago Lawyer Warns of D.C. Terror Plot." The moment he saw the name Snyder it set off bells. Bart Snyder was accusing a man named Thorn of being involved in the murder of his son, James, in Washington, D.C. The old man had held a news conference. The story was brief, only six short paragraphs, but it was enough to make the hair on the back of Thorn's neck stand up. "Mr. Snyder stated that the man he identified only as Thorn, also known as Dean Belden, is believed to have extensive ties to international terrorist organizations. He claims that his son, James Snyder, may have inadvertently discovered evidence of terrorist activities, and believes that he was killed for that reason. Mr. Snyder told reporters that he is conducting his own investigation and will be releasing further information early next week.

"A spokesman for the FBI confirmed that James Snyder was the victim of an apparent homicide in Washington, D.C., earlier this summer, but declined further comment, stating that the matter was under investigation by the Metropolitan Police. A spokesperson for the police department confirmed that Bart Snyder had been attempting to assist police in the investigation of his son's murder, but that at this time police have no credible information concerning any terrorist activities in connection with the case."

Thorn's blood ran cold. How in the hell did Bart Snyder get his name? And what else did he know? This was trouble with a capital T. From the tone of the story it sounded as if the cops weren't taking Snyder seriously, unless they were playing it cool.

It was now Thursday. One thing was clear. If Snyder was planning to go public with further information early next week, Thorn didn't have much time.

TWENTY-NINE

Liquida was smiling from ear to ear as he looked at the tracking data on the laptop computer.

After crawling out from under Madriani's house and dusting himself off, Liquida went home and retrieved one of the other GPS trackers. This one was called a Lightning Spark Nano. It was highly sensitive and didn't require an external antenna. You could put it in the glove compartment of a car and track the vehicle anywhere in the world and all you needed was an Internet connection to find it. It ran on a small internal battery that gave it five days of continuous tracking.

Liquida packaged it in a small cardboard box, the kind you might use for a piece of jewelry, and included a short printed note:

Dear Sarah,

This is something I found on my travels. I wanted to send it to you because it may help us keep in touch. Put it in your purse and hang on to it. <u>And don't tell Harry because I have one coming for him as well, and I want it to be a surprise!!!</u>

Love,

Dad

He wrapped the small box in brown wrapping paper and taped and tied it with cotton twine, but not before he switched on the tracking device. He addressed it to Sarah Madriani at the home address in Coronado, using Madriani's law office as the return address. Then he hand-carried it to the post office, where he sent it express overnight delivery. Liquida knew it would take longer than that to reach its destination, probably one or two days because of the change of address. But he didn't care. The battery would still be running by the time it arrived.

He watched the tracking data for three days and when it stopped moving, Liquida knew it had arrived.

The GPS image on the computer showed not only a street map, but a low-level satellite image similar to Google Earth. As he scanned out on the computer to get a smaller scale, he could see that the farmhouse in the satellite photo was located on a rural road just outside a place called Groveport, in the state of Ohio. Express overnight mail from the postal service wasn't too bad.

* * *

The trip to the aviation boneyard in Victorville turned out to be a dead end. Nobody in the office or the shop recognized Thorn from any of the photographs we showed them. It was nearly noon by the time we got back on the highway and headed south toward Arizona.

Joselyn had tried to contact Bart Snyder to see if he had any other information on Thorn and to find out who his source was on the boneyard lead. But she couldn't get hold of him. Her calls kept ringing through to his voice mail. She left a message along with her cell number.

The trek across the desert turns out to be long, hot, and dry. To top it off, our timing wasn't good. After two days of hard driving, we reach the outskirts of Tucson on Friday evening. We take a shot and drive out to a place called Evergreen Maintenance. It is the larger of the two airplane boneyards in the Tucson area. According to their Web site, they are a major hub for leasing and sales and are used by federal agencies for some maintenance.

The office is closed, and except for overhead lights in the parking area, the place is dark. The storage area, which we can see in the distance, seems to run for miles. It is loaded with planes, too many to count, all parked neatly under overhead arc lights. An ocean of tall tail rudders with airline logos from around the world stretches toward the horizon as far as I can see. According to the online news articles, we are looking at one of the largest grounded fleets of commercial jetliners in the world.

The storage area, runway, and hangars are gated off, locked behind chain-link fencing, all topped off by taut strands of barbed wire. We have no choice but to cool our heels and wait.

* * *

Early Monday morning we head back to Evergreen. By the time we reach the parking lot in front of the office, the asphalt is already starting to warm up. The mirrored gleam of polished aluminum airframes in the bright Arizona sunlight is almost too much for the eyes. In daylight, looking at the planes in storage is like staring into a solar collector.

We make for the office and do the routine with several of the employees at the counter. We show them Thorn's photographs and I give them the spiel. I use my business card and tell them I represent a bank Thorn owed money to and that we are pursuing assets under a court order on the belief that Thorn is purchasing airplanes with bank funds, a loan that was obtained through fraud. We also tell them that he might be using a different name.

The staff in the front office takes a hard look at the photographs, all with the same result. They shake their heads. Nobody recognizes him.

We head back out to the parking lot.

We cross town and head to the second boneyard in Tucson. I'm beginning to think that maybe we're wasting our time. He may be active again, but Thorn hasn't come near any of these places.

Herman is wondering if we should even bother to push on to New Mexico if we bomb out at the two shops in Tucson. He tells Joselyn and me that we should take the car and head back to California. He'll leave his pistol in the trunk of the car and fly on to Kingman in New Mexico, check out the boneyard there, and catch a flight back to California, where we can compare notes.

"Have you heard anything back from your man Snyder?" he asks Joselyn.

"No. Not yet. I left messages on his landline, his cell phone, and sent him a short e-mail from my iPhone. And so far no reply."

"You called him when, Wednesday morning?" says Herman.

"Whenever we left L.A. . . . . Was that Wednesday?"

"Time flies when you're having fun," I tell her.

"It's been five days," says Herman.

"I know. Maybe he's busy," she says.

"Maybe he doesn't like you anymore," I tell her. "What did you do, shut him down on a date?"

"Not that it's any of your business, but no."

Joselyn has the brush out in the back-seat, stroking the locks, trying to get the knots out.

"Bad-hair day?" I ask.

"Something like that."

"Dry air, it splits the ends. Does it to me all the time," I tell her.

"If I were you, I wouldn't fret about it. In a few years you won't have any hair to worry about."

"Says who?"

"Says that little budding bald spot in the back."

"What bald spot?"

"In another year the back of your head is going to look like the moon over Miami," she says.

"You noticed that too," says Herman. "I was gonna refer him to my barber."

"Don't you give her any moral support," I tell him. "She's enough trouble on her own."

"You don't believe me, check it out with a mirror," she says. "Better yet, let me take a picture with my cell phone and I'll post it on the Internet so you can see it." She leans forward in the backseat and grazes my scalp through the hair with a long feline fingernail. Right there." She giggles. "You need to start using Rogaine or those few feeble little hairs you use to cover it up are going to die of loneliness pretty soon."

"When you're done taking pictures with that phone, why don't you call Snyder again?" says Herman. "I'd like to know if we're chasing our tails before I hop a flight to New Mexico."

"If you like." She takes out her cell phone and begins pushing buttons. I can see her in the rearview mirror, all cross-legged and sexy. She takes off her earring, shakes out her hair, holds the phone up to her ear, and listens for several seconds. "Mr. Snyder, this is Joselyn Cole again. I left a message for you last Wednesday and I haven't heard back. Mr. Madriani, his investigator, and I are on the road. We could really use some help if you could give me a call.

You've got my cell number. I'll be waiting to hear from you." She drops the phone in her purse. "Sorry, but he's still not answering."

"Maybe you should use a more sultry tone," I tell her. "Next time he asks you out, at least tell him you'll think about it. That way he'll take your phone calls."

"You're the one who keeps talking about him. Maybe you should go out with him," she says.

"He's not my type. It seems that I tend to argue with male lawyers."

"From what I've seen, you don't do too well with female lawyers either," she says.

"No? Now that all depends."

"On what?"

"On who's on top."

"Oh, jeez," says Herman, "let's not go there."

"From back here it looks like you dropped a flare in your investigator's lap," says Joselyn. "That is blushing, or do those little veins in your ears always throb like that?"

I look over. With Herman it's hard to tell. But she's right. His head's turned the other way, one hand covering part of his face. He's shaking his head and laughing.

"That'll teach me to get in the car with two horny men," she says.

"Who's horny?" I say.

"You," says Herman. "Shut up and drive before you get us in an accident."

The other Tucson storage facility is about twenty miles out into the desert. It is much smaller, nestled against some low-lying sandstone cliffs. By the time we get there, it's almost ten. I pull up in front of what looks like the office, an old wooden building that was a barn at one time. The Dutch gambrel roof is missing enough wooden shingles that it looks like a toothless hag.

The planes in storage look older and not as well maintained. The entire facility has a kind of seedy appearance, faded paint on the wooden facade of the office, scrapped-out parts lying around, and some old airplane tires piled against the fence. There is a single long runway and about twenty planes, some of them parked on an apron in front of the hangar, and others on a diagonal along the far edge of the runway. Six of these are jetliners. The rest are all prop jobs, and from the faded paint and dust, none of them looks as if it is in great shape.

"Let's get it over with so we can get some lunch," says Herman.

Joselyn and I open the doors and step out at the same time. "You want to be the lawyer for the bank this time?" I ask.

"No. I'm not good at telling lies." She looks at me with an innocent smile.

"Right. This way, Pollyanna." She follows me up the rickety wooden steps to the porch that leads to the office. The window air conditioner is rattling a few feet away, vibrating in the wall, dripping condensation, and expelling hot exhaust.

I open the door and the three of us step inside. It's a small office with two desks, a lot of paper clutter and dust.

"Looks like there's nobody home," says Herman.

There is one of those antique bells with a button on top of the desk. Herman walks over and slaps it a few times and a voice from the bowels in the back hollers, "Be there in a minute."

A few seconds later a guy I would guess is in his late forties comes through the door in the back. "What can I do for you?" Dark stringy hair, and oil ground into his fingers.

"We're looking for someone," I tell him. I

pull the photographs from my leather portfolio, the enlargement of Thorn on top, and
hand them to him. I can tell the moment
he looks at them that he recognizes Thorn.
You can smell the rubber burning behind
his eyes. He looks at me and then back at
the pictures.

"Who are you?" he asks.

"I'm a lawyer." I give him my card, and
then lead him through the story of my client the bank and Thorn's fraudulent loan,
the fact that we're chasing assets, trying
to nail anything that moves to the ground.

He stands there impassively looking at
my card and then says, "Is that so? Sorry,
but I don't think I can help you."

"Do you recognize him?" I ask.

"I see a lot of people in here," he says.
"It's hard to remember all of 'em."

"Yeah, I can see you're doing a booming
business," says Herman. "Gonna have to
take a number next time we come in. Why
don't you just make it easy on yourself?
Tell us when you saw him last. And what it
was that you sold him."

"I didn't say I did," says the guy.

"No, but your eyes don't lie as good as
your lips," says Herman.

"Is that so?" says the man.

"What's your name?" I ask.

"Why do you want to know?"

"So I can forward it to the FBI along with your place of business. You see, there's a federal warrant out for this man's arrest. And the FBI is going to want to talk to you and take a close look at your records of sale."

"I see," he says. "Let me take a look at the pictures again."

"Take your time," I tell him.

"Could be this guy was in here early last week," he says.

"That's better," says Herman.

"But he wasn't using the name Thorn. He called himself George Michelli. It looks like him. He was representing a buyer out of Latin America. He bought an old 727-100C. And he got a good price. He paid with a certified check drawn on a corporate account down in Colombia. That's all I know."

"Did he take the plane?" I ask.

"Yeah. Flew it out of here himself that day, along with some onboard equipment."

"What kind of equipment?" says Herman.

"A generator, a new-model transponder. I can't remember what else," he says.

"Where was the plane headed?" says Joselyn.

"I assume Colombia," says the man.

"Did he file a flight plan?" says Herman.

"Not with me," says the guy. "As soon as I was sure the certified check would clear, he was out of here. Now that you mention it, he seemed to be in a hurry."

"Do you have the contract of sale and the rest of the paperwork?" I ask.

"Yeah, but I'm not sure I should be showing it to you," he tells me.

"Your choice," says Herman. "You can either show it to us or to the FBI."

The guy thinks about it for a second. "All right, you can look, but I'm not making any copies until I talk to my lawyer."

"Agreed," I tell him.

He rummages through one of the filing cabinets behind his desk.

The chances of finding anything useful in the contract or the other papers is slim. No doubt Thorn used a false front, an empty corporation in Colombia, solely for the purpose of buying the plane. I doubt that's where it's headed. Thorn wouldn't leave that kind of a trail.

"Here it is." The guy turns around holding a manila folder, reading the label on the tab. "Gallo Air, SA. That's the name of the company. Bogotá, Colombia." He carries it over to the other desk, wipes off some of the dust with an old rag, and sets the file down. "You want to take notes, that's fine, but don't take anything out of it," he says. "I'm gonna have to call my lawyer."

In which case Joselyn, Herman, and I are going to move fast, before his lawyer can step in and start asking particulars about my client and the bank. The contract lists the tail number of the plane. Herman makes a note.

"How much fuel did the plane have when he left?" I ask.

"Full load," says the guy.

"What's the range of that particular plane?" I ask him.

He thinks for a moment. "Cargo plane, stripped, no seats, light load, I say maybe five thousand nautical miles."

"He could be anywhere in the Western Hemisphere," whispers Herman.

Joselyn and I page through the pile of forms in the folder, transfer of title documents, most of them NCR forms, pink copies, meaning that the top sheet on the multipage forms went somewhere else.

"Who got the original top copies?" I ask him.

"The seller. A bank in Texas," he says. "I mailed them out late last week."

I am flipping pages when Joselyn stops me. "Wait a minute. Go back."

I flip back one page.

"What's this?" She points to a handwritten note in the margin on one of the pink forms.

"Numbers. Looks like somebody made a note," I say.

"That's not the purchase price," she says.

"Is this your handwriting?" I ask the guy behind the desk.

He comes over to take a look, shakes his head. "It's not mine. Lemme see." He turns several pages. On each one of them the same numbers are there in the same location in the margin, ten digits, spaced out three, three, and four.

"It's gotta be his writing 'cause nobody else was involved," says the man. "He did receive a phone call when we were doing the signing. As I recall, he took out a slip of paper, wrote something on it, and put it back in his pocket. Conversation didn't last long."

"And he got a copy of these?"

"Yeah. Original and five copies in all. Original goes to the buyer, bottom copy to the selling title holder. We keep everything in between," he says.

"Thanks," I tell him.

Joselyn looks at me. "If he put the slip of paper on top of the original form before the copies were separated, he wouldn't notice that his note bled through onto the NCR copies underneath."

She's right.

"Could be a phone number," I say.

"Took the words right outta my mouth." Herman's looking over my shoulder.

"If so, it's a 787 area code. Where's that?" I say.

"I don't know," says Herman.

"Gimme a sec," says Joselyn. She fishes her cell phone from her purse and starts to press buttons.

"You're not going to call the number," I tell her.

"No. I'm just going to Cha Cha the area code."

"What the hell is that?" I say.

"Watch and learn, or talk to your daughter. Every kid in America knows Cha Cha," she says. Joselyn sends a text message to the number 242 242, better known as Cha Cha. She types the question "Where is area code 787?"

A few seconds later the answer comes back: "The 787 area code belongs to Puerto Rico (PR) . . ."

THIRTY

By the time he arrived home in Chicago, it was after midnight. Bart Snyder was exhausted. He had spent five days in Washington in a fruitless effort to light a fire under the cops and get them to move on Jimmie's murder investigation. The fact was that after almost two months, he was still unable to get the police to say officially that it was murder. The specter of a drug overdose still hung over Jimmie's head.

On top of everything else, Snyder held a sparsely attended news conference that made him look like a fool.

Only one of the two daily metro newspapers showed up, along with a single camera from one of the cable news affiliates. When Snyder saw the poor turnout, he started out lecturing the media for their lack of interest in an "important case." At one point he lost his temper. It was that single ten-second snippet that they ran under the label "Emotional Father" that was recycled on the cable network for two days. They never even mentioned Thorn's name on TV, only in the newspaper.

Going public with the news conference had backfired. Now the police were not only refusing to share information, they were laughing at him.

Snyder was forced to double down. He hired a public relations firm in D.C. so that his next foray in front of the cameras would go more smoothly, and hopefully garner more coverage.

By the time he dragged himself and his luggage from the car in the garage and into his kitchen, he was angry, tired, and depressed. He dropped his bags and briefcase in the middle of the kitchen floor, stepped back into the garage, and pushed the button to close the garage door.

All he wanted to do was take a shower and go to bed. Instead he hauled his weary body toward the study to check his home voice mail and see if there were any last-minute messages on the computer.

Snyder had been dodging phone calls from Joselyn Cole for four days. She was on the road somewhere with Madriani and was looking for more information. Snyder was beginning to think that he'd made a mistake by trusting her with the lead on the boneyards.

It was starting to look as if Cole and Madriani had known each other for some time, and that he, Snyder, was the odd man out. She was probably already aware of the Liquida-Madriani connection to the attack on the North Island Naval Base. Snyder didn't trust Madriani. The lawyer from Coronado had too many secrets. He suspected that Madriani knew more about Jimmie's murder than he was saying, and he wasn't about to share more information with someone he couldn't trust. It was easier to simply ignore Cole's calls than to get into an argument with her over the phone.

Within a few days Snyder would know whether the stuff on the boneyards was a dead end or not. His investigator, Dimmick, should have somebody burning up shoe leather now, checking them out.

Snyder plunked himself down into the webbed Aeron chair in front of his computer and opened his e-mail. There were several messages but nothing new. There was one from Joselyn Cole. According to the note at the bottom, it was sent from her iPhone, and implored him to call her on her cell as soon as possible.

There were four flashing voice-mail messages on his home-office line. Snyder reached over and pushed the Repeat button to play them.

The first was nothing, just a hang-up. Snyder erased it. The second was from the maid who cleaned his house, saying she couldn't make it next week but would be by early the next morning. Snyder wasn't happy but he had no choice. She would be waking him up in the morning. He erased the message. Someone at Dimmick's office called and wanted to know which address to use for billing statements, Snyder's home or his law office. Snyder remembered that he'd given Dimmick one of his firm's business cards when they'd first met. He made a note to call him back in the morning. The last message was from Joselyn Cole asking that he call her. They needed some more information. Snyder erased it.

If he was going to cut her off, it was better to do it in writing, and to keep it brief. He turned to the e-mail from her cell phone and hit the Reply button at the bottom just as the loop of hemp went over his head and flashed in front of his eyes.

Before Snyder knew what was happening, it dropped around his throat and tightened like a steel band. He reached up with both hands and tried to pry his fingers between the rope and the skin on his neck. But he couldn't. The three-eighths-inch hemp line was cutting a deep groove in the flesh around his throat, and was being pulled up high at the back of his neck.

Snyder felt something solid, a knee in his back, as he was jerked up straight in the chair, his back arched like a bow. The abrasive fibers of the hemp cut into his flesh like wire. He fought to get a breath, reached up with his hands, and tried to grab whoever was behind him. He felt a tight cotton slipover shirt but couldn't get a grasp on the fabric.

He struggled to get out of the chair. If he could stand, he could turn and perhaps twist free. Feet planted on the floor, he pushed on the arms of the chair with all of his strength. He started to rise, then suddenly the knee was again driven into his back. The sharp bone could be felt through the thin web that formed the back of the chair. Snyder was jerked down hard into the chair as it tilted backward, and his feet came off the floor.

Reflex drove his hands back to the futility of the rope around his throat. Snyder could feel the veins in his face bulge as panic flooded his brain. In one violent heave he threw his head back against his assailant's chest, cast his gaze toward the ceiling, and saw the pockmarked cheek and the dark malevolent eyes.

Snyder's sight began to dim as his heart pounded in his chest, pumping for air. He reached forward with his hands, grasped the board on the stand in front of him and felt for the positioning of the keys, and touched four quick letters.

His right hand left the keyboard and grasped the mouse. The assailant saw the gesture. He jerked the rolling chair away from the computer, but not before Snyder had clicked the button.

Liquida jerked the wooden handles he'd fashioned for the garrote with all of his strength. His gaze fixed on the flashing yellow sign on the computer's screen— MESSAGE SENT.

In a fury, Liquida pulled the chair over backward, slammed it to the floor, placed his right knee on the side of Snyder's head, and jerked the ends of the rope with all his might. He heard a snap, looked down, and saw the tongue protruding from Snyder's mouth, his lifeless eyes bulged open.

Liquida held tight for another few seconds until he was sure there was not a hint of respiration coming from the man's chest. He released his grip on the wooden handles of the garrote, stood up, and tried to catch his own breath.

With his foot he moved the lolling head back and forth one time, making sure that Snyder's neck was broken. Then he reached down and removed the garrote, slipped it into his pocket, and lifted the body, hoisting it onto his shoulder.

Still panting from the battle with his victim, Liquida carried the dead form out into the garage. He turned on the light and maneuvered around behind the back of Snyder's car toward the empty bay at the far end of the three-car garage.

Liquida had already set up a five-foot ladder and tied off a short section of the same hemp rope he'd used to fashion the garrote, looping it over one of the rafters in the garage.

Snyder, who had driven in, never saw the ladder or the rope with the noose all the way down at the other end because the overhead door light didn't illuminate that part of the garage. Liquida had made a note of this. He had been waiting for Snyder for more than three hours, napping on the bed upstairs, waiting for the noise of the garage-door opener to wake him the moment Snyder arrived home.

He carried the lifeless body, climbed up two steps, and centered Snyder's chest over the top of the ladder. Careful to make sure the body was balanced, Liquida reached up, grabbed the noose, and slipped it over Snyder's head. He positioned the knot behind the left ear, tightened it, and checked to make sure that the noose was aligned with the rope burns and abrasions left by the garrote.

When he was finally satisfied, Liquida stepped down, stood there for a moment looking, then reached out and pulled the ladder sideways. Snyder's body lurched free, swinging in the air as Liquida laid the ladder carefully on its side on the concrete so as not to make too much noise. He stood there watching until the body hung motionless, twisting only slightly on the rope as it searched for its point of ultimate rest.

Liquida checked the garage one last time to make sure he hadn't left anything behind, then went back inside. He left the light on in the garage. Not even the most despondent soul would hang himself in the dark.

He went back into the study, picked up the toppled desk chair, and with a gloved hand grabbed the computer mouse off the floor where it had fallen.

Liquida then used the mouse to maneuver the cursor on the screen to the folder that read SENT MESSAGES. He clicked and opened it and looked at the top message on the list. It was sent to someone named Joselyn Cole.

Liquida opened it. It was a reply to an earlier e-mail and it was there that Liquida saw a name he recognized. This woman, Joselyn Cole, was traveling, where she didn't say, but she was on the road with Madriani. Liquida had been headed to Ohio to kill Madriani's daughter when he was called away by his employer to clean up a loose end. It was now becoming a generational thing. The fellow who over-dosed in D.C. had a meddling father. To Liquida it all came down to the same thing, money. Business before pleasure. The law-yer's daughter would have to wait. He would have to do that one on his own time.

It would have been a nice touch to send Madriani another message, leaving the mystic thumbprint on Snyder's computer. But that wouldn't do. It would cause com-plications. And besides, the digit was be-ginning to smell. The print Liquida had left on the lawyer's business card, the same one he had left at the scene of Afundi's body dump, was not his own. Liquida wasn't that stupid. The cops didn't have his picture and they sure as hell weren't going to get his prints. The print belonged to the thumb of one of Liquida's earlier victims. Liquida had cut it off to use like the sealing stamp on a signet ring, storing it in formaldehyde when it wasn't needed. Like the Mexicutioner, the victim was not an American citizen and had no prior criminal record. So Liquida knew his prints would not show up in the FBI database.

He turned his attention to Snyder's farewell message, his abrupt reply to Joselyn Cole. It was very brief. Whatever Snyder was trying to communicate, you might say, was cut short. But then only Liquida knew this. Still, it wasn't bad. The cops might even see it as a suicide note. After all, the four-letter word "evil" is not such a strange farewell for the fevered mind of a man about to hang himself.

THIRTY-ONE

They were now in the home stretch, and like a buzz of electricity running through his veins, Thorn could feel it. He was finally back at the airfield in Puerto Rico. The clock was running. He had only days to go and a mountain of work to complete before the plane could be airborne again.

Thorn had received word that morning that the Mexican had done his job. Snyder was dead. There would be no more news conferences. Whether he knew anything or not, the old man's lips were now sealed, and Thorn was free to concentrate on the task at hand.

To help him he had two of his regular crew, along with the two others, Western-educated Saudis, both of whom were trained as pilots and who would fly the plane. They were Muslims from the Mahdi Army, recruited through contacts that Thorn had developed during his years in Somalia.

But it seemed there was always one more problem. This one was driving Thorn crazy. Ahmed, the senior pilot, came fully equipped with his own caste system. He indicated a strong resentment toward any-thing that even remotely resembled man-ual labor. And, of course, the moment this affliction was made evident, his copilot, Masud, developed the same disease.

Between prayers they would sit on their asses all day under the trees, watching Thorn and his crew busting their behinds to get the plane ready. When Thorn tried to explain to them that there was painting to be done and a ramp to finish, they turned up their noses.

The one job they agreed to work on was the pylons under the two wings, and only because these were weapons-related. This seemed to appeal to their native warlike in-stincts in the same way possessing a rifle and shooting it into the air had appealed to their ancestors.

Thorn had no choice but to put them to work on the pylons while he and his crew hauled cans of paint, masked the exterior of the plane, and went to work firing up the compressor that was stashed inside the plane.

Every time the two Saudis took a break, Thorn would have to stop the compressor and look at them to get them back on the job. Sometimes even that didn't work. He would say chop-chop as if they were Chinese. Ahmed actually spoke perfect American English. He should, as he had been raised for eight years in the borough of Queens in New York.

The two pylons were mounted, one under each wing. The alignment was critical. The mounts had to be perfectly straight, otherwise you were inviting a midair catastrophe because of the aft-situated wing configuration and the long fuselage. Thorn was forced to break away several times to check on the Saudis and their work. In the end it would have been easier to do it himself.

In between painting and running herd on his two pilots, Thorn turned his attention to the small toy he had dubbed "the little brown bat." In military parlance it was known as an MAV, a micro air vehicle.

Seeing Thorn with the toy as they worked on the big jet, the two Saudis would look at him, talk to each other, and then laugh. Thorn didn't pay any attention as long as they got their work done.

The model airplane was just slightly larger than the size of Thorn's right hand, which now held it. The wingspan, just over six inches from tip to tip, was curved, somewhat like a bat, hence the name. The entire craft was clad with a thin layer of a bright, shiny copper compound. This had been sprayed on to save weight. The tiny plane had been specially crafted for Thorn by a master model maker who assured him that the copper-pigmented paint would react chemically in the same manner as if the model were made of the metal itself.

The plane was powered by two tiny electric motors, each capable of spinning a small propeller at more than fifteen thousand revolutions per minute. Using two nine-volt batteries, it could carry the necessary payload to an altitude of five hundred feet, and then stay aloft for a little over six minutes. This was more than enough time to do its job.

In flight, the little brown bat was virtually silent. On a dark night you would have to know precisely where it was, and even then you would have to strain your eyes to see it.

Thorn carefully placed plastic tape over the electrical components, the tiny motors, the wires, the battery housing, and the circuit board that formed the spine of the little craft between the two wings.

There was still more work to be done on the small bat before it was finished—the installation of the pinhole camera, a servo-motor to swivel and maneuver the camera, and a small light-emitting diode slightly larger than the camera that would be wired into the circuit board. But that work would have to wait until Thorn had completed this part of the processing.

He finished masking the electrical parts, then carefully patted the tape in place to make sure it was sealed and that there were no openings. Then he placed the small aircraft on the ground and stepped back a foot or so. Thorn then pulled down the zipper on his jeans, fished out the man in the turtleneck sweater, and began to pee all over the model.

When the two Saudis behind him saw this, they began to laugh. "If you like, we can come over there and help you," said Ahmed, smiling.

"I think I can handle it," said Thorn. "You just get the pylons finished."

"Whatever you say, boss." They laughed some more.

Thorn didn't care. He knew that in less than two weeks they would both be dead and he would be sitting on a beach somewhere drinking mai tais while tallying up the bottom line for his numbered account in Lucerne.

Thorn looked down at the little model. In a day or two the uric acid would begin to patina the copper pigment in the paint. By the end of the week, with another bath or two, the little plane would be the color of an old, worn penny. Precisely what he needed.

* * *

Joselyn begged off and went to the ladies' room while Paul and Herman grabbed chairs at the American Airlines gate at Miami International. They had two hours to kill before their connecting flight from Tucson would carry them south to Puerto Rico. Herman was feeling naked without his pistol, particularly now that they had a lead on Thorn's whereabouts.

The phone number, the Puerto Rico area code and the seven digits that followed on the hand-scrawled note that bled through onto the contract for the plane, rang at a hotel in a town called Ponce on the west side of the island, the Hotel Belgica.

Joselyn wanted Paul to contact the FBI, but Madriani wanted confirmation that Thorn was actually at the hotel in Ponce. If he wasn't there and the FBI was called in, whatever credibility they still had with the feds would evaporate.

As she stepped out of the ladies' room Joselyn reached into her purse for her cell phone. She had forgotten to turn it back on following their flight from Tucson.

She fired it up and checked her messages. When she saw it, her eyes lit up. She'd missed a call from Snyder. He had called less than an hour before. She touched the message and hit the Callback button. The phone rang twice before it was answered.

"Hello."

It didn't sound like Snyder's voice.

"Hello. I wonder if I have the wrong number?"

"No. No," said the voice. "Are you calling for Mr. Bart Snyder?"

"I am," said Joselyn.

"Then you have the right number," said the voice. "My name is Peter Montoya. I am a lieutenant with the Chicago Police Department. May I ask who's calling? Is this Ms. Joselyn Cole?"

Obviously he could see Joselyn's caller ID on Snyder's phone.

"Yes, it is."

"I'm afraid I have some bad news for you. Mr. Snyder is dead."

"What?"

"It happened early this morning," said the officer. "The maid found his body when she arrived for work. We are not sure, we are still investigating, but it appears likely that it was suicide."

"I don't understand. He called me not more than an hour ago," said Joselyn.

"No," said Montoya, "that was me. I have been calling recent contacts, people who left messages on his cell phone, to see if any of them might have spoken to Mr. Snyder in the last few days. Did you talk to him recently?"

"No," said Joselyn. "I didn't know him well. I met him only once, earlier this month."

"I see. Where was this?"

"In California, near San Diego."

"May I ask the circumstances of this meeting, was it business or social?"

Joselyn thought for a moment. The shock of Snyder's death unnerved her. Something deep down told her it wasn't suicide. "Neither," she said. "I just happened to be seated at a table where Mr. Snyder was also having lunch."

"Did you talk to him?"

"Yes."

"Did he seem despondent? Upset by anything?"

"Yes. His son had been murdered," said Joselyn.

"I see. Then you were aware of this."

"Mr. Snyder talked about it," said Joselyn. "And it did upset him, obviously."

"Of course. According to our notes you made several attempts to contact him. May I ask why, what the reason was?"

"I don't have time to discuss this right now," said Joselyn. "I'm trying to catch a connecting flight."

"I see. Where are you now?"

"Miami International."

"I would like to get a statement from you. Are you headed home?"

"No," said Joselyn. "I'm headed to Puerto Rico with friends."

"And when will you be returning?"

"I'm not sure."

"Can you give me the name of the hotel where you will be staying?"

"I don't know yet," said Joselyn. "We're going to pick a hotel when we arrive. But you can reach me at this number."

"Of course. I will do that. I don't want to hold you up any longer. You will be there tonight in Puerto Rico?"

"Yes," said Joselyn.

"Have a good flight. And I am sorry to have to convey such bad news."

"Thank you," said Joselyn. She hung up and jotted the name "Lt. Peter Montoya" on a small pad in her purse. Then suddenly she realized that the only number she had to reach him at was that of Snyder's cell phone.

* * *

Liquida walked the short block from where he'd parked his rental car to one of the bridges over the Chicago River. Joselyn Cole was with Madriani and their next stop was Puerto Rico. It was a safe bet this wasn't a vacation. Liquida smiled, wondering how much this information would be worth when he offered to sell it to his employer.

Word of Snyder's death had been all over the local airwaves. A prominent lawyer committing suicide was hot news, that and the video of the babbling maid who found the body.

Liquida walked halfway across the bridge and leaned against the railing. Lawyer with a scrambled brain, no one would even notice that his cell phone was missing. And even if they found records showing calls made on the phone after Snyder's death, an inquiry like that wasn't likely; given the virtual certainty of suicide, the call records would lead them nowhere, only to Joselyn Cole and a cop, Peter Montoya, who didn't exist. Liquida felt the stiff breeze against his back as he unfolded his arms and casually dropped Snyder's cell phone into one of the swift-moving eddies of the river below.

THIRTY-TWO

It was one thing to wait until we had confirmation of Thorn at the hotel in Puerto Rico, but the minute Joselyn came over and told me that Snyder was dead, we all knew this was no suicide.

There is no sense in waiting any longer. I call Thorpe in Washington and wait until his secretary answers.

"Hello, this is Paul Madriani calling for Mr. Thorpe. Is he there by any chance?"

"I'll have to check. Just a moment." The line goes dead for a second as she puts me on hold.

"You might give him the name Peter

Montoya," says Joselyn. She hands me a notepad where she has written this down.

"Hello, Mr. Madriani." It is Thorpe on the other end. "I'm afraid you caught me at a bad time. I'm on my way to another meeting."

"I understand. Did you hear that Bart Snyder is dead?" I ask him.

"Yes. I received a phone call from the Chicago field office this morning. I have to say it doesn't come as a great surprise," says Thorpe.

"What do you mean?" I ask.

"Of course, I am sorry for him, but he was around the bend, off the rails. You saw what he did up here in the news conference?"

"No. I'm sorry, I've been on the road," I tell him.

"Well, you didn't miss anything," says Thorpe. "He went off on a rant against the police, us, the media, anybody and everybody within reach, claiming there was a cover-up involving his son's death. And if that wasn't enough, he shot off his mouth about this guy, Thorn, saying he was involved in some vague plot to blow up the Capitol. Snyder was bonkers," says Thorpe.

"It happens. I'm sorry for him, but there's nothing we can do."

"You don't really think he killed himself?" I say.

"What do you think? They found him hanging by a rope in his garage with a ladder knocked over underneath him. Given the evidence and his bizarre behavior over the last several days, I'd say suicide is a pretty good theory."

"Overdoses and suicides, those are Liquida's specialties," I tell him.

"Yeah. Right behind knifing young girls in their sleep," says Thorpe.

"Listen to me," I tell him. "We've tracked Thorn to Puerto Rico and he has a plane."

"What are you talking about?"

I tell him about the boneyard in Arizona, the 727 and the phone number in Puerto Rico.

"And how did you come by all of this? Who put you on to the boneyard?"

"Snyder," I tell him.

"Oh, that's good. And how did he find out?"

"I don't know," I say.

"That should tell you something," says

Thorpe. "How do you know it's him?" He means Thorn. "Did you see him?" he says.

"No. But the guy at the boneyard ID'd him," I tell him.

"Based on what?"

"Based on the photographs your agent gave to Snyder," I tell him.

"I thought your lady friend, Ms. Cole, told you those photographs were not a good likeness of Mr. Thorn."

"She did, but the guy at the boneyard still recognized him," I say.

"Bully for him. We've looked at those pictures and compared them to our old file photos on Thorn. I hate to tell you this, but we don't see the resemblance," says Thorpe. "We're having experts look at them to see if maybe there's been some facial reconstruction, but it takes a while. We told Snyder this, but he was impatient. He didn't want to wait. According to our agent who interviewed him in Chicago, Snyder's law career was over. He was a man at an end. People at his office said he was chronically depressed. I hate to tell you this, but it's a classic case of depression and suicide."

"I hope you're more inquisitive when

Liquida hangs me," I tell him. "By the way, I assume it wasn't your people who put the GPS tracking devices on our cars?"

All I hear is silence from the other end.

"No, then who else but Liquida?" I ask.

"These tracking devices, do you still have them?" he asks.

"Why?"

"Because if you do, we might be able to trace them, find out who bought them, or contracted for satellite service."

"We assumed it wasn't healthy to hang on to them."

"What did you do, throw them away?"

"Something like that," I say.

"That's too bad. And the photographs, the ones you say are of Thorn, I assume Snyder gave them to you?" he says.

"That's right."

"I should have killed the agent," says Thorpe. "He had no business giving those photographs to anyone, let alone to a loose cannon like Snyder. Where are they now, the photographs?" he says.

"I don't know where Snyder kept his, but we have ours," I tell him.

"They're not yours," says Thorpe. "They belong to the federal government. They're part of an ongoing investigation, and I want them back. Now!" he says. "Where are you?"

"I'm not sure I should tell you."

"Why not?"

"Because you seem to be in a foul mood."

"Sorry, but I have a full calendar today. I don't have time for this. But I want those photographs back. Do you understand?"

"Stop dithering over the photographs and listen to me," I tell him. "Do you have a pencil and paper?"

"Why?"

"Write this down. From what we know, Thorn is in Puerto Rico in a town called Ponce." I spell it for him. "Unless I'm wrong, he's staying in a place called the Hotel Belgica." I spell it again. "Did you write it down?"

"What am I, your secretary?" says Thorpe.

"Did you write it down?"

"Listen, I'm late for a meeting. And I want those photographs. Do you hear me?"

"I'm telling you he has a plane, a 727, and he's up to something."

"Right," says Thorpe. He thinks for a moment. "All right. I'll have somebody check it out. What's the name of this boneyard?"

I give him the information.

"We're going to have to continue this some other time. I gotta run. Take some advice and go home," he says.

"I can't. I'm flying south."

"You're going to get in over your head," he says.

"I already am."

"Try not to get in any more trouble, and call me when you get back." Thorpe hangs up.

THIRTY-THREE

The second he got off the phone with
Madriani, Thorpe grabbed his jacket and
was out the door. One agent held the elevator for him while another waited for them
in a car down in the garage. Thorpe was
pressed for time, and what he was dealing
with couldn't wait.

It was Victor Soyev, a Russian arms
merchant who had been arrested in Los
Angeles. The FBI had received an anonymous tip as to Soyev's whereabouts and
had taken him into custody at LAX just as
he was getting ready to jump on a flight to

Asia. Immediately, they hustled him off to Washington on a government jet.

For two days agents had been moving him around, from one location to another, trying to keep him out of the news and away from the clutches of defense lawyers. If the honchos at the Justice Department found out, Thorpe would be looking for a new job.

Based on the anonymous tip, the FBI checked Soyev's voice against the NSA voiceprints from the telephone conversation between North Korea and Cuba. The Russian's voice was a match. Soyev's was the voice on the North Korean end of the conversation. He was one of the operatives moving the massive thermobaric device that got grounded in Thailand. Thorpe wanted answers, and he wanted them before Soyev had a chance to lawyer up.

The problem was the constantly changing rules for interrogation laid down by the White House. The guidelines were as clear as mud, and designed with enough political wiggle room so that members of Congress and the White House could run for cover and point the finger at underlings the minute anything went wrong. Everything was on a case-by-case basis. The minute Thorpe told the White House he had Soyev and what the case involved, the Russian would be put in a holding pattern, and the FBI would be told not to question him until a decision had been made by a higher authority as to the process to be used.

It was fashionable to quote Truman as to where the buck stopped, but in reality, every White House since had become increasingly expert in the art of plausible deniability. And every one of them could spin like a weather vane when it came to the blame game.

For the moment, Soyev was in a hotel room six blocks from FBI headquarters. Transported in a blacked-out van and taken up to the room in a service elevator with a hood over his head, the Russian had no idea what city he was in. He would be in the hotel for no more than two hours before they moved him again. Interrogation was captured on multichannel microphones and video in case they missed something the first time through. At night they held him in a safe house just across the Maryland state line, where questioning continued. Thorpe would devour the interrogation transcripts each morning.

So far Soyev wasn't giving up much. He denied that he was ever in North Korea. He claimed he was a Moscow businessman dealing in heavy industrial equipment. He demanded to see the nearest Russian consul, and when that failed, he asked for a lawyer.

Thorpe had his people giving Soyev only the best when it came to food and drink. They would give him Stolichnaya vodka whenever he asked for it. It was available only through one importer in the States. The agents told him if he wanted a lawyer they would get one, but that if they did, Soyev would have to be locked up in a federal facility pending trial, and the booze and steaks would all go away. The Russian withdrew his request for a lawyer. Thorpe knew he couldn't keep the movable feast going forever. He was running out of time.

When Thorpe arrived at the hotel that afternoon, interrogation had already started. The room had been sanitized to remove everything that might tell Soyev where he was. The curtains were pulled and only a single light from a lamp illuminated the room.

It was the third time Soyev had seen Thorpe, though the two men had never talked. All questioning was conducted through a set of three interrogators. But the Russian seemed to know that Thorpe was someone important. Like a bitch in heat, he could smell an alpha male.

"Mr. Soyev, why don't you tell us what we want to know?" said the interrogator. "We have the tape and the transcript of your telephone conversation from Pyongyang to Cuba. We know that it was your voice coming from North Korea based on voiceprint identification."

"So you say," said Soyev. "And I tell you I have never been to North Korea. Check my passport if you don't believe me."

"We are well aware that an arms merchant of your stature can avoid the normal processes of customs and immigration in places like North Korea. Let's stop playing games. Tell us who the man was on the other end of the telephone conversation. The man in Cuba."

"I don't know what you're talking about. I am a Russian citizen and I demand to see the Russian consul. Also I would like a drink if you don't mind. I'm getting thirsty. How long is this going to go on? I am very tired. As you know, I haven't been able to sleep in two days. You keep waking me up every few minutes to ask more questions."

The interrogator nodded toward one of the other agents, who immediately opened an attaché case and came up with the bottle of Stolichnaya.

"I hope you have ice?" said Soyev.

"Stop," said Thorpe. "Enough." Thorpe reached over and flipped on the switch for the overhead lights in the room.

Soyev looked at him, squinted, and shaded his eyes.

"Mr. Soyev, I am Zeb Thorpe, executive assistant director for the National Security Branch of the FBI. We've carried on with this as long as we can and I'm putting an end to it right now. Upon leaving here, you're going to be transported to a federal detention facility for maximum-security prisoners. You will be charged with numerous crimes, including violation of international weapons embargoes, terrorism, conspiracy to commit terrorism, and arms smuggling for starters. I'm sure that there will be superseding indictments with other charges that will be added in the coming weeks. Suffice it to say that there will be enough charges and convictions that you are almost certain to spend the rest of your life in a federal penitentiary in this country. That is, unless one of these thermobaric devices that you're dealing in goes off in a major metropolitan area, killing a number of people, in which case we will be seeking the death penalty. Do you understand?"

Soyev just looked. He didn't say a word.

"There will be no more vodka and no more rich meals. Now, the only way you are going to change any of these circumstances is by cooperating with us. And to do that, you have a very brief window of opportunity. You see, your compadre, your comrade, the man on the other end of that telephone conversation with you, the one in Cuba . . ."

Soyev followed every word.

". . . he not only ratted you out and turned you in . . ."

Soyev's brow furrowed, and his eyes turned to little slits.

". . . he is also, I assume, operating on

some kind of a timetable, a schedule," said Thorpe. "That means that the minute he uses any of the weapons that you shipped to him, the window of opportunity for you to cut a deal with me is going to come down on the back of your neck just like a sharp blade. That means that you will be charged as an accomplice with any and all of his deeds. You will be subject to the same penalties as he is. Since he did you the favor of landing you here, why don't you do the same for him?" Thorpe stood there, looking straight at the Russian.

"You know this?" asked Soyev.

"As a matter of fact, we do. The phone call that gave us your name and flight number came into our field office in Los Angeles. It was taped. Voiceprint analysis confirms that the voice on that telephone conversation is the same voice as that from Cuba during your telephone conversation from North Korea."

"Shit!" said Soyev. "Bastard never paid me. Second half of money."

Thorpe was lying. The call fingering the Russian was placed to the TSA, the Transportation Security Administration, at the airport. And it wasn't taped.

"Who is he?" said Thorpe.

"If I knew, believe me, I would tell you," said Soyev. "I don't know his name. I call him Chief. He calls me Tonto, but he never uses the name. Whenever I call, he knows my voice."

"You've never met him?"

"No. This is not unusual," said the Russian. "I never meet most of my customers. Just voices on the phone."

"And the money?" says Thorpe. "I assume he paid you something. How? An overseas numbered account?"

Soyev nods.

"I need the name of your bank and the number of your account," said Thorpe.

"Fat chance." Soyev laughed. "Next you're going to tell me you have a bridge you wish to sell me."

"We won't touch the funds," said Thorpe.

"And for this what do I have, your word?" said Soyev.

"I need the number. With your account number I can have the Treasury Department turn the screws on the bank and trace his last wire transfer back to his bank and his account number. With that number we may get a name."

"If we are going to be doing this, I need to talk to a lawyer," said Soyev.

"While you're conferring with your lawyer, he could be setting off one of the devices. How many are there?" asked Thorpe.

Soyev sat back in the chair and folded his arms. "What kind of a deal do I get? Life in prison does not sound like bottom line to me," said Soyev.

"Do you know what he was doing with the bombs? Do you have any information on targets? If you know, now is the time to tell us. Afterward it's going to be too late."

"I know nothing about that," said Soyev. "All I did was obtain items he asked for. He tells me nothing about anything else."

Thorpe turned to one of the interrogators. "Gimme the transcript of the telephone conversation, Pyongyang to Cuba."

The agent went to his briefcase, found it, and handed it to Thorpe. Thorpe flipped a few pages. "Here it is. You talk about 'the big guy' and 'the kid'—Fat Man and Little Boy, is that correct?"

Soyev looked at him but didn't say anything.

"I'm going to assume that it is. You told

the man in Cuba that 'the kid' will take a later flight. Meaning that the smaller of the two devices was not on the Russian plane that was forced down in Thailand." He looked at Soyev. "So I'm assuming it was shipped some other way?"

Soyev was now refusing to make eye contact.

"That means that the 'Fat Man,' or 'big guy,' was the one we found on the plane in Bangkok. But then you go on to volunteer to your compatriot, to your coconspirator in Cuba, and I quote, 'the man has a brother.' Look at me when I'm talking to you!" Thorpe shouted at him.

The Russian's head and eyes jerked to the right to engage Thorpe.

"That means there was a replacement for the 'Fat Man,' doesn't it? Doesn't it?"

Soyev didn't want to, but he nodded, almost by reflex.

"Has that device been delivered?" asked Thorpe.

This time Soyev nodded more deliberately.

"Where did you deliver them?" said Thorpe.

"I want to talk to a lawyer," said Soyev.

"Later," said Thorpe. "Right now you talk to me."

"All I know is that one of them was shipped to New York. The other I don't know about because it was transshipped. I delivered it to Havana. From there I don't know."

"New York?" said Thorpe. "Where? Did you have an address?"

"It was a bonded warehouse on the docks. It was to be picked up."

"Which one of the devices went to New York?"

"The replacement," said Soyev.

"Fat Man? The big one?" asked Thorpe.

Soyev nodded.

Shit, thought Thorpe.

"And you have no idea what the target is?"

"I don't know that there is a target. People buy munitions for all kinds of things."

"You don't need a lawyer. You're doing fine on your own," said Thorpe. "He never mentioned a possible target? Think!"

Soyev paused for a moment, if for no other reason than to make it look good.

"No. As I say, I have no idea what he was going to do with any of this equipment."

"What equipment?" said Thorpe. "You sold him two bombs. According to my experts, these things are just half a step down from nuclear devices."

"No. No. They are wrong," said Soyev. "I have never dealt in nuclear materials or any weapons of mass destruction."

"I see. You're a merchant of death with moral standards, is that it . . . ?"

Before Soyev could answer, Thorpe said, "Are you going to give me the number for your overseas account or not?"

"Not until I talk to my lawyer," said Soyev.

"Yeah, and by the time he gets through, the account won't exist because he'll clean it out for his retainer. Take him away. Lock him up, and get him a lawyer. And make sure the court knows he can afford to pay for his own. If he's going to kill a bunch of taxpayers, the least we can do is make sure they don't have to pay for his legal defense."

THIRTY-FOUR

The flight time from Miami to San Juan, Puerto Rico, is listed as two hours and forty-three minutes. Today's flight takes us more than three hours. According to the pilot, we have been bucking heavy head-winds all the way.

We sit three abreast in the center section, Joselyn between Herman and me, and we look over her shoulder at a photo of the Hotel Belgica in Ponce on Joselyn's laptop. She found the Web site and down-loaded it to a file before we left the airport in Miami.

The hotel is two stories, something from the plantation period of the last century. It has an upscale ambience, even from the outside, pastel masonry with white trim, arched windows, and green wrought-iron railings. There are awnings over all of the windows as well as the main entrance on the ground floor. The building could pass for one of the better establishments on Royal Street in New Orleans.

"Looks like a nice place," says Joselyn. "Too bad we can't stay there."

"Can't take the chance," says Herman. "Not if Thorn's there. All we need is for him to recognize you."

That Thorn may be there is a long shot, but it's the only lead we have. We have to assume that he penned the note with the hotel's telephone number for a reason. Either he or someone he is dealing with is staying there.

Joselyn has also downloaded a map of the town of Ponce onto her computer. It looks like a vacation spot with an abundance of hotels and cultural exhibits, and a sizable port facility. There is a museum of art, and a central plaza with a cathedral as well as a number of tourist sites, mostly eco tours and snorkeling according to the information on the computer.

"Where we stayin'?" says Herman.

"I booked us at a small hotel downtown, not far from the Belgica," I tell him. "I reserved a car at the airport. When we land I'll get the car, you guys can get the luggage, and we'll meet out in front."

"I have to make a phone call," says Joselyn. "I need to contact my office, let them know I'm alive."

"I'll grab the luggage," says Herman.

A half hour later we're on the ground, inside the terminal. "Catch you guys later. Out front at the curb." I point.

"I've got to go to the ladies' room," says Joselyn. "I only have the one checked bag."

"I got it," says Herman.

I walk toward the rental-car counter and Joselyn heads the other way.

Just inside the door to the ladies' room, Joselyn stops, reaches into her purse, and pulls out her cell phone. She turns it on, punches in a name, and highlights it when it comes up on the screen. She hits the green button and places the call. It rings three times before it is answered by a familiar voice.

"Hello, Joselyn here. Is your boss in? I need to talk to him. Tell him it's urgent." She waits on the line, tapping her pointed high heel on the floor nervously as she holds the phone to her ear. She glances under the stalls to make sure no one is within earshot.

"Hello. Thanks for taking my call. I don't have much time. I'm in Puerto Rico at the airport . . .

"I know. I know. I didn't know myself that I was coming down here until late yesterday. Unfortunately, I haven't had a moment alone since then to make the call, not during the day when I could reach you. And I didn't want to commit any of this to an e-mail or a text message . . ."

She listens for a moment as he agrees that texting or e-mail would be unwise.

"Listen, we've got a problem. Remember the lawyer I told you about and our last conversation about Thorn? You wanted me to keep you informed . . .

"Yes, well, the lawyer's been nosing around with the FBI. I'm not sure exactly what he told them or how much they believe, but he's managed to track Thorn to a hotel in a small town called Ponce in Puerto Rico."

She listens to the voice on the other end.

"Yes, that's what I said. There are the two of them, Madriani and his investigator, a man named Herman Diggs. They were armed, but they're not any longer. I don't think Madriani got the FBI to follow through, but I'm not sure. That's why I'm calling you, to give you a heads-up."

She listens for a moment.

"I'm not sure what he knows," says Joselyn. "But he may be about to find out, and it could get pretty hairy. Do you understand?" She listens again.

"Exactly. That's why I called," she says. "I would like you to take care of it. A single phone call from you would do it."

Joselyn listens for a moment. She gets the reply she was hoping for. "Good. Then I'll leave it in your hands. You'll take care of it . . . ?"

"Good. I can't stay on the line. They're gonna start wondering where I am. I'll call you when I know more. Take care." She pushes the red button, drops the phone in her purse, and heads back out to the luggage-claim area.

* * *

There was a reason Thorn had picked the ancient Boeing 727-100C, and strangely, it wasn't because of the price of the plane. The old rear trijet design had everything he needed.

Dating to the early 1960s, the 727-100C included an internal auxiliary power unit for starting its own engines on the ground. This eliminated the need for a heavy external power source on the remote runway in Puerto Rico.

The "C" designation meant it was convertible and could be used for either freight or passengers depending on how the interior of the plane was configured. It had a large freight door on the forward left-hand side of the fuselage that could be used or not, depending on whether the air carrier was flying passengers, freight, or a combination of the two.

The 727 had been the workhorse for most U.S. domestic short-haul flights during the 1960s and '70s because it required very little ground maintenance. Its wing design incorporated leading-edge flaps that gave the plane greater lift, allowing it to remain stable in flight at low speeds. For all of these reasons it could service smaller cities with shorter runways, resulting in one of the plane's most distinctive features, the built-in drop-down ramp, or airstair, near the tail section of the plane. For Thorn, this was critical.

The drop-down stairs were lowered from under the rear belly and allowed passengers to get off the plane without the need of roll-up steps or a connecting jetway. Some airlines came to love it when they discovered that passengers could be de-planed from the front while cleaning crews could climb on board from the lowered air-stairs at the rear, thereby shortening the turnaround time.

But this love affair came to an abrupt end in 1971 because of one man, a ghost who called himself Dan Cooper. An early aviation hijacker, Cooper waylaid a North-west flight claiming he had a bomb in his carry-on luggage. He demanded and got $200,000 in twenty-dollar bills along with four parachutes. Cooper used one of the parachutes to make the leap into criminal history by jumping from the steps of the rear drop-down ramp at ten thousand feet with the flaps lowered to reduce speed. He was never seen again.

Some claimed that he died in the jump or soon thereafter, either in the snowy mountains of the northwest or by drowning in one of the many rivers in the area. Others claimed they had seen him since. The FBI was still looking for him. Like Jacob Waltz and the "Lost Dutchman Mine," D. B. Cooper had acquired the status of a myth.

For this reason he was one of Thorn's heroes. Cooper left two enduring monuments to his brief criminal career. The scanning of all carry-on luggage for bombs and weapons, and another that was linked to his name, the so-called Cooper Vane.

This morning Thorn was busy at the airfield in Puerto Rico removing the old Cooper Vane from the tail section of his plane. The vane was a deceptively simple mechanical device. Federal law required its installation on all commercial planes with rear airstairs after Cooper's crime.

The vane consisted of an oval-shaped control surface that stuck out from the underbelly of the plane like an oversize

Ping-Pong paddle. This was connected to a rectangular steel plate on a pivoting bolt that was spring-loaded. When the plane was on the ground, the paddle remained perpendicular to the fuselage, its flat edges facing the front and rear of the plane. But in flight, when air speed hit the forward face of the paddle, it would turn parallel to the fuselage, pivoting the steel plate with it. The plate acted like a gate latch, preventing the airstairs from being lowered in flight.

The ability to lower the airstairs in flight was critical to Thorn's plan. Hence the vane had to come off.

While Thorn worked on this, his ace welder was busy working on the rear ramp itself. He used an arc welder to fix two heavy steel rails, one along each side of the ramp, about six inches above each step. These steel rails had been prefabricated and had a slight curve, higher at each end and lower in the middle. Affixed to each of the two rails were heavy steel rollers, four on each side.

Thorn drilled out the post pivot on the Cooper Vane and removed the steel plate. Then he patched over the hole with an aluminum panel, sealing it with a special epoxy to ensure that the patch wouldn't leak when the plane was pressurized. He then turned his attention to the next task, the bomb—Little Boy, still resting in its wooden crate.

Thorn had done considerable research before settling on the plane and the type of ordnance to be used. One of the most insightful pieces of literature, strange as it might seem because it was so dated, was a postwar analysis based on captured classified documents from the Japanese of their attack on Pearl Harbor.

Thorn was particularly impressed with the detailed analysis regarding the destruction of the USS *Arizona*.

The Japanese bomb that did the job was about eight hundred pounds, less than half the weight of Thorn's device. Contrary to popular belief, it wasn't an aerial bomb at all. It was a modified naval artillery shell, armor piercing, with a box-fin stabilizer attached to the tail and a delay fuse added to the nose. The Japanese were an entire generation ahead of any other warfaring nation in their conception of how to retread old ordnance with new technology.

When it hit the ship, it sliced through the top weather deck of solid teak. It then passed through two armor-plated lower decks, each one four inches thick, before it came to rest in the forward magazine of the battleship. There it exploded, igniting almost a million pounds of gunpowder used to fire shells from the ship's fourteen-inch guns. The blast melted iron bulkheads and literally lifted the ship out of the water.

For the Japanese bombardier who dropped it, it was a lucky shot. Thorn couldn't afford to rely on luck. He would compensate for this with a combination of laser-guidance systems and advanced control surfaces that would dramatically in-crease the glide ratio of the ordnance he was using. Like the Japanese, he would marry old technology to new.

The answer was the Paveway, a series of laser-guided add-ons made by Texas Instruments, Raytheon, and a number of other corporations starting in the 1960s. The various versions included large tail-fin assemblies and nose-cone attachments with laser seekers. These could be at-tached to any dumb iron gravity bomb, transforming it into a precision-guided system with a glide ratio in some instances exceeding fifteen nautical miles.

The defensive perimeter around the target was twice this range, thirty nautical miles. But the government had already compromised this protective zone by their demonstrated and repeated indecision regarding the rules of engagement. Thorn was well aware of these incidents, one of which had involved a state governor whose pilot drifted into the protection zone through ignorance.

It's what always happened when the airspace over a target was too often inhabited by people of power and influence. It was one thing to shoot down a planeload of three or four hundred taxpayers. It was another to shoot down one of the privileged political class flying in their ego-containered government jets. The pattern had been set to hold their fire and try to escort the violator to the nearest airport where their ass could be gently hauled off in a limousine of state to the nearest five-star hotel.

To Thorn, this was invariably the case. The defensive systems and the people operating them seldom failed. But the pampered powerful whose minds were focused on their own wealth, comfort, and continued power could sabotage anything, and almost always did.

THIRTY-FIVE

Joselyn, Herman, and I checked into the Hotel Melia in downtown Ponce. The Melia is in the historic area, about ten blocks from the cathedral and the Hotel Belgica. Joselyn checked into her room while Herman and I took the car and headed toward the Belgica to see what we could find out.

It took a few minutes to make our way through town, Herman behind the wheel with me navigating. Ponce is a larger and more congested area than it looked like on the map pictured on Joselyn's computer.

When we finally found the street that went in front of the Belgica, traffic was one-way, and by the time we got in front of the hotel we were almost past it before we realized. There were cars parked on both sides of the street, with nowhere for us to stop. Then we got lucky.

A car pulled out of a spot at the curb across the street about a half block down from the entrance to the hotel. Herman blocked traffic, with horns blaring behind us, to let the guy out, then pulled forward, backed in, and turned off the engine.

"You got those photographs of Thorn?" he says.

I reach over to the backseat and find the three photos in my briefcase. "I thought we agreed we weren't going to use these?"

"Sit tight." With that, Herman takes the photographs from my hand and is out of the car. He slams the door, leaving me in the passenger seat as he strolls down the sidewalk in the shade until he is just opposite the entrance to the hotel. I watch as he slips between traffic, crosses the street, and disappears through the entrance under the awning.

We had already decided that we would use the photographs of Thorn to question the clerk at the front desk only as a last resort. Innkeepers are generally protective of their guests. Any word that someone was asking questions about him and Thorn would vanish like a puff of smoke. And any hopes of finding a trail that might lead to Liquida would vanish with him. Of course, all of this assumes that Thorn is even here.

While I'm waiting in the car I feel the cell phone on my hip and I'm wishing I could call Sarah. I could, but I don't. I haven't spoken to her in several days, and by agreement we haven't called each other. It's a problem. I have had to delete all contact information on her from my phone in case either I or the phone falls into Liquida's hands. There are simply too many records maintained on cell phones and computers to feel safe. Even without information in your contact lists, a call made or received showing an area code can leave an indelible record that can be traced. I am glad that Harry is with her.

Herman is inside the Belgica for a while. It's starting to warm up in the car.

Just as I reach for the door handle I see Herman step out from the hotel's entrance under the awning. He has some literature in his hand and a smile on his face. He crosses the street, sashaying between the cars, making his way back, and opens the driver's-side door. Then he settles in behind the wheel.

"You look satisfied."

"It's hot in here."

"I know."

He puts in the key and turns on the engine and the air conditioner. Then he closes the door.

"What did you find out?"

"We got lucky," says Herman. "Our man's there."

"Did you see him?"

"No, but Joselyn said Thorn had an Australian accent. The kid behind the registration desk was very helpful. I told him I was lookin' for a man with an Australian accent who was supposed to be stayin' at the hotel. I slipped him a couple of twenties, showed him my PI credentials, and told him I was serving process in a divorce case."

"And?"

"He says, 'You mean Señor Johnston?'" Herman looks at me and smiles. "So much for hotel privacy. I showed him the close-up photo of Thorn and the kid says, 'Yeah, he checked in two days ago.'"

"How do you know he won't tell Thorn?"

"Best reason in the world, economic stimulus," says Herman. "I told him the two twenties I gave him had brothers. If he kept his mouth shut until after I served Johnston, I'd make it an even hundred. I stuffed another twenty in his pocket on the way out just to keep him happy. So you know what that means?"

"Yeah. I owe you sixty bucks," I tell him. "And if you pay him the other forty it's coming out of your own pocket."

"Don't worry. You don't have to pay me right now," he says. "I'll put it on my next billing statement."

"Is Thorn in the hotel now?" I ask.

"No. He leaves his key at the desk when he goes out and picks it up when he comes back. The clerk checked. The key was in one of the slots behind the counter, room 219," says Herman. "Guess who's in 221?" He opens his hand and flashes me the key. "Looks like you and I won't be snorin' in the same room tonight. And by the way, you can tell Joselyn that, for the record, you do snore."

"Did the desk clerk have any idea when Thorn might be back?"

"No, but he said Señor Johnston seems to be on some kind of a schedule and appears to be working very hard."

"How's that?"

"According to the clerk, he leaves every morning between six thirty and seven and doesn't get back until after dark. Kid says he doesn't know where he goes or what he does. Johnston keeps to himself. But he's gone all day. Tell you what, I'll drop you back at the Melia, then I'll have to bring the car over here. I'll need it in case Thorn shows up and leaves again, so I can follow him. My room's right next door to his, so I should hear him when he comes in."

"Do you want me to call Thorpe again, tell him we think we found Thorn?" I ask.

"We got this far, why don't we wait and see what's goin' on? Besides, he didn't seem that enthusiastic the last time."

"He was busy," I tell him.

"He's always busy," says Herman.

"I'd feel a whole lot better if we hadn't had to leave the pistols in my car at the airport in Tucson," I tell him.

"Makes two of us," says Herman. "I'll just have to be extra careful and keep my distance till we find out what Thorn's up to.

In the meantime, I need to park the car in the back. You were right. The clerk says there's a lot back there. He gave me a parking pass. He says it's where Johnston parks his car. He asked me if it was possible to serve him with the process back there in the parking lot, can you beat it? He says his boss wouldn't want anything unpleasant to happen in the hotel."

"What did you tell him?"

"Told him I would. Why not? This way the clerk won't be asking any questions when he sees me follow Thorn out of the hotel. I told him it could take a day or two to find the right moment, so I could lay the papers on him without causing any embarrassment."

"And the kid bought it?"

"Oh, yeah. I got him believing process servers are all jet-setting chichi types. Personally, I always fly in early, check into a swank hotel, taste the wine, and lay around the pool for a few days so's I can practice to see which hand I'm gonna use to lay on the paper." Herman glances at me and laughs. He starts the car and looks over his shoulder to check for traffic. "Young clerk's gonna be mighty disappointed when we have to call 911 and SWAT shows up with Thor's hammer to take Mr. Johnston's door off the hinges, burn holes in the carpets, and smoke the place up with flash bangs. That kinda stuff tends to knock a few diamonds off your rating with three A," he says.

"I'd like to keep it to ourselves until we know what Thorn's up to and hopefully get a lead on Liquida," I tell him.

Herman ignores me. "You need to get some rest. I'll get you back to your hotel. Listen. You go upstairs, knock on her door wearing your jammies and dragging a blanket behind you with a pillow under your arm, and tell her you want to take a nap. Wipe a little sleep from your eyes when she opens the door." He looks at me, and for a moment I think he's serious. Then I realize that he is.

"Trust me, it'll work," he says. "Women love that shit. They can't resist it."

"You don't know Joselyn. I think she can resist anything. And if not, she'll just analyze the hell out of it until it dies."

"No. Trust me. She won't be able to say no. It's something about the maternal instinct."

"What, and tell her I'm having a nightmare, so I can crawl into her pants? If I tried to manipulate her like that, she'd shrink-wrap my brain, tell me I'm suffering from an anal-retentive disorder, and spin me around like a compass until my dick was pointing back to my own room." I shake my head. "Listen, I'm not sure there's anything real happening between us. I mean, sure I'm attracted to her. I'm a red-blooded male. What's not to like? She's beautiful, sexy, cute, smart . . ."

"Listen to yourself," says Herman. "You're not sure there's anything happening between the two of you, but you're about to have an orgasm all over Avis's front seat."

"It takes two before you have a relationship. I'm not sure she has any deep interest in me."

"She's got the hots for you."

"Says who?"

"Says who? Says me."

"Did she tell you that?"

"She doesn't have to. I got eyes. I can see and I can hear. And everything I see and hear tells me she's got a lock on you like a radar beam. Why do you think she's trailing along with us?"

"Because of her past dealings with Thorn. She wants to see him get nailed," I tell him.

"Sure, she hates the guy. She's scared to death of him. But that's not the reason she's here. She's worried about you."

"You think so?"

"When it comes to women, you're pretty damn dense," he says. "No wonder you haven't gotten married since your wife died."

"That's a tender subject," I tell him.

"And it's an old one, ancient history. You gotta move on. From what I can see, you got one hell of an opportunity dangling in front of you right now. If I were you, I wouldn't let it die on the vine, not without tasting the wine, sampling the vintage, to see if you like it."

"I'm not sure I . . ."

"Don't tell me you're not interested. I've seen the way you look at her. And if I die in my sleep tonight, I wouldn't want the last words I hear from your lips to be a lie. So bite your tongue," he says.

THIRTY-SIX

After a short but silent ride, Herman dropped me back at the Melia. He told me one more time to knock on Joselyn's door and at least be friendly. Then he turned around and headed back toward the downtown plaza.

I haul my luggage upstairs, fishing for the room key in my pocket. When I find it, I finally drag my weary body inside the room and dump my bags at the foot of the bed.

Before the spring on the door can close it, I hear her voice behind me. "So what's going on? Where's Herman?"

I turn and Joselyn's standing in the doorway, her left arm dangling at her hip as her
right hand holds the door open. She is
barefoot, wearing a kind of silky-slinky red
chemise that clings to her body and ends
midthigh under a longer thin duster, open
and unbelted in the front. Her curving hips
form a lazy S against the steel frame of the
door as she stands there.

"Come on in. Herman took a room at the
Belgica."

"Told you it was a nice place," she says.

"We think we found Thorn."

Her gaze suddenly turns serious. She
steps inside the room and lets the door
close behind her. She has her room key in
her hand.

"So he is there?"

I nod. "According to the desk clerk. He
ID'd him from one of the photographs. He's
booked under the name Johnston. But
he's not there now. Herman took the room
next door. According to the clerk, Thorn's
been at the Belgica for two days. He leaves
early in the morning and doesn't get back
until after dark. Herman's going to try to
listen through the walls, pick up his movements when he comes in tonight, and track

him when he leaves in the morning. He'll call us on my cell as soon as he knows what's going on."

"You think that's safe?" she says. "I mean, you don't think Herman's in any danger, do you?"

"Herman knows what he's doing. He'll take precautions, keep his distance." I don't share with Joselyn my concern about the desk clerk. That if he says anything to Thorn about Herman asking questions, there are only two possibilities: one, that Thorn will disappear and we'll never find him again, and the other, which is more ominous. If Thorn is heavily invested in whatever he's doing on the island and he thinks Herman is acting alone, he may decide that it's easier and more profitable to dispose of Herman than to run.

"If I don't hear from Herman by ten o'clock tonight, I'll call him. If I think he needs backup, I'll grab a taxi and go over."

"And then what are you going to do? You don't have a gun," she says. "This is crazy. The two of you are going to end up dead. I'm telling you, he is a dangerous man. You're worried about Liquida. Thorn is just as deadly. Trust me on this."

"Yes, but at the moment he's all we've got and we can't let him go. Tiger by the tail," I tell her. "Thorn is the only link we have to Liquida. And if I can't lead the cops to Liquida and get him off my back, I don't have a life. And neither does my daughter, or, for that matter, Harry or Herman. I don't have to remind you that Liquida has shown a pathologic willingness to kill people who are even remotely associated with me. You might want to think about that," I tell her. "In fact, it might be a good idea if you got on a plane and headed home. I'll keep you posted on what happens. I promise."

"You look exhausted," she says.

"Yeah, well, you should be tired too."

"I got a little rest. Why don't you sit down?" she says.

I step around my bags and settle down on the side of the bed.

"Take a deep breath," Joselyn says. She approaches and puts her hands on the shoulders of my polo shirt and starts to massage.

I roll my head back, move my shoulders. "That feels great." Then she pushes my upper body back until I'm lying flat on the bed with my feet on the floor.

"What are you doing?"

"Never mind, just relax." She reaches down, grabs my ankles, and swivels my body until I am lying with my head on one of the pillows, my feet up on the bottom of the bed. Joselyn unties my shoes and pulls them off, tossing them on the floor. The release of tension and stress is palpable as she rubs my feet.

"You don't have to do that."

"I know. Focus on your mantra."

"My what?"

"Relax. Don't tell me you've never done any meditation?"

"Sorry," I tell her.

"Your mantra can be anything, an image, a word. It can be a tone, like this: Aommmmmmmmmmm."

She does it two or three times, holding the tone until, like a bellows, the air goes from her lungs. The gentle, low tone of her voice is something strange, almost intoxicating. But I'm afraid it's not meditation that I'm thinking about.

"If you do it repeatedly and focus your consciousness, you can reach a transcendental point where monks believe the mind and the soul meld," she tells me. "Practiced regularly it can lower blood pressure and reduce stress. And stress kills, in case you haven't heard."

"I know."

"Trial lawyers don't like it," she says. "They believe meditation dilutes their aggression. And, of course, they're right. It's the fight or flight thing. When you don't want to do either, resort to your mantra."

"I will."

"There's a time to talk and a time to be quiet." She puts a finger to her lips. "This is the time for silence. Just lie there and relax."

She rubs my feet, and then my lower legs, and I begin to drift off.

"There is no restaurant or bar in the hotel, but there are some good restaurants a few doors away. We can order out later if you want. They'll deliver. I've got a menu."

"I'm trying to be quiet," I tell her.

"Good."

"Are you hungry?" I ask.

"Um, no. I have an appetite but not for food."

I open one eye and look at her. She fixes me with a winsome smile, stops massag-

ing, and gazes at me from the foot of the
bed with almond-shaped eyes.

"That was very nice. Thank you."

"We're not done yet," she says.

At the moment she looks like the spider
about to attack the fly. I watch her as she
moves gracefully, almost floating on air,
around toward the other side of the bed.
Halfway there she drops her hands to her
sides and gently thrusts her shoulders back.
The robe slides from her body and disappears like a silk puddle, past her thighs and
onto the floor.

As she walks through it, the body-
hugging red chemise clings to her form,
set off by two thin straps over her shoulders and a filigree of lace at the tawny
satin smoothness of her thighs.

"I really didn't want to stay in my room
alone tonight," she says. "I hope you don't
mind."

"No. Why should I mind?" I think to myself, I love being raped by beautiful women.

"Missing Herman, are you?" she says.

"Umm, no. Not exactly."

"Good. That makes two of us."

"You don't like Herman?"

"He's a very nice guy," she says. "But that makes two of you, and when I'm added to the mix, three is a crowd."

"I see. He speaks highly of you."

"Thank him for me." As she reaches the other side of the bed she raises a tanned, shapely knee and plants it deep in the soft muslin bedcovers. Then in a flowing feline motion she traverses the width of the bed on her hands and knees. When I look up I see her face hovering just over my left shoulder, pursed sensuous lips and oval eyes.

"Don't look so frightened," she says.

"Do I look scared?"

"I won't bite," says Joselyn. "I promise. Not unless you ask me to, and then you may have to beg."

"That sounds kinky."

"Silence, remember?" Joselyn has bathed and washed her hair. I can smell the perfumed soap and the scent of strawberries floating in the ether above me.

"Pick a mantra, anything, and focus on it. It will help break the fear."

"Really?"

"Aom, aom."

I look at her eyes, her pursed lips, almost pouting, as she stalks me on her hands and knees, staring down at me. "Before I settle in, would you like something to drink? Something from the minibar, perhaps?"

"Sweetheart, if you think I'm going to allow the moment to slip away and let you slide off the hook by bringing me a cocktail, you're out of your mind."

She laughs. "What do you think is going to happen?"

"I don't know, but I'm dying to find out. At the moment I'm feeling just fine." In fact, looking up at her face, her body encased in the tight chemise, kneeling above me like a tigress, I am feeling almost euphoric, as if someone has shot me up with heroin.

She settles down with the sweet fragrance of her hair dulling my senses and her head on my shoulder. "Do you mind?"

"Oh, yeah. I hate it." As I lay sprawled on my back, Joselyn snuggles up against me, displacing every void of air between our bodies. Lying on her side, she raises a bent knee and rests it gently on top of my thigh. The tension causes me to stir in that place down below. She knows exactly what she's doing. She smiles and rhythmically rolls her knee gently across my groin.

I take a deep breath and arch my back.

"Relax," she says. "Focus on your mantra."

"I'm trying to, but they're pressing into the side of my chest at the moment."

Her breasts planted in my side, her back gently arched, she starts to laugh as her body stretches out and sculpts the perfect form of sensual desire.

I lift my right arm over her head so that I can cradle her. She stops laughing and snuggles in tighter.

Like a schoolboy, my heart pounding, I slowly move my hand down the smooth, silken finish of her chemise until my fingers reach the small of her back. They come to rest in that heaven above the arch of her buttocks as my fingers start to dance. Lazily they skim across the satin finish, feeling only the bump of a single chord, the waistband of her thong under the smooth, red-silken sea of the chemise.

"I'm glad that Herman found another room tonight." The warm, moist breath of her words in my ear ignites a sexual tingle of electricity that traverses my spine.

"Herman says I snore."

"I wouldn't call it snoring," she says. "They're actually just cute little occasional snorts."

"How do you know?"

"I heard it every once in a while between Herman's foghorn."

"When?"

"When I was outside your door at night."

"What were you doing outside the door?"

"I was beginning to wonder if you were ever going to come to my room. Obviously not," she says.

"I didn't . . . I mean I wasn't sure . . ."

She puts her finger over my lips. "Now is one of those moments when silence is best," she says. Her lips seal over my ear, her pointed, wet tongue penetrating to its inner depth as she quickly slides her hand from my lips down my chest and stomach under the open bottom of my shirt. Her nails, like talons, rake my stomach and chest. Passion seizes my lungs. I arch my back as her knee presses into the hardness at my groin. I listen and feel her hot, moist breath in my ear until her lips move, grazing my cheek.

Like a magnet, I turn my head, finding

her lips with my own, rolling up onto my side as I grab her in my arms, pressing her body to my own, our legs intertwined, our tongues doing a dance.

Suddenly she pushes with her hands. I don't want to let go. It feels so good to hold her, as if nature itself had reached a point of equilibrium, a tender balance of two human souls.

Suddenly she disengages. She's back up on her knees. I lay there wanton, baffled and befuddled. Then I realize her need and she starts to pull the shirt over my head. While I'm finishing with the shirt, her frenzied hands go to work feverishly at my belt.

"Maybe I should take a shower," I tell her.

"Later," she says. "Unless you want me to leave, in which case you better make it a cold one."

"Later would be best," I tell her. Before the words clear my lips, she smothers them with an openmouthed kiss as she pulls my pants down. Together we finally shed them over the edge of the bed, where the red chemise and Joselyn's thong join them.

She is back in my arms, the warm, tawny

glow of her nakedness against my flesh. Her lips press to my ear in a husky, sensuous voice: "If Herman calls now, he won't have to worry about Thorn. I will beat him to death with his own phone."

THIRTY-SEVEN

What they say about hell and good intentions is true. I had intended to call Herman by ten o'clock.

When the phone rings, somewhere muffled and distant, I gaze over and the clock on the nightstand reads 9:10. I rouse from a deep sleep to the feel of her warm body against me. Joselyn's tousled hair covers her face as it nuzzles into the cranny of my neck, her limp arm and sharp nails draped across my chest. Each time I move she sticks her claws in me like a cat.

When I see the sliver of bright light breaching the blackout curtains, I panic.

"Oh, shit." The phone is still ringing. But it's not night, it's the morning after.

I struggle to get up.

"Emmmmm!" Joselyn stirs and digs a fingernail into my nipple. "What time is it?"

"Morning," I tell her. I free myself from the claw.

"Where are you going?" She yawns, covers her mouth, and stretches under the covers.

"Looking for my phone." It's not on the nightstand. When it rings again I realize it's still strapped to the belt on my pants, down on the floor under the tangle of garments.

I lean over and fish my way through the red sexy thong and the chemise, trying to focus my eyes. I find my pants and feel for the phone, slide it out of the holster, and check the screen. It's Herman. I push the green button. "Hello!"

"Where were you? Took you long enough," he says.

"Couldn't find my phone."

"Hope you slept well, 'cause I've been up since six," he says.

"Where are you?" I swing my legs over the edge of the bed and sit up.

"I been on the road since six thirty," he says.

"You're tailing Thorn?"

"Yeah, and you're not gonna believe what I'm lookin' at right now."

"Where are you?"

Joselyn kneels up behind me on the bed and puts her arms around my chest, her chin on my shoulder from behind, and starts to graze me with her nails again. "What's happening?"

"Stop it."

"You didn't seem to mind last night."

"Is that who I think it is?" says Herman.

"Yeah. Tell me what's going on."

"You first," he says.

"Never mind. Just tell me where you are."

"Well, right now I'm on a narrow ledge of ground, on a hillside off a dirt road, lyin' on my stomach lookin' at some farmer's field through a pair of binoculars," says Herman. "According to the odometer, I'm about 12.8 miles south of Ponce and about a half mile east of the main highway. Thorn's got himself a makeshift landing strip out here."

"Is the plane there?"

"Yep. I'm looking at it right now. He's got it tucked away under some camouflage netting and a bunch of equipment down there. He's got one, two, three guys working with him. Looks like they're getting ready to do some painting and one guy's doing some welding."

"How do I get out there?" I ask.

"You want me to come get ya?"

"No. Stay there. Keep an eye on Thorn. If he leaves, follow him. I'll grab a taxi."

"Not without me you won't." Joselyn pushes off behind me, pulls the top sheet off the bed, and wraps it around herself. Then, as if in a gown with a long trail, she parades toward the bathroom, where she closes the door.

"I need to take a shower," I tell her.

"Go ahead, the door's unlocked," she hollers. "And you don't have anything I haven't already seen."

"Sounds like you had a better night than I did," says Herman.

"Yeah, well, what can I say?"

"You can give me a briefing," he says.

"Later. First tell me how to get out there." I grab a pen and the pad from the nightstand. Herman gives me detailed directions. I write it all down.

"Do me a favor," he says. "Have the driver

stop so you can get me a cup of coffee and somethin' to eat. Thorn gets up early and he moves fast. I can smell military all over him," says Herman. "I didn't get any breakfast."

"What do you want?"

"Steak and eggs, hash browns, side of pancakes, and a pot of coffee."

"Are you sure you don't want me to have this catered?" I say.

Herman laughs. "Driver might know where there's a good doughnut shop. Get me a big cup of coffee, one of those sixteen-ounce jobs, and a dozen doughnuts."

"You know those aren't good for you."

"Have 'em throw in some tofu," says Herman. "And make it two dozen if you guys are eatin'."

I check my watch. "It'll take me at least forty-five minutes to get there."

"Hurry up. I'm hungry," he says.

It takes us twenty minutes to shower, clean up, and get dressed. We grab a cab out in front and have him take us to a doughnut shop with a small market next door. Joselyn buys a couple small containers of fresh cut-up fruit and two plastic cartons of yogurt at the market while I get the doughnuts and three coffees.

She and I sit in the backseat of the taxi feasting on yogurt and fruit as we down our coffee. When I lift the lid on the dough-nut box for an inspection, she slaps my hand and seals the box shut.

"You sapped my vital juices," I tell her. "I need to keep up my strength."

"Sounds like Superman needs Viagra," she says. "There's nothing in that box but kryptonite. I noticed last night that your speeding bullet is already a little too quick." She glances at me sideways and smiles. How fast women become possessive.

"Is that so?"

"Uh-huh."

"Maybe I just need more time at the range," I tell her. "It could be that I'm out of practice." I squeeze her thigh through her jeans and she jumps, dropping a piece of fruit off her plastic fork into her lap.

She starts to laugh, wiping her mouth with a napkin. "Yeah, well, you start eating doughnuts and you'll be shooting blanks," she tells me. "And I got a flash for you. You won't be jumping me in a single bound.

Stick with me and I'll keep you healthy," she says.

"And what about happy?"

She turns to look at me. "I don't know. You'll have to judge that for yourself," she says.

THIRTY-EIGHT

The taxi driver finds the dirt road and a few hundred feet in I see Herman's rental car parked halfway into the brush off to the side.

We pull up. I pay the driver, grab Herman's coffee and the doughnut box, and Joselyn and I get out.

"Over here!" I hear Herman's voice beyond the brush.

We make our way between some bushes where Herman's big feet have beaten the grass down to make a narrow path.

He rolls over off his stomach and sits up as soon as he sees us. "Thought you guys were never gonna get here," he says. "I'm dyin'."

"Not to worry. Your friend brought you a box of poison," says Joselyn.

He reaches up and takes the coffee in one hand and hands me the field glasses with the other. I give him the doughnuts. He sets them on the ground and plucks the lid off the coffee. "Ah, good, cream," he says. "You remembered. Any sugar?"

"In the box with the doughnuts," I tell him.

He opens the lid and finds six packets. Herman holds them together in his big fingers and rips the tops off all of them in one move. Then he pours the contents into the hot coffee, stirring it like syrup with a plastic fork.

"We could just get a long needle and inject twenty pounds of sugar into your heart," says Joselyn. She stands there motionless looking at the steaming cup in Herman's hand as if it were a viper.

"What did I tell you when I first saw her?" says Herman. He talks without looking at us, picking through the box of doughnuts for his first victim. "All shapely and sexy like that. She's gotta be a health nut. Don't say I didn't warn you. Course there are advantages . . ."

"Yes, one tends to live longer," says Joselyn.

"That wasn't the advantage I had in mind," says Herman. "But I suppose it'll do. Watch the glasses." He looks at me as I scan the open field down below through the binoculars. "You're not careful, Thorn's gonna pick up glare off the front lens. Morning sun," he says.

I lower them. "So what do I do?"

"Baseball cap on the ground there," says Herman. "Use it to shield the front end a little bit. Keep the sunlight off them."

I settle onto the ground on my stomach, lay the baseball cap over the top of the fifty-power glasses with the bill sticking out over the two lenses. Then I focus them.

"Look to the left there, in the trees up at the end of the field," says Herman. "See the camouflage?"

"Oh, yeah. I see the plane but he's got it covered pretty well. Unless you were looking for it, you wouldn't see it."

"Wouldn't see it at all from the air," says

Herman, "not with the naked eye anyway. My guess is that's what he's worried about. Drug interdiction flights. Last few years that's become a heavy part of the action down here. If the cartels can bring their product in here, they're already inside the U.S. Customs zone."

"So what do you think Thorn's up to?" I ask.

"Haven't seen enough to know yet," he says. He grabs another doughnut and gulps some coffee.

"I don't know, but I doubt that it's drugs," says Joselyn. "Not unless he's changed. It's true it's been a long time. But I don't think so." Joselyn sees a small rock outcropping a few feet away. She steps over and dusts it off with her hand, very feminine, then turns and sits on it. "Do you see him down there? Thorn, I mean?" She looks at me.

"I don't know. I see three men working around the plane. One of them is up on a ladder, big extension thing, against the tail section," I tell her. "Another one's got a shorter ladder working against the side of the plane up forward, just in front of the wing."

"Yeah, he's been taping down paper," says Herman, "some big pieces. Looks like they painted the fuselage white, then did the whole tail section that dark blue. Sort of a cone shape on an angle all the way down underneath the tail."

"I see it," I tell him.

"Now they're gettin' ready to put up a logo or some letters. I'm not sure," says Herman.

"Yeah, I hear the compressor, but I don't see it," I tell him.

"They must have it in the plane to keep the noise down. You can hear that thing all the way out here every time they fire it up," he says. "They had it going a few minutes ago, just before you got here. They were clearing two spray guns. Shot a lot of red and blue paint all over the grass."

"Looks like we got company."

An old beat-up Ford F-250 pickup truck is coming down the runway, moving fast, coming this way. For a moment I wonder if the driver has seen us.

"That's Thorn's truck. I followed it on the way out here," says Herman. "We better get out of here."

"Hold on. He's stopping," I say.

Herman turns to look.

Joselyn is on her feet, standing next to him, shading her eyes with one hand and staring down at the field.

The truck is stopped, no more than a quarter of a mile away. The driver is getting out. He goes in the back to the open bed of the truck and lifts out a cardboard box. He carries it over and sets it down on the field. Then he walks back to the pickup.

"I don't think he's seen us," I tell them.

This time he reaches inside the cab. He steps back and closes the door. He has two items, one in each hand. The one in his right hand looks like a laptop. I can't make out what the other one is. It's too small.

"What's he doing?" says Herman.

"I don't know." I have the field glasses fixed on his face at the moment. "I think that's our man."

"Let me see," says Joselyn.

I hand her the glasses.

She raises them to her eyes. "How do you adjust them?"

"The toggle on top." I show her.

She focuses in. Then suddenly takes a

deep breath. "Yes. That's him. I would know that face anywhere," she says. When she passes the glasses back to me, her hand is trembling.

By the time I refocus and acquire his image once more, Thorn is down on one knee in the field. He is working on something, but I can't see it. His back is to me, shielding whatever it is that he has on the ground. He reaches into the cardboard box with one hand and takes out two wires. They look like leads connected to something in the box.

A few seconds later he stands and flings something into the air. He does it almost casually, backhanded, with a flick of his wrist. Whatever it is, it doesn't fall to the ground. Instead it flies off, like a bird, silent and fast into the distance, where I lose it.

"What the hell was that?" I ask.

"I don't know," says Herman. "I saw it too, then it just disappeared."

"What's he doing?" I ask.

"He's flying it," says Joselyn. "What you just saw is an MAV."

"What the hell's an MAV?" I ask.

"Micro air vehicle," she says. "It's military

hardware. Latest cutting edge. Like a model airplane, only smaller."

"I don't hear any motor," I tell her.

"It's electric. High speed. They use them for surveillance, but use your imagination. With the advances in miniaturization, almost anything's possible."

"How do you know about this stuff?" I ask.

"Part of the new generation of weapons systems," she says. "Designers, kids from Stanford, get hung up on it because it's novel and looks cute and the military tells them it's harmless. But the range of possible applications is insidious. I think we should be going."

"Why?" says Herman.

"Because we can't see that thing," says Joselyn, "but if it's what I think it is, it can probably see us."

"You mean it's got a camera?" I say.

"A camera, infrared sensors, I don't know, but look at him." She gestures toward Thorn out in the field.

I train the glasses back on him. He's standing up, holding the laptop in one hand while he manipulates what looks like a small joystick with the other.

"He's not looking up in the air, is he?" she says.

"No. He's looking down at the computer screen."

"So?" says Herman.

"So he's flying whatever it is using the eye that's on board that little devil," she says. "Which means he can see everything on the ground as he flies over it."

It's hard to know where it is because we can't follow Thorn's line of sight to track the small model in the air. Then suddenly Thorn turns and looks across the field.

"I got it." In the sunlight with the glasses I pick up the glint off one of the wings. The only reason I can see it is because it's almost stationary in the sky, doing a tight circle, hovering over an area on the other side of the field.

"Where?" says Herman.

"There." I point. "See the little metal shed over there? Looks like a pump house?"

"Yeah."

"Look directly above it."

"Oh, yeah," he says. "Looks like a little dot."

Suddenly the little plane darts away. It moves off just a bit and then drops down quickly and starts to fly in a slow, lazy circle at rooftop height around the corrugated-steel pump house. The building is more of a box, perhaps four feet square and eight feet high, with a slanted shed roof that pitches this way. The metal is all rusted, as if it's been there for a hundred years.

The model turns, heading toward the building. I expect it to fly over the shed roof but it doesn't. Instead, the model noses up just as it gets there and stalls. Suddenly it falls like a rock, hits the roof, and slides off and hits the ground.

"So much for that," I say.

Thorn grabs the box, gets in the pickup, and races across the field. He parks close to the pump house, then retrieves the little plane. He checks it out.

"Maybe he broke it," says Herman.

"I don't know. It looks like he's adjusting something under the wings," I tell them. "That's got to be the smallest model plane I've ever seen. It's not much bigger than his hand. It looks like four bent wires coming out underneath. They look like the legs on an insect."

"Let me see," says Joselyn.

I hand her the glasses. She focuses and looks. "Climbing, perching, and jumping," she says. "It's what they're working on."

"What?" I say.

"There're like feet or something attached to the ends of the wires."

Within seconds he flings it into the air again, opens the computer, and starts all over.

"What's he doing, playing?" I ask.

"I don't think so," says Joselyn.

Thorn flies the model around the shed twice and then approaches from the same direction, straight in toward the roof. At the last second he noses up and the little plane falls from the air once more. Only this time it doesn't slide off the roof. It stays there, upright, as if there is something holding it in place.

"Son of a gun. He did it," she says.

"Did what?" says Herman.

"He perched it on the roof," she says. "From everything I've read, they haven't been able to do that yet."

"What?" I ask.

"The military has been putting out RFPs, requests for proposals, to contractors for

several years. They're looking for somebody who can design a micro air vehicle
that can perch on the side of a building."

"Why would they want to do that?" says
Herman.

"Because if you can attach enough things
to the side of a building and equip them with
listening devices, you can pick up everything going on inside. The power to recharge
the batteries you get from a photoelectric
cell. A fly on the wall could stay there for
years," she says.

"You work with some very insidious
people," I tell her.

"I don't work with them. I just know about
them."

"You think that's what he's doing, trying
to pick up surveillance?" says Herman.

"I don't know," says Joselyn. "I know they
have stuff that can fly and climb. And they're
working on weapons systems, some of
them no bigger than the tip of your finger.
They say within a few years they'll have
robotic insects the size of a grasshopper
armed with lethal toxins and heat sensors
to home in on the human body. They could
release them by the millions using missiles

tipped with cluster bombs. If they can do that, they can do anything."

"Where do you guys get this stuff?" I ask.

"It's not science fiction," says Joselyn. The second she says It I hear a high-speed whirring sound. It comes from behind us, sounds like the wings of a hummingbird, and races over our heads. It's gone before we can even see it.

"Son of a bitch," says Herman.

When I look out at the field, Thorn is standing there holding the computer, looking down at the screen. The little model is no longer perched on the roof.

"Let's get out of here," says Joselyn.

"It's too late. He's seen us," says Herman, who is already halfway to the car.

I lift the binoculars up to my eyes with one hand. "What the hell is that?" I am looking back at the jet under the camouflage netting. The rear ramp is now down. The man who was doing the welding is testing the motor that lifts the ramp up and down. As I look at it I realize why. The ramp was never designed to carry the kind of weight represented by the bomb. Resting on a steel cradle just above the stairs is the massive casing of a torpedo-shaped device.

"I gotta call Thorpe," I tell her.

"Later," she says.

I pull out my cell phone.

"Not now," she says.

"Just a second." I fumble with the applications until I find the camera. I look at the screen on the phone and wait for the ramp to come down again. It won't be a great picture but it's better than nothing.

"We don't have enough time," she says.

Thorn is down on one knee out in the field with the open cardboard box next to him.

The ramp starts to come down.

Thorn is charging up the little bird for another look. He finishes and then slowly stands, turns around, and looks up. Like a flashbulb going off in his head, he suddenly realizes what's on display under the belly of the big plane. He spins around and looks up toward where Joselyn and I are standing. I don't think he can see us, but he knows we're here.

I wait until the end of the ramp reaches the ground, like a yawning mouth, and then I snap the picture.

It's a footrace for the car, with Joselyn out in front. Herman is already behind the wheel, with the engine running.

We jump in the back and Joselyn yells, "Move!"

"Do you think he saw us?" I ask.

"I don't, but I think we better find another way out of here," she says.

THIRTY-NINE

There's a map in the glove compartment," says Herman.

He is ripping along the dirt road doing at least fifty miles an hour, fishtailing in the sandy soil. Joselyn and I are bouncing around in the backseat. My head hits the ceiling of the car.

"Get the map," he says.

"I'm trying. Slow down or you're going to kill us. We won't have to worry about Thorn," I tell him.

"Where does this road lead?" says Joselyn.

Herman is driving farther into the brushy

hillside, away from the pavement we came in on.

"It'll take us back to the highway," says Herman. "There's a turn, but I'm not sure where."

"How do you know?" I ask.

"'Cause I checked the map to make sure I had a way out before I parked," he says. "But I don't want to make a wrong turn."

He slows for a few seconds and I reach over from the backseat, into the glove compartment, and pull out a folded single-page Avis map.

Herman glances over. "No, not that one. The one underneath."

I fish around inside and find another, thicker map. As soon as I slump into the backseat I unfold it and it opens up like an accordion, enough paper to seal off the backseat. It's a geodetic survey map showing the island in sections. "Did this come with the car?"

"No. Bought it yesterday while you guys were napping," says Herman. "One of the little shops next to the hotel. Look for the exit off the highway you came in on and find the dirt road."

Joselyn and I search for it until we find

the right quarter section and then home in. "Here it is." She points with her finger. "Let me have it." She plucks it out of my hands.

We are climbing higher on the hillside, well above the trees at the end of the airfield. The plane is no longer visible down below, lost in the morass of foliage and the camouflage. But in the distance behind us I can see a trail of dust in the air. "Somebody's on our tail," I tell him.

"I see him," says Herman.

"I hope you're right about there being a way out of here."

"He is," says Joselyn. "There's a fork up ahead, take it to the right."

"Good girl," says Herman. He gooses the engine and we start to slide around in the backseat.

"There's another turn to the right about a quarter of a mile beyond that," she tells him. "Then it looks like it turns to pavement. You take it all the way to the highway."

"That's the one," says Herman. "It's Thorn behind us. I got a glimpse of the pickup when he rounded one of the bends back there."

I turn and look. I see the dust, maybe half a mile behind us and closing fast, like a cyclone.

Herman takes the fork to the right and a quarter of a mile beyond it takes a sharp right, nearly lifting the car up on two wheels.

"Maybe he'll take the wrong cut at the fork," I tell them.

"No," says Herman. "He's still behind us."

I turn to take a peek. Herman's right. The looming dust devil is still behind us and getting closer.

A hundred feet beyond the turn, the wheels grind over gravel and onto solid pavement. The road smooths out and Herman pushes the pedal to the floor. The midsize four-cylinder picks up speed, but we'll never make it to the highway. The minute Thorn hits the pavement, the big Ford V-8 will run us down in less than a mile. And I am guessing that Thorn is probably armed to the teeth.

We swing around a curve, coming down the hillside. I can see the highway in the distance, maybe two miles off. The road we are on rolls over the hillocks like a ribbon leading right to it.

"Hang on," says Herman. Suddenly the car swings to the right, skids on the pavement, and rolls onto a gravel road.

"Where are you going? It's a dead end," I tell him.

"I know," says Herman. He pulls up about fifty feet and turns to the left into some heavy brush, then slams on the brakes and turns off the engine. "Get out of the car." Herman grabs the field glasses and opens his door.

Joselyn and I follow him over the rough ground into the brush.

"Come on," says Herman. He leads us toward a small rock outcropping, kneels down, and sets up with the glasses.

Joselyn and I really don't need them, we can see the ribbon of paved road leading down to the highway just off to our left.

"Shhh . . ." Herman holds a finger to his lips and listens.

I hear the high-speed rush of rubber on the road, and a second later the rush of air as a vehicle races past the gravel turnoff. An instant later I see the Ford pickup as it blasts into the open and races down the road toward the highway. I'm guessing that he's doing close to a hundred miles an hour. It takes Thorn less than a minute to reach the intersection on this side of the highway. You can see the truck's tail end lift up as the brake lights come on. Thorn screeches to a complete stop right in the middle of the road.

There's a little chuckle next to me. Herman is looking through the field glasses. "That's the problem with the dust when you're chasing somebody. You can't be sure how far behind you are. It's not like being out in front. That's why I pulled off," he says. "The curve back there. Once he rounded it we were dead. He woulda seen us and run us down before we got to the highway. Now he's sitting there getting whiplash, lookin' both ways 'cause he can't be sure which way we went, right toward Ponce or left toward San Juan. Wanna look?" He hands me the glasses.

"I'll take your word for it. I'm still trying to keep my breakfast down," I tell him.

"You got a bad inner ear. There he goes." Herman is back looking through the field glasses.

As I look toward the highway, I see the pickup truck speed across the double lanes and turn left, heading north.

"He figures we're running for the big city and the airport," says Herman.

"Aren't we?" says Joselyn.

"Not till we make a phone call," says Herman.

* * *

Part of what Thorn was being paid for was to think on his feet, and to do it quickly. He'd raced no more than three miles north on the highway before he realized that he'd lost them.

He turned around and sped back to the airfield. Thorn knew that by now the trio on the hillside would be calling the cops.

He and the two Mahdi pilots loaded the jet with four empty fifty-gallon paint drums, along with two others that were half full of the diesel fuel used to run the compressor. They strapped everything down so it wouldn't move.

They grabbed as much of the large brown masking paper as they could and tossed it on board, and then ripped off what was left on the side of the plane.

Most of the painting was done, though not all of it. They would have to finish the rest when they got where they were going.

They threw the air hoses and spray guns inside the plane. Thorn grabbed the large attaché case containing the little brown bat and the laptop that controlled it as well as the battery-charging unit that was in the cardboard box. He put it all on board the plane. The only thing he couldn't get was his luggage at the Hotel Belgica. He would have to take care of that later by phone. He was confident there was no way the authorities could connect the mysterious missing jetliner to the Charles Johnston who checked out of the Hotel Belgica by telephone.

All the heavy work on the plane was done. The bomb in the tail section was strapped down and concealed inside the closed airstairs. Anyone looking at the plane from the outside would conclude that the rear ramp that once existed was now sealed up and no longer functional. This was the fate of many of the ramps on the old planes, most notably those that weren't equipped with a Cooper Vane.

The two pylons were problematic, but they were relatively small, designed for jet fighters. They were lost under the large wings of the big airliner. On the ground, especially without attached ordnance, no one would notice them.

The two small air-to-air missiles were still in crates in the back of the plane. They had been easy to obtain, and relatively cheap. Whereas a shoulder-fired ground-to-air missile could cost upward of two hundred thousand dollars on the black market, an air-to-air missile like the two old French Magic heat seekers, which were now considered obsolete, could be picked up for a few thousand dollars. They weighed less than two hundred pounds each and required no sophisticated target-tracking system to use them.

A well-armed terrorist with an airframe like the 727 could have armed it with a load of obsolete Magic missiles under each wing, set out over the Atlantic beyond ground-based radar, and in a single day taken down a score of commercial jetliners flying in and out of the East Coast.

Thorn had already trained the two Mahdi pilots in how to mount the missiles on the pylons and how to pull the arming ribbons before they took off. And where they were headed, it wouldn't matter, because there

would be no one around to see them
do it.

* * *

I start calling from my cell phone before
we reach the rental car still parked behind
the bushes near the dead-end gravel road.
I call 911 and wait for the dispatcher's
voice to come on. Then I explode all over
her in a litany of information, drowning her
in details, everything we've seen during
the last hour.

"Wait, wait, wait," she says. "Is this an
emergency? Is someone injured?"

"No," I tell her. "But a lot of people are
going to be dead real soon if you don't
send somebody out here now."

"I don't understand. Slow down, calm
down, and tell me one more time," she says.

I take a deep breath and then in a calm
voice tell her about the plane, the bomb,
the camo netting, and the grassy airstrip. I
tell her what we know about Thorn and,
halfway through what must sound like an
incredible tale she stops me and says,
"Who are you? What's your name?"

I tell her.

"Where are you right now?" The way
she says this makes me wonder if she's

about to dispatch a few male nurses from a local mental institution to come and pick me up.

"We're standing on a hillside about fifteen miles south of Ponce, just off the main highway."

"And you're telling me you've seen all of this?"

"Yes, damn it!"

"Just a minute," she says. She puts me on hold.

Herman, Joselyn, and I stand by the car.

"What are they saying?" says Joselyn.

"Nothing. I'm on hold."

* * *

In less than half an hour, Thorn and the two Madhi pilots had buttoned up the plane, turned it around, and were jetting down the runway, leaving the welder to load up his equipment in the back of Thorn's pickup and disappear.

The jet had enough fuel for about three hours of flight time. Thorn intended to make the most of it. He needed a cover story, one that would fit like a glove into everything his visitors were about to report to the cops. If it worked, it would put a quick end to the search for the plane.

As soon as the wheels cleared the runway, he lifted the landing gear, started to climb to altitude, and reached down and turned on the mode C transponder. He dialed in a number at random.

This immediately gave away their location. The instant the plane showed up on radar in the control tower at Mercedita Airport, three miles outside Ponce, the controllers in the tower went nuts.

Thorn was flying directly into the approach pattern of incoming planes and he knew it.

Frantically they tried to reach him by radio using the squawk number from the transponder. "Unidentified 2416, come in! You are entering controlled air space. Come in!"

Thorn ignored them as the two Mahdi pilots looked on, fear and puzzlement written all over their faces.

"Not to worry," said Thorn. "I thought you were prepared to die."

The 727 continued to climb. Off in the distance Thorn could see a large wide-bodied jet, its wheels and flaps down, its landing lights on. It was descending, steaming this way on a clear approach to Mercedita.

Thorn gently eased the 727 to the right until it was virtually nose on to the incoming plane. By now the chatter on the radio was frantic. "Do me a favor, turn that off," said Thorn.

Ahmed, the Saudi flyer now sitting in the right-hand seat, looked as if he was about to wet his pants. He reached over and turned off the radio, then turned his gaze, his eyes wide like saucers, back toward the front windscreen.

"Put your hands on the throttles," said Thorn.

Ahmed looked at him and tentatively reached for the throttle controls.

"Gimme full power, when I tell you. Not before! You got it?"

Ahmed said nothing. He was frozen with fear.

"Answer me. Do you understand?"

"Yes." Ahmed's fingers turned white strangling the plastic tops of the throttle controls as the nose of the giant wide-bodied plane suddenly filled the glass panel in front of him. He looked down and winced, and hunched up his body for the impact as Thorn yelled: "Now!"

Ahmed pushed the throttles all the way forward as Thorn pulled the yoke back hard. The nose of the 727 soared upward. The colliding air turbulence from the massive jet hit them like a brick wall. It rattled the old airframe and shook it nearly to pieces. Thorn could feel the pressure on the foot pedals as the two rear elevators flapped like bird wings. "God damn, that's a rush!" he yelled. The old plane jolted as if it were strapped to the back of a bucking bull.

"They don't make 'em like that anymore, hey, Ahmed?" He looked over at the Saudi. "What am I asking you for? You wouldn't know."

Ahmed glared at the infidel and then gave him a ghost of a smile and nodded. It was always best to humor those who were insane. God often protected them.

* * *

"I talked to my supervisor. We can dispatch a squad car from Ponce but it will take a while for them to get there," she tells me.

"We don't need a squad car!" I say. "We need a tactical unit. You send a cop out to that field alone, he's going to get killed."

"Are you telling me that they're armed?" she says.

"Lady, they've got a bomb. What do you call that?" I ask. As I am talking, I hear the jet engines approaching from the distance.

"You don't have to yell," she says. "I'll see what I can do. But I will tell you that the nearest tactical unit is in San Juan. It would take them at least an hour to get there, maybe longer."

"Isn't there a military base at this end of the island that can scramble planes?"

"There was, but no more. There's a DEA unit at Ramey," she says.

"Well, then, damn it, tell them there're drugs on board that plane," I tell her.

"You didn't say nothing about drugs before."

"I am now."

"Listen," she says. "It's a serious matter to make a false report. You can get into a lot of trouble. Do you understand?" As she is talking I see the giant airliner already in the air heading straight up over our heads. I can no longer hear her on the phone. For almost half a minute the noise of the jet engines drowns her out.

"Yes, and if there's a tape of this conversation and Thorn drops that bomb on a population center, somebody is going to want to boil you and your supervisor in oil," I tell her. "Never mind, it's too late."

"We have limited resources. There's only so much we can do," she says. "And as I tol' you, we don't have no tactical unit at that end of the island. I'll do what I can."

"Thank you," I tell her. "In the meantime, do you have the local number for the FBI?"

"You can get that through information," she says. She tells me that we should wait out on the highway for the police to show up.

I hang up and tell Herman what's happened and he laughs. "Maybe we should just go home," he says.

"At least one of you is beginning to talk sensibly," says Joselyn.

FORTY

By the time the cops show up and we get to the airfield, everything is gone, including the plane, Thorn, and his comrades. All that is left is some abandoned equipment—a generator, a compressor, some spray rigs, and a lot of trash.

I try to show them the photo taken on my cell phone but they are not impressed. You have to use your imagination to make out the plane, and the bomb is virtually invisible.

There is a large empty wooden crate marked MACHINE PARTS. I try to convince them that the bomb must have been shipped in it. The crate looks about the right size.

The cops tell me it could have been drugs. They will bring the dogs out in the morning and have them sniff around. If there are drugs or munitions, the dogs will pick up the scent.

They tell us they will make a report and conduct an investigation.

Before they could even get started, a call comes in on their radio that a large multiengine jet has gone down out over the ocean following a near collision with another plane.

I look at Herman. "There goes our only lead to Liquida."

"Look at it this way," says Joselyn. "At least Thorn's dead. And that bomb is gone."

"There was no bomb," says one of the cops. "According to the tower, the pilot admitted there were drugs on board."

"If you say so," says Joselyn.

A half hour of driving, and an hour of paperwork, filling out and signing reports at the police station in Ponce, and we finally make it back to the Hotel Melia. The steady flow of adrenaline has left us exhausted, strung out, and depressed.

We put everything we saw in the police

report, though the cops virtually dismissed any thought of a bomb. They told us that the Coast Guard would search the waters until dark and go back out in the morning, but that hope of finding anything was slim. The plane had gone down over the Puerto Rico Trench, one of the deepest areas of ocean in the world.

Joselyn, Herman, and I sit around in the bar downstairs having drinks, trying to figure out what to do next. It was a stone wall. With no leads, there was nothing left.

"I'm gonna have to call Sarah and tell her," I say.

"Tell her what?" says Herman.

"I don't know."

"You think it's safe to bring her home?" he says.

"No."

"Then what are you going to do?" says Joselyn.

"I don't know."

"Well, I know what I have to do," says Herman. "I'm not sleeping over at the Belgica after what's happened today. Is that extra room still open upstairs?"

"Yeah," I tell him.

"I gotta go over and pick up my stuff," he says.

"I'm going to head up and take a shower," says Joselyn.

I give her the room key. "Guess I'll go with Herman to pick up his bags."

"Where are you sleeping tonight?" she says.

"I don't know, any ideas?" I ask.

"See you upstairs," she says.

"Bless you," says Herman.

She laughs and heads the other way.

Herman finishes his drink and we head for the car.

*   *   *

From years of experience Thorn had learned that in his line of work, you never did anything without a backup plan. And if you were smart, you had more than one.

After the near midair collision Thorn took the plane up to twenty thousand feet and flew due west until he was about thirty miles out over the ocean. He turned on the radio and called in a mayday. He reported damage from the near collision and acknowledged that there were drugs on board. He told the air-traffic controllers he was having engine trouble and reported a hydraulic leak.

A couple of minutes later Thorn nosed the plane into a steep dive, but not before lowering his flaps and dropping his wheels to slow his speed. At a thousand feet he turned off the transponder and leveled off. With his speed still reduced and watching his fuel, Thorn lowered the ramp at the back.

The bomb was bolted in place. The rollers that released it from its cradle wouldn't move unless the safety bolts were pulled and the two metal straps holding the bomb in place were removed.

The drag on the plane from the shifting weight and the air resistance from the lowered ramp were considerable. Thorn put the plane into a mild turn, dipping the port wing and adjusting the throttles to give the plane enough power to keep it in the air. Thorn checked the altimeter.

He turned the flight controls over to Ahmed and told him to maintain altitude at five hundred feet and to hold the turn.

Over the horizon and under the radar, the controllers in the tower at Mercedita would assume that the plane went into the water.

"Okay?" He looked at Ahmed, who glanced at him nervously and nodded as he gripped the controls.

Thorn watched him for a few seconds until he was satisfied, then he and the other pilot went to the back of the plane. They gathered all of the brown paper masking panels from the paint job and tossed them out through the open airstairs in the back. The empty paint drums followed. Thorn was careful not to allow any of them to strike the area near the tail of the bomb where the snap-out fins deployed.

Finally he grabbed the two fuel cans and poured enough diesel fuel out the back end of the plane to leave a sheen on the surface of the water below. Then he tossed the two empty fuel drums out. He took one last look to make sure everything was floating nicely on the surface of the sea down below. "Good!"

Then he went back up to the flight deck and closed the airstairs, bringing up the ramp. Thorn lifted the wheels, brought up the flaps, and took over the controls again. Checking his fuel, he goosed the throttles and brought the plane onto a heading due south.

He hopped the waves, hugging the water for more than eighty miles, and didn't turn on the transponder. He did turn on the radio and listened while the tower at Mercedita called in the Coast Guard and launched a search and rescue for the downed plane.

Thorn stayed under the radar and didn't pop up again, not even when he reached his destination. It was the small island of Vieques, off the southern tip of Puerto Rico. There was a fair-size general aviation airport on the eastern side of the island. From there Thorn could take one of the twin-engine commuter flights to San Juan and catch a direct flight to D.C. in the morning. But at the moment that wasn't where he was headed.

On the western side, near a beautiful cove, the azure waters and white sand beaches concealed a deadly secret. The island was badly polluted. For fifty years the western side of Vieques had been a bombing range for the U.S. Navy. Tons of high-explosive ordnance had been dropped all over the island, and heavy metals, including mercury and lead, now contaminated large parts of it.

The people who lived there were territorial subjects. They lacked the wealth and political influence to launch the kind of "not in my backyard" movements that had shut down most of the military bombing ranges on the U.S. mainland. It wasn't until the base closure commissions began shutting down military facilities across the country that a coalition of environmentalists and islanders finally waged a successful battle to oust the navy. The old bombing range was turned over to the Department of the Interior, while bureaucrats argued over who was going to clean up the mess.

Meanwhile, the buildings at what had been the navy's old Camp Garcia lay abandoned. All that remained was a five-thousand-foot runway and a small unmanned weather station. It was the perfect location for stashing the plane.

All Thorn needed to buy two nights, two days, and a load of Jet A fuel from the airport on the other side of the island was a plausible story. The empty jet was under a lease arrangement, a replacement craft deadheading from Houston to San Juan to carry freight. The partially completed paint job would enhance the story, and they painted the logos on the side of the plane as they waited. The story would be that they had developed a serious engine problem and that Thorn had to set it down on the abandoned runway when he found it available on his charts. No one would be looking for him there. It would be at least a day or two, maybe longer, before they realized there was no real wreckage in the waters west of Mercedita. By then the plane would be gone, the mission completed.

Ten minutes before landing, just off the southern tip of Puerto Rico, Thorn checked his cell phone for a signal. When he got one he made one phone call, to the front desk at the Hotel Belgica.

FORTY-ONE

The Belgica is one of those cozy boutique hotels you often find tucked away in the old world cities of Europe, only this one has a Latin flavor to it.

When I walk through the front door behind Herman, I see that the lobby is small, and at the moment there is no one at the front desk.

Herman and I go up to his room. It takes him five minutes to throw his dirty underwear in his bag and gather his shaving kit and other toiletries from the bathroom. He does one last check of the closet and looks

around to make sure he hasn't left anything, and we head out.

As I turn toward the stairs, Herman is
behind me.

"Hold on a second," he says.

I turn. "Did you forget something?"

He shakes his head, puts his finger to
his lips in a sign of silence, and then points
back behind us down the hallway. "That's
Thorn's room," he whispers. The door is
wide open and the light is on.

"You think maybe the cops?" I'm up close
in his ear.

He shakes his head. Herman's not sure.

We move slowly down the hall toward
the open door. When we get there we see
some luggage assembled on the floor, a
large black roller and a smaller one. The
bed's been stripped, all the sheets and towels in a pile on the floor. The closet door is
open and there is a light on in the bathroom
but no sign of anyone inside.

Herman slowly steps into the room, looks
one way and then the other. He doesn't
see anyone. I step in behind him. He checks
the closet. There are two shirts hanging
inside.

While he's doing that, I check the luggage tags. They are only temporary, paper, the kind of tags you get from the airlines when you check your luggage. The name on them is Charles Johnston, 113 Calle Once, Havana, Cuba.

I look at the smaller case, reach down and start to unzip it.

"Excuse me! What do you think you are doing?"

The voice sends me out of my skin. I turn around and there's a guy standing in the bathroom door looking at me. "Who are you?" he says.

Herman steps out of the closet. The guy looks at him. "Oh, señor, it's you." The guy in the doorway seems relieved.

Herman says: "Ah, my friend. This is the young man I was telling you about." Herman looks at me and smiles. "Pablo, correct?"

"That's right," says the kid.

"This is the young man at the desk," says Herman. "Very enterprising fellow. This is one of my associates. Pablo, meet Paul. Two Pablos, how about that?" he says.

I laugh and step away from the bag that

I was about to rifle, so that I can shake his hand. Perhaps for a smile and a few dollars he'll let us search the bags.

"Were you able to deliver your papers to Señor Johnston?" asks Pablo.

"Sadly, no," says Herman.

"That's too bad, because I'm afraid he's checked out."

Herman starts to laugh as if the kid has made a joke about death.

"I take it you've talked to the police?" I say.

"No." The kid turns serious. "Why would I talk to the police?" It's obvious he doesn't know that Thorn is dead.

"You said he checked out," says Herman.

"*Sí*, about an hour ago."

Herman looks at me.

"He was here?" says Herman.

"No. No. He called to say that he couldn't make it back to the hotel. Tol' me to put all the charges on his credit card and have his bags forwarded to his new hotel."

"Where's that?" I say.

"Oh, well, I'm not sure I should say," he says.

"Did he say where he was when he called?" I ask.

The kid makes a face, like maybe yes, maybe no.

"Listen, you've been very helpful," says Herman. "Lemme show you how much we appreciate it." Herman steps in front of me, then turns his back to the kid and rubs his thumb and forefinger together—the international gesture for money—as I reach for my wallet.

I pull out four twenties. Herman reaches around my hand and plucks out two crisp one-hundred-dollar bills from my open billfold. Before I can say a word, he is over in front of Pablo, stuffing them in the kid's breast pocket.

"Oh, thank you, señor."

"It's nothing," says Herman. "After all, we're all in business to make a profit, and you are a very good businessman."

"Oh, yes, I wish to be one day."

"Oh, you already are," says Herman. "It's the information age. The most valuable commodity there is."

"Yes, of course," says the kid. "I dunno where he is. He called on his cell phone."

"When exactly?" I say.

"As I say, maybe an hour ago. Perhaps less."

"You're sure it was him?" says Herman.

"Oh, yeah. He thank me for putting the muffins and fruit in the bag for him this morning. We're not supposed to open the continental breakfast until seven. But as you know, he left early. He tol' me to put all the room charges on his credit card and ship the bags to a hotel in Washington, D.C., overnight," he says. "I tol' him we can ship them air freight, express overnight, but it's expensive. Besides, they won't ship until tomorrow, and they don't deliver on Sunday, so he won't get it till Monday. He said he didn't care. To put it on his hotel tab, and to give myself a nice tip. He didn't say how much."

"I'm sure you'll figure it out," says Herman.

I am thinking that it probably won't matter, as Thorn no doubt stole the credit card from somebody else.

"I wonder if you could get the address for us, the hotel in Washington where the bags are going?" says Herman. "It would be a big help."

"It's downstairs. I'll go get it," he says. He takes two steps toward the door and stops. "Maybe I should take the bags down first."

"We'll watch them," says Herman.

"Okay. Be right back."

The second he leaves the room, Herman and I open both bags. Dirty clothes, two pairs of shoes, one of them dress shoes polished like a mirror, a shaving kit, neatly packed, almost anal. Herman is right. Thorn is military. Everything packed in its proper place.

"The kid didn't pack like this," I say.

"No," says Herman.

It's obvious that Thorn was getting ready to leave.

We dump everything out on the bed and start pawing through it. I check the pockets of the pants for anything left behind. They are all empty.

I slide my hand along the inside edge of the small case, into the elastic pouch where small items are sometimes stored. I find a plastic sewing kit, needles and thread, some matches, and a unique folding knife. It has a clear plastic handle through which you can see the blade.

I wonder how Thorn gets it through airport security until I open it and realize that the four-inch razor-sharp blade is ceramic. The handle is formed from a clear solid block of acrylic. To a scanner the knife would be virtually invisible.

I continue my search along the inside edge until I feel something solid rub against the back of my hand. It's not inside the elastic pouch but behind the lining of the suitcase itself. I open the ceramic knife and slice the lining of the case, reach inside, and pull out not one, but three separate passports: one French, one British, and the last one U.S. I open them. They all have the same photograph of Thorn but different names.

"From my recollection, they look better than the ones you and I bought down in Costa Rica," says Herman. "And a much clearer picture of the man. No wonder he wants the suitcase back." Herman grabs all three of the passports and slips them into his pocket.

We're running out of time. I hear the kid coming up the stairs.

Herman grabs the knife, folds it up, and slips it into his pocket. "Keep goin', I'll keep him busy." He steps out into the hallway. A second later I hear the two of them talking, this time in Spanish, down the hall near the head of the stairs.

I run my hand along the liner until I feel something else. It's not a passport. It's too small. I try to reach it with my fingers through the slit in the lining, but I can't quite get it.

I look for the knife and realize it's gone. The voices are moving this way.

Herman tells Pablo he wants to check out. He tries to draw him back toward the stairs.

"Okay, but I should lock up," says Pablo. "I must not leave Señor Johnston's bags unattended."

I rip the lining and reach inside. It's a small black book the size of a pocket calendar. I don't have time to open it. I just jam it in my pocket and start throwing clothes and shoes, the shaving kit, all of it in a jumbled mess inside the suitcases. I zip up the large bag, set it on the floor, and pull the zipper around on the smaller one just as I hear them approach the doorway. I set it on the floor, then turn and smile.

"Did you get the address?" I ask.

"Absolutely," says Herman. "Pablo is very efficient and professional. He assures me that he said nothing to Señor Johnston about our efforts to serve him."

"Good man," I tell him.

"Of course, that is your business," says Pablo. "When I give my word, it is important that I keep it."

"Yes, indeed," says Herman. "Let's let Pablo lock up so I can go down and check out. Then we gotta get out of here."

"Yes, we do," I tell him.

Less than an hour later, we're back in the room at the Hotel Melia. Joselyn dries her hair with a towel and watches over my shoulder as Herman and I pore over the booty from Thorn's suitcases.

Herman opens up one of the passports and shows her a more current picture of Thorn.

"He hasn't changed much at all," she says. "That's how I remember him from Seattle. Dorian Gray."

"What's this, I wonder?" I'm looking through the little black book. The first page is covered in a long series of numbers, dark blue ink pressed firmly into the paper as if the writer has a tendency to push too hard.

"It looks like a code of some kind," says Joselyn.

There is a separate set of numbers on each line.

"Could be dates," says Joselyn.

"What do you mean? There're too many numbers on each line," I say.

"Turn the page," she says.

I do it and the numbers continue, for two more pages. The writing is precise, very neat, but looks hard, as if the ballpoint engraved itself in the fine paper.

"What it looks like to me is a series of dates," says Joselyn, "at least the first six numbers on each line. Look, they're set off by a space from the rest of the numbers on the line. It's like two columns. The dates could be international style, not like we do it in the States. The number of the day followed by the number of the month, and then the last two digits for the year."

"Then what's the rest of it?" I ask. "The other numbers?"

Joselyn uses her finger and counts the numbers on each line. "Assuming the first six numbers represent dates, then there are ten additional numbers on each line. Could be phone numbers," she says. "Area code and then seven more for the local number. Give me a second," she says.

She tosses the towel on the bed and gets her cell phone out of her purse. "Take the numbers on the first line, forget the first six and just give me the last ten," she says.

I read them to her and she keys them into her phone. She listens for a second, then hangs up. "Nope. It's disconnected. Give me the next one."

We try again.

"No, it can't be phone numbers, must be something else," she says.

I flip the pages. "Not necessarily. Try this one." I read it to her and watch as she dials.

I hear it ring. She gives me a wide-eyed look and a thumbs-up. It answers, a kind of synthesized voice, not human but computer generated. It is loud enough to make out the words from where I am sitting. "Speak clearly in order to be identified."

"Hello," says Joselyn. Suddenly the line goes dead. She looks at her phone. "I think I dropped the call."

"Let me try." I dial the same number on my cell, get the same synthesized voice with the same message "Speak clearly in order to be identified." The second I say, "Who is this?" it hangs up.

"What is it?" says Herman.

"It must be set up on some kind of voice-identification system," I tell him. "If the wrong person calls in, it hangs up. It's obviously a system for Thorn to communicate with someone. Probably a backup copy. He must have another one he works from and keeps this one in the suitcase in case he loses it."

"How come that number answered but the other ones didn't?" says Joselyn.

"It's the phone number for today's date," I tell her. "And there is one more for the day after tomorrow, and that's it."

"So what does that mean?" she says.

"Either Thorn gets another set of communication codes," says Herman, "or else by then whatever he's up to is gonna be finished. What's today's date?"

"October second," I say.

"So that means the fourth, which is what, Monday?"

"Yeah," I say.

"And all we know, at least according to Pablo, is that sometime Monday his luggage is supposed to be in Washington. What's the name of the hotel?" I ask.

"The Washington Court," says Herman.

"I know it well," says Joselyn. "It's right downtown, walking distance to the Capitol."

"So what do we do?" I slowly flip each page of the little book as we talk. After the code, the book is blank, not a mark on it.

"Be a waste of time to call the cops again," says Herman. "We tell them that Thorn's still alive, they're just gonna say so what. That means he wasn't on the plane. As far as they're concerned, maybe he wasn't even involved in it."

"I agree," says Joselyn. "Listen, if Thorn's headed to Washington, why don't you let me make a phone call. I have a contact who I believe should be able to get some action."

"Who's that?" says Herman.

"I can't tell you. You'll have to trust me. But I know he can reach all the way to the highest levels of the Justice Department."

"You got that kind of juice, do it," says

Herman. "You have any problem with that?" Herman looks at me.

"One question. Will we be able to get information back from your contact?" I ask her.

"What do you mean?" she says.

"I mean, if they pick up Thorn in D.C. and he lawyers up, we may lose any hope of identifying or locating Liquida. Will you be able to get information from your man regarding Liquida?"

"That's a good point. Let me find out," she says.

"Go ahead and call him," I tell her.

Joselyn takes her phone and heads into the bathroom. She closes the door to make her call.

"Secretive," says Herman.

"I suspect that's her big source on weapons systems," I tell him. "That's how she got all the details after the attack in Coronado. Leaks from friends in high places."

I reach the last page of the little book, not a single mark, only the communications code on the first three pages. I'm about to flip it onto the table when I notice that the last page has been ripped out. The front and back cover of the moleskin pocket book is stiffened with cardboard.

"Herman, do me a favor. In my briefcase you'll find a pencil in the pocket up top. Get it for me, will you?"

Herman gets the pencil as I examine the inside of the back cover, holding it up at an angle to the light.

"Whatya find?" Herman hands me the pencil.

"I don't know. Have you got that knife?"

Herman fishes it out of his pocket. "I want it back," he says.

"I found it," I tell him.

"I'll arm-wrestle you for it."

"I value my elbow joint too much. You can keep it." I open the knife and shave the pencil point on one side to expose more of the lead. Then I take the flat edge of the pencil and rub it gently back and forth over the impression carved in the white paper covering the inside of the back cover of the little book. Slowly the writing from the missing page emerges in the form of white letters from the growing panel of slate gray graphite. It is in the same neat hand as the coded numbers: "Waters of Death, Second

Road, Pattaya, Thailand." A group of numbers follow, nine digits in all, separated in sets of three with a space between each set, and the name "J. Snyder, 214 S. Pitt St., Alexandria, VA."

FORTY-TWO

Liquida found himself bundled onto the last evening flight out of Columbus, Ohio, the seven o'clock headed for Dulles, in D.C. He'd received the e-mail that afternoon that his services were needed on another job and he wasn't happy about it.

He had spent the last three days and a chunk of his own change watching the small farm outside Groveport where Madriani's daughter and his law partner were holed up. The little GPS tracker that Liquida had mailed to the girl had done its job. The device was so sensitive that at times he was able to follow it in transit, even in the package. The second she opened the box, the tiny tracker gave Liquida a read-out including latitude, longitude, and street address, and then plotted it all on a map. And if she had swallowed the thing, Liquida was sure that it would have performed an upper GI series.

He believed firmly that technology was a wonderful thing, as long as he didn't have to use it. It was why he didn't carry a cell phone, and why he changed his e-mail address more often than his underwear. Anything science could make, government could abuse.

He had staked out the farmhouse and identified the girl's daily schedule. She never left the place. And the old man who owned the farm had friends. Half the time the driveway out in front of the house looked like a police convention. If Liquida had a dime for every car with a set of light bars on top that visited the house, he could have retired.

If that wasn't enough, there were dogs, and not just any kind. The farmer raised Doberman pinschers. Liquida wasn't a "dog kind of guy," and he hated any breed that was German. You could poison most junkyard hounds. But a forty-dollar hunk of Chateaubriand salted with enough Ambien to put an elephant down wouldn't raise an eyebrow on a good Doberman. And if you were stupid enough to cross the line and try to hand-feed him, you'd better be wearing a Kevlar body stocking.

The last time Liquida had tangled with a pinscher he'd ended up with his head in the dog's jaws, being humped and thrashed like a stuffed bunny. Until the dog finally let go of his head, Liquida thought he was engaged, well on his way to becoming Muerte Liquida-Doberman. And he wasn't anxious for a rematch.

But these dogs were confined by an invisible fence. A wire circled the property and was buried just inches under the ground. It emitted a signal that was picked up by a diode on the dog's collar whenever it got within a few feet of the wire. If the dog tried to cross the wire, the animal would get a severe jolt of low-amperage electricity. The dogs had been trained and conditioned to stay inside the fence.

By now Liquida knew the precise boundaries of the invisible fence. He watched the property from a tree in an empty field across the road.

For the last two days, Madriani's daughter had slipped into a pattern. Each morning around eight she would come out of the house carrying a colander to pick berries from some wild bushes that ran along the front of the property.

Madriani's law partner would come out with her carrying a shotgun. But he usually sat on a chair on the front porch and kept an eye on her from a distance. And each day, as the berries became sparser, the girl wandered farther. She was already within the warning zone of the invisible fence. The dogs no longer followed her. By tomorrow she would be outside the fence and fair game for a needle-sharp stiletto hiding in the brush.

Liquida had been called away, but at least he knew where she was, and from all appearances, she wasn't going to leave. He could only hope and pray that the berries would hold out until he got back.

* * *

Thorn approached the U.S. Capitol Building from the north, walking toward what many tourists called the back of the immense, sprawling structure, the steps on the east side.

He had spent Saturday finishing up the logos on the 727 and arranging for the delivery of a truckload of Jet A fuel from the airport on the east side of Vieques Island. After pumping the tanks full and paying for the fuel, Thorn hitched a ride with the driver of the tanker back to the airport, where he caught a flight to San Juan, and from there to Washington.

It was now late Sunday night. The area around the Capitol was quiet, but well lit. Thorn was carrying an attaché case. He had lied to the two Saudi pilots on board the plane back in Vieques about many things, including their ultimate objective. As far as he was concerned, they didn't need to know. And as long as he was packing the item in the briefcase, Thorn was in control.

At Capitol Street he turned left, away from the domed monolith, and headed instead toward the intersection of First Street. He ended up kitty-corner from the Library of Congress and stopped at the traffic light.

Standing at the curb waiting for the light to change he had to keep himself from looking up.

Thorn knew that he was being watched and, no doubt, recorded by at least three or four, and maybe as many as half a dozen, surveillance cameras.

He was standing in the middle of Government Square. Except for the area around the White House and parts of North Korea, it was probably the most heavily watched patch of ground on earth.

The feds had installed cameras, night-vision equipment, and God knows what else under the cornice of every building. Rumor had it that there were antimissile missiles deployed around the Capitol as well as the White House. During the daytime, tourists could stand on the steps of the Supreme Court and look across to see snipers in their black garb as they milled around with their rifles on the roof of the Capitol Building.

On his last visit Thorn had seen metal domes on the roof of the Capitol that looked suspiciously like the housing for the MK-15 Phalanx installed on naval war ships. The

Phalanx was a twenty-millimeter chain gun, radar directed and capable of rapid fire to take down incoming missiles or planes if they penetrated the outer defenses around Washington. None of this particularly bothered him.

When the light changed he crossed at the intersection and continued straight on, along the south side of the Supreme Court Building. Across the street was the Library of Congress with its Beaux-Arts architecture and shallow dome topped by an ornate windowed cupola and capped by the Torch of Learning. This and the light from the windows in the cupola lit up the night sky with the old-fashioned feel of the nineteenth century.

The dome and the cupola were clad in copper that had long since acquired the brown patina of a dirty penny. Half a block down he stepped off the sidewalk and through the gate of a low, iron picket fence bordering the front yard of one of the old Victorian houses that lined the block. Most of the stately old homes along the street now housed lobbying groups and other organizations with regular business before Congress.

It was Sunday and late enough at night that the lights in the old Victorian were out. Only the streetlamps provided illumination, and Thorn avoided these by huddling in the shadows under a tree in the front yard. Quickly he went down on one knee, opened the attaché case, and removed the little brown bat.

His hands were trembling. Thorn knew that this was perhaps the riskiest part of the entire venture. He would either succeed or fail within the next three or four minutes, and he would be likely to get only one shot. Damage or loss of the bat and his only backup was virtual suicide. He would have to take the large laser designator and find a way to get up into the building. Given the tight security, this was virtually impossible; chances were he would be either caught or killed. If Thorn had to make a choice, it would be the latter.

He pulled out the laptop and turned it on. A few seconds later there was a slight vibration and a gentle whirring sound from the little bat as Thorn tossed it into the air. A second later the sound disappeared. Thorn watched the computer screen as he piloted the little brown bat with the small joystick using the mounted camera as his eyes.

Quickly he climbed above the streetlights and over the trees. In the distance he could see the bright lights on the Capitol dome as the bat gained altitude. It crossed over the intersection at Second Street just as a Capitol police car cruised by beneath it.

Thorn maneuvered the plane with the joystick, varying the speed of the motor with a small wheel that he rolled back and forth with his other thumb. Banking to the left, he saw the brown copper dome of the Library of Congress illuminated by the torch on top of the cupola. He aimed the bat directly at it. He wondered if he should circle around one time just to get the lay of the land and then decided against it. The brightness from the cupola was too much. Thorn needed to get it down and out of the light as quickly as possible.

As he approached the dome, he lined it up with one of the crosshatched ornamental iron pieces. These ran from the balustrade at the base of the cupola down to the lower edge of the dome. There were eight of them. Thorn had studied the photographs for weeks. As he approached within a foot of the ironwork, he abruptly pulled the joystick and rolled the power wheel back. The nose of the little plane, along with the camera, suddenly pointed straight up. A flash of blinding light filled the camera's lens from the Torch of Learning, followed by the blackness of the night sky.

The plane stalled. Then it fell tail first. The image on the screen shook and pixilated as the bat hit the domed roof. Thorn sucked in air and held his breath as he winced. The plane teetered on its tail. If it flipped onto its back, it would be over. The little brown bat would slide down the dome until it either fell onto the walkway below or became wedged behind one of the ornamental pediments at the edge of the roof. Either way, it would lose its signal and Thorn would no longer be able to control or retrieve it.

A second later the plane flopped forward, and the image shook and broke up a little as the camera's tiny transceiver absorbed the shock. A few seconds later the picture stabilized. The four powerful magnets on the feet of the little bat clung to the ornamental iron like glue.

Thorn smiled. They would have to pry the little beast off if they wanted to get their hands on it. He let out a palpable sigh of relief, then laughed. He had to catch himself before he made too much noise or wandered out into the glare of the street-lights. He felt absolutely giddy. The rest would be a piece of cake. Unless the Arabs flew the jet into a ditch, the mission was a lead-pipe cinch. All they had to do was deliver the package.

Thorn had been training for the maneuver with the bat for almost a month. But until he actually put the little plane at risk, there was no way to be sure if he could pull it off.

Peering into the computer's screen, Thorn was looking up into the lights of the cupola over the main reading room of the Library of Congress. The balustrade around the base of the cupola was no more than ten feet away. Hunting and pecking he hit a few keys on the computer.

He could throw the joystick away now. Instead he ran his finger over the laptop's touch pad. The tiny servomotor kicked in and the small camera began to pan. The camera and the laser diode were mounted on a gimbal, like a compass on a ship. They could turn in any direction, right or left, up or down. He aimed the camera at the target, lifted his finger off the pad, and looked at the screen. It was perfect. He couldn't believe it. A few adjustments in the morning and he would be set.

He held his breath. One final test. He clicked a few more keys on the computer and suddenly he heard the signal, a periodic beep. He had to turn down the volume on the computer, otherwise somebody on the street might hear it. It was like a human pulse. The only thing pounding harder at the moment was Thorn's heart.

Quickly he turned off the diode to save the battery, shutting down all the power to the little bat. It was settled into its nest for the night. Now if only the wind stayed calm and the weather clear, Thorn had it made. He had already checked Weather Underground, one of the major weather prediction sites on the Internet. The forecast for tomorrow was bright and clear, with a high of seventy degrees. All they had to do was deliver the bomb, and Thorn would take care of the rest.

* * *

By the time we reach the Hotel George in downtown Washington, it's already late. Joselyn and I are exhausted. Herman slept on the plane while Joselyn and I talked, so by the time we land, Herman has gotten a second wind. He wants to go and at least take a gander at the Washington Court Hotel, where Thorn is checked in.

"Listen, leave it alone," says Joselyn. "Everything is under control. The FBI has already confirmed that he's checked in, and they have him under surveillance."

Joselyn has assured us both that her contact in the Capitol has everything in hand, and that Thorpe is on board. According to Joselyn, Zeb Thorpe has received firm instructions from the director of the FBI as well as the attorney general. They have Thorn under round-the-clock surveillance. They would pick him up, but they want to know if he is working with anyone else. So for the time being, they are watching and waiting.

Joselyn's source has warned us to be

careful, not to take any chances. He has assured her that the Hotel George, where we are staying, only half a block from the Washington Court Hotel where Thorn is booked in, is now under full protection. Both city PD and federal authorities are now watching it.

FORTY-THREE

It was five A.M. and Flannery and Son's cement contractors were scheduled for a major pour. The framing crew was finishing up the last few forms as the cement-pumper truck set up over the site at the Fulton Street subway station.

There was already a line of seven heavily laden cement trucks queued up on the street outside the gate, each one waiting to disgorge ten cubic yards of concrete. More trucks were on the way. They would be rolling in and out all day, dropping their load into the hopper of the pumper truck as the cement crew moved the hydraulic-

powered chute around, pouring the concrete as they spread and leveled it.

"Hey! You got a problem." One of the
drivers milling around outside the gate
yelled over the sound of the idling diesels.
He pointed to the second truck in line. Its
giant mixer barrel on the back was not re-
volving.

The driver of the truck leaned out of his
open window. "I know. Batch plant didn't
give me enough water. Had to shut my mixer
down. How about I get inside to use your
hose to get some more water in the mix?"

The guard at the gate looked at the officer in charge. Both private guards and
transit police provided security for the construction site. The transit cop nodded, and
the private security man with the clipboard
wrote down the license number of the truck
as well as the owner's name and contractor's license number from the driver's-side
truck door. He then swung open the gate
and waved the truck inside.

The guard raised his hand and stopped
the truck just as it was about to enter. "Two
water trucks parked over there." The guard
pointed off to the left, a fair distance from
the site of the giant open hole over the

subway. "Tell 'em to give you a hose. They should have more than enough water."

The driver smiled, nodded, and drove through the gate.

*   *   *

Ahmed sat in the left-hand seat as the 727 climbed through twelve thousand feet. He could see the white surf and the azure blue shallow waters just off the beaches on the southwest coast of Puerto Rico as he and Masud held the plane on a steady course headed north.

They had a full load of fuel. The two air-to-air missiles were now slung under the wings, attached to the pylons that Ahmed and his comrade had helped to install.

The two Saudis were mystified by how easily Thorn had managed to bulldoze his way past the inquisitive onlookers on Vieques after the plane landed. A handful of bureaucrats from the U.S. Department of the Interior who worked at Camp Garcia came by to look when they heard the plane come in.

The workers made the trek a half mile or so from the dilapidated offices at the camp to the airfield, some of them in cars and a few on foot. Thorn took charge, showing them some papers and telling them that he'd already called in the incident to the FAA, and that a Federal Aviation Administration inspector was being dispatched from Washington to Vieques to investigate. He would be there Monday morning.

This put an end to all their questions. A few of them lingered, wandering around the outside of the plane for a few minutes, and then disappeared.

As soon as everything calmed down, Thorn went back to work on the plane. He finished the spray job on the company logos just forward of the wings and skipped the big one on the tail section. He told the two pilots it wouldn't matter.

Thorn arranged for a load of fuel. As soon as it was delivered, he started up the engines and turned the plane around so that its nose was pointed down the runway. Finally he went over last-minute instructions with them and then departed for the airport on the other side of the island.

For two nights Ahmed and his comrade slept on the plane. They were armed and instructed to kill anyone, quietly if they could, who approached the plane or tried to get on board.

Then early Monday morning before daybreak they broke out the two air-to-air missiles from their crates inside the plane, mounted them to the pylons under the wings, and armed them both. Within a half hour they had the engines warmed up and were headed down the runway. It was six thirty A.M. None of the government workers would show up at Camp Garcia for another hour and a half.

Ahmed piloted the plane on a northwest course sixty miles out to sea before heading due north. The plane climbed over puffy patches of tropical clouds casting shadows on the water below. He kept his transponder turned off and stayed well out over the ocean. The plan was to avoid ground-based radar from Puerto Rico and the frequent radio inquiries from the island's air traffic control towers. Forty minutes into the flight, he turned ninety degrees to starboard and put the plane heading over the ocean forty miles north of Rafael Hernández Airport on the extreme north end of the island.

Formerly known as Ramey Air Force Base, the field had been turned over to civilian use as part of the base closure program a few years earlier. The Air National

Guard and the Coast Guard still retained a presence there. It was also used by the airfreight carrier FedEx as its hub for the Caribbean Basin.

Ahmed climbed to twenty-five thousand feet and put the 727 into a circling pattern out over the water as Masud listened to their VHF radio receiver. They had plenty of fuel. He was scanning the frequencies, searching for their quarry.

"Federal Express flight 9303—Squawk 1423, runway two north. You are cleared for takeoff."

"There it is!" said Ahmed. He couldn't believe it. It was exactly as Thorn had said. The airport at Rafael Hernández usually didn't have FedEx flights any farther north than Miami or Memphis, but today they did.

Flight 9303 was headed for Newark Liberty Airport in New Jersey. The wide-body DC-10 would dwarf the smaller 727. And anyone familiar with the FedEx flight schedule would know that the carrier never used smaller planes on such long-haul routes. But by the time anyone on the ground or in the air saw the plane, the 727 would be so close to its target that this would be the last thing on their minds.

Ahmed continued to circle, holding his altitude at twenty-five thousand feet and waiting as the huge wide-body took off and slowly climbed toward its cruising altitude.

Almost twenty minutes later Masud spied the larger plane cutting through a cloud deck eight thousand feet below them and still climbing. Ahmed continued his arc around in the circle and fell in behind them, still five thousand feet above the larger jet. He went into a shallow dive and used his altitude to pick up speed and close the distance on the other plane.

When he got within a half mile, he eased back on the throttles and flew fifty feet above the tall tail of the DC-10 to avoid the air turbulence off its wings and its jet wash.

The bigger plane had a slightly slower cruising speed than the 727 and Ahmed wanted to be careful to avoid getting on top of it. He hugged in as close as he dared, knowing that with his transponder turned off, the collision avoidance system on the DC-10 was blinded. From out in front there was no way that the crew on the flight deck of the large wide-body could see them.

In less than a half hour they were more than a hundred miles off the north coast of

Puerto Rico, well beyond the range of ground-based radar, in an area approaching no-man's-land, the heart of the Bermuda Triangle.

* * *

Once inside the chain-link gate, the driver of the large cement truck made a broad-arcing turn toward the two parked water trucks. But instead of continuing on, he stopped. He turned the wheel and started to back up. The reverse safety bell on his rear wheels started to clang and by the time the guard at the gate turned and saw him, the truck was moving backward on a direct line toward the open cavern over the subway.

"Where the hell's he goin'?"

Two of the transit cops looked over. One of them shook his head, then started to wave his arms back and forth. "No. No. Not there." He took a few tentative steps toward the moving truck. "Hey, dimwit!" he yelled at the top of his voice.

The driver looked at him for an instant before pressing the accelerator to the floor. The weight in the back of the truck was the only thing that slowed it down. The cement truck started to back up faster, its reverse safety bell now ringing frantically. As the transit cop realized there was something wrong, both he and his partner started to run toward the moving truck.

One of the workmen, still hammering forms, hearing the bell bearing down on him, looked up and threw his body out of the way as the rear wheels barely missed him. They rolled right over the wooden forms, crushing them, and kept right on going. The forms didn't even slow down the heavy quad set of dual wheels.

"Stop!" The workman leaped to his feet and jumped up onto the truck's running board as it passed by. He reached inside and tried to grab the steering wheel.

The driver wrestled him for control of the wheel, but the framing contractor was big and burly and by now was flowing with adrenaline.

The Somali driver grabbed the Sig Sauer nine-millimeter pistol next to him on the seat, pressed the muzzle against the workman's forehead, and pulled the trigger. In a cloud of bloodred spray, the workman's gaze fixed as his body tumbled backward off the truck. A second later the driver felt the steering wheel pull to the right as the front left wheel of the massive truck rolled over the dead laborer.

The two transit cops pulled their pistols and started firing at the truck's windshield. They unloaded their full clips on the fast-moving vehicle. Two of the rounds hit the driver in the head and chest.

His right foot went all the way to the floor as his body fell forward onto the wheel.

The truck careened to the right and caromed off a pile of steel I beams. The impact jarred the dead driver's foot off the gas pedal. But the truck didn't stop. Instead it slowly continued to roll toward the open pit.

One of the transit cops launched himself onto the running board at the driver's-side door. He pulled on the door handle and found it was locked.

He reached through the open window and opened the door from the inside as the truck continued to roll. He jerked the dead driver out of the seat, threw him to the ground, and climbed up into the cab.

The rolling dolly on the rear end of the truck slid over the edge of the open cavern. It disconnected from the tow gear on the back of the truck and tumbled down into the open shaft.

The cop hit the clutch and jammed his foot on the brake just as the first set of rear wheels went over the edge.

* * *

About two hundred miles out, over the dark blue water of the Atlantic, Ahmed told Masud to dial in the transponder numbers and to be sure that the altitude button was pressed.

Masud turned each of the four knobs until he dialed in the squawk number for the big DC-10, the numbers 1423, then he pressed the button that would disclose to ground radar the 727's altitude. But he didn't flip the button to turn the transponder on, not yet. "Ready," he said.

Ahmed eased back on the throttles. He wanted to maintain altitude but increase the distance between himself and the bigger plane. The 727 fell back three-quarters of a mile. The fear was that if he was too close, the jet intakes on the smaller Boeing would suck in debris and stall out.

"What do you think?" said Ahmed.

"A little farther," said Masud.

Ahmed eased back on the throttle a

little more. Suddenly the smaller plane was buffeted by the swirling turbulence off the wingtips of the big DC-10. Ahmed shook his head and adjusted the throttle forward again. "Do it."

Masud opened the lid on a metal box bolted to the floor at his feet. He lifted the two red plastic switch covers, looked over at Ahmed one last time, bit his lower lip, and flipped both switches.

The two wing-mounted missiles fell from their pylons and an instant later their rocket motors flared on. They streaked forward on each side of the cockpit, leaving a contrail like a running torpedo as Ahmed lifted the nose of the 727 and pulled to the right.

Two seconds later a massive ball of fire erupted just over the nose of the plane, to the left. Ahmed pushed down on the right pedal and turned the wheel. He lifted the left wing as streaks of smoking-hot debris flew past the window and made a rat-a-tat pattern like flack striking the aluminum skin along the side of the fuselage.

"Transponder!" Ahmed had his hands full with the controls.

Masud reached over and flipped the transponder button on. It was unlikely that ground radar from anywhere would have had them on the screen, but any loitering AWAK flights that might have them on the screen would have noticed only a momentary flicker in squawk signature on their screen for 1423, and only a slight adjustment for heading and altitude.

Ahmed looked out his side window and watched behind him as the flaming debris fell toward the sea.

FORTY-FOUR

It is sometime Monday morning when I hear the familiar and now detested ring tone from my cell phone. At least this time I know where it is, on the nightstand somewhere behind me.

I can sense the satin smoothness of her body stir as I move my hand like a blind man along the surface of the table feeling for the phone. The blanket lifts up just enough to allow some of the chilled air from the register of the hotel's air conditioner to spill between the sheets.

"Turn that thing off. It's cold." Joselyn

presses her warm back up against me like a hot spoon under the heavy covers.

My hand finds the phone and I pull it to my ear. "Hello!"

"You might want to be getting your ass outta bed," says Herman. "Thorn's on the move and unless they're ghosts, I don't see any cops or the FBI."

"What are you talking about?" I am half asleep. "They told us to leave it alone," I tell him.

"Yeah, I know. But I got hungry. Got outta bed to come over and see for myself Thorn's hotel," he says. "They got a bar with a small restaurant, so I decided to get some break- fast. While I was eating Thorn came out of the elevator carrying a briefcase." Herman is breathing heavily.

"Where are you now?"

"Just across the street. I'm out in front of a liquor store on the corner, place called Kogod's Liquors," he says. "There's an old firehouse next door."

I toss the blankets off, throw my legs over the side of the bed, and sit up. "What are you doing?"

"Following Thorn," he says. "Nobody else seems to be interested. I'm just across the

street from our hotel, corner of E Street
and New Jersey Avenue. I followed Thorn
from his hotel half a block to the corner
where you turn to go to ours. He walked
across the street, went up to the door at
the liquor store, but it was closed. It's not
open yet. It's just after nine. I think he knew
it wasn't open but was lookin' at the mirror,
you know—the glass door, to see if anybody was following him."

"Which means he probably saw you,"
I tell him.

"No," says Herman. "I had the angle on
him. I'm not that stupid. Then he went down
the street and ducked into a garage that's,
like, right across the street from the front
door to our hotel. I hope to hell he's not
gettin' into a car, 'cause if he is we're about
to lose him."

"Listen, don't go in there," I tell him.
"Wait for the cops."

"There are no cops," says Herman.

"What's going on?" says Joselyn.

"Herman is following Thorn. He says
there's nobody tailing him."

"No, that can't be right," she says. "Let
me talk to him."

I hand her the phone. She's still lying

down under the covers, head on the pillow.

I start to get dressed.

"Herman, this is Joselyn. What are you doing?" She listens for a moment. "Yeah, but my people told us to stay away from him. They have it covered. Give them some credit. You're going to mess things up. Now get back over here."

He says something to her, but I can't hear it.

"Here, he wants to talk to you." She gives me the phone back. "Tell him to come back to his room," she says.

"Paul!" Herman is shouting into the phone.

"Yeah." I put the phone up to my ear as I hold my pants up with the other hand. "The sign out in front of the garage says 'Colonial Parking,' right over the door. Big white block letters. If you step out of the hotel and turn right, you can't miss it. It's right across the street."

"Wait for me," I tell him.

"I'm just gonna stick my nose inside to see if he's there. He might be tryin' to slip out another door. And if he's got a car, at least I'll get the license plate number."

"No!"

"Get over here as quick as you can," he says. Then he hangs up.

* * *

Herman smiled at the attendant in the glass booth as he walked into the garage. He strode with confidence, as if he was heading to his parked car inside. Then as soon as he made the turn where the attendant couldn't see him anymore he immediately slowed down.

Herman knew he'd made a mistake the moment he passed through the door. The light was all wrong. But it was too late. He was already committed. He moved toward the wall and tried to stay in what shadow there was as he moved toward the line of cars in the second aisle. From what he could see from the outside, that was the route Thorn had taken when he entered.

Herman slipped one hand into his pocket and tried to melt his huge frame into the concrete wall while he inched his way along. He walked until he was opposite the long, narrow driveway that made up the second aisle in the parking garage.

From here he could see straight down

the long row of vehicles, all the way to the other end of the building. There were cars parked nose in on both sides, with the painted arrow on the floor pointing in this direction. The garage was one way, with traffic weaving up and down each aisle.

Herman listened for the noise of an engine starting and scanned the aisle on both sides looking for backup lights. But he didn't see or hear anything.

* * *

"Damn it!" I tell her.

"What's he doing?" says Joselyn.

"Herman followed Thorn to the garage across the street, now he's going inside."

"Who, Thorn or Herman?" she says.

"Both of them."

"Why didn't you tell him to stop?"

"I did. He wouldn't listen." I pull my shirt over my head and slip on my shoes sans socks.

"You're not going over there?"

"I have to." I press my phone into the holster on my belt and strap it down.

Joselyn throws the blankets off and starts to get up.

"Where are you going?" I ask.

"With you."

"No, you're not."

"Why not?" she says. "If the two of you can be terminally stupid, why can't I? Herman has rocks in his head. And you're not much better. Neither of you listen," she says. "The FBI and the police have Thorn covered. I have it from on high. You can trust me on this."

"Tell that to Herman," I say.

"I did. He wouldn't listen. In other words, he doesn't trust me," she says.

"It's not just you. Herman doesn't trust anybody," I tell her. "Herman believes what he sees with his eyes and smells with his nose. I think that's how he's stayed alive this long."

"So it'll serve you right if the FBI busts both of you for interfering with their investigation." She has her bra on and is pulling up her pants, searching for a top. "And if they do, don't call me to come post bail," she says.

I glance at her and smile. "You mean if I called, you wouldn't come?"

She looks at me, trying to maintain a stern expression. "I don't know. What I want to know is why men are so stupid."

"Probably has to do with the yin and the

yang," I tell her. "Testosterone versus the female hormone."

"You mean estrogen?"

"Yeah, that's the one. It's why women find it so easy to manipulate us. It gives you that whole sexy package," I tell her.

"Yes, that along with intelligence," she says. "Don't try to patronize me and don't change the subject. If you guys want to think with your dicks, that's fine, but don't ask me to put my body on the block with friends in the future unless you're willing to cooperate."

"You stay here," I tell her.

"Oh, sure." She has her top unbuttoned and no shoes on her feet. "I'll just lie back down and go to sleep," she says.

"I'll grab Herman and be back in a flash." Before she can answer or follow me, I'm out the door. I hear one of her shoes slam against the inside of it before it can close.

* * *

Thorn was down on one knee between two parked cars about twelve vehicles down the aisle in the garage. He looked at his watch to check the time. This morning he was on a very tight schedule, and he had to keep moving.

Thorn knew that the three of them had been following him since before his last trip to Puerto Rico: the lawyer, his investigator, and the bitch Joselyn Cole. Thorn had been tipped off, been given detailed information and then told not to worry, that everything was taken care of. It wasn't then, but it would be now. He had to get them off his back and keep them off for at least one hour. That was all he needed. After that it wouldn't matter. By noon it would all be over.

In the meantime his luggage from Puerto Rico would catch up with him at the hotel. Thorn would be free to select any one of the three fresh passports from his suitcase and disappear, vanish forever into the luxury of a multimillion-dollar retirement.

He didn't have to wait long. A few seconds later he heard footsteps moving in the shadows of the garage. They were coming from the direction of the sunlit entrance at the ticket kiosk out in front. He saw the large silhouette as the man moved slowly. He stayed away from the cars as if he knew that the blind spaces between them represented a risk. Instead, he kept his back to the front concrete wall of the

building, where he knew there was nothing behind him.

The man stalking him tried to stay in
the shadows, but given the bright morning sunlight and the fact that he was back-
lit against the opening of the garage
entrance, it was impossible.

Thorn could have easily threaded the
silencer on the small Walther PPK in his
pocket, and even at this distance could
probably hit the man at least three times
without missing. The guy was that big. But
he didn't want to take the chance, not with
the ticket attendant in the kiosk out in
front. Besides, the Walther might not drop
him. Instead, Thorn stuck to the plan,
waited, and watched. He would use the
gun only if one or both of the other two
showed up. Thorn had arranged it all in
the garage directly across from their hotel
to make it as convenient as possible.

Herman started to wonder whether he
might have lost him. He scanned the distance across the garage over the tops of
the cars and noticed at least one lighted
exit sign on the back wall as well as a
bank of elevators leading to the offices up-

stairs. Thorn could have taken either one and slipped away.

The garage was quiet. Most people were already at work. Herman looked back toward the entrance, thought for a moment, then turned and started toward the next row of cars, the third aisle down.

Before he could take a second step, he heard a scratching sound on the concrete somewhere behind him and off to the right. He stopped, turned, and looked. He was certain that the noise had come from the aisle in front of him, and close.

Herman took a tentative step toward the line of cars, then decided he couldn't be sure which side of the aisle the noise might have come from. He moved as silently as he could on the rubber soles of his running shoes, one hand plunged deep in his pocket, the other balled into a fist.

Thorn slipped down onto his chest and looked under the car. He could see the shoes of the big man as he came straight down the center of the aisle between the two lines of parked cars. No doubt he was checking between each vehicle on each side as he passed them, trying to make sure that no one got behind him. It was a good tactic as far as it went, but Thorn could see that he had already blown it.

Thorn waited until the man was almost even with the other side of the car he was peering under and then, without warning, he suddenly bolted upright, stood straight up, and looked right at him.

Herman stood there wide eyed. Adrenaline shot through his body. He recognized Thorn immediately. The only thing he couldn't see was the man's hands, to tell if he was holding a gun.

Thorn took a step out from behind the car and Herman realized that the only thing in the man's hand was the briefcase.

Liquida would have preferred Madriani. But he knew that unless he could get the lawyer alone, sooner or later he would have to deal with the big investigator. So it might as well be now, when he had the element of surprise. He came at him with catlike quickness, the deadly stiletto in his gloved hand behind him.

Herman took half a step forward and was about to lunge toward Thorn when the searing pain in his back, up under his ribs, froze the soles of his shoes to the concrete floor. Suddenly Herman couldn't move. He reached with his one free hand behind his back and felt the warm blood as it pulsed from his body. Herman knew instantly who it was and that the sharp point still jammed in his back had pierced a main artery.

Liquida's blade found that magic place that paralyzes with pain. The big man's knees buckled. As he went to the concrete floor, Liquida went with him, holding the knife in place and moving it around for maximum damage.

Herman tried to call out, but he couldn't. It was as if his voice was paralyzed. He realized he could no longer draw air in his lungs, as the blade had punctured one of them and blood began to fill it.

"You got him?" said Thorn.

"He's mine." Liquida withdrew the knife from its victim, straightened up, and looked over at Thorn. "Go. I'll finish up." Blood dripped off the tip of the stiletto as he stood there like a butcher over his quarry.

"Good work," said Thorn. He turned and ran toward the exit sign at the back of the building.

Liquida watched him as he went. He

stood there, his feet straddling the big, bald black man he had seen in every dark dream since that night in Costa Rica almost a year before. Liquida looked down at him. "I will make it quick, but you must know before you die that I have found the girl. Madriani's daughter will die next, before he goes into his own grave."

Liquida leaned down, drew the nine-inch stiletto back for the death plunge into the man's chest, and felt a searing fire erupt from his right shoulder blade, all the way through to the muscles under his arm. He jumped back quickly, like a man who's been snake bitten. He reached across his body with his left hand to grip his dead right forearm at the wrist.

The bloody stiletto toppled from his numb fingers and rattled onto the concrete pavement at his feet. His right hand had no feeling. Liquida was unable to grip or even close the fingers of his right hand into a weak fist.

Blood poured from the wound under Liquida's arm as Herman lay on his back, his head raised up off the pavement. He was smiling. The open four-inch ceramic blade from Thorn's exotic folding knife was in his right hand as his vision began to blur. He reached out feebly with the blade and drew it across the fading form of Liquida. In his final delirium his sight had lost any sense of depth.

The Mexican was standing three feet away from him, fury in his eyes.

Herman's head settled back onto the concrete as his vision went dark and what shallow breath was left abandoned his body.

With his right arm hanging limp at his side, Liquida kicked the knife out of Herman's hand. It skidded across the concrete and under one of the cars.

Liquida was breathing heavily as he heard the pounding of feet on the pavement coming this way. He turned and looked and saw the form of a man running into the dark parking structure from the sunlit outside. He looked down at the dying form at his feet, reached around and felt the warm blood oozing down his own back, and decided that discretion was the better part of valor.

* * *

I get only a fleeting glimpse of a running form in the distance as I walk and then run down between the lane of parked cars. I see the spreading pool of blood from under Herman's body as I jump and curse and pound my hands on my thighs.

"HELP!" I yell at the top of my lungs. "Anybody! I need help now!"

I am down on both knees hovering over Herman, the man who has saved me so many times. There is blood on his chest but I see no wounds, yet the pool on the concrete beneath him is spreading. "Call an ambulance! I need help!"

Herman is trying to say something, but he's unable to speak. He mouths the word "Liquida" and points with a trembling finger toward the bloody stiletto lying on the concrete. He tries to say something else: "Ssss . . . Sa . . ." and loses consciousness.

I roll him over onto his stomach. It takes all my strength. As he goes over I see the wound in his back still oozing blood, then a spurt and bubbles of air.

"That's good," I tell him. I get down in Herman's ear. "Stay with me," I tell him. I tear off my shirt, pulling it over my head. "Damn it! Can you hear me?" I scream at the guy in the kiosk out front. "There's a man dying, I need HELP NOW!"

I press my shirt against the open wound to seal it, using my knees to apply as much pressure as I can, then grapple for my phone with a bloody finger. I hit the button and look for a signal. Nothing. The concrete of the garage has my phone sealed off. I drop it onto the concrete and yell for help.

"What's happened?"

I turn my head. It's the guy from the kiosk.

"Call 911. Get an ambulance. He's been stabbed."

He runs for the door.

I press down on Herman's back, trying to clear the blood from his lungs while pressing the shirt against the wound with my knee.

I am wondering where the police and the FBI are as I try to stanch the bleeding and get him to breathe. I still see bubbles from the wound as I press down on his back.

"They're on their way." The parking attendant from the kiosk is behind me. Then suddenly two or three more people. One of them is a nurse. She grabs her large handbag, reaches inside it, and finds a sandwich in a plastic bag. She opens up

the bag, tosses the sandwich, flattens the
bag out, and says: "Move that!" She's talking about my bloody shirt.

She lifts Herman's blood-soaked shirt,
pulling it out of the way, and places the
plastic sandwich bag directly over the
open wound. "Here, help me get his belt
off."

I roll him up onto his side, reach underneath, and unbuckle it.

She grabs the buckle end and yanks it
several times until it comes free from his
pants. She puts the belt under his chest,
tells me to lay him down flat on his stomach,
and fastens the belt directly over the plastic
bag and the wound. She runs the open end
of the belt through the buckle and pulls it as
tight as she can. She puts her knee against
the center of his back and pulls harder. "I
know this looks bad, but it's a sucking chest
wound and I have to seal it off or else he'll
drown in his own blood."

I notice that the bubbles stop.

She opens Herman's mouth, reaches
between his teeth with two fingers, and
scoops out blood. She does this two or
three times, each time reaching back farther toward his throat to clear his airway.

We roll him onto his back and she starts doing heavy compressions on his chest as I open his mouth, move his tongue out of the way, and try to blow air into his lungs.

FORTY-FIVE

Zeb Thorpe had been in the command center at FBI headquarters since shortly after six that morning. He was called in early on an emergency in New York and was busy watching live images on a screen as transit authorities, police in New York, and construction workers tried to stabilize a cement truck and pull it away from an open cavern over the Fulton Street subway station.

Transit police had managed to stop the truck, but four of the eight rear wheels on the dual doubles were already over the edge of the hole.

Thorpe believed he already knew what was on board the truck, and it wasn't cement. Victor Soyev, the Russian arms merchant, had given them leads, all of them pointing to New York as the target. Thorpe's people had turned over every rock until they found the garage in upstate New York where the work had been done. From there they were within hours of running the thing down when the cement truck turned up at the building site.

The bomb squad had already confirmed that the mixing drum on the back of the truck was welded into position so that it couldn't turn. And there were wires leading from the drum through holes in the cab to a metal box that appeared to be a triggering device. Transit police had shot the driver dead before his hands could reach the trigger.

But if the rear wheels slid a few more inches, the front end of the truck would lift up and the entire vehicle would tumble into the open cavern below. The bomb squad was concerned that a trembler switch might be connected to the detonator. If so, any sudden jarring would set it off.

Authorities were desperately trying to

clear the subway below, to get everyone out, as workers used a heavy cable from one of the construction cranes and a D9 Caterpillar bulldozer to try to stabilize the truck and pull it back from the opening. The question was whether the bulldozer was heavy enough, or if the weight of the truck and the mammoth air-fuel bomb might pull the entire truck down into the hole.

"Mr. Thorpe, telephone call for you on line one." It was Thorpe's secretary, her head through the door. "Caller says it's urgent."

"Not now," said Thorpe. "Who is it?"

"Mr. Madriani."

"Take a message," said Thorpe. "Tell him to turn on his television, cable news. Tell him I'll call him back."

"He says his investigator has just been stabbed. It happened right here in the city, near a hotel downtown just a few minutes ago. He says a man named Liquida did it."

"Tell him to call the police," said Thorpe.

"He already has. He says paramedics are working on the man who was stabbed, but that it doesn't look good. He wants to know why our agents weren't there."

"What's he talking about? The last I

heard, Madriani was headed out of the States somewhere. Puerto Rico, as I recall. Are we supposed to be everywhere?" said Thorpe.

"He says somebody by the name of Thorn got away. And that he's up to something near the Capitol."

"Tell him not now. I'll have to call him back. Get a number."

* * *

Joselyn finished getting dressed, then checked her watch. It was almost ten o'clock. She was wondering how Herman could be so sure that the police and the FBI had fallen down on the job and that Thorn was running free. After all, Joselyn had had assurances direct from the lips of god that the authorities were on top of it.

Still, it wouldn't hurt to check, but she didn't want to insult him. After all, he was the one who'd fed her the highly secretive information on the loose nuke in Coronado involved in the attack on the navy base. He was her compatriot in crime when it came to insider stuff whenever the government was trying to hide things under the nutshell of national security.

The man knew where all the bodies

were buried because of his status, his position and unique access to information.
And for that reason Joselyn had to protect
him. Portions of what he had told her over
the years were sufficiently sensitive that
he could go to jail if the facts were known.

Because of the risks he took in a worth-
while cause, she considered him a true
patriot. It was too early to reach him in the
office, but Joselyn had his private cell
number.

She had to tell him that Thorn was on the
move, roaming near the Capitol. He would
want to know, even if the FBI had everything under control. She called up the contact list on her iPhone and thumbed in the
first three letters. She hadn't even gotten to
the *h* when the words "Joshua Root, Chairman, Senate Select Committee on Intelligence," popped up on the phone's screen.

*   *   *

As soon as the paramedics arrived, the
nurse and I moved back and allowed them
to take over. There was no FBI, and the
only police on the scene were the first re-
sponders who had come in just ahead of
the ambulance.

Nobody other than Herman was watching Thorn. According to Thorpe's secretary, he had no agents on the ground tracking Thorn. What was worse, he didn't have a clue as to what Thorn was up to in Washington. What had happened to all of Joselyn's phone calls and the assurances from her contact?

Herman lies on the ground surrounded by a growing throng of gawkers as the paramedics work furiously trying to keep him alive. Swallowed up in the emerging crowd, I have never felt so alone in my life.

My blood-soaked shirt lies balled up on the concrete next to Herman's body. One of the firemen from the pumper truck that accompanied the ambulance hands me a yellow fire jacket from the back of the truck. I put it on to cover my bare, blood-streaked upper body.

The ambulance and fire truck block the garage entrance and exit as police cordon off the entire area around the building with yellow tape. The paramedics have now been at it for more than ten minutes. You can read it in their eyes, see it on their faces as they work feverishly; Herman isn't going to make it.

He lies unconscious on his back on a

flat body board as they work on him. His head is back, Adam's apple protruding, eyes half open in that glazed look of death. They are having trouble finding a pulse. They started an IV but his blood pressure keeps dropping until the monitor finally flat-lines.

One of the paramedics rips Herman's shirt down the middle with a pair of scissors. He reaches over, grabs the portable paddles from the defibrillator, and then flips the dial. "Clear!" Everybody backs away. He places the paddles diagonally across Herman's chest and pulls the trigger. Herman's upper body heaves as his back arches up off the body board.

The monitor beeps and a weak pulse jots across the screen and then goes flat.

"Again." The paramedic lifts the paddles and hits the switch on the defibrillator. The machine makes a whining sound as it recharges the coil. "Clear!" They back away once more. Herman's body arches up again and the monitor picks up the blip as his heart muscle convulses with the electrical shock.

"Sir, please step back. Let them do their

work." One of the cops in uniform starts to push me back.

I can see the ragged edge of a weak pulse as it blips across the screen, like a car on a cold morning trying to start.

"Is he going to make it?" I ask.

"I don't know," said the paramedic. "Internal bleeding, sucking chest wound. Got his heart going but we gotta get him to the ER now. Let's move. Check that belt across his chest. Make sure it's tight. Who put it on?"

"I did," said the female nurse. "With help from the man standing behind you."

"You guys did a good job," he says.

Four of the firemen lift the body board with Herman on it as one of the paramedics holds the bag with the IV in the air so that gravity can continue to feed fluid into Herman's body. "Keep pressure on that wound."

"Sir!" One of the uniformed cops is standing behind me. "Did you see what happened? The nurse over here says you were the first one on the scene."

"He was already down when I got here," I tell him. "But I know who did it."

"Who?"

"A man named Liquida," I tell him. "A Mexican contract killer who works with the drug cartels."

"Can you spell the name for me?" he says.

"It's not his real name. It's what he goes by, an alias," I tell him. I spell it for him.

"How do you know this man did it?"

"Because Herman told me."

"So you knew the victim?" he says.

"He works for me. Scratch that," I tell him. "Herman Diggs is my friend."

"I'm going to need a detailed statement from you, and some identification," says the cop.

"I don't have time right now," I tell him.

"You're gonna have to make time," he says.

I try to tell him about Thorn, the fact that Herman was following him, that he apparently escaped from the garage, about the jet down in Puerto Rico. And that unless I'm mistaken, something major is about to happen here in Washington. "There is no time to talk," I tell him. "We need to move and move quickly to find Thorn."

The cop looks at me like I'm crazy. He

tells me to calm down, to give him my name and address, or perhaps better yet, we should go downtown where they can get a more detailed statement. He asks for my driver's license, some ID.

There is no time for this. Thorn is on the loose. So is Liquida, and Joselyn is back in the room, alone.

I tell the cop to give me a minute, that I have to make a phone call and to get a signal I'm going to have to go over by the door.

He says fine, tells me not to leave, and turns his back for a moment.

I walk over toward the kiosk at the entrance and take out my cell phone. It is spotted with blood and scratched where I tossed it on the concrete. I call Joselyn's cell number to tell her what's happened. The call goes directly through to her voice mail. Either her phone is turned off, or it's busy, or else . . .

FORTY-SIX

Two hours after the fiery wreckage splashed into the Atlantic, and eleven hundred miles to the northwest, the phantom FedEx 727 passed over the outer continental shelf just a few miles north of Cape Hatteras.

Ten minutes later Ahmed and Masud saw the coastline as it passed beneath them somewhere near Virginia Beach. They could see the mouth of the Chesapeake yawning directly in front of them.

Suddenly the onboard VHF radio came to life. "Squawk 1423, this is Potomac air traffic control. Please identify yourself."

"Take over." Ahmed turned over the flight controls to Masud, reached over, and flipped the switch on the radio. "Potomac, this is FedEx flight 9303, on route from Rafael Hernández Airport in Puerto Rico bound for Newark Liberty Airport. We're showing a serious hydraulic problem, requesting permission to land at Reagan National."

"Flight 9303, this is Potomac air control, say again? Are you reporting an in-flight emergency?"

"Affirmative," said Ahmed. "We have shut down starboard engine overheating and show loss of hydraulic controls. Requesting permission to land at Reagan National."

Ahmed looked at Masud, who glanced over at him.

"Flight 9303, this is Potomac. Descend to eighteen thousand feet and await further instructions."

Ahmed reached over and pushed the throttle controls all the way forward. He goosed their speed to just over six hundred miles an hour and told Masud to maintain their present heading and altitude. They were on a beeline flying directly toward downtown Washington, D.C.

Ahmed knew that air traffic control would never clear them to land at Reagan National Airport. The tactic now was to stall for time. The plane was nothing more than an aerial platform for the fuel-air thermobaric bomb tucked away in the ramp of the airstairs in the rear. In order to deliver it to the target, speed and elevation were everything.

Ahmed did some quick calculations in his head. They were roughly a hundred and twenty miles out; at six hundred miles an hour, ten miles a minute, they only had to stall for twelve minutes to reach the target, and not even that if they could maintain altitude. At their current altitude with its front-end canard controls and big rear fins, the bomb had a glide range of almost thirteen miles.

"Potomac air control to flight 9303, you are instructed to descend to eighteen thousand feet, do you read?"

"Potomac, this is flight 9303. We are having problems with flight surfaces due to hydraulic failure. Trying to descend at this time," said Ahmed.

"This is Potomac air control. How serious is the emergency?"

Ahmed looked at Masud, shrugged his shoulders, and smiled.

"Potomac, we're not sure at this time. We are having some difficulty with flight controls."

He muted the radio for a second. "Descend. We'll give them two thousand feet and then report more problems," he told Masud.

It was as if the bottom fell out of the plane. They dropped quickly down to twenty-three thousand feet.

"This is Potomac air control. One moment."

The air defensive zone around Washington had been beefed up and expanded following the attacks on 9/11. The no-fly zone had been extended out to a radius of between fifteen to seventeen statute miles from the Capitol and the White House. But politicians had already compromised the system, and the military had tipped their hand concerning their willingness to use dire tactics in the event of aircraft violating the zone.

At one point the governor of Kentucky had accidentally wandered into the defensive zone in a private plane, which had

caused the entire Capitol to be evacu-
ated.

It was the problem with Washington.
Wherever there were people of wealth and
power, you could expect that rules would
be broken. It was one thing to shoot down
a commercial jetliner with a few hundred
tax-paying drones on board, all strapped
into their seats so they couldn't even pee
for the last hour of the flight. It was another
to fire on a jet-powered ego container
taking members of Congress to some
lobbyist-paid junket. And around Washington, odds were that if you shot down a
plane, there was more than a fair chance
it might have somebody important on
board.

Ahmed was banking on all of this, vacil-
lations, indecision, and delay just to get
the nose of the 727 under the tent. All he
needed was just a few miles inside the no-
fly zone, and at ten miles a minute that
wouldn't take long.

"Flight 9303, this is Potomac control.
You're being diverted to Dover Air Force
Base in Delaware. Dover tower has been
advised of the emergency. They have

facilities and a long enough runway to allow a landing if your brakes fail."

Masud gave Ahmed a worried look.

"Potomac control, this is flight 9303. We may not be able to make Dover. We're having problems with the rudder controls, a lot of vibration."

"This is Potomac control, are you sure your starboard engine is shut down? Radar control shows your current speed at approximately 520 knots."

Ahmed reached over and switched off the radio. "Take it back up to twenty-five thousand feet." He pushed the throttles all the way forward. The plane screamed toward Washington.

* * *

After more than an hour of desperate work, transit authorities managed to pull the cement truck back from the brink and away from the open hole over the Fulton Street station.

They emptied out the subway down below and one of ATF's bomb-disposal units was gingerly moving in on the vehicle. ATF had already been briefed by the military on the fuel-air device that authorities believed was on board. If Thorpe was right, it was the big one from North Korea, the one that Soyev called Fat Man.

The mixing barrel on the truck was about the right size. Thorpe wanted to know if the cement truck could be safely moved from its present location to somewhere outside the city where the bomb could be safely defused. But the bomb squad said no.

While the manual triggering device in the cab could be controlled, and the trembler switch, if there was one, wouldn't present any particular difficulties since the truck had already been driven to the site, they couldn't be sure until they looked whether there was a timing device.

Given the size and potential destructive power of the fuel-air device, the bomb squad couldn't guarantee that if they moved the truck through the streets of New York it wouldn't go off.

They could try to move it onto a barge and haul it out into the Hudson. But it would take time to get all of the necessary equipment together. And time was the one thing they didn't have if the bomb had a clock on it.

They were probably lucky in one respect.

If whoever put the device together had mounted a pressure switch under the driver's seat, the bomb would have gone off when the transit cop pulled the dead driver out from behind the wheel. They were guessing that the bomb maker probably didn't want the device to go off until it was down in the hole, where it would do the most damage.

The short answer to their dilemma was that they couldn't move the truck. Instead they would have to move all of the news helicopters and anybody with a television feed away from the scene so that viewers wouldn't be able to see what was happening when one of the members of the bomb squad crawled inside the tumbler of the cement truck and tried to defuse the detonator.

The fear was that the detonator could also be remotely controlled by someone close enough who, if he saw what was happening, might set it off.

They assumed, given the nature of the device, that the detonator was probably electronic. If they could safely clip its power source, they could then cut the wires to the manual trigger, make sure there was no secondary detonator, and then haul the truck away to dispose of the massive bomb somewhere safe.

* * *

I'm standing near the exit to the garage still trying to reach Joselyn on the phone as they roll Herman into the back of an ambulance. Half of the blood from his body is now on the concrete floor near where he lay. But sadly, I don't have time to think about it.

On the third ring she finally picks up.

"Hello, Paul, where are you? I thought you were coming right back."

"Never mind," I tell her. "Are you still in the room?"

"Yes."

"Stay there, and don't open the door unless you hear my voice. Do you understand?"

"What's wrong? What's happened?"

"I'll be there in a minute. Just wait for me." I hang up and look over my shoulder. The cop who was taking my statement is busy talking to somebody else.

I step out into the sunlight, take off the yellow jacket, and hand it to one of the firemen. "Thanks." And before he can say anything, I skip across the street and scurry down the sidewalk on the other side under the chrome marquee and through the front door of the Hotel George.

Shirtless and speckled with Herman's blood, I draw stares from curious onlookers as I make my way through the lobby to the elevator. One older woman is standing there waiting for a car to arrive. She looks at me wide eyed.

"An accident," I tell her.

"I take it someone was hurt?"

"Yes. He's on his way to the hospital."

"What a shame," she says.

"Yeah, it is." We walk into the elevator together and I lose her on the third floor as I get off and head for my room. I knock on the door. "It's me." Then I use my key to get in, but the door is locked with the safety bar.

"Just a minute," she says. Joselyn comes over, closes the door all the way, then opens it again. "What happened to you? Where's your shirt? Are you cut?"

"No. But Herman's been stabbed. It's bad," I tell her. "He's on the way to the hospital."

"What do you mean, it's bad?" she says.

I head for the bathroom to wash my hands. "I don't know if he's going to make it. It was Liquida. Herman was able to tell me before he passed out. And Thorn got away. Slipped out of the garage somehow." I grab a facecloth, wet it down, and start to mop the blood off my body, then notice that the knee of my pants where I pressed it into Herman's back is stained a dry brown. I strip my pants off.

"Let me get you some clothes," she says. A few seconds later Joselyn is back at the bathroom door with a clean shirt and a pair of pants. "Here."

"What I need to know from you is who you called," I tell her.

"What do you mean?"

"I mean your source who gave you all the assurances that the FBI and the police had Thorn under glass. Because there was nobody there. Thorn led Herman into a trap in the garage. And the only way he could have done that was if someone tipped him off and he knew that we were following him."

"What are you talking about?" she says.

"It's possible Thorn might have seen Herman following him," I tell her, "but I doubt it. Herman was too good to let that happen. But even if he did, that doesn't explain Liquida. Herman didn't say anything on the phone this morning when he called about anyone else tagging along with Thorn. According to Herman, when Thorn came out of the elevator in his hotel this morning, he was alone. If anybody had been with him, Herman would have mentioned it, especially if it looked like it might be Liquida. But he didn't. That means Liquida was already waiting for Herman over in the garage. And the only way that could have happened is if someone tipped Thorn off that we were here. And the only person we've talked to besides Thorpe, and he didn't know where we were staying, was your contact."

I look at her as all the computations are being made in that sharp little brain behind her eyes. "I . . . I find that hard to believe," she says.

"Hard to believe or not, it's a fact. Who else knew we were here?"

She shakes her head. "I don't know."

"It's time to cough it up. The name," I tell her. "Who have you been talking to?"

*   *   *

"Zeb, sorry to break in, but we got another problem." This time it wasn't Thorpe's secretary but Ray Zink, his assistant. And from the look on Zink's face, Thorpe knew it was trouble.

"We've got reports that there's a commercial air-freight flight, a FedEx plane originally bound for Newark, reporting some kind of onboard emergency and requesting permission to land at Reagan National. Air traffic control tried to divert the flight to Dover Air Force Base and then lost radio contact. But the plane is still in the air and bearing down fast on Washington."

"Well, there's nothing we can do? Did they scramble fighters?" said Thorpe.

"Yeah. Two F-16s out of Andrews," said Zink.

"Okay, well, keep me posted."

Zink turned and started to leave.

"Just out of curiosity," said Thorpe, "where did the wayward FedEx flight originate?"

Zink turned and looked at him. "Puerto Rico."

It took about two seconds of cold fusion before all the circles and rings began to link up in Thorpe's brain. He slapped his forehead with the heel of his hand. "Of course. That's it!"

"What is?" said Zink.

"The plane from the boneyard," said Thorpe. "It was where Madriani was headed the last time we talked, Puerto Rico. Madriani told me that Thorn had purchased a commercial jet. I didn't pay any attention. We had Soyev, a bird in the hand. But he didn't know anything because his client kept him at arm's length. He'd never met him. The phone call from North Korea to Cuba. It would be the perfect location for Thorn to hide out while he waited for the two bombs. And Little Boy is still out there."

"You think it's on that plane?" said Zink.

"I'd bet my life on it," said Thorpe. "Madriani and I have been chasing the same man. We just didn't know it. Thorn was Victor Soyev's other half. The client who stiffed him and turned him in. It all makes sense."

Thorpe jumped up from his chair. "Ray, get me Madriani's cell number. My secretary has it. Do it now."

Thorpe's attention suddenly turned toward the White House and the Capitol

Building. He was confident that the fighters and the other layers of air defense deployed since 9/11 could take down the plane. The question was whether they could defend against whatever was on board.

FORTY-SEVEN

My contact is Senator Joshua Root," says Joselyn. "I am telling you this only because I am certain that he has nothing to do with what happened to Herman. I am telling you in confidence and I expect you to keep the secret. Do you understand?"

"I understand."

We are in our room at the Hotel George. I'm still changing my clothes.

"I can't believe what you're saying," she says. "I've worked with him for years. There has to be some mistake."

"Did you tell him where we were staying, here in D.C.?"

She nods. "Yes, but why would he do anything like that? What possible involvement could a man like Joshua Root have with someone like Thorn? What would he possibly have to gain? It's not like him. Josh Root is a dove. I know him. He is a gentle man. He hates violence. True, he's had some bouts with serious depression in the last year or so. But he has been treated for that. We all have times when we're not ourselves. God knows what I'll be like when I'm his age. But there's no way he'd be involved with someone like Thorn."

"What else did you tell him?" I ask.

"I told him about Thorn and the plane, what happened down in Puerto Rico. I told him everything we knew, and I asked for his help, and he agreed."

I pull on my socks and put on my shoes as we talk.

"When's the last time you talked to him?"

"I tried to call him this morning, just a few minutes ago. I tried his office. They said he wasn't there. I called his house. There was no answer, and his cell phone didn't answer either. I'll try again in a few minutes."

"Root was the source of your information on the nuclear device in San Diego?" I ask.

She nods. "And his information has always been accurate. He has been nothing but truthful every time I've dealt with him. And he takes a considerable personal risk in sharing such information because it's classified. He could go to prison and he knows it. But he's willing to take that risk because he knows that the dangers the country and the world face by remaining silent are much greater."

"How did he know about the nuke?"

"He chairs the Senate Select Committee on Intelligence. There isn't much he doesn't know. There was a Senate investigation after the attack at Coronado. Root's committee held two weeks of hearings behind closed doors. He told me some of the committee members wanted to go public with the information about the bomb. But the administration convinced them that until they knew more about who planned the attack, and how they carried it out, it would be unwise to disclose the fact that there was a nuclear attempt. All it would do would be to cause needless public panic," says Joselyn. "At least that was the argument."

"Yeah, and would probably raise a lot of questions about how the administration screwed up," I tell her. "Wait a second. Wasn't that the committee Snyder's kid . . . ?"

"Yes. I thought about that when I read the news reports on the murder," says Joselyn. "Jimmie Snyder worked for Root's committee, but it didn't have anything to do with his death."

"How do you know?"

"He was on staff, but he was new. He'd only been there a short time. I'm sure he didn't have any security clearance, so he wouldn't have had access to any significant information. He was a gofer. Besides, he wasn't working there at the time he met Thorn, when those security photographs were taken."

"How do you know that?" I say.

"His father told me. He and I talked after you left the office that day. The day I got sick."

"So where were the photos taken?" I ask.

"I asked him that," says Joselyn. "He told me he'd rather not say. He said Jimmie had made a mistake and paid with his life."

"Violated security protocols, as I recall."

"Yes, by showing Thorn something he wasn't supposed to see," says Joselyn. "Snyder made it clear that unless discussing the details would lead him to Thorn, he didn't want to talk about it."

"Why?" I ask.

"Sheltering his son's reputation, I suppose. Even in death."

"Where are the pictures Snyder gave us?"

"They are in my briefcase," says Joselyn. "Why?"

"Why don't you get them?"

"Sure." She walks over to the other side of the room, looks in her briefcase, and pulls out a manila folder. She opens it and takes out the photos.

We spread them out on the bed. Joselyn lays down on her stomach. I sit. We look at all three photographs for the umpteenth time, two of them showing Thorn and Jimmie Snyder together, the third one, the enlargement of Thorn by himself.

The images are almost ghostlike

because of the stark white walls behind them. They look like film frames from one of those movies in which some mortal character plays God in some whitewashed ethereal corporate office that represents heaven. There is nothing on the walls except the one sign partially obscured behind Thorn's shoulder.

"What's this? It's been bugging me since the first day we saw the photographs, just before lunch at the Brigantine." I point to the sign over Thorn's shoulder, the words "basketball and weightlifting" clearly visible.

"It looks like a gymnasium," says Joselyn.

"It has to be here in this city someplace. Are you sure you don't recognize it? You're the Washington insider," I say.

She shakes her head. "No. I've never seen it before. It doesn't ring any bells." She tries to read the line below it, the last few words of which are visible over Thorn's shoulder but lost in the glare of light. "It looks as if there's some kind of a plastic sheet or cover over the sign," she says. "The rest of the sign is blocked by part of Thorn's head and body. Give me a minute."

Joselyn rolls over, sits up, and again walks to where her briefcase is. When she returns, she has a small plastic case about an inch and a half square and half an inch thick in her hand. She pulls on it and a small magnifying glass slides out. She reaches across the bed and picks up the photograph with the sign in the background. She holds the magnifying lens close to the photo and examines the image as if it were a fine piece of jewelry. "Oh, my God! What day is it?"

"Monday. Why?"

"The first Monday in October, right?"

"Yeah."

"The sign. It's the highest court in the land," says Joselyn.

"What?"

"We don't have time to talk," she says. "Come on." She grabs me by the arm and pulls me toward the door.

FORTY-EIGHT

He sat in the small, dark room watching a tiny television set, the breaking news of the unfolding events over the subway in New York.

"Information is sketchy at this time but it appears that something has happened at a construction site out near the Battery on the tip of Manhattan. There are reports of a shooting between transit police and an unidentified suspect involving some kind of large vehicle, a heavy truck of some kind, and that the area around this construction zone has been cordoned off by police.

"Jim, as you can see, I am near the site. But police have now moved us back three blocks from where this is happening, so our camera really can't see anything. And now I'm getting word that our helicopter, which was en route, will not be able to get a visual of the location because authorities have cleared the airspace above the site, for what reason we're not sure.

"In addition, subway service into and out of the area has been shut down, and police and emergency services workers are moving as quickly as possible to get people out of the subway. According to the subway system, they have closed all stations from midtown down to the Battery."

"Mike, can you tell us, are you able to see any portion of the construction site from where you are right now?"

"Jim, actually I'm not."

"Mike, we're being told that according to the authorities it's the site of the new Fulton Street transit station."

"That would be about right, but as I say, they've pushed us back so far that we really can't see anything. Excuse me . . . just a moment."

The Old Weatherman watched as the

reporter on the screen pressed his finger to his ear and listened as one of his producers told him what was happening.

"We now have a report that the vehicle in question is a large cement truck and that the driver of that vehicle exchanged gunfire with police at the site. According to the information, the driver and a third party were shot, and police sources are now confirming that the driver is dead. As to the identity and condition of the other shooting victim, at this time we have no information.

"And there is more. According to one source, a bomb squad has been dispatched to the scene. For what reason we don't know. But coupled with the fact that the authorities are now evacuating the subway, it doesn't look good. Over to you, Jim."

"Thanks, Mike. We'll be back to you momentarily. As soon as there's any more information."

The Old Weatherman reached over and turned off the set. The only thing he needed to know was the fact that the driver was dead. The FBI and local law enforcement would waste the next several hours tinkering with the truck before they extracted the detonator.

They probably wouldn't find out at least for a day or so, until after it was carefully examined, that the detonator itself was defective. The bomb was in fact inert. Its sole purpose was to draw the attention of the FBI away from what was happening in Washington.

The last thing the Old Weatherman wanted to do was kill thousands of people in a perfectly senseless act of mayhem. He was not a terrorist, no matter what others might think. He had suffered through years of regret for the one senseless act of violence in his youth, the bombing of the bank that had accidentally cost a human life. It had twisted his psyche in ways that he still did not fully comprehend. It was the reason he'd sent Root to warn his old friend Nicholas Merle that it was time to retire, to give up his seat on the Supreme Court. He wanted him out of the way before the man lost his life. But Merle wouldn't listen. The Old Weatherman tried to shake off the thought.

Where was he? He couldn't remember

where his mind had left off. It was the detonator. That was it. The bomb's ignition source. The detonator was the key because the FBI would trace it from the manufacturer in Germany to a purchaser in the Middle East. At that point the government would start looking at all the usual suspects. And in all the wrong places.

They would see the whole thing, the distraction in New York, and the real attack in D.C., as inspired by Middle Eastern terrorists, but this time they were using professional mercenaries to carry out the attacks. It all fit. Frustrated by the increasing security and unable to get their own people into position in the United States, the Islamic radicals now would be seen as hiring Western mercenaries who would have less difficulty gaining access and traveling in America.

It was the cover that the Old Weatherman needed, not for himself, but for the president, who knew nothing, but who would now have a free hand to fill all nine positions on the U.S. Supreme Court.

Decapitate the executive branch and the effect would be short term, if at all—but only until the next election. This was true of Congress as well. The present corrupt system of money and politics, of a Washington aristocracy utterly out of touch with the people they ruled—the fiction of a representative republic that no longer existed was far too resilient to bring down in this way, and the Old Weatherman knew it.

But there was one institution of the federal government for which this was not true—the Supreme Court. Because of the lifetime tenure conferred on members of the high court, and the fact that these nine justices held the final word on most if not all of the social and economic controversies confronting the country, it was the one controlling pressure point that could alter the long-term direction of America.

Franklin Roosevelt had realized this during the dark days of the Depression when he contemplated packing the court with additional members all of his own choosing. But politics conspired against him and he dropped the idea.

The court had been badly divided now for years. Most of the controversial decisions depended for their legitimacy on razor-thin five-to-four votes with too many of the decisions going the wrong way. In the eyes of the Old Weatherman, the national economy was dictated by five members of the Federal Reserve Board, none of whom were elected by anyone, with political and social policy determined not by the rule of nine, but by a tyranny of one, a single deciding swing vote on the U.S. Supreme Court.

The court was divided along partisan lines in the same way the nation was. Aging liberal members of the court had been required to survive and to defer their retirement until a like-minded president was in the White House in order to preserve their numbers on the court. Conservative members would now be required to do the same, waiting for the next conservative president to retake the White House.

But most of the conservative members of the court were young and would be in place for decades. And while liberals now had their chance to retire, this would not change the balance of power on the court. The only exception to this waiting game was death, and for the Old Weatherman this happened all too infrequently to alter the formula of justice. He was tired of waiting.

He realized that the opportunity for real change was at hand. A well-timed precision attack on the court, taking out all nine members in a single stroke, would transform the course of history in ways that even the most wide-eyed radical of the sixties could never have dreamed of.

The incumbent president would be able to fill all nine seats on the court at a single stroke, and conservatives in the Senate would be powerless to stop him. The time to strike was now.

The Old Weatherman started coughing, covered his mouth, then looked at his hand and saw blood. It was getting worse. When he'd declined the radiation and the chemotherapy, the doctors had warned him that he wouldn't have long. And for that he was grateful.

As he glanced at the dark screen on the television, the mirrored image was haggard and old. He had been weaning himself from his other medications now for almost three months. It was a cocktail of psychotropic drugs that gave Root the upper hand over the Old Weatherman. Without them the Old Weatherman was the master. Unshaven, and unkempt, wearing a tank top T-shirt, with hair sprouting from under his arms, he saw the image of a traitor and a coward. He saw in that moment of clarity the face of Senator Joshua Root.

FORTY-NINE

Ahmed was back in the rear of the 727, huddled up against the raised ramp over the bomb on its custom-built carriage. Using a ratchet and a set of sockets, he first unbolted the three metal straps holding the bomb in place.

Thorn had trained him thoroughly on all of the preattack procedures and had provided a checklist.

As soon as Ahmed removed the last strap, he went to work on the four long bolts holding the rolling carriage in place. Before he removed that last bolt, he replaced the third one with a soft piece of pine doweling the same length as the missing bolt.

When he was finished the only thing keeping the rolling carriage and the bomb that was on it from moving was the single wooden dowel. When the ramp was lowered, the shifting weight of the carriage, and the two-thousand-pound bomb resting on it, would snap the dowel like a twig. Their fearless leader, the Australian who ran the show, had tested it on the ground using simulated weights, not once, but several times, and each time the dowel snapped as if on cue.

The only difference this time was that the carriage and the bomb would roll down the rails and sail into the open sky from the lowered airstairs of the plane. The carriage would fall away, free, as the large rear fins and the front canard on the bomb slowed its descent and the laser sensor in the nose cone began searching for the signal.

Ahmed put the ratchet and sockets back in the toolbox and placed the box, along with loose bolts and metal straps, into a storage bin in the plane's cargo area. He made sure the lid on the bin was latched and locked. Then he checked all of the other equipment in the cargo bay to make sure that it was all lashed down tight.

When the airstairs opened at their current speed and altitude, the plane would experience a sudden loss of pressure. This would suck anything and everything that wasn't secured or tied down out through the open door. One loose piece of equipment colliding with the bomb in midair could destroy the entire mission.

Ahmed took one final look and then headed back to the flight deck. He wasn't a minute too early. Just as he settled into the left-hand seat and started to buckle up, two jet fighters screamed past the nose of the plane.

Ahmed nearly got whiplash trying to turn his head to follow the path of their flight. He saw one of them start to take a wide, arcing turn to come around behind the 727, then lost sight of him.

Ahmed took over the controls. A few seconds later one of the F-16s pulled up alongside the nose of the larger plane, about forty feet off the port-side window of the cockpit. The fighter pilot turned his head and looked directly at Ahmed.

"Take the controls," said Ahmed.

Masud did as instructed.

Ahmed reached down and picked up his radio headset, held it up to the side window, and then signaled thumbs-down, a sign that their radio was out. As far as Ahmed was concerned, he would now use anything just to buy another minute of flight time.

The fighter pilot looked at him, stern eyes from over the top of his oxygen mask, nodded, then maneuvered to wave his wings, the sign that Ahmed was being instructed to follow him. Both of the Saudi pilots knew they were on a suicide mission. But the goal was worth it. What they had been told was that the bomb was destined for downtown Washington, and the destruction of the United States Capitol Building.

*   *   *

Thorn sat on one of the concrete benches along East Capitol Plaza just above the ramp to the Capitol Visitor Center. The subterranean monstrosity was a disaster. Its construction was nearly 1,000 percent over budget and three years late, but it did have a consistent theme.

Forcing taxpayers in a hole to see their government in action couldn't help but remind them of the bottomless pit Congress kept digging with their galactic budget deficits.

As far as Thorn was concerned, the last building any reputable terrorist would want to blow up would be the Capitol. Why kill your most potent ally? Congress had done more damage to the country in the last twenty years than a legion of suicide bombers. And they were still hammering away.

He knew that Joselyn Cole and the two men with her had been tracking him since before he'd left Puerto Rico. His employer had kept him informed through the elaborate telephone code system. How the employer found out about the trio Thorn didn't know. Nor did he care. In ten more minutes it wouldn't matter. By then it would all be over.

He opened the snap locks on the attaché case and checked his watch. He lifted the lid and punched the power button on the laptop inside. Thorn scooted a little sideways to make sure that the computer's antenna would have a clear line of sight to the copper dome over the reading room in the Library of Congress across the street. He watched as the screen lit up and the program booted. The computer battery had plenty of life. The only one he had to worry about was the small NiCad battery on the little brown bat.

Thorn held his breath and hit the keys. A few seconds later the camera on the back of the bat came to life. He breathed easy and glanced around a little to make sure no one was watching. He pulled the lid on the attaché case closed just a bit to gain shade on the screen and to conceal it from prying eyes. Gently Thorn put his finger on the track pad and the camera lens began to move as the gimbal rotated on the back of the bat.

To Thorn, who had been at war for thirty years, the new microtechnology was nothing short of stunning. During the First Gulf War, doing what he was doing now would have required a device known as a "mule." It was a cumbersome black blunderbuss, a sawed-off shotgun on electronic steroids. It had a shoulder stock so you could steady the laser beam on the target. And when the words "light 'em up" were used, it didn't mean "smoke 'em if you got 'em." It was the order to paint the target with the mule, a laser designator, to aim it and turn on the switch so that the receiver on the incoming ordnance could home in on the laser beam and strike within an inch of its center.

To anyone standing near a target that was painted, the laser was invisible. The target designator, unlike a laser pointer in a classroom, did not emit a continuous beam. Instead it sent out laser light in a series of coded pulses. These signals were designed to bounce off the target and into the sky. There the pulse would be detected by the seeker on the laser-guided ordnance. The incoming bunker buster would steer itself toward the center of the reflected signal, and unless the people inside had access to laser-detection equipment, the only thing they would hear would be the ear-splitting detonation from the blast that killed them.

Because the device emitted no heat signature and only a tiny radar profile, the gravity-directed bomb would be largely immune to antimissile defense systems, including other missiles and Phalanx, a high-speed radar-directed Gatling gun designed to destroy incoming missiles in flight.

To Thorn, size was everything.

Laser designators came in a number of

sizes, generally ranging from a black box that resembled your grandfather's eight-millimeter movie camera mounted on a tri-pod to a sleeker model that looked like a squared-off set of large binoculars. But the little brown bat could never carry that big a payload.

The key for Thorn was miniaturization. The answer had come from a small firm in Delaware. The company had lost out on a bid with the army to design a miniaturized laser designator. They already had two pro-totypes, laser-targeting diodes not much bigger than a watch battery. In fact, it was a large watch battery mounted on the back of the bat that provided the power for the cam-era and the optically linked laser. Thorn had already turned on the camera just for a few seconds in order to train it on the section of roof across the street from the Library of Congress. The beam, when it was turned on, would pulse off the roof of the Supreme Court Building, the area directly over the courtroom. The small watch battery would last only about ten minutes, but for Thorn's purposes that would be long enough.

The reason Thorn's small point-and-shoot camera did not set off the metal detector the day he scoped out the target from inside, the gullible Jimmie Snyder in tow, was that it wasn't a camera at all. It was a laser range finder capable of measuring minute distances with amazing precision. It was made of carbon fiber and plastic.

What Thorn needed to know was the exact distance between floors, from floor to ceiling at each level, as well as the distance from the front edge of the gabled roof to the bench in the courtroom. What bothered him most was the area of the gymnasium with its basketball court. What they jokingly referred to as "the highest court in the land." Thorn had to be sure that the bunker-busting munitions would "breach the monastery" and penetrate to the correct depth, where it would detonate on cue, directly over the angled bench.

The bunker buster was designed to penetrate up to one hundred feet of earth and twenty feet of steel-reinforced concrete before detonating. To receive his final payment, he had to be certain that the fuel-vapor charge would level the building and leave not a single survivor among the nine justices sitting at the bench.

The rapid consumption of oxygen resulting from the firing of the mixed-fuel mist in a confined area would produce a near vacuum followed by shock waves that would collapse the entire structure where the blast occurred.

Those caught inside a hardened structure by such a blast, if not incinerated or suffocated by the depletion of oxygen sucked from their lungs, would likely die of massive concussive injuries to internal organs resulting from the heat-driven pressure wave.

FIFTY

The opening day of the Supreme Court's new session, the first Monday in October, is always high ceremony. The chief justice first welcomes any visiting judges and lawyers from abroad. He then swears in lawyers applying to become members of the Supreme Court bar. All of this takes time before the court begins to hear the argument in the first case of the day.

I can see from a block away as we run through the East Plaza behind the Capitol that a crowd has already assembled out in front of the Supreme Court Building, in the distance across the street.

I glance at my watch. The court would already be seated at the bench. This must be the overflow, members of the public who have been turned away because the court-room is full.

There is a line of television cameras up on the west plaza, facing the building's white stairs and portico. Reporters are staged in front of them using the stark white glare of the temple's gleaming marble as a backdrop.

"Thorn could be anywhere," says Jose-lyn. "We'll never find him."

"I don't think so. He's going to have to be close by somewhere."

"Why?"

"The model plane," I tell her.

"Stop," she says. Joselyn is out of breath.

"He was practicing against that shed out in the field for a reason. That little toy has something to do with his plan. If that's the case, he won't be able to get beyond the range of the radio controls."

"You don't understand," Joselyn says. "The military can fly their drones from any-where in the world."

"Yes, but they have satellites. Thorn's not the U.S. military," I tell her. "He wouldn't have access to satellites. He's going to have to stay within the line of sight to maintain radio control. If his little bird gets behind a building, he's going to lose it. That means he has to stay somewhere close to the target."

"But he could be in a building or a car," she says. "We may not be able to see him. Let's call 911."

"And tell them what?" I say.

"That there's a bomb in the Supreme Court Building." She looks at me and arches an eyebrow. "The worst that can happen is that they arrest us. But at least they'll have to clear the building."

We are directly in front of the east steps behind the Capitol. I look at her. "Do it," I tell her.

"I can't. I don't have a phone. I left my purse back in the room."

I grab my cell phone off the clip on my belt and flip it to her. "You stay here. I'm going to keep looking for Thorn." I turn and start running toward the Supreme Court Building three hundred yards away.

"How do I stay in touch with you if you don't have a phone?" she says.

I turn, palms up, shrug my shoulders,

and shake my head as I skip away and start to run again.

* * *

"Potomac air control. This is VNG 118. That's affirmative, he's got all three engines burning hot and fast. No sign of any engine trouble." The F-16 flying behind the FedEx flight had a clear view of all three engines and could see that they were throwing heat.

The other F-16 alongside hit his afterburner and pulled out in front of the big 727. He wagged his wings a couple more times in a clear indication that the larger plane was to follow him. Then the fighter made a long, slow, sweeping turn northeast, toward Dover Air Force Base in Delaware.

* * *

Ahmed reached down, tightened his seat belt, and told Masud to get his oxygen going. Ahmed put on his own mask, tightened the straps behind his head, and then pulled back hard on the yoke. The nose of the 727 started climbing as Ahmed watched the dial on the altimeter start to turn like the second-hand sweep on a watch. Every thousand feet added range to the bomb. The plane had already penetrated both the outer and inner defensive zones. Anything Ahmed could get now added insurance. He put his fingers on the lever controlling the airstairs in the back.

*   *   *

"This is VNG 118. I have a lock on the target."

"VNG 118, you have authorization to launch. Repeat, you are authorized to launch."

The fighter pilot flipped up the cap cover on the trigger and pressed the button. The sidewinder fell away from his right wing. Just as the rocket motor cut in and the missile began to streak ahead, the rear ramp on the 727 suddenly yawned open. A large bomb fell away, separated from its metal carrier, and before the fighter pilot could react, both the bomb and the carrier were below and behind him.

Two seconds later the sidewinder streaked into the exhaust port of the 727's starboard engine and exploded. The F-16 pulled skyward, and a second later a massive yellow fireball filled the air where the

FedEx flight had been. Hot shards of flaming metal streaked from the fiery blast as the debris pattern left curling contrails in the sky.

"Andrews control, this is VNG 118, target destroyed, but incoming ordnance is in the air."

"Andrews control to VNG 118, say again."

"This is VNG 118. The target was able to release ordnance."

"Can you describe, kind and type?"

"Negative."

"Any chance you can get a radar lock?"

"No, sir. Item was too small, and from what I could see, there was no heat source."

"Tower to VNG 118. See if you can pick it up."

"VNG 118 to Andrews control, will do."

* * *

On the east side of the United States Capitol, East Capitol Street is like a broad bridge, a concourse for pedestrians only about a hundred and thirty yards long until you reach First Street.

At that intersection, cars cross it going north and south, and vehicles can drive in an easterly direction on East Capitol. On the north corner of First and East Capitol

Street is the Supreme Court Building. On the south corner sits the Library of Congress.

I jog past tourists milling in each direction on the pedestrians-only walkway until I am about sixty yards from First Street, when I see him. At first I am not sure if it's Thorn. From this angle I can see only a portion of his face. He is sitting on a concrete bench near the end of the concourse, no more than twenty yards away.

I stop running so as not to draw attention to myself and wander over toward the railing on the left-hand side of the walkway to get a better look. I lean against the railing with my back to him and then slowly turn.

At the moment his head is down. He has an attaché case on his lap with the lid open, both hands inside. Whatever he is doing, his attention is focused inside the case. He is wearing dark glasses and his face is shaded. Then suddenly he looks up, turns his head the other way, and for several seconds he stares across the street, not in the direction of the Supreme Court Building. Instead he is looking toward the Library of Congress, up high, toward the copper dome.

In that instant it clicks, the copper wings on the model plane. He has already landed the little brown bat. What it's doing up there I have no idea. But there is no time left. Without thinking I push off from the railing and run straight at him.

Thorn hears my footfalls on the hard concrete and starts to turn his head. Running at full bore, six feet out from the bench I launch myself into the air.

Just as Thorn's startled eyes turn to fix on me I roll my right shoulder into his upper body and smash into him.

* * *

The impact moves Thorn's thumb on the computer track pad and sends the servo-motor for the camera gimbal on the back of the little brown bat gyrating. The laser signal darts skyward just as the sensor in the bomb's nose cone homes in. The servo-motors on the canard and tail fins suddenly rotate, lifting the nose of the bomb from its sharp dive to a more flattened trajectory as the control surfaces bite into the air.

* * *

The impact of my body drives Thorn off the bench and sends both of us sprawling across the pavement. The attaché case

flips into the air and slides across the concrete as the laptop flies out of it and skit-
ters along the ground.

A woman screams and tourists suddenly
move away from the bench as if it were the
entrance to hell.

Even before he hits the pavement, Thorn's
hands are reaching out, trying to grab the
flying computer as if it were a fumbled foot-
ball. He hits the ground and instantly rolls
up onto one knee.

Before I can move, he scrambles ten
feet across the cement to the computer.
Single-minded and focused, he tries to get
his fingers on the controls.

Just as he picks up the computer
and starts to finger the keyboard, a moving shadow crosses the ground. A whoos-
hing sound streaks overhead. Thorn looks
up, a kind of pleading expression in his
eyes. Two seconds later a flash of light followed by a massive concussive explosion
rocks the ground.

* * *

Joselyn connected with the dispatcher at
911, and reported that there was a bomb
in the U.S. Supreme Court Building.
She was watching, wondering what was

happening, as she saw Paul race across the sidewalk maybe a hundred and thirty yards away, and careen into someone seated on a concrete bench.

"Who is this?" said the dispatcher. "I need your name."

"There's no time to talk," said Joselyn. "Just evacuate the building and do it now!"

Before she could even press the button to hang up she felt the ground rock beneath her feet with the force of the explosion. Her gaze turned toward the flash of light and she saw the rising mushroom cloud as it billowed two hundred feet into the air little more than a half mile away.

* * *

The VRE, Virginia Rail Express, had just pulled out of Union Station, headed for Fredericksburg, in northern Virginia, when the blast ripped up the rails a quarter of a mile behind it.

The explosion sent a mound of dirt and debris high into the sky as the concussion rattled the trailing truck on the last passenger car off the rails. The slow-moving train immediately applied its brakes and came to a screeching halt as flames and an immense plume of black smoke rose into the sky just down the tracks behind the train.

* * *

With the concussive blast, all eyes around us suddenly turn away from the brawl on the concrete toward the north and the rising plume of smoke. A couple of women are screaming. A few of the tourists start to run. Others seem frozen in place.

I look into Thorn's eyes. What I see is desperation and anger. Only he and I know that the collision on the bench and the massive explosion were connected.

He looks at me for only a second before he darts toward the sidewalk on First Street. Suddenly he realizes he has a chance to escape. He looks at me with a scowl, turns, and starts to walk away.

In an instant I'm on my feet.

He turns, sees me, and starts to run.

"Paul, let him go!" It's Joselyn behind me, running to catch up. "Let the police get him."

I turn, look at her. "Stay there!"

She cups her hands around her mouth. She's still a hundred feet away. "Let him go. The police will find him."

But by then it's too late. Adrenaline has

taken hold. I turn back toward Thorn, and with the chase instinct of a cat, I find myself in a footrace. We run down the sidewalk on First Street dodging tourists and government workers.

Thorn is maybe two hundred feet ahead of me, running at full speed. He reaches Independence Avenue and doesn't even slow down. He runs out into the intersection against a red light, dodging cars with honking horns.

By the time I get there, he's opened up a lead of almost half a block. I continue running. I can see him in the distance. Suddenly a car pulls up next to me. It's a cab and Joselyn is in the back. She opens the door. "Get in!" she says.

I turn and look back at Thorn just as he runs between two barricades blocking cars from turning onto First Street across the intersection up ahead. "Go around and head him off," I tell her. "Don't get out of the car. Use the phone to call the police."

She nods, slams the door closed, and the cab speeds away.

I continue running down the block until I reach the traffic barricade, then step between the two gates and start to jog again. I am in a canyon between two House office buildings, in the shade. I catch a fleeting glimpse of Thorn as he steps off the sidewalk to the right and disappears somewhere beyond the next intersection up ahead. I begin to wonder if he has a car parked in a garage or a lot. I pick up the pace and start to run.

As I clear the barricade at the other end of the block, I see the yellow cab coming this way. Now if he has a car we can follow him and call in the location to the cops. The cab screams up the street and stops at midblock. A few seconds later I reach it just as Joselyn is getting out of the backseat.

"I hope you have some money. All I have in my pocket is some change, a credit card, and my Metro pass," she says. "And we'll need that."

"Why?"

"Hurry up. Pay the driver," she says.

I do it and she grabs me by the hand, pulling me across the street. Then I realize where we're going. The sign says CAPITOL SOUTH. It's an open, cavernous concrete hole in the ground with escalators. We jump on the one going down.

"You sure he went in here?"

"I saw him," she says. "I just hope he hasn't gotten on one of the trains yet or we'll lose him for good."

The escalator drops into the bowels of the earth, maybe two hundred feet below-ground. When we reach the underground station, it's a milling madhouse with vending machines and a ticket kiosk that has a long line in front of it.

"Follow me." Joselyn reaches into her pocket.

I stay right behind her.

She reaches the turnstile and slips a plastic card into the slot then steps through. She grabs the card as it's spit out on the other side then reaches and hands it to me. I do the same and within seconds we're running for the platform. I'm looking both ways, scanning the crowd to see if there's any sign of Thorn.

Joselyn sees two uniformed cops patrolling the station on the other side of the tracks. "Give me a moment, I'll have to go back up and over the top so I can tell them what's happening. I'll be right back." She leaves me standing on the platform as she heads back toward the ticket area.

I turn again and look for Thorn, but I don't see him. I am beginning to think that he caught one of the Metro trains and disappeared before we got down here.

I look back toward the ticketing area where Joselyn was headed and notice that she's still on the platform, and she's not moving. She is stopped near a pillar, standing there motionless, not saying anything and not moving.

I start to walk in that direction and suddenly Thorn steps out from behind the pillar. He has one hand on her arm and the other in his coat pocket. The way he holds it there I can tell he's handling some kind of weapon.

* * *

"Never mind that your friend's seen us," said Thorn. "This way." He held her arm, gripping it hard above the elbow, and pulled her behind him, retreating toward the far end of the platform.

Thorn had already seen the two cops on the other side. He got up close in Joselyn's ear from behind. "Don't say anything," said Thorn, "just motion with your hand.

Tell him to stay away. Do it or I'll kill you right here. Trust me—I can shoot you and nobody's even going to hear it."

* * *

Joselyn moves her right hand out, her palm facing me, away from her waist, her fingers open and extended, and while Thorn grips her arm tightly, she waves me off, a sign that I should keep my distance.

All I can do is stand there and watch as Thorn, with his hand around Joselyn's arm, retreats toward the other end of the platform.

Suddenly I hear the rush of air coming from the open tunnel behind them. A train pulls up and stops at the platform. The automatic doors open and a flood of passengers disembark while others wait to get on. In the press of bodies, the invasion of a new army onto the platform, I lose sight of Thorn and Joselyn. Then I see his head. I move a few feet toward one of the open doors of the train in case he tries to get on.

He sees me and stops. Before he can move again, the doors close and the train starts to move. Thorn realizes that his best chance to escape has just pulled out of the station. Instead he backs up toward the open tunnel, pulling Joselyn along behind him. As I stand there and watch, he pushes her off the platform, down onto the tracks, and then jumps down behind her.

In the rush and commotion of the train pulling out, I look across to the other side. The two uniformed cops are gone. When I look back at the tunnel, both Thorn and Joselyn have disappeared into the darkness.

I run for the end of the platform, lean over, and try to peer into the tunnel, but I can't see a thing. I hear footsteps shuffling in the gravel along the bed near the tracks, somewhere off in the distance.

I jump down and enter the darkness. It takes a minute or so for my eyes to begin to adjust. I can make out warning signs, red lights facing in this direction in the distance. I start to make my way deeper into the tunnel. Every few seconds I stop and listen for the shuffling of feet on the gravel. And I keep moving. I worry that if I get too close and a train comes, Thorn may throw Joselyn in front of it and try to escape amid the screeching steel wheels and chaos that follows.

I look down. There are two sets of tracks.

One on this side and one on the other, three
rails for each set. Two of them are safe, the
third one, off center and just inside the rail
nearest me, carries high-voltage electricity
for the train. It is deadly. Touch it, even wearing a rubber-soled running shoe, and you're
toast.

* * *

As soon as they were enveloped in darkness, Thorn pulled the silenced Walther
PPK from his coat pocket and held it firmly
against the side of Joselyn's head as he
pushed her through the tunnel. He kept
her moving as fast as he could.

He had no idea how far it was to the
next station. His plan was to kill her with a
single silenced shot to the head the moment he saw any light at the end. That
way he could emerge alone into the station, where he could take the escalator up
to the street and disappear. He wasn't sure
what he would do about his passports or
his luggage. That he would have to think
about, and figure it out when he got there.

As all of this was running through his
mind, Thorn looked up and saw a bright
light in the distance. For a moment he
thought it was the next station coming into

view. Then he realized it was a train coming his way.

*   *   *

I see the lights approaching. I jump the
two rails next to me, skip over the other
rail, and then clear the opposite set of rails
carrying traffic in the other direction. I want
to get to the far side of the tunnel before
the train lights me up for Thorn to take a
shot. With me on one side and him on the
other, the train will be between us, at least
momentarily. If I can move fast enough,
running down the other side of the track, I
can be on top of him before he realizes it.

I wait until I feel the rush of the wind, the
pressure wave in front of the train as it fills
the tunnel. Then I start to run full tilt down
the other side of the tracks. I hear the squeal
of the wheels on the steel rails as the head-
light flashes in the darkness. The noise of
the train drowns out everything except the
pounding of my heart in my ears.

As the train reaches me, I sprint as fast
as my legs can carry me. My feet kick up
gravel. But Thorn won't be able to hear a
thing, not with the sound of the speeding
train in his ears. The lighted windows race
by, like a falling ladder. The instant they

pass I am once more immersed in darkness. But the sound of the retreating train still covers the noise of my feet on the gravel.

I jump the two rails closest to me, then the outside rail and the other set, and within a few seconds my back is pressed against the side of the tunnel, into an alcove formed by one of the large steel reinforcing ribs that arches overhead and supports the tunnel. I strain my ears, listening for the sounds of feet shuffling on gravel.

Then I hear it. I can't tell how much distance I have made up, but it doesn't sound right. Suddenly I realize why. Joselyn and Thorn are no longer out in front. They are behind me, coming this way. I can hear Thorn talking to Joselyn, telling her to keep moving.

I realize what has happened. They had stood stationary, probably pressed against the wall of the tunnel as the train approached and then went by. All the while I was running past them on the other side.

Thorn must have been looking back for me, using the lights of the train to try to scope me out in the darkness. Instead, I am already past him.

Now they are closing in on me. I can't tell

how close, maybe no more than ten or fifteen feet away. I can hear Joselyn breathing heavily as he pushes her along. "Keep
moving, bitch!" He shoves her and she
stumbles forward, landing on her hands and
knees almost at my feet. She looks over
and sees the bottoms of my pants legs.
There is an expression of shock on her face
when she sees me. Then she looks away.

My body presses against the side of the
tunnel. The only thing between Thorn and
me in this instant is the arching steel I
beam.

Joselyn gets to her feet, takes two steps,
and just as Thorn clears the I beam she
begins to run. Her sudden action must have
startled him, because it takes him a second
before he realizes. He focuses all of his en-
ergies on the pistol in his hand. He raises it
and takes aim just as I reach out and grab
his wrist with both hands, forcing the muzzle
of the gun up.

Thorn pulls off the round. The pistol
coughs and the bullet ricochets off the
ceiling of the tunnel.

Thorn, startled, tries to wrestle the muzzle of the gun in my direction. But I have
one hand on his wrist and the other on the

small flat frame of the pistol with his finger trapped inside the trigger guard. He fires another round and the bullet flashes off the concrete just over my head. It is like having a tiger by the tail. If I let loose for an instant, he will draw a bead on me and I will be dead.

He raises one leg and tries to knee me in the groin. Instead he misses and hits my thigh. A rock comes from out of nowhere and hits him squarely on the side of the head. Blood begins to trickle down his temple. Then another rock and another. Most of them hit him in the upper body. He lifts his left hand and tries to fend off the rocks while he holds on to the pistol with his right.

He glances over and looks at Joselyn with fire in his eyes. She unloads on him with a machine-gun barrage of rocks, venting the anger of a decade as she tries to stone him to death. She catches me on the hand with one of them. It stings like hell. But I can't let go of the pistol.

Thorn lifts his right foot and tries to knee me one more time. As he does it I hook my right foot behind his left ankle and push him away, releasing his wrist and the pistol in the same motion.

His eyes widen with glee as he begins to go over backward, gripping the pistol with both hands to take aim. A green arc lightens up the cavern as six hundred volts and four thousand amps hiss through his body.

Thorn writhes like a snake on the third rail as Joselyn runs into my arms and buries her face in my shoulder.

FIFTY-ONE

The minute Joselyn and I are able to slip away from the police down inside the tunnel we grab a taxi and head for the hospital.

I've had no word on Herman since the ambulance took him away that morning. By the time we get there and check in at the front desk, I have to arm-wrestle with one of the nurses to get any information at all. Not being family, the hospital is reluctant to release anything.

The only family Herman has, to my knowledge, is a sister in Detroit, and I don't have her number. It would be in Herman's cell phone, which of course the hospital won't give me.

An hour later Thorpe shows up with an entourage of FBI agents and a million questions. While he wants to closet both Joselyn and myself until he can vacuum our brains for all of the details of Thorn's dealings, whatever we know of them, he does at least take the time and use his authority to cut through the red tape at the hospital.

On Thorpe's authority they give me Herman's cell phone. I call his sister and give her the news. In turn she authorizes the doctors to give me whatever information they have concerning Herman's condition.

According to the surgeon, it was touch and go when Herman arrived in the ambulance. Following surgery he appears to be out of immediate danger, but the long-term prognosis is guarded and he is not out of the woods.

In any event, it will be at least two days, possibly longer, before anyone will be allowed to see him, let alone talk with him. There is substantial damage to his right lung and the doctors are concerned that any effort on his part to talk or to move could result in a resumption of internal bleeding. For the time being he is recovering in the intensive care unit and is likely to be there for the better part of a week.

With that news, and the knowledge that Joselyn and I are not going anywhere, Thorpe and his agents throw a net over us. They gather our luggage, along with Herman's, check us out of the Hotel George, and put us up in a penthouse in one of the downtown high-rises near FBI headquarters while they proceed to grill us around the clock.

Thorpe is a little sheepish, and cuts us some slack due to his own failure to take us seriously when I called him from Arizona about Thorn and the plane from the boneyard. We give him the three passports pilfered from Thorn's luggage along with the small black notebook with the coded phone numbers, and tell him what little we know about Liquida, and that Herman had told me with his last conscious breath that it was the Mexican who'd stabbed him.

Thorpe informs me they already checked the bloody stiletto dropped in the garage for prints and that they found none. They are anxious to talk to Herman to see if they can get a description. But that will have to wait.

The minute Joselyn mentions her communications with Senator Joshua Root, and the fact that she had requested his assistance with the FBI, Thorpe's antennae goes up. He listens intently to the details of her conversations with Root, and Root's assurances of help and guarantees that Thorpe and his men were on board.

"Root is dead," says Thorpe. "According to reports he took his own life about two hours ago. It's all over the news. I can tell you with certainty that he never contacted us, the cops, or anyone else. The story is still breaking, but according to reports he was in the final stages of terminal cancer. And there's rumors of serious mental problems. We don't know all of the details yet."

I give him a questioning look.

"He was supposed to be taking medication, that's all we know. Why the leadership in the Senate hadn't taken steps to ease him out we don't know, especially given the classified nature of the information handled by his committee. At the moment everybody is running for political cover. But we'll get to the bottom of it, you can be sure of that."

That night after Thorpe left us alone, Joselyn showered as I sat in the room and examined the only document I had left from the trove of items Herman and I had taken from Thorn's luggage. It was my handwritten note jotted down after I had lifted the final invisible note from the back cover of Thorn's little black book: "Waters of Death, Second Road, Pattaya, Thailand." There was a phone number along with a note of the instructions that Liquida had been given when Thorn told him to kill Jimmie Snyder, including the kid's address in Alexandria, Virginia.

I pick up the hotel room phone on the nightstand next to the bed and dial Sarah's cell phone. It rings several times before she answers.

"Hello."

"Hi, babe, it's Dad."

"Oh, God, I have been so worried. I haven't heard from you in so long," she says. "Where are you?"

"In Washington. We're okay." I don't tell her about Herman. That would unravel her. I will wait until he is out of the hospital and back on his feet. "How's Harry?"

"He's bored. He has cabin fever. The original grumpy old man. What can I say? When can we go home?"

"Not just yet," I tell her. "Pretty soon."

"Did they catch him?" Sarah is talking about Liquida.

"They'll get him. He can't get far. How's life on the farm?" I try to change the subject. We talk for several more minutes. It is strange that after all the tension, there isn't all that much to say. If I talk too long, sooner or later she is going to ask me about Herman and I will have to lie. So we cut it short.

"See you soon," I tell her. "I love you."

"Love you too. How's Herman?"

I ignore the question. "Say hello to Harry for me. Bye-bye."

"Call me again soon, please. Bye." She hangs up.

* * *

The moment Sarah hung up she realized— Damn! She'd forgotten to mention the little package he'd sent her or ask him what it was for. It was supposed to be so they could stay in touch. According to the note in the box, he was sending another one to Harry and it was supposed to be a surprise. She wondered for a moment whether she should call him back. She decided against it. She made a mental note to ask him the next time he called.

* * *

Liquida gripped the wheel in obvious discomfort as he steered the rental car north up I-70. The doctor who'd stitched him up had done a pretty good job, though he could not guarantee that the feeling in the fingertips of Liquida's right hand would ever fully recover.

Liquida thanked him and then cut his throat. The doctor, at an all-night clinic in downtown Washington, was far too inquisitive as to how the injury had occurred. He had seen too many knife wounds to buy Liquida's story that it was an industrial accident.

For the moment all Liquida wanted to do was to put distance between himself and Washington, and he didn't want to fly. The last thing he needed was TSA running their hand-wand metal detector over the staples in his back. Besides, this way he could stop every few hours. And whenever he wanted to he could layover for the night. Liquida was in no hurry. The investigator was dead, and no one knew where the Mexicutioner was headed. He had business to finish, a labor of love at a farm outside Groveport, Ohio.

ACKNOWLEDGMENTS

Many people provided encouragement and support in the writing of this book, including family and friends.

At the very top of the list of those I wish to thank is my assistant, Marianne Dargitz, who for years, on those long lonely days when I stared bug-eyed at empty manuscript pages, offered her boundless patience, constant encouragement, and ever-diligent work to make this and other books possible.

For particular assistance on technical aspects for this book, I thank Bruce Wilson, whose voluminous research and attention to detail were of incomparable help. In addition, I appreciate greatly the help of Dick Gerry, whose long experience, knowledge, and guidance as a retired commercial airline pilot made possible the crafting of those flight scenes that are so pivotal to this story. That said, Mr. Wilson and Mr. Gerry are in no way responsible for any errors that may have crept into the book, since neither had a hand in the actual writing of the manuscript. For any errors in these regards, the author is solely and entirely responsible.

Among others to be thanked are my publisher, William Morrow, and all the people at HarperCollins without whose unstinting care and love of publishing nothing would be possible. Most of all I wish to thank my editor, David Highfill, who has been a friend and constant source of encouragement and patience; editorial assistant Gabe Robinson, who fielded my phone calls and handled so many technical aspects during the transition from paper to digital editing; my agent, Esther Newberg, and attorney, John Delaney, of International Creative Management, and my New York lawyers, Mike Rudell and Eric Brown, of Franklin, Weinrib, Rudell & Vassallo, for their constant attention and guidance to the business aspects of my publishing career.

Finally, and not least for their caring interest, love, and constant encouragement, I thank Al and Laura Parmisano, who have been there for me always during good times and bad; my friends Jan Draut, Anna Aleynikova, John Garrison, Mike Padilla, and Jim Bryan; and for her constant and unconditional love, my intelligent, beautiful, and wonderful daughter, Megan Martini, who in my eyes makes all things possible.